the

SISTERS OF
ALAMEDA
STREET

the
SISTERS OF
ALAMEDA
STREET

a novel

LORENA HUGHES

Skyhorse Publishing

FIRST EDITION

Skyhorse Publishing books may be purchased in bulk at special discounts for sales promotion, corporate gifts, fund-raising, or educational purposes. Special editions can also be created to specifications. For details, contact the Special Sales Department, Skyhorse Publishing, 307 West 36th Street, 11th Floor, New York, NY 10018 or info@skyhorsepublishing.com.

Skyhorse® and Skyhorse Publishing® are registered trademarks of Skyhorse Publishing, Inc.®, a Delaware corporation.

Visit our website at www.skyhorsepublishing.com.

10 9 8 7 6 5 4 3 2 1

Library of Congress Cataloging-in-Publication Data

Names: Hughes, Lorena, author.
Title: The sisters of Alameda Street : a novel / Lorena Hughes.
Description: New York : Skyhorse Publishing, [2017]
Identifiers: LCCN 2017001225 (print) | LCCN 2017014966 (ebook) | ISBN 9781510716018 (ebook) | ISBN 9781510716001 (hardback)
Subjects: LCSH: Suicide victims--Fiction. | Family secrets--Fiction. | Sisters--Fiction. | Identity (Philosophical concept)--Fiction. | BISAC: FICTION / Historical. | FICTION / Sagas.
Classification: LCC PS3608.U367 (ebook) | LCC PS3608.U367 S57 2017 (print) | DDC 813/.6--dc23
LC record available at https://lccn.loc.gov/2017001225

Cover design by Erin Seaward-Hiatt

Printed in the United States of America

To Esthela, my wise and kind mom

Ecuador, 1962

Papá had been many things: forgetful, cryptic, melancholic. But never duplicitous. Malena had always overlooked his flaws—they seemed so minor then—but this was not something you could just ignore. She sat on the bed, light-headed. Her hands had turned clammy and cold. She couldn't believe that her father, the mathematical genius respected by all who knew him, had lied to her all her life.

The letter was curled around the edges and faded to a vanilla white. The professional letterhead made it seem like a business correspondence and so did the fact that it was typed, but its content made it personal. Judging by the stains on the sides, someone with dirty hands had once held it. Who knew how many people had read it before her or how many times, but this was the first time she'd laid eyes on it.

Platas Jewelers
Alameda Street #345
San Isidro, Ecuador

November 20, 1947

Dear Doña Eva,

Please forgive me for writing. I know I promised I would never contact you or Malena, but I've now realized the huge mistake I've made. Giving my daughter away was a deplorable, unforgivable thing, but it was my only option at the time. Please don't think I want to take the girl from you. You are the only mother she's ever known and pulling her from your side would be cruel. Besides, I could never give her what she needs. All I ask is that you let me see her one more time. She doesn't have to know anything. I won't even speak to her. I just need to see her one last time to keep my sanity, to know that she exists. We could meet anywhere you'd like. Please let me know if this is possible and if so, set a place and a time, and I'll be there.

With warm regards and utmost respect,
A.

What in the name of everything holy was this? Her mother had died in childbirth! At least that was what both her father and her grandmother had said. And as far as she knew, dead people didn't go around writing letters! Could she still be alive now, fifteen years after this letter had been written to La Abuela Eva? Had her grandmother agreed to the request? Malena had no memory of her mother whatsoever, but she must have been five years old when this encounter took place, if it ever did. Would it have been too much to ask to include a photograph with the letter? Then again, her father had buried this correspondence in the depths of his trunk. Clearly, he hadn't meant for Malena to find it.

A metallic taste filled her mouth. First his suicide, now this.

She sifted through mountains of paper in the trunk in search of her birth certificate. *Her mother might still be alive and only a few hours away. Her mother, alive?* Malena couldn't grasp this concept, no matter how many times she repeated it.

Years of arduous studies were compiled in her father's trunk: diplomas, student lists, graph paper covered with numbers and never-ending equations. Photographs of herself as a child kept popping up—most of them with those stiff braids her grandmother had weaved to tame her curls. Underneath this mix was an unmarked manila envelope. It was filled with canceled checks made out to someone called Cesar Villamizar and signed by her own father. The amount was always the same: half of his teaching salary! And it seemed like he'd been paying this man every month for the last year. No wonder they'd been so tight on money! But who the hell was Cesar Villamizar?

She tossed the envelope on the floor and let out a groan.

Her father's bedroom was so silent now, so void. A musky scent of cedar and mothballs had taken over the room after a week of being closed off. If only Papá's things would give away the answers she needed. There was the calculus book he'd written and would never open again, the *guayaberas* gathering dust in the armoire, and his precious Gardel record collection, which would forever sit silently under his phonograph. She ran her hand by his indigo bedspread. To think that Papá now lay inside a frigid, hard casket instead of this bed. The thought didn't let her sleep the night of the funeral.

On top of his desk was the note he'd left for her—a series of rushed words that didn't explain a thing. This paper was supposed to be her consolation, the answers that would keep her satisfied for the rest of her life. But, honestly, what was she supposed to do now that he was gone? For as long as she could remember she'd been the Daughter of Hugo Sevilla, acclaimed mathematician.

Ha! If only the dean of mathematics and her father's other devoted followers would know about this double life of his, about his lies. And what about this mother she'd never heard of, the woman who "could never give Malena what she needed"?

She picked up the letter again. They said her mother had been a nurse and that her name was Malena, like hers—obviously another lie. But perhaps *she* had some answers, if not about her father's suicide then about why Malena had been raised by her grandmother and father, or why they had moved from one city to another her entire life until they landed in Guayaquil.

She ought to just take the first bus to San Isidro and demand an explanation.

But who knew if her mother still lived in this town. What if she had died, too? It was now 1962. So many things could have changed since this letter was written. Going on a wild chase across the country with such little information would be crazy, and she still had so many things to take care of here: this apartment, her studies, her father's things. She wasn't reckless, like her father. She was an anchor, like her grandmother—not that any good had come out of that.

Abuela, if you're up there pestering the angels to sit up straight and tune their harps, send me a sign and tell me what to do.

Chapter 1

The taxi's rearview mirror revealed enormous bags under Malena's eyes. No amount of foundation had been able to cover them up. Well, what else could be expected after a ten-hour bus ride? Her night at the humble hotel she had found by the bus station had been anything but restful, with all that panting and moaning next door. It had taken all her might to lie on those coffee-stained sheets. She could have sworn she saw lice in there, too. She scratched her head. Who knew what kinds of germs inhabited that rickety mattress. Now that she thought about it, this cab looked like it hadn't seen a feather duster in months either.

"Are we almost there?" she asked the taxi driver.

"Yes, *Niña*, almost."

Malena reapplied her carmine lipstick, which she kept for special occasions, and squeezed a drop of almond oil onto the palm of her hand—not that she was excessively vain, she just needed *something* to do with her hands.

The town of San Isidro was larger than she'd expected. And she hadn't expected much after nearly missing it on the map altogether. Nestled in a valley in the Andes Mountains, a gothic cathedral towered over hundreds of high, pitched roofs.

1

Concrete balconies filled with red geraniums lined the narrow, winding streets. Behind the colonial houses, a majestic volcano rose over the town.

Had her father lived here, too? It would make sense. Where else could he have met her mother? The thought of him still brought a lump to her throat. But that was it, she refused to shed a single tear after what he had done. Not that she *could* cry, even if she wanted to. She'd wept so much after her grandmother had passed away—had it been ten years already?—that she seemed to have dried up inside, at least that was what her father used to say. (Once in a while, when you least expected it, Papá would say something insightful, something that made you think he was actually paying attention.)

A daunting cliff divided San Isidro in two, but a dangly bridge joined the two parts. Malena's stomach seemed to float as the taxi crossed it, but the nonchalant driver whistled the entire way. They continued a few more blocks uphill until they reached a park surrounded by a green metal fence. A monument of a noble man or conquistador—she couldn't tell who it was— overlooked a garden of blushing lilies. Lottery ticket vendors, ice cream carts, newspaper stands, and shoeshine boys filled the park. Malena wouldn't have minded switching places with one of those carefree ladies enjoying the sunny morning on a bench.

This trip was insane. She still hadn't thought about what she was going to say. She didn't even know her mother's name, for God's sake. Who was she going to ask for? Mrs. A? Perhaps she had rushed too much when she took the first bus to San Isidro, but she was already here, wasn't she? And now she had to discover who this mysterious woman was and why she'd given her away, preferably without leaving a trail of destruction and scandal in this little Sierra town.

The taxi turned into Calle Alameda and stopped in front of a whitewashed two-story house attached to a jewelry store. Above the glass door was a sign in black bold letters that read JOYERÍA PLATAS.

Her mother might live in this house. There was, of course, the possibility that she might have moved somewhere else, but what if she *were* here, at this very moment? Malena could be a few minutes away from meeting her. Seconds even. A tremor started in her gut and traveled all the way down her legs.

What if her mother didn't want to see her?

"We're here," the driver said.

Malena paid for her fare and stepped out of the taxi. She moved slowly, as if prolonging the moment would give her the courage to ring the doorbell. But her courage left with the departing cab and she remained glued to the paving-stone sidewalk, squeezing her old leather purse. She stood in front of the jewelry store with only one thought in mind. *Leave before it's too late. Get out.*

She forced her legs to cross the street and caught her reflection in the store's glass door. Only now did she realize the miserable state of her grandmother's wool suit—it was old-fashioned, faded, and two sizes too big for her. You would think she'd have bought a new outfit to meet her mother, but her father had left her nearly destitute.

She adjusted her pink headband. Maybe she should go back to the hotel and think about this some more. Do something about those worn-out shoes of hers. She turned to leave, but a male voice stopped her.

"Are you lost?"

The owner of that deep, raspy voice was a young man holding the door open. His eyes—somewhere between green and gray—seemed to be smiling at her. He was just a notch taller than her and a few chest hairs escaped the top of his collar.

"I'm looking for someone," she said. "Mrs. . . . Platas?"

"Ana Platas?"

Great, an *A* name.

"Yes," she said.

He examined her as if she were an art piece at a museum. "You must be Liliana Paz."

Liliana?

"I thought you looked familiar," he said. "Though you probably don't remember me. We were so small when we met."

"No, I'm—"

"Javier!" A man's voice came from inside the store.

"I'll be right there!" He returned his attention to Malena. "I'm Ana's son, Javier."

Her son.

Javier smiled and a pair of dimples—identical to hers—framed both of his cheeks. This could be her brother.

"Come on in. My mother has been waiting for you since yesterday."

Malena peeked inside the store, but couldn't distinguish any shapes through the glare in the glass. She was about to clarify the mix-up, to say her name, but something stopped her. This moment of confusion could be a way in. If she came as Malena, she risked being turned away without ever being able to talk to Ana. This was a delicate matter, after all; she couldn't just blurt out to her son: "*Maybe* I am your mother's daughter?"

No, she must speak to this woman first, in private.

Javier opened the door wider. From the back of the store came a man who stopped behind a U-shaped glass counter filled with silver jewelry.

"There you are," he told Javier.

"Papá, Liliana is here."

The man looked at Malena. His face was pale, his nose slightly crooked. A mustache framed his upper lip and his hair was slicked back. He could pass for a thin man were it not for the paunch extending over his belt.

"Welcome, Señorita. I'm Rafael Dávila, Ana's husband." They shook hands. Not once did he smile.

"She's waiting for you in the house," Javier told her. "Follow me."

Javier led her into a sterile room furnished with a desk, a chair, and a metal vault. Her heels echoed behind him into a hallway with two shut doors. A frog seemed to be hopping inside her stomach. From one of the doors came the muffled noise of a drill. Javier pointed at yet another door at the end of the hall.

"That's the door to the house."

Her pulse raced as though she'd run a kilometer. What if they discovered she was not Liliana? It would be so humiliating. Plus, she was not prepared to meet her alleged mother yet. She hadn't decided what she was going to tell her. *God, please make her happy to see me.*

He opened the door.

"Madre, someone's here to see you!"

Malena followed Javier into a spacious living room with a grand mahogany piano and a chimney. Two women sat on an off-white couch, needlework in hand, while a third one sat on a rocking chair across from them.

The woman in the chair set her embroidery on the coffee table and stood.

"Lili?" She approached her. *This must be Ana.* "It's so nice to finally have you here." The woman raised her hand to adjust her spectacles. The sleeve of her dress pulled back and exposed a purple and yellow patch wrapping her wrist like a bracelet. *Was that a bruise?* She glanced at Malena before hastily covering her arm with her maroon shawl. "Don't you remember me? I'm Ana Luisa."

Malena remained stiff as Ana hugged her. For years, she'd longed to have her mother this close. She wanted to hug her back, but couldn't bring herself to do it. This woman was a stranger, after all. She examined Ana's features behind her glasses. Her eyelashes were long. Her eyebrows had a decent shape, though they could use some tweezing. Fine lines emerged from the corner of her eyes, but she was younger than she appeared from afar, and not bad looking. Without the glasses and the scarce gray hairs in her bouffant, she would be much more attractive.

"This is my older sister, Amanda, and my daughter, Claudia." She pointed at the women on the couch. "You probably don't remember them either. You were just a toddler when we last saw you."

Wait. Did she say Amanda?

The older sister stood up and gave Malena a kiss on the cheek, leaving a sweet scent of gardenia in the air.

Amanda didn't look older than Ana. And she didn't look much like her either. This woman exuded elegance through every pore of her body. Not a hair out of place or a wrinkle in her exquisite cream-colored suit. Her makeup was impeccable and her legs enviable.

Amanda and Ana. One of these two women had to be her mother.

"I wouldn't have recognized you," Amanda said. "It's amazing how much you've changed. I didn't remember you having curly hair."

It had to be her Medusa hair that would ruin everything! Malena searched for something in Amanda's appearance that would resemble herself, but this woman was worlds apart from her, in style and confidence.

Ana turned to the young woman named Claudia.

"Aren't you going to say something?"

Claudia adjusted the golden cross on her necklace and stood up, examining Malena through a pair of blue eyes, the bluest she had ever seen. Her hair was up in a ponytail and a pair of pearl earrings dangled from her ears. Claudia flattened the creases on her skirt and extended her hand.

"Welcome," she said.

Malena held Claudia's frail hand in hers. She reminded her of a porcelain figurine—like anything could break her petite frame—a younger version of Ana in demeanor and coloring but without the glasses.

"Have a seat, please." Ana pointed at the couch. "Javi, could you bring Liliana's luggage inside?"

"Sure. Where is it?" Javier asked Malena.

Luggage? So this Lili person was staying here. Malena wanted to scream the truth. But if only Ana's children weren't here. They probably didn't know what her mother had done (and certainly Ana wouldn't want them to). And what if Amanda was her mother? She'd probably hid it from the family. It was obvious that Malena was someone's secret. If she blurted out her suspicions, her mother—whomever she might be—may never forgive her.

They all watched her. She had to say something, anything.

"I accidentally left it on the bus," Malena said.

"You mean the train?" Ana said.

So Liliana lived far, maybe further than Guayaquil. "Yes. The train."

Ana frowned. "How did that happen?"

Of course she would be frowning, only an idiot would forget her valise on the train! Malena looked at Javier and remembered what he'd said about expecting Liliana the previous day.

"It's very foolish, really. I stepped out at one of the train stops and lost track of time. The train left without me, and my valise was in there, so I had to wait for another train and travel all night. That's why I'm late."

"You poor thing," Ana said. "Did you tell someone at the station?"

Malena caught Amanda watching her in silence. *She knows I'm lying.*

"Yes, but they couldn't find it." Malena said. "I'm supposed to go back later today."

"Great." She nodded toward her son. "Javier can take you."

"Of course," he said.

Malena avoided the inquisitive looks upon her. She had to get out. She needed time to think about what she was going to do. "May I use the lavatory?"

"Sure, *hija.*" Ana stood up. "Come this way."

Malena followed Ana to a bleach-smelling bathroom beside the staircase and locked herself inside. Like the living room, the lavatory was spotless. She approached the sink and splashed her cheeks with cold water.

What was she doing here? This was not at all what she'd expected. She ought to just go out there and say who she was, demand that these women tell her if one of them was her mother. She washed her hands and ran her fingers over the veins in her milky wrists, thinking about Ana's bruises and what could have caused them. A fall? But there would be no reason to hide them or get so nervous then. Had someone done this to her?

Her husband?

If it had been him, who knew what he would do if he found out his wife had a daughter with another man—given that Ana might be her mother. Malena couldn't just come out and announce to the entire family who she was. Ana might not even admit to it. She might just send her away.

Things started to make sense now. Ana could have been unfaithful with Malena's father. But what about her sister? Her name also started with an A.

She squeezed the towel. What was she going to do? They could catch on to her any minute, but she didn't have many options. She could confess who she was and risk being thrown out without an explanation, perhaps even cause a terrible feud. Or she could play along until she could be alone with the sisters. This confusion could buy her some time.

"Are you okay, Liliana?" Ana asked from behind the door.

She had to make a decision. Now.

"Yes."

Malena flushed the toilet and opened the door. Gently, Ana pulled her by the arm in the direction of the front door.

Oh, no, she knew. She was throwing her out.

"I know your secret," Ana whispered. "But don't you worry. Only Amanda and I know, and she's very discreet." She held Malena's hand. "María Teresa told me about that . . .

unfortunate incident back in San Vicente. I was young once. I understand these things can happen. I just want to ask you not to talk about this with anyone, especially with my Claudia. She's very innocent."

Malena nodded, too confused to say anything. San Vicente was in Manabi, a province north of Guayaquil. And whatever this Liliana had done was apparently serious.

"Now come with me," Ana said. "I'm going to show you around the house."

Ana turned around before Malena had a chance to say anything. She followed the older woman up a varnished staircase. A glimmering chandelier hanging from the ceiling caught her eye—she'd never seen one of those outside a movie screen.

Claudia stood atop the stairs, waiting for them. Behind her was a long hallway with doors on both sides. The hall curved to the right. Ana, holding Malena's arm, opened the first door.

"This is Claudia's room," she said. "You will stay with her."

Malena and Claudia followed Ana inside the bright room. There were two beds separated by a night table and a wooden cross hung above one of the beds.

"Oh, I don't want to impose," Malena told Claudia.

"I don't mind." Claudia touched the golden cross on her chest. "It's my duty."

They held each other's stare for a moment, but Malena couldn't read anything in Claudia's serene expression.

"Claudia is the best roommate you could ask for," Ana said. "She's clean, quiet, and respectful."

Claudia lowered her head in apparent humility.

"*Hija*," Ana said. "Why don't you pick a dress for Lili to change into?"

"No, no. That won't be necessary," Malena said.

"I'm sure Claudia won't mind."

Claudia ran her fingers over a jewelry box on the vanity table. "Of course not, Mamita. Liliana can have anything she wants."

Things were getting out of hand. If only there were fewer people in this place!

Amanda joined them in Claudia's bedroom. "So what do you think of the house, Lili?"

"It's great, you're all great."

"Isn't she sweet? Just like her mother," Ana said.

Of course Ana was talking about Liliana's mother, whoever that might be, but Malena glanced at both sisters.

Ana pushed her glasses up with the tip of her index finger. "I was asking Claudia to lend Liliana one of her dresses."

Amanda's laughter disrupted their hushed conversation.

"What's so funny?" Ana asked.

"You're crazy if you think Claudia's dresses would fit Lili. Look at her bosom!"

Malena couldn't believe Amanda had said that aloud! And in front of her! She eyed the handwoven rug under her feet.

"Amanda, please . . ." Ana said.

"Come with me," Amanda told Malena. "I have some dresses that may fit you."

Malena folded her arms across her monstrous chest and followed Amanda down the hall. She noticed then that Amanda walked with a slight limp.

———— >∘< ————

If Claudia's room had been simple and plain, Amanda's was the exact opposite. A large bed with a purple bedspread, matching cushions, and a tulle canopy took most of the space. A full-length mirror sat near the window.

Amanda opened an armoire in the corner of the room and looked through her blouses. "I have the same problem trying to fit into dresses."

Malena searched for a wedding photograph or something in the room that would tell her about Amanda, but aside from a photograph of Carlos Gardel—the tango king—there was nothing.

"So you live here, with your sister's family?" Malena said.

"Yes. But it's not their house," Amanda said. "It's my mother's. Ana's husband has managed the family business since my father passed away."

"And you're not married?"

"I'm a widow."

Amanda watched her for moment. Her examination made her nervous.

"So you like the tango." Malena pointed at Gardel's portrait. "My father does . . . did, too." She had no idea if Liliana's father was dead or alive, but she hoped Amanda wouldn't notice her hesitation. Why had she even brought up her father?

"Of course. Old people like us love the tango."

"You're not old." She wrapped her hand around the bed pole. This was her chance. "Amanda, I need to ask you something."

"Sorry, *querida*. I'm not telling you my age."

"It's not that."

"I know what you're going to say. Ana talked to me about it. Don't worry. I won't say anything about that man. I promise." Amanda returned her attention to her packed armoire. "Young people make mistakes. You shouldn't feel too bad about it."

"No, listen . . ."

"You don't have to justify yourself to me." Amanda handed her two shirtwaist dresses and a beige coat. "Here, try these on, and hurry because I want you to meet my mother. She had a little episode with her arrhythmia this morning, but I think she's awake now."

Arrhythmia? From what little Malena had learned about medicine, she knew that condition had to do with irregular heart rhythms, or something like that.

"I'm sure they'll fit." Malena just wanted to talk to the sisters, not try their clothes on.

"I apologize. I forget you young women are shy about your bodies." Amanda wrapped her fingers around Malena's arm. "Just leave those here and come with me."

The two of them entered the first room around the corner. The curtains were drawn, but it was bright enough to see an old woman sitting on the bed with a rosary in her hands. The room was larger than Claudia's or Amanda's. A lingering scent of medicine and old furniture reminded Malena of her grandmother, Eva.

"Mamá," Amanda said. "Someone's here to meet you."

The woman lifted her head. Her hair was reminiscent of a cotton ball and wrinkles grew like spider's legs from the corner of her eye to her temples. She looked so fragile.

"This is María Teresa's daughter, Lili," Amanda said. "Remember we told you she was coming? She's going to stay with us for a while."

The woman didn't blink. "Come here, child, so I can see you better."

Malena approached the bed and extended her hand. "It's nice to meet you, Señora."

"Call me Mamá Blanca." The woman watched Malena's every move. "You remind me so much of . . ." Her eyes moistened a bit and her gaze drifted away from Malena to a fixed spot in the wall for a few seconds. Then, she sat up as straight as her crooked back allowed her. "How is your mother? I haven't seen her since she got married and moved to Manabí."

Malena shrugged. "Fine. I guess."

Ana walked into the room. "Oh, here you are," she told Malena. "Please join us downstairs. Lunch is served."

Goodness, now she had to have lunch with the *entire* family. Well, she needed to eat at some point. She hadn't had any breakfast and her stomach was silently protesting.

"I'll have Trinidad bring you your lunch, Mamá," Ana told her mother.

"Oh, no. I'm not eating in my bedroom as though I was some decrepit mummy. As long as my legs work, I'm eating downstairs, with the rest of the family."

The exquisite aroma of *hornado* welcomed Malena to the dining room, where the family had already gathered around an oval table. A replica of Da Vinci's *Last Supper* hung on the back wall and a side window revealed a Spanish-style courtyard outside.

On the center of the table sat a long tray of sliced pork surrounded by hominy, fried plantains, sliced avocados, and potato patties. A lanky woman with a lengthy braid and a light blue uniform greeted Malena.

"Liliana, this is Trinidad," Ana said. "She's been with us for twenty years."

"Twenty-seven, Niña Ana." Trinidad wiped her hands on an apron as white as the snow at the tip of the Cotopaxi volcano before disappearing through a swinging door.

After twenty-seven years, the maid ought to know something about the family. If the Platas sisters weren't willing to talk, maybe the maid would.

Ana's husband, Rafael, and Mamá Blanca sat at either end of the table. Malena scrutinized Rafael's face, as though something in his features would reveal if this man was capable of hitting a woman. Javier dragged his chair away from the table to sit down, scraping its legs against the floor with a deafening squeal. All the women in the room protested. Javier smirked. Amanda ruffled her nephew's hair and sat beside him while Ana instructed Malena to sit next to Claudia.

One empty space remained.

"Where's Alejandra?" Mamá Blanca asked.

"She's coming," Javier said.

Malena couldn't hold her tongue. "Who's Alejandra?"

"Didn't María Teresa tell you about us?" Amanda said. "She's our younger sister."

Good God, another A. Was this some kind of joke?

"Let's begin," Rafael said. "Alejandra knows our schedule."

All eyes set on Claudia, who made the sign of the cross and intertwined her fingers together. Before she could say a word, Javier took a monumental bite of pork.

She scowled. "Is it too much to ask for you to wait until I say grace before you start eating?"

Javier picked up another piece of meat and shoved it in his mouth, watching his sister as he chewed.

"Oh, that's beautiful, Javier!" Claudia grimaced. "You can't even mind your manners when we have company?"

Javier's sole response was a wink for Malena.

Claudia turned to her mother. "Mamita . . ." But Ana was smiling at her son.

"That's enough, Javier," Rafael said. "Continue, Claudia."

"In the name of the Father, the Son, and the Holy Ghost—"

"Look who's honoring us with her presence!" Rafael said to someone behind Malena. "You're only five minutes late today."

Malena glanced over her shoulder. A thin woman stood on the threshold. But this was no ordinary woman. She wore blue jeans and an oversized black shirt. Malena was by no means the fashion authority, but she would never be caught wearing pants in public. Wiping her hands on her trousers, the woman took a seat by Mamá Blanca.

"Don't mind him," Mamá Blanca told her.

Ana unfolded her napkin and placed it on her lap. "Alejandra, this is Liliana Paz."

Alejandra looked up, but didn't say a word.

"Nice to meet you," Malena said, although the shock of meeting another possible mother was anything but nice.

"Continue, *hija*," Ana told Claudia.

Claudia said grace in a soft voice. All eyes were fastened onto the feast they were about to enjoy. Malena studied Alejandra discreetly. She looked young, perhaps too young to be her mother. She had short hair and no makeup on. Her features were delicate, too feminine for her attire. Dressed properly, she might have been as beautiful as Amanda. Her nails were short,

14

her fingers long and not fully clean. Patches of paint were scattered throughout her hands. An artist. Malena looked at her face and flinched. Alejandra was staring at her.

Malena glanced at Amanda and then Ana. People often said this kind of thing was intuitive. She should just know who her mother was, feel it somehow. Well, her intuition wasn't working properly. None of these women were anything like she'd imagined her mother—the nurse—to be. In her mind, her mother had been as warm and self-assured as the Mona Lisa. But all of these women were too human, too imperfect. Even Amanda, who was gorgeous and poised, didn't seem motherly enough.

"Amen," Javier interrupted Claudia's prolonged prayer. He lifted the pork tray and offered some to Malena. Then he picked a large piece for himself with his hand.

"*Por Dios,* Javier! Teaching you etiquette is harder than having a gorilla sip tea from a cup!" Claudia said.

"Liliana," Ana said in a loud voice, glaring at Claudia and Javier. "How is Don Hernán doing?"

The room turned hot. Who could this be? Lili's father, maybe? She ran her finger up and down her glass.

"Fine," she guessed.

Everyone was silent.

"That's strange," Ana said after a moment. "María Teresa said the doctor only gave him a few weeks."

Malena took a long sip of water, wishing it were something stronger. "Well, considering his . . . condition, he seems to be doing better."

Silence returned to the room, and she didn't know whether it was good or bad. She had to do something. She concealed her eyes with her hand, pretending to cry.

Ana held her hand. "I'm sorry, *hija,* I didn't know you were so fond of the foreman."

Malena blew her nose with her paper napkin, a gesture that apparently offended Claudia, judging by her wrinkled nose.

"That's life in the country for you." Rafael added more *salsa agria* to his pork. "If they would have taken him to Quito or Guayaquil, he would have been cured for sure."

"Some illnesses are incurable." Amanda poured Pilsener beer into her glass. "No matter where you get treated."

"You don't know what you're talking about, Amanda. I know the country." Rafael said. "It takes days for a doctor to show up. And if you're lucky, they take you to a dispensary to get treated by a resident with expired medication." He waved his index finger at Malena. "I always thought it was a mistake for your parents to move to the middle of nowhere. The country is only for cows and uneducated fools."

Malena was oddly offended for María Teresa and Liliana.

"You didn't say that when you inherited your uncle's ranch," Amanda snapped.

Rafael set his glass on the table, glaring at Amanda.

"Is that all you're having?" Mamá Blanca asked Alejandra. "You're so thin you're going to disappear any day now."

Alejandra smoothed her napkin over her lap. "Can't I eat in peace?"

"Better too thin than too fat," Amanda said.

"Mamá Blanca just wants what's best for Alejandra," Ana said.

"No man is going to look at her with those thin legs!" the older woman said.

Alejandra tossed her napkin on her plate. "I lost my appetite."

Nobody spoke until the youngest sister left the room. What a strange group of people. So hostile to one another. They had no idea how lucky they were to have each other. Malena would have given anything to grow up in a large family such as this one. Ironically, these strangers were her family and one of these three women, her mother.

"When are you going to stop harassing her, Mamá?" Amanda said. "She's never going to get married."

"Of course not," Rafael agreed with Amanda for once. "She's nearly forty. She'll always be a *solterona*. Speaking of that, Claudia, when is that boyfriend of yours going to propose? He's cancelled the engagement party twice already."

"What did you expect?" Amanda was already on her second glass of beer. "Sebastian's father was dying. He couldn't possibly have had a head for engagements."

"If you don't mind, I was talking to my daughter." Rafael turned to Claudia. "I don't like long engagements nor do I want another old maid in the family. At your age, you should've already given me two or three grandsons."

"Claudia is only twenty-one!" Amanda said.

Claudia blushed.

"Can't we have a pleasant conversation for once?" Ana said. "Lili is going to wish she never came to San Isidro."

Malena hoped it didn't come to that, but this trip might not end so well after all. As harsh as these people were, they would have no qualms in telling her to leave and never come back once they found out who she really was. And who knew what Rafael would do to Ana then.

Chapter 2

From the passenger seat of the 1956 Chevy Bel Air, Malena racked her brains for a reason as to why her luggage wasn't at the train station. She'd already done more lying in one day than in her whole life, and coming up with logical explanations wasn't easy. As Javier drove, he tapped the steering wheel of his father's automobile to the rhythm of a *guaracha* on the radio.

"Javier?" Malena's voice cracked a bit. "You don't have to wait for me while I get my valise. I can take a taxi back."

"There's only a few taxis in San Isidro. You would have to be very lucky to find one when you need it, and besides, my mother would kill me if I left you alone." He shifted gears. "Don't worry about me. I'm grateful for anything that keeps me away from those four walls at the store."

"You don't like your job?"

"I wouldn't mind it as much if I didn't have to work for my father."

"Even more reason for you to go back to work soon. I don't want to cause you problems."

She ought to just ask him to stop the car so she could hide in the marketplace at the end of the block. Never show her face in the Platas house again.

"It's no problem. Really," he said.

No, she couldn't leave San Isidro without answers. Not when her mother was so close. It was surreal to know that she'd already met her. It gave her a small thrill despite the anxiety building up inside her gut. She hoped all the lies were worth it, though. If Lili showed up at the house while they were gone, Malena would be boarding the bus back to Guayaquil before the day was over.

Through the windshield, she spotted a run-down two-story building with pink trimmings and a row of windows. Four large columns stood before the entrance and an old sign in gold letters read THE GUAYAQUIL & QUITO RAILWAY CO. Her father had once explained that in some stations, there was still an English sign because an American company had built the railway at the beginning of the century.

Javier parked by the building and removed the key from the ignition.

Maybe she should just tell him the truth. He might know something.

"Wait, Javier. I have something to tell you." She focused on the Bel Air logo on the dashboard.

"What's wrong?"

"My valise is not at the train station." She squeezed one of the gloves sitting in her lap. "It's in a hotel room."

He frowned. "Why?"

How could she think for a moment that Javier might know anything about his mother's indiscretion or his aunt's secret lives?

"I arrived last night but didn't want to show up at your house so late."

"You shouldn't have done that." His eyes looked darker than they had earlier. "It wasn't your fault if the train arrived late."

She was afraid he could see right through her, quiet as he was. She didn't know him well enough to know if he was irritated or if he didn't believe her.

19

"Which hotel is it?"

"It's near"—she swallowed—"the bus station."

Javier started the car and turned on the radio. "Nuestro Juramento," one of her father's favorite boleros by Julio Jaramillo, filled their silence. *Her father*. If he hadn't been so secretive, none of this would be happening.

In the light of day, the hotel appeared worse than it had at nighttime or even in the morning. The outside paint was peeling, the windows were cracked and dirty, and graffiti marred the walls.

"You stayed here?" Javier asked.

"I know it's humble." She eyed the burnt-out *H* in the hotel sign. "But I needed a place to stay and it was raining when I arrived."

Thank God for last night's rain, which had provided her with the perfect excuse.

"It's not that it's a humble hotel, it's just not . . ." He lowered his voice. "A very decent place."

The noises next door made sense now. "Please don't tell anyone."

Javier unlocked the door and stepped out of the Chevy. He walked around the car, tapping the hood as he went by, and opened the passenger door for her. She hesitated before taking his hand. She was not used to holding men's hands, much less a stranger's. Good thing she had gloves on to cover her sweaty palms. For once she was grateful for her grandmother's fussiness about wearing gloves at all times (it was a true sign of a lady, she would say, even in scorching weather).

In the restaurant across the street, an impeccably dressed young man stared at her from one of the outside tables. Malena had only seen suits like his in movies and magazines. In her hometown, men always wore *guayabera* shirts or light suits—anything else would have made them sweat like a Turkish bath. This man, however, looked like he had stepped out of one of those American comedies and didn't belong in this town, much less in such a modest neighborhood.

His dark eyes never left her face, not even when he took a sip from his drink. She headed for the entrance, where Javier held the door for her, and walked inside.

There were voices in the living room of the Platas household. Malena froze behind Javier. Lili could be there. The front door was still close enough to flee before having to go through the humiliation of explaining herself to the family.

"Are you coming?" Javier set her valise by the staircase.

She followed him into the living room. Ana, Amanda, and Mamá Blanca were the only ones in the room. Malena exhaled. Lili had not arrived. *Yet.* The women stopped their chatter as soon as they saw her, the way people do when they are caught gossiping. Probably about her.

"What took you so long?" Ana asked Javier, picking up a pair of socks from a handwoven basket sitting on the coffee table. "Your father has been asking about you." She inserted a burnt-out light bulb inside a sock, stretching the hole on the tip so she could mend it properly.

"Well," he said, "the valise wasn't exactly where we expected it to be."

Malena fanned her cheeks with her gloves.

Amanda sat back, rubbing the sides of the rocking chair. "Doesn't surprise me. As disorganized and crowded as the train station is."

Javier's gaze set on Malena. *Please don't say anything.*

"Well," Ana said. "Go back to the store before your father comes again."

"Yes, go," Amanda said. "Poor Claudia is all alone with him."

"Amanda . . ." Ana said.

Only when Javier had left the room did Malena remember to breathe again. She was safe. For now.

Mamá Blanca patted a spot beside her on the couch. "Come here, child. Tell us everything about your mother."

Her mother? How ironic for them to ask about her. "There's not much to say about my mother." Her glance traveled from Ana to Amanda, who picked up a *Burda* magazine from the coffee table. *Say it. Just ask them.*

"I don't really know her," she blurted out.

Ana sighed, but kept her gaze on her needle.

Mamá Blanca shook her head. "For once I would like to meet a mother and daughter who didn't quarrel," she said. "But it would be abnormal."

Mamá Blanca rested her palm on her chest for just a second. No. This wasn't a good time to talk. Not in front of Mamá Blanca. What if she gave the woman a heart attack with the news? It would be better to wait for Alejandra to be present anyway.

"Well? What are you waiting for?" Amanda told her. "Grab a sock and sit here."

Malena picked up a pair of socks and a needle from the table, even though she'd never mended a pair of socks in her life. La Abuela hadn't been around long enough to teach her. Ana handed her a roll of olive thread. Her wrist was now well covered with the sleeve.

"Is your mother coming any time soon?" Mamá Blanca said.

"I don't know, Doña." Malena hadn't thought of the possibility of Lili's mother coming until now. Great. Now she had one more thing to worry about.

Amanda leafed through her magazine. "Must be hard for her, living among men."

Malena tried to pass the thread through the needle's tiny eye.

"Let me see that." Mamá Blanca took the needle and thread from Malena's hands. Squinting, she licked the tip of the thread and attempted to introduce it into the needle.

"I told you, Mamá. You need new glasses." Ana took the needle from her mother's hands. She did the task effortlessly and returned the needle to Malena.

"There's always something with you," Mamá Blanca told Ana. "First it was the teeth, now it's the glasses."

"And you never listen." Ana renewed her sewing. "You need dentures and you know it."

"I'm not dying with someone else's body parts," Mamá Blanca said.

Amanda laughed. "They're not real teeth."

Mamá Blanca tilted her head, admiring her work. "If God wanted me to die with teeth, He would have never taken them from me."

Amanda sighed. "*Ay, Mamita.*"

"Lili, we should call your mother to tell her you arrived," Ana said.

"Good idea," Mamá Blanca said. "The poor soul must be worried."

Malena jabbed her finger with the needle. She couldn't talk to María Teresa. She couldn't fool her. But there was no excuse not to call her. Ana stood up.

"Come on."

"Now?"

"Of course."

Malena's legs obeyed Ana, even when her brain ordered them to stay in the living room, where she was still safe. But her legs, her quivering legs, were done listening to her. They followed Ana to a room between the stairs and the kitchen door, a small study filled with bookshelves. A sky blue telephone and a typewriter sat side by side on the desk. Perhaps the same typewriter where her mother had written the letter now buried in the bottom of Malena's purse. Ana pointed at the phone.

"Would you like to call her yourself?"

"No."

Ana studied her face for a moment before picking up the receiver. Still watching her, she told the operator María Teresa's number. They waited in agonizing silence for the call to go through.

"Hello? Yes, this is Ana Platas de Dávila. Is María Teresa available?"

Malena dug her nails against her palms. What was she going to tell this woman? Ana nodded as she listened to the person at the other end of the line.

"I see," Ana stared at Malena.

What did she see? *What?*

"All right, thank you." Ana put the receiver down. "Your mother went into town. We'll try again later."

Malena let out a slow, quiet breath and released her fists. She followed Ana to the door but a framed black-and-white picture hanging by the door caught her eye. Four young women and a teenage boy sat by a fountain looking straight at the camera.

"Who are they?" Malena asked before Ana walked out of the room.

Ana glanced at the picture. "My sisters and I."

"But there are four girls here."

"We used to be four."

Ana pointed at a young woman in the center of the frame. "This was Abigail. She died ten years ago."

Abigail. Her heart sank. How many prospective mothers was she going to have? Worse yet, her mother might be dead after all.

Sitting on the bed, Malena brought the coral bedspread to her legs, running her fingers over the sea of creases her body had created under the covers. She didn't want to upset any part of Claudia's room, including the bed that would only be hers for the night. Only tonight. Tomorrow, she would somehow gather the courage to speak to the Platas sisters. Assuming, of course, that Lili wouldn't arrive at this very moment and demand her spot in this bed. She looked at her enlarged shadow against the wall. She shouldn't be here, in this strange house, in a room that didn't belong to her, using a name that wasn't hers.

At least this place didn't smell like a public restroom, like the hotel room had. It was a minor consolation that she didn't have to spend another night there. Just thinking about it gave her an itch in the back of her head.

Claudia, in her pink nightgown and robe, entered the bedroom. She had her wavy brown hair down and her clothes in her hand. She looked like an angel floating into the room. She hung her clothes on the back of the vanity table's chair. Malena's presence had taken away that small privilege from Claudia, the privilege of undressing in her own room. The silence between them lingered. *Say something.* But she couldn't think of anything to say. Under normal circumstances, she would have been elated to share the room with another girl. For most of her life she'd wished she had a sister to talk to in the darkness, just before dozing off. And now she had Claudia, who could be that sister she had longed for, or at the very least her cousin.

"Your family is very nice," Malena said.

Claudia raised an eyebrow.

Malena reconsidered her words. Maybe *nice* was not the best way to describe Claudia's family. That evening, during dinner, Rafael Dávila had gotten into another dreadful argument with Amanda over Carlos Gardel's true nationality. Apparently, there was a big controversy over whether he'd been born in Argentina, Uruguay, or France. Unable to reach an agreement with his sister-in-law, Rafael had scolded Javier for his lack of productivity at the store, at which point Alejandra had left the dining room. No, they weren't exactly nice, although Malena had been grateful for Mamá Blanca's smiles across the table and Ana's attentiveness.

"You've always lived with your aunts?" Malena said.

"Ever since I can remember." Claudia removed her robe and set it on the foot of her bed. Her movements were controlled, slow, as if she didn't want to break or upset any of the objects around her.

"Your Tía Alejandra . . . she never married?"

"No."

"And . . ." Malena caught a glimpse of the rosebuds in the wallpaper. "Your mom said they had another sister . . . Abigail?"

Claudia opened her night table's top drawer. "Did you bring your rosary?"

"No."

Claudia handed her a white marble rosary and knelt by her bed, facing the cross on the wall.

"Come here," she told her.

Malena obeyed. The floor was cold against her knees. In Guayaquil, the floor was always so warm she'd never imagined it would be different anywhere else. She crossed herself, after Claudia, mimicking her solemn demeanor. She hadn't prayed since her grandmother died. But maybe prayer was exactly what she needed now.

Claudia started the *Credo*. Just when Malena had brought her crossed hands to her forehead and closed her eyes, a strident sound wrecked her momentary peace, as though God Himself was scolding her for her web of lies and deceit.

The chime of the doorbell vibrated in her ears, in her head, in her entire body. She didn't dare look at Claudia. She didn't trust herself to conceal her fear—the fear of being discovered now that Liliana had finally arrived.

Chapter 3

Amanda sat on the rocking chair with her eyes shut, enjoying Libertad Lamarque's rendition of "El Tango de Malena"—her favorite tango. Her throat ached. This song always had the power to unlock buried emotions in her, especially when Libertad sang it. Thank goodness she was alone.

The shriek of the doorbell removed her from her trance. Damn. It was so rare to hear this version on the radio anymore. She hoped whoever was at the door would go away.

The doorbell went on again, and this time it was a long, impatient sound.

The kitchen door opened and Trinidad crossed the living room threshold, tightening the strings of her apron. Amanda heard a man's voice at the front door, but couldn't detect what he was saying. She sighed. Libertad would have to wait for another day. She stood up and shut the radio off.

"Who is it, Trini?"

She recognized Bernardo's stocky frame behind Trinidad.

"It's Mr. Bernardo." Trinidad's eyes shone and a smile she never used appeared on her plain face.

"*Bernard*," he corrected with a French accent and brushed past the maid, his old brown hat between his hands and his complexion darker than the last time Amanda had seen him.

"Good evening, *Madame*. Forgive me for coming this late."

"This is a surprise," Amanda said. "I didn't expect to see you until next month."

"I know, *Madame*, but we need to talk."

Amanda pointed at the couch in front of her. Bernardo sat on the edge of the seat, his hat resting on his knees.

"May I take your hat, Señor?" Trinidad offered.

Bernardo brought his hat closer to him. "No."

"Trini," Amanda said. "Would you bring some coffee, please?"

"Just water for me, *s'il vous plaît*."

Trinidad hurried to the kitchen, her lengthy braid bouncing back and forth as if attempting to catch up with her quick stride. She was only this lively when Bernardo came. Trinidad always reminded Amanda of a Mannerist portrait without the elegance. Her body was exaggeratedly elongated. Long enough to look awkward: oval face, ostrich neck, and bony fingers.

Amanda returned to the rocking chair. "So, what is it?"

"I'm quitting, *Madame*."

"What?"

Bernardo wiped the sweat off his forehead with a mended handkerchief. "I can't continue to work for that Italian brute."

Trinidad reentered the living room with a pitcher of water, glasses, and two generous slices of *flan de coco*—her specialty.

"You've been saying that for years," Amanda said. "What's changed?"

"I can't sit back and watch your brother-in-law destroy the business your husband worked so hard for. Besides, he's vulgar."

Destroy the business? No, surely Bernardo was exaggerating. He always did when it came to Enzo. Trinidad stood by Bernardo, like a statue, while he tried a bite of custard.

"He begged me not to tell you anything," Bernardo said. "But after today I owe him no loyalty."

"Not tell me what?"

Bernardo ate another spoonful, not granting Trinidad a look, much less a compliment.

"How bad the business is doing. It's losing a lot of money."

"But I don't understand," Amanda said. "I've been getting my check the first of every month."

"Yes, he's been borrowing money from the bank to make those payments."

Amanda uncrossed her legs. "Why didn't you tell me before?"

"I told you, he asked me not to say anything." Sweat trickled from his hairline. "Besides, he said it was temporary. But I don't believe him anymore—he's been firing a lot of people lately."

Amanda slammed her fist on the side of the couch. "Damn Enzo! How could Nicolas have had such an incompetent brother?"

"Not only incompetent: loud, perverted, you name it."

"So, what happened today?"

Bernardo glanced at Trinidad over his shoulder. Amanda dismissed her. When Trinidad left the room, her braid no longer bounced and her shoulders drooped. Bernardo leaned forward.

"I was scolding a waiter for coming in late when that . . . Enzo showed up and defended him. He not only made me look bad in front of an employee but he also called me a low-class, fake Frenchman."

Amanda rubbed her forehead. *Here we go again.*

"You know, *Madame*, that I am a quarter French. My grandmother was from a little town near Nice. I wouldn't make that up."

Amanda had heard this story a million times.

"And her father was—"

"So, what else happened with Enzo?"

He devoured the remaining flan.

"That waiter, the one I told you, has a younger sister Enzo has his filthy eyes on. Obviously he wanted to get on this man's good side. *Madame*, he humiliated me in front of all the employees." Shreds of coconut flew all the way to Amanda's lap. "Anything to get a woman in his bed. You know how he is."

"Yes, I know."

"So different from his brother." He sighed. "Ah . . . *Monsieur* Nicolas. Now there was a gentleman: smart, hardworking, elegant. What a pity he had to die so young."

Amanda stared at the flower vase sitting on the coffee table, attempting to suppress the image of her late husband from her mind. "Bernardo, I need you to stay there. You're the only person I trust in the entire restaurant."

"To be honest with you, *Madame*, I doubt Il Napolitano will be opened much longer."

This was more serious than she thought. She was going to have to pay a visit to that rotten brother-in-law of hers.

A cold chill ran down Amanda's spine when she walked into Il Napolitano, the first Italian restaurant in San Isidro. Back when Nicolas Fornasieri was alive, it was the most exclusive, elegant, and crowded place in town. Everybody wanted to try its famous shrimp cannelloni, listen to the quartet of violins, and admire its owner, one of the most charming men ever to set foot in San Isidro.

She could picture her husband with his impeccable black suit standing by the entryway, welcoming customers with his thick Italian accent. Tonight, the room was empty, except for a waiter without a tie or a jacket, sweeping the floor. The last time she had been here at this hour, people were waiting in line to be seated. But that had been nearly a year ago. She glanced at the chandeliers. They needed a feather duster and a polish. The tables were not even set now. Old chairs sat upside down on a corner table while raggedy tablecloths were piled up nearby. Amanda glanced at the velvet curtains that had once hung proudly beside two gigantic glass windows. Now they were faded and dirty. It was fortunate Nicolas had never lived to see the miserable state the place was in.

She walked to the waiter.

"Where's Enzo?"

"At the office." The man studied her from head to toe. "Who wants to see him?"

She pulled her shoulders back. She was the wife of Nicolas Fornasieri, the legend, the man who had created the trendiest place in town. How dare this little man talk to her with such disdain? There was a time when every employee in this restaurant had bowed to her when she walked in. Back then, nobody would have even thought of answering her in that tone.

"Tell him Nicolas Fornasieri's widow is here."

The waiter dropped the broom and rushed to the office. His reaction didn't surprise her. None of the employees knew her, except for Bernardo, and it was all her fault. She shouldn't have trusted Enzo to manage the business for so many years. Instead of waiting comfortably for her check every month, or for the yearly report, she should have checked up on the business frequently. It was out of the way, it hurt too much to go, she didn't want to put up with Enzo—whatever her excuse, it was never the right time to go.

"*Cara mia*, what an honor!"

Amanda had to hold on to the back of a chair when she saw Enzo. He had grown to look just like his older brother. Never before had their resemblance been so pronounced. His head was now filled with gray hairs, his nose had acquired the same length and shape as Nicolas's, and his green eyes had the same shine—that same mischievous expression. At fifty, Enzo was looking better than ever. He hugged Amanda and gave her a kiss on the cheek, tickling her skin with his warm breath.

Butterflies in her stomach? At her age? She took a step back, reminding herself of the reason for her visit.

"What happened here?" she said.

"What do you mean?"

Amanda hated that Italian accent that grew stronger whenever he wanted to charm someone or get out of trouble. He had used it hundreds of times with female customers.

"Why isn't anybody here?" she said.

"Oh, because we're closed. We don't open on weeknights anymore."

"Really? Then why is the 'open' sign on the front door?"

"Well, maybe people aren't hungry."

"Oh, please, you can think of a better excuse."

"What are you doing here anyway? Didn't the fake Frenchman take your check on the first?"

"Yes, but he also came to see me today and told me what was going on."

"Nothing is going on. It's been a slow month, that's all."

She headed for the office. "I want to see your bookkeeping."

She could hear him cursing in Italian under his breath as he followed her into the office.

A woman with a blonde wig sat on the desk filing her nails, the top three buttons of her blouse undone. Startled, she buttoned her shirt as Amanda approached the desk. Enzo nodded toward the front door. The woman immediately jumped off the desk and left.

Amanda opened the desk's top drawer.

"This is ridiculous, Amanda."

She shuffled through various papers.

"Come on, *sorella* . . ." Enzo mellowed his tone. "This is just a misunderstanding."

"Don't call me that. I'm not your sister."

In the second drawer, she found a leather-bound accounts book. Enzo paled. As soon as she opened the notebook, an ocean of red ink spread throughout the pages.

"What is this? You barely have enough to pay the employees."

"Well, you know how people are. It turns out my last accountant robbed me."

"I don't believe a word you're saying. Aren't you man enough to admit the truth? You're a lousy administrator and instead of working, you waste your time with women and parties!"

"You mean her?" He pointed at the door. "She's just my secretary."

"What do you need a secretary for? Nicolas never had one back when the business was doing well!"

"It's easy to sit back in your comfortable chair and criticize everything when you're not doing any of the work!"

Amanda knew he had lost his patience when he started gesticulating with his arm and twitching his right eye, just like his brother.

"You have never moved one finger to help with the business. How dare you come here and throw all these insults at me?"

Enzo had a point. He had been in charge of the restaurant for over twenty years, and she hadn't granted him more than a yearly visit.

"The only reason I haven't been involved," she said, "is because Nicolas left you in charge of all his businesses. If I had been in charge, I am certain this restaurant wouldn't have turned into the garbage that it is now!"

"You?" Enzo chuckled. "A woman could never manage a business like this."

"Of course I could."

His laugh was so loud Amanda was sure that stupid fake-blonde could hear them from the hallway. The thought of that woman smiling enraged her.

"It doesn't take a genius to run a restaurant," she said. "All it needs is someone to work."

Enzo looked at her with an amused smile, his arms crossed in front of his tight chest. "Talking is easy, *sorella*. Doing is something else."

"What do you mean?"

"Well, if you think you can do a better job than I can, then do it."

Amanda looked about the crammed office. She couldn't run a restaurant. She'd never worked before.

Enzo rubbed his eyelids. "I don't have time for this. Let me get back to work."

"You mean screwing your secretary?" She regretted her words as soon as they came out.

Enzo leaned on his desk. "Jealousy is an ugly thing."

"Oh, please . . . I'm not jealous of her. Why would I be?"

"For one, she's young. Her life is like a blank page. Not one filled with strikes and blots, like yours." He unfolded his arms. "Oh, don't get me started."

Amanda lifted her chin up. "Say it. Say what you've been thinking all these years."

He held her stare for a long time, his eyes glimmering with contempt. He blamed her for everything. That, she knew. She thought he was going to start his accusations, but surprisingly, his glare softened and the wrinkles on his forehead released.

"You know? It really is a good thing you came. I'm glad this is finally out in the open." He walked toward his jacket, hanging by the door. "I'm tired of having to deal with creditors and employees." He searched inside his pockets for a set of keys and threw them at her.

"Here. Il Napolitano is all yours." He put on his hat and turned to the door. "I expect my check the first of the month."

Chapter 4

When Malena woke up, she was alone in Claudia's room, a neatly made bed by her side. Somewhere in the neighborhood, a dog barked. So it hadn't been a dream; she *was* at her mother's house. Incredible she'd been able to fall asleep after spending most of the night staring at the ceiling, listening to Claudia's breathing and waiting for Liliana to show up in the room. But Lili never came. How strange that she hadn't arrived yet. If something bad had happened to her, no one would even know to look for her. Oh, Christ. She couldn't think of that now. Guilt was something she couldn't deal with at this moment.

She pulled her valise from under the bed and set it on top of the covers. Her clothes—what little she had brought—were neatly organized by colors. She slipped into one of her better shirtwaist dresses and scrambled out of the room. The sooner she talked to the sisters, the sooner this deceit would be over.

The house was quiet, and the dining room empty. Malena pushed the swinging door that led to the kitchen. The temperature here was warmer than any other part of the house and a mélange of smells filled the room, among them spices and coffee. Trinidad stood by the sink, peeling potatoes. This morning, she had fixed her hair in two long braids instead of one.

"*Buenos días, Niña Lili,*" she said.

"Good morning, Trinidad. Where's the family?"

"The men are at the store, Niña Claudia went to mass, and Doña Ana and Doña Amanda took their mother to the doctor for a checkup."

And Alejandra? People in the house rarely mentioned her. It was almost as if she were another object in their beautiful home.

"Do you know when they'll be back?" She didn't have a lot of time. Lili could show up any second now.

"They didn't say, Niña. Would you like some breakfast?"

How could anyone eat at a time like this? She should have spoken to the sisters last night! She didn't even want to think about the chaos that would ensue if Lili arrived before Malena had a chance to clarify her situation.

Trinidad brought a basket of bread to the counter and a jar of marmalade—no labels on the jar.

Then again, there might never be another opportunity to speak to the maid.

"Did you make this?" Malena raised the jar to eye level.

"Yes, Niña. It's blackberry."

Her neighbor Julia prepared her own marmalade, too. Perhaps she should call her soon and tell her she was fine—at least for now—and maybe get some advice from her only friend in Guayaquil.

Malena sat on a stool. "After twenty-seven years, you must know the family well."

"That I do." Trinidad placed a cup of *café con leche* in front of Malena.

"And you've met my mother, right?"

"Yes. Before she got married, she spent a lot of time in this house with Doña Ana. She was her only friend." So María Teresa was Ana's friend, not a relative. "But we haven't seen her in fifteen years, at least. She never comes to San Isidro anymore."

"My mother is a very busy woman." Malena poured sugar in her coffee. "But she always talks about Ana. She also talks about another friend. A family friend. But she lost track of him years ago and asked me to find out what happened to him. So I thought that maybe . . . you knew him, too." She set the spoon on the saucer. "His name was Hugo Sevilla." It felt weird to say her father's name aloud.

"I've never heard of him."

"Are you sure?"

"I never forget a name, Niña." She dried her hands on a hand towel. "And now if you'll excuse me, I have to go upstairs to tidy up the rooms."

The woman darted out of the kitchen before Malena could say another word. Had Trinidad been honest? She seemed in an awful hurry to leave. Then again, if Malena's mother had an illicit relationship with her father, it wouldn't be so strange if Trinidad had never met him.

There had to be something in this house to prove that one of the sisters had a baby or at least knew Malena's father. Photographs, letters, or maybe the birth certificate she hadn't been able to locate in her apartment. There was that picture of the sisters in the study. She'd better take advantage of nobody being home and go there. Who knew how much longer before Lili arrived.

She fled to the study and pushed the door open.

"Do you need something?"

Malena flinched. She hadn't seen Claudia standing by the front door, hanging her coat on the tree-shaped hanger.

"I just need a piece of paper," Malena said. "To write a letter to my mother."

Claudia removed the black lace veil covering her head while staring at Malena for an unnerving moment. The temperature rose in Malena's face. *Just one more lie. Soon this will all be over.*

"Go ahead, then." Claudia inserted her gloves in her purse and headed for the stairs.

Through the spaces in the staircase banister, Malena waited for Claudia's thin legs to disappear onto the second story. Then, she entered the study and searched for a clue in all the desk drawers and underneath stacks of stationary paper, envelopes, and store documents. She found an address book, but her father's name was not in there.

She removed the Platas sisters' picture from the hook. Judging by the girls' dresses and hairdos, it must have been more than twenty years old. Yet Malena could still recognize the mole on Amanda's cheek, Ana's pointy chin, and Alejandra's big brown eyes. At the center of the frame, Abigail looked directly—almost defiantly—at the camera. Malena looked for a resemblance between the dead woman and herself, and identified the same unruly hair and full mouth. A teenage boy stood by a very young Alejandra. He was handsome and oddly resembled Mamá Blanca.

The peal of the doorbell made her drop the picture to the floor. *Liliana!* She picked it up, wiped the glass with her sleeve, checked for cracks, and returned it to the hook. The doorbell rang again. She had to open it before Trinidad or Claudia did. She had to talk to Lili, *beg* her to help her.

She dashed to the front door and pulled it open. The face in front of her wasn't Lili's. It was a man's face, and she had seen those sad eyes before. She recognized him then. He was the man sitting in the restaurant across from the hotel; the man staring at her; the man drinking by himself; the man in the fancy suit. He wore a similar suit today, and he had an armband on.

"Good morning." He seemed confused. "I'm looking for Claudia."

She lowered her gaze, as if that simple motion would prevent him from recognizing her. If he did, if he said something, she would have to explain herself, to lie again. Under his polished black shoes lay a piece of paper, an envelope. She could read a portion of the sender's name: Liliana. Her palms moistened. *It must be a letter from her.* He followed her glance to the ground and, upon seeing the envelope, moved his foot.

"Oh, I'm sorry. I didn't see it."

She picked up the envelope so he wouldn't read the name.

"Please come in. I'll go get Claudia for you," she said.

She kept the envelope behind her back while holding the door for him.

He walked into the foyer. "Have we met before?"

"Oh, no, I don't think so. I just arrived here. I'm a family friend." She pointed at the stairs. "Claudia is upstairs. I'll go tell her you're here. I'm sorry. Your name is?"

"Sebastian Rivas." He extended his hand.

She switched the envelope to her left hand and shook his firm hand. This close, she could smell his citric cologne mingled with a mild cigarette scent. He was tall, a head or so taller than her, and so she focused on his thin black tie as they shook hands.

"Please make yourself comfortable." She took two steps back, still holding the envelope behind her.

All her instincts forced her up the stairs before he could say another word. Had she stayed there any longer, he might have remembered seeing her, or asked about the letter. She held onto the rail as she read the addressee's name on the now wrinkled envelope. *Sra. Ana de Dávila Platas.* Her address was scribbled underneath. In the upper left corner, that girl's name: "Liliana Paz." It was printed, not handwritten or typed, and no return address was given.

Malena folded the envelope in half, unbuttoned the top two buttons of her blouse, and inserted it inside her brassiere. Then, she opened Claudia's door without knocking.

Claudia stood by her bed with Malena's valise on top of it, her hands on the zipper as if she was about to open it, or maybe she was closing it.

"What are you doing?"

Claudia ran her palm by her forehead. "I was going to put your valise in my armoire. So it wouldn't be in the way."

"I don't think it's in the way *under* the bed."

Claudia gripped the handle and placed the valise on the floor. "I was just trying to do you a favor, but if you don't want it there, that's fine."

Malena made a brief inventory of her valise's contents. Her mother's letter was inside her purse in one of the night table's drawers.

"Forgive me," she told Claudia. "I didn't mean to be rude."

Malena shoved the valise under her bed.

"Someone called Sebastian is waiting for you downstairs."

"Sebastian? Why didn't you say so?" Claudia examined her reflection in the vanity mirror, pinning the loose hairs in her ponytail and pinching her cheeks. "How long has he been waiting?"

"Not long."

"Should I change?"

Malena shrugged. To her, all of Claudia's clothes seemed nice, and the pink cashmere sweater she wore was no exception.

"I don't think you should keep him waiting."

Claudia sighed. "You're right." She put on her necklace and straightened the cross. Before stepping out, she turned to Malena.

"There's a piece of paper sticking out of your blouse."

Chapter 5

Sebastian's head would explode any second now. He brought his fingers to his temple and pressed it hard, as if he could squeeze away the pain. He would never drink again. Especially not in that filthy place where they only served *puros* and *canelazos*. In the end, it hadn't been worth it. He hadn't been able to forget, like he'd intended to in the first place. The pain was still there. And this pain was far worse than any migraine. This pain you couldn't fix with an aspirin or any herbal tea Juanita prepared.

He felt his shirt's front pocket for his Lucky Strikes. *Maldición!* He'd forgotten them. He would have to stop by El Turco's store and get a new box.

He paced around the foyer. Claudia was taking a long time to come down. Maybe she was talking to that girl, the one who opened the door. The one he couldn't place. He'd seen her face before, and that wild hair of hers, but where? His head throbbed again. He would remember—eventually. Just not now. Not while his brain attempted to break open from his skull.

The noise of heels against the guayacan floor became louder and Claudia's petite figure appeared on the staircase. Her lovely

41

eyes shone—those bewitching eyes that reminded him of the ocean he loved so much.

He met her at the bottom of the stairs and his lips sought hers, but she moved her face so the only thing his mouth found was her cheek.

"What a nice surprise, Sebastian," she said. "You should have told me you were coming so I would have changed into something more suitable."

"You don't need to change. You're perfect they way you are." His fingers rested on her elbow as he led her toward the living room.

"Can I bring you something to drink?"

"Not now, thank you."

They sat by each other on one of the couches.

"How is your mother?" she asked.

He shrugged. The subject of his mother was not one he wished to think about right now. It would only worsen his headache.

"The poor thing," she continued, "she didn't look well at the funeral. I've been praying every day that our Lord would help her come to terms with her loss."

She'd come to terms all right. Just not the way Claudia had been praying for.

"Since you're mentioning my mother," he said, "she thinks we should reschedule the *Pedida de Mano* for this Saturday. Do you think your father would be fine with that?"

Claudia appeared to be fighting a smile. "I don't know, Sebastian. Your father's passing is so recent."

"Yes. But this is what he would have wanted."

"Whatever you'd like is fine by me."

He caressed her cheek. Claudia, his eternal bride, the angel who'd been waiting for him to propose for the last four years. How could he, with all his imperfections, have lucked out with such a perfect woman? How could he ever doubt that she would be anything but the best wife a man could want?

She was always so compliant, so ready to please him. Never a scorn, never a disagreement. Best of all, she was the complete opposite of his mother.

"Sebastian? Did you hear me?"

He moved toward her. He needed to feel close to another human being now that the only person he'd counted on had died. He held her face between his hands and kissed her. She welcomed the kiss for a moment, but as he pulled closer, her body tensed. With his tongue he attempted to break the barrier of her lips, but she tightened them and pulled her head back. She pushed his chest with her hand.

"Sebastian," she whispered. "Your father just died. How could you even think about . . ."

He moved away from her, rubbing his temple with his hand.

"You're right, you're right. I apologize."

She glanced over her shoulder at the living room doorway. "Anyone could have walked in."

He sat back. He needed to control these urges with Claudia. She was a decent woman and his future wife, not one of the girls at the Zona Roja.

And yet, sometimes Claudia could be so passionate, but when he least expected it, she would stop him and remind him there were rules of conduct to follow. Oh, when was that aspirin going to start working?

"Are you all right?" she asked.

"Yes. I'm fine." He needed a smoke. Badly. "Who's the girl who opened the door?"

Claudia rested her hands on her lap. "Do you remember María Teresa Santos?"

"I think my mother has mentioned her."

"Well, Liliana is her daughter. She's staying with us for a few weeks."

He recalled the name from one of his mother's idiotic conversations. "That's right. They live somewhere in the Coast."

"Manabí."

He'd never been to Manabí. So where had he seen her then?

"She seems . . . a little different," he said.

She raised her voice. "Different? How?"

"I don't know. The way she carries herself, the way she dresses."

"Yes, she's different," she said. "But you know how *monas* are. People from the Coast don't value the same things we do. Traditions, family, you know." She rubbed her palms on her skirt. "Morals."

"I've never thought of them as immoral people, just more blunt and outgoing than us."

"Oh, she is immoral." She bit her lower lip.

"How come?"

"Why are you so interested in her now?"

"I don't know." He set his arm on the sofa's backrest. "Curiosity, I guess."

"You want to know the real reason why she's here? Well, I'll tell you why." She talked faster than usual. He'd never seen her this animated before. "Her mother sent her here to keep her away from her married lover." She covered her mouth with her hand, as if this gesture would take her words back.

"Señor Sebastian! I didn't know you were here. I would have brought you a slice of flan," Trinidad said from the threshold.

Claudia placed her hand on her chest. "Trinidad, you need to make your presence known in a less strident way. You nearly gave me a heart attack."

"I'm sorry, Niña," the maid said. "But you know your mother's rules."

"Yes. You don't need to remind me." Claudia walked past her. "I'll go get the flan."

Trinidad stood behind the couch, like she did every time Sebastian visited his future wife, not that Claudia herself would ever let him do anything more than hold her hand for five seconds.

The headache continued after Sebastian left Claudia's house, and the heat was only making it worse. He stopped by El Turco's store on his way to the newspaper, but Turco himself told him they were out of Lucky Strikes. His supplier hadn't brought him any this week. He offered him another brand, for free, but Sebastian declined. It had to be his Luckys, his precious American cigarettes, nothing else would do. He loosened his tie a notch. The thought of spending the entire day without a smoke made his head hurt more, but he had to go to work. He'd been avoiding his responsibilities for too long already.

On his way downtown, he fought an obstacle course of condolences. Being a public figure in a town like San Isidro wasn't always easy. Not that he had ever wanted the notoriety that came with having a father who'd owned the town's only newspaper. In fact, he hated it. He despised having to get drunk in isolated dumps so nobody would see him, or lock himself in his room for hours.

He stopped in front of the ugliest building in town, and his father's second home. His first, really. *El Heraldo de San Isidro* sat across from the Iglesia de Santo Domingo in the heart of downtown. The five-story building had been built forty years ago by Sebastian's grandfather. Back then, it had been a proud display of modern architecture with its electric elevator, high ceilings, glass windows, and decorative cast iron in the façade— the greatest source of pride for the Rivas family.

Not for Sebastian. He'd always thought it was out of place in a colonial town. It didn't match any other buildings around it and was unnecessarily flamboyant. Growing up, he'd been embarrassed to be associated with such a pompous construction. Ironically, now he had to spend eight hours a day locked inside those cold walls and persistent moldy odor.

He walked into the building and waved at the guard at the desk. He didn't stop—he didn't need any more condolences— and climbed the stairs, already missing his old crowded office and the loud noise of the press humming in his ears for hours on end. He never took the elevator, even though his father's office was on the fifth floor. But he wouldn't have taken it even if it was on the tenth, fifteenth, or twentieth floor of a skyscraper. It was only a matter of time before someone got stuck inside that trembling contraption. He'd made that mistake before, back when he was a little boy, but it wouldn't happen again.

Breathing hard, he reached the fifth floor. Pamela Torres sat at her desk. Pleasant, gentle, a lady if ever there was one, she'd been his father's secretary for as long as he could remember. She stood up as he approached her desk and waddled on wide hips toward him. Sebastian had always thought Pamela's body belonged to two different women. Her torso was petite, her breasts unnoticeable, and her arms, two bones scarcely covered with skin. Her lower body, on the other hand, held probably seventy percent of her weight. Her legs were thick, her derriere stuck out like a duck's tail, and her hips stretched horizontally in a way that caused creases in any skirt she wore.

Pamela offered a warm hug. "I'm sorry for your loss." Her voice broke. "Your father will be missed."

Sebastian believed her words. He had seen the way she adoringly stared at his father over the years.

"I'm so glad you're back, Sebastian. Things have been very . . . different around here lately."

A male voice behind him interrupted the hug.

"Sebastian! I'm sorry, Señor Rivas, what are you doing here so soon?"

Sebastian greeted Cesar Villamizar, his father's right-hand man.

Cesar was a small, quiet man with black-frame glasses and a trim beard. He had worn a white shirt and suspenders since Sebastian first visited the newspaper back when he was five or six years old. Cesar had been his father's most loyal employee. Originally a reporter, he'd morphed into several different positions within the organization—as often happened in small newspapers—including photographer, and most recently managing editor.

"Don't call me Señor. I'm Sebastian, like always."

"But you're the owner now."

Sebastian didn't want to be reminded of that. "Newspaper Owner" was not a title he was looking forward to. As production manager all he had to do was make sure the printing press worked well, the ink didn't bleed, and the paper didn't get stuck. He didn't want to have to worry about stories, salaries, and advertisers.

Cesar stretched his suspenders with his thumbs. "Sebastian, I wanted to apologize for not attending your father's funeral, but I had to go to Guayaquil for . . . personal reasons."

"I understand, Cesar. You don't need to apologize."

When Sebastian glanced at Pamela, her smile had faded. He headed to his father's office, followed by Cesar. A blend of scents including leather couches, cigarettes, and bleach gave Sebastian a sudden vision of his father. He could picture him sitting behind his desk with his arms stretched behind his head, displaying the confident smile people in town, especially women, found so charming. How different from the Ignacio Rivas of the last three months, when that damn cancer had consumed him. Sebastian reached the cherrywood desk and rubbed the surface. He waited until Cesar closed the office door before speaking.

"I need to know in what state my father left the company."

Cesar's smile dissipated. "You mean the bookkeeping?"

"Yes."

"Well, your father said I would be in charge of the finances after he . . . passed."

Sebastian sat behind his father's desk. "Cesar, I'm sure my father had a good reason to tell you that, but I'd rather keep you in your current position. You've done such a wonderful job for us." He rested his palms on the sides of the leather chair. "I'll take care of that tedious stuff."

Frowning, Cesar walked toward a file cabinet in the corner of the room and removed a pile of leather-bound folders. He placed the stack in front of Sebastian.

Sebastian exhaled. This looked like hours of work.

"Do you have any Luckys?"

"I don't smoke, Sebastian."

His head throbbed again.

Chapter 6

Nobody had followed her to the park, it seemed. Fortunately the place was crowded enough to get lost among the faces of these strangers.

With one of her gloves, Malena wiped the dust off a bench and sat down across from the statue of Juan León Mera, one of the country's most prolific writers and the author of the National Anthem—if she remembered correctly. Then, she removed the letter from her purse; the letter with Ana's name on it, not hers. She hadn't dared open it yet, not only for practical reasons—Claudia or Trinidad could have walked into the room—but also because it wasn't hers. Tampering with other people's correspondence was a serious offense, and it was also unethical. Not that she'd behaved in the most honest way since she'd arrived.

She traced the edges of the stamp with her finger, reading the faded postmark on top. The letter had been sent from Quito two days ago, the day Lili was supposed to arrive. If only she could open the envelope without tearing it, but it was tightly sealed. No matter how carefully she tried to unglue the flap, it would rip. She took a deep breath; there was no turning back now. She tore the side of the envelope and removed a white piece of paper folded in three parts.

Doña Ana,

I'm unable to accept the invitation to stay at your home in San Isidro. I've decided, instead, to start a new life with the man I love, even when it's without my family's blessing. Please tell my mother not to look for me. Juan Pablo and I will make sure she can't find us. Tell her, also, that her plans to separate us didn't work, and that it will take a long time for me to forgive and forget the pain she caused.

I apologize for the trouble this situation might have caused you.

Sincerely,
Liliana Paz

Malena allowed herself a smile of relief in spite of the guilt and shame of her dishonesty. Lili was not dead or wounded. She had eloped with her boyfriend. And she wouldn't be coming to San Isidro. *Ever.*

The honest thing—the *responsible* thing—to do would be to return this letter to Ana and confess. But it was too tempting, this interesting twist of fate, too easy to be seduced by the possibilities this letter offered. Lili's secret could be hers. Nobody would have to know, nobody would even suspect who she really was.

The image of her grandmother Eva came to mind. La Abuela would never approve of this deceit. But who was she to criticize her? Hadn't she lied to Malena all her life? Hadn't her father lied, too? And her mother, for that matter. Everyone lied, it seemed. Then why couldn't she do it? Malena had always been the good girl, she'd always followed the rules, and look where that had taken her: nowhere. And besides, it was for a good cause. There must be a powerful reason why her mother had hidden the truth for so long. She must have kept it from the rest of the family, too. It would be devastating for all if Malena exposed her in public.

As Lili, Malena could find out what happened, approach her mother in private (given that she was one of the living sisters), and then go back to her normal life. Whatever was left of it, anyway: no father, an empty apartment, and her second year of nursing school, which, let's face it, was a problem. Not only did the sight of blood or nasty little frogs' guts revolt her stomach, but she couldn't stand being around needles either—much less pushing them through someone's flesh! Sure, it had been her decision. Malena herself had chosen this smart, practical profession—just like her mother. God, she was so pathetic. It was likely that her mother had not been a nurse at all! But there was only one way to find out if this had also been a lie. She *had* to stay in San Isidro. It didn't have to be long. Just until she could confront the sisters and learn the truth.

Just a little while longer.

And now, she had to dispose of this letter. It would be too risky to take it back to the house. She read it again and again, trying to memorize every sentence, every word, for she would never lay eyes on it again. When she was done, she shredded it into tiny pieces and dumped them inside a wide wastebasket by the bench. As she released the last piece of paper, her pulse slowed down, and she had a sudden urge to laugh, to hug someone. She had time now, all the time she needed. She picked up her purse from the bench and headed home, admiring the clear sky for the first time in the day.

The confidence Malena had gained at the park faded as she approached Calle Alameda. The fear of being discovered returned. Too many things could go wrong. She could say something inappropriate, Lili's mother could call, or someone could ask a question she didn't know how to answer. There were just too many variables she couldn't control. How could she think for a moment that she was safe in this role?

She rang the doorbell to the Platas home. Not a minute had passed before Trinidad—flushed cheeks and sweaty forehead—opened the door.

"Niña Liliana! Where have you been? Doña Ana was so worried." She held the door for her. "They're all waiting for you."

Waiting? For *what?* Malena followed Trinidad to the dining room, where the entire family had gathered—a soup of some sort in everyone's bowls.

"Good afternoon," she said. "I apologize for the delay."

Ana set her spoon aside. "Where were you?"

"I went out for a walk." She looked at all the somber faces staring back at her. "To get acquainted with the town."

Rafael faced his wife. "Haven't you told her the rules of the house yet?"

Ana nibbled at her thumbnail. Today she wore a white long-sleeved blouse with buttoned cuffs.

"Well, Señorita," Rafael told Malena. "Lunch and dinner in this house are served every day at the same time. One and seven o'clock, respectively. Tardiness is not tolerated here, nor is it appropriate for a young lady to take walks by herself without permission. Next time you want to go for a walk, you would need to go with Claudia, Javier, or anybody else in here."

Malena bit the inside of her cheek. Not even her father had imposed a schedule on her. In fact, *she'd* been the one to run the schedule in her house. And if she'd waited for a chaperone, she would have never left her apartment!

"Leave her alone, Rafael," Amanda said. "You're going to scare the poor girl." She turned to Malena. "Come join us, please."

Everyone had taken the same seats from the previous day and Malena's chair sat empty. *Her chair, her spot at the table.* The spot she should have always used, and was finally claiming now, after twenty years, under false pretenses. She sat down. Trinidad promptly set a bowl of *caldo de patas* in front of her.

"As I was saying," Amanda said. "Il Napolitano is not going to survive much longer under its current administration."

"I've been telling you for years to sell your half to your brother-in-law, but you never listen," Rafael said.

"Well, it's too late now," Amanda said. "Enzo won't have anything to do with it anymore."

Ana turned to her sister. "Why not? What happened to him?"

"He's burnt out," Amanda said.

"It's understandable," Ana said. "After so many years."

"Maybe." Amanda stirred her soup. "At any rate, I've made a decision." She looked around the room. "I'm going to manage it."

Everyone talked at the same time, their heads shaking.

"But that's not all." Amanda's voice rose above the rest. "I'm going to turn it into a tango nightclub."

Silence sucked the air out of the room. For the first time during the discussion, Malena became interested in what Amanda had to say.

"Have you lost your mind?" Rafael said. "Do you want to drag your family name through the mud? You know that Pope Pius X forbid the tango, right?"

"That was decades ago!" Amanda said.

"So what? It's still indecent."

"Oh, she's not serious," Ana said. "She's just teasing, right, Amanda?"

Amanda's face was grim. "No, I'm serious."

Mamá Blanca smoothed out the creases on her napkin. "Oh, dear."

"But Amanda," Ana pleaded. "Nobody here dances the tango. It's an Argentincan dance."

"No one dances the tango?" Amanda said. "The whole world loves it!"

"You'd better talk your sister out of this madness," Rafael told Ana, throwing his napkin on the table and getting up from his seat. He darted by a wide-mouthed Trinidad, who stood anchored behind the table with a tray of rice in her hands, and slammed the door behind him.

"You see what you've done?" Ana told Amanda.

"I'm sorry if my decision makes your husband uncomfortable, but I'm not going to change my mind."

"Don't you see? Everybody is going to start talking about you . . . about us. It's shameful, Tía." Claudia's voice broke. "What am I going to tell Sebastian?"

"A woman running a cabaret! Imagine that!" Ana said.

"A nightclub, Ana," Amanda said. "A classy one."

"Well, I would be more concerned over the fact that you've never managed a business before." All heads turned to Alejandra as she voiced her opinion in a sweet but strong voice.

"Yes, but I lived with a businessman for five years. I saw how he did things. If an idiot like Enzo managed the restaurant for twenty years, I'm sure I can do it. Frankly, I'm surprised at all of your reactions. I expected more support."

"It's a man's world, Amanda," Ana said.

"Women can work, too," Amanda said. "In fact, I know of some who are more competent than most men." She looked at Alejandra.

"You know that's different," Ana said.

"I would have never guessed you had such a low opinion of me, Ana," Amanda said sadly. "You must think I'm a moron."

"*Madre,*" Ana faced her mother. "Aren't you going to say something?"

Mamá Blanca finished chewing. "Amanda is an adult and she knows what she's doing."

"I think it's a great idea," Malena said—tango was so swell!

Ana and Claudia frowned. Amanda seemed to notice Malena for the first time.

"I do, too," Javier said.

"Javier!" Ana's high-pitched voice reached new heights.

"Have you thought of a name yet?" Malena asked Amanda.

"I have a few ideas."

Ana stood up. "I've lost my appetite."

Claudia stood after her and followed her mother out of the room.

Mamá Blanca set her napkin by her plate. "I don't feel so good. I'm going to rest."

Malena rose. "I'll help you upstairs."

She held the older woman's plump arm and helped her out of the chair. The two of them climbed the stairs carefully. Mamá Blanca used Malena's arm as a cane, while Malena held on to the rail for balance. Mamá Blanca was heavier than she looked. Still, the experience of holding her grandmother moved her. *Her* grandmother. At this point, she could only be certain of one thing about this family. Whoever her mother might be, Mamá Blanca was her grandmother.

For a moment, while helping the old woman lie down on her bed, Malena felt as though La Abuela was back, except that Mamá Blanca had a sweetness that Eva Sevilla had never had. La Abuela had been a pillar of knowledge and a strict disciplinarian, whereas Mamá Blanca reminded Malena of a child; someone who needed protection and care.

Malena brought a blue wool blanket to her grandmother's legs. "Better?"

She patted the side of her bed. "Come here. Let me see you."

Hesitantly, Malena obeyed. With cold fingers, Mamá Blanca lifted Malena's chin, examining her entire face. Malena fought the urge to move away, to prevent the woman from discovering something about her. She focused on the old lady's bosom as it moved up and down in rhythmic breathing.

"You don't look anything like María Teresa or Manuel," Mamá Blanca diagnosed after a thorough study. "It's so strange. You look more like my Abigail."

"Abigail was your daughter, right?"

"Yes. The light of my life."

"I saw a picture of her in the study."

Mamá Blanca picked up her knitting needles. "Yes. She was lovely, wasn't she? Even on her deathbed."

"What happened to her?"

"Kidney failure." Her eyes filled with tears.

"I'm sorry," Malena said sincerely. She knew everything about the loss of loved ones. "Did she ever marry?"

"She was engaged once, but fortunately that ended. It was best that she didn't marry."

Mamá Blanca leaned back on her pillow and closed her eyes. *No, don't go to sleep. Not now. Why was it best that Abigail never married?*

Her grandmother opened her eyes again, as if she'd heard her.

"There is a young man in the picture," Malena said. "Is he your son, too?"

"No, that was Fausto, my nephew. My husband and I raised him after my sister passed away. I loved him like a son. He also . . ." She shook her head.

Malena placed her hand on top of Mamá Blanca's and looked at the woman with compassion, understanding now why she always wore black.

"He was wonderful," she said. "He brought so much life and joy to this house. When he left, a part of all of us died."

"Was he also sick?"

"No. A despicable man killed him when he was only nineteen. Alejandra was never the same after he was gone." She paused for a moment. "Well, none of us . . . but it affected her the most. She adored him."

Deep wrinkles framed Mamá Blanca's mouth. Malena didn't want to press the issue any further, though this knowledge had raised more questions in her mind. The old woman looked exhausted, physically and emotionally.

Malena stood up. "I'll let you rest now."

"Lili?"

"Yes?"

"Don't ever mention Fausto in front of Alejandra."

Malena tightened her grasp on the rusty metal chains and kicked her legs harder, swinging higher and higher above the sparse patch of grass under her feet. The cool breeze on her face was a blessing; the scents of moist grass and eucalyptus were comforting. She glanced at her bare tanned calves and her white and blue checkered uniform skirt waving with the wind. Her socks were pushed down to her ankles and her white sneakers were untied.

She looked around the park for the familiar voice nearby. La Abuela Eva was sitting on a bench, a few steps away, in that two-piece gray suit Malena despised. She was looking up at a woman standing in front of her, immersed in conversation. The woman had her back to Malena, and wore a hat with a white feather.

That has to be her. That has to be my mother. She needed to reach the woman before she left. Oh no, they were shaking hands and La Abuela was saying *"Hasta luego."*

Malena jumped off the swing, landing painfully on her palms and knees. The ground was harder than she'd expected. She stared at her palms, now filled with soil and blood. It was hot out here. Why had she jumped? It was so refreshing on the swing. She looked for the woman. She was walking away. Malena tried to get up, but her legs wouldn't move fast enough. They were heavy, and they ached.

"Mamá!" she yelled. "Wait!"

She stood up in slow motion. Her scratched knees burned.

"Turn around," she muttered. If only she could see her mother's face.

"What are you doing here?" a male voice asked her.

Malena met her father's glare. "Papá, you're back. You're alive!"

"You're supposed to be at school, Lili."

Lili? "No, Papá, I'm Malena."

Her father looked angry, and old. Older than ever.

"Whose handkerchief is this?" he asked.

Handkerchief? What was he talking about? Malena looked at her hands—they were still bleeding—but there was no handkerchief. "I need a handkerchief," she said. "Don't you see I'm bleeding?"

She searched behind him for her mother. Where had she gone? Why had she let her father distract her?

He repeated the question. "Whose handkerchief is this?"

Malena opened her eyes and looked around the bright room. *Claudia's room.* She was alone and it was eight in the morning, according to the bedside clock.

She heard the male voice again.

"Are you going to tell me whose handkerchief this is?"

A female voice answered him. "Please keep it down, someone could hear you."

Was that Ana's voice? Malena removed the covers from her legs—her knees were intact—and stepped out of the bed. She tiptoed to the door and opened it.

Rafael's voice sounded louder in the hallway. "I don't care. Answer the question. Whose is this?"

Malena followed the thin burgundy rug leading to the adjacent room.

Ana spoke in a soft voice. "I don't know. It probably belongs to one of my sisters. Trini always mixes our things."

"Then how come it was hiding in your bottom drawer?"

"Since when do you look through my things?"

"I wasn't looking *through* your things; I was just trying to find a blessed handkerchief! Is it too much to ask to keep my things in order?"

Malena couldn't hear Ana's answer. She took a step closer to the door. Ana was reduced to a wordless sobbing while Rafael's voice was tight and hard.

"I always suspected there was another man."

Malena stood very still.

Ana managed to get a few words out. "Would you keep it down?"

"No, I don't care who hears us! I'm not the one at fault."

They were quiet for a moment. Malena even considered knocking at the door to interrupt whatever he was doing.

"Rafael, listen to me," Ana pleaded. "I've never been unfaithful to you. I swear."

"I don't believe you. And don't think this is going to end here. I'm going to find out who gave you this."

The door opened without a warning, without a sound. Ana stepped out.

"Lili! I didn't know you were here."

"I'm sorry." Malena hugged her arms, covering up the thin fabric of her nightgown.

Ana closed the door behind her. "I'm sorry about that. We were so loud. Did we wake you?"

"No. I was just . . . going to the lavatory. Excuse me."

She locked herself in the bathroom and washed her face with cold water, unable to erase the image of the white handkerchief poking out of Ana's tight fist.

Chapter 7

Ana, 1936

Ana had always known there was nothing special about her. She wasn't ugly, when compared to the rest of the girls in town, and her body had a decent shape, but she had accepted early on in her eighteen years of life that she would never be one of those beauties who caused men to turn their heads as she walked down the streets of San Isidro. A beauty like her sister Amanda, for example.

Yes, she'd finally accepted it and lived with it. Except for times like this, when standing by her older sister turned out to be an unbearable ordeal. Times when Amanda's beauty pained her, made her physically uncomfortable. She glanced at her sister in the backless silver rayon dress that Mamá Blanca had made for her, grumbling, since she didn't approve of the design. It ought to be illegal, the way the silky looking fabric molded her waist and hips like a second skin. After endless pleas from Amanda and her sisters, it had been Amanda's best friend, Ofelia, who ultimately convinced Mamá Blanca to sew the dress for the radio dance contest.

"You want your daughter to win or not?" she had told her. Ana's mother had agreed to it, with the condition that Amanda would only wear it this one time.

So here they were, on their way to the contest, as soon as the photographer finished taking the family portrait for their parents. The photograph had been Amanda's idea, but she was probably regretting it already. Ana covered up her one-piece crepe frock with her coat and looked straight at the camera, while Amanda argued with Fausto.

"Be still," Amanda told him for the third time. But there was no way to control their younger cousin. Every time the photographer stood behind the camera and pressed the shutter, Fausto tickled Alejandra. Their younger sister would burst out laughing, testing not only the old photographer's patience but also Amanda's.

They should have known better. Put a young boy, a park, and his devoted cousin together, and you get exactly this: an explosion of mischief.

"Excuse us," Amanda told the photographer, who was already loosening his bow tie.

Amanda grabbed the thirteen-year-old Fausto by the arm and dragged him aside.

"If you keep up with this nonsense," she told him. "I am not teaching you how to tango."

Fausto's grin faded. With that serious expression on his face, his navy blue suit, and the shadow of a mustache above his upper lip, he looked like a man already. And what a handsome man he would turn out to be one day, with those enormous hazel eyes and curly eyelashes.

"You promised, Amanda."

"I did. But now I'm promising a beating if you don't shape up."

"Fine."

He dragged his feet back to the concrete fountain and stood stiffly by Alejandra. Amanda turned to Ana and Abigail, clapping her hands.

"Come on, girls. Sit up straight."

Resting on a nearby bench, the photographer continued fanning himself with a newspaper. "I'm not getting up until you're ready."

"We are," Amanda said. "I promise."

The man uncrossed his legs and lifted himself from the bench with extraordinary effort. He resumed his position behind the camera and buried himself under a thick black cloth.

"Everyone still—and smile," he ordered without a trace of kindness.

Ana didn't smile. It was too hot to smile. She merely held Amanda's arm and sat still.

After a moment, the photographer removed the cloth from his head, revealing a mass of messy hair.

"Perfect."

"Thank you, Sr. Valencia," Amanda told him, pulling Ana by the arm. "Come on, we're late."

Abigail rushed behind them. "Can I come, too?"

Amanda took longer strides and whispered into Ana's ear. "Pretend you didn't hear her."

But their sister caught up with them and seized Amanda's arm. "Please."

"No!"

"It's not fair, I'm already fifteen." And she was, but didn't look it. Her breasts had hardly developed yet and Mamá Blanca continued to dress her like a child. That pink ribbon around her waist would simply not do at such an important dance contest. Amanda would never consent to take Abigail with them.

"Don't you have to go to the pool or something?" Amanda said.

Abigail pouted. "Yes."

"Then? Get going! You still have to go home and change."

Amanda dragged Ana across the street. "And make sure Alejandra and Fausto go home with you!"

Ana gave Abigail one last glance as she stood by the curb, kicking a light post. If she could have switched places with her, she would have done it in a heartbeat. There was nothing more dreadful than dancing, especially under Amanda's stern eye.

Amanda made them stop a block before reaching the radio station to fix their hair and dresses. "Take off that coat," Amanda told her. "You look like an old woman."

Ana eyed her mother's coat. It was an old woman's coat, but at least it covered her dull dress. "But I'm cold."

"In this heat? Are you crazy? Come on. Hurry up."

Ana removed her coat and hung it on her forearm.

"Amanda!" a man's voice called at the end of the street.

Joaquin Nasser, Amanda's best friend and eternal admirer, approached them. He wore a black suit and his hat covered the edge of his dark eyebrows.

"What took you so long?" he asked; no hellos or even a glance of acknowledgment for Ana. That's the way things were when she stood by her sister: men didn't see her.

"We were having our picture taken," Amanda said.

"It had to be today?"

"Yes," Amanda said. "My parents' anniversary is coming up and I wanted to surprise them with a picture of us."

As they approached the radio station, they encountered a long line of youngsters in their best outfits. Joaquin handed Ana and Amanda safety pins and two pieces of white cloth with numbers printed on them. Ana returned her number to Joaquin.

"I'm not dancing."

"Of course you are," Amanda told her.

"Yes," Joaquin said. "I brought Rafael with me."

Joaquin pointed at his friend, standing at the front of the line. Ana bit the corner of her thumbnail—a habit that appeared every time she was nervous. Despite his extreme thinness and that serious expression he always displayed, Ana found Rafael to be an attractive young man. She'd only seen him smile once, at her—not at Amanda—and his eyes often lingered in her direction—not her sister's—which was more than she could say of any other man.

Joaquin held Amanda's hand and caught up with Rafael. Ana followed a few steps behind.

"*Flaco*," he told Rafael, "you know Amanda Platas, right?" Rafael nodded.

"This is her sister, Ana."

Rafael gave her a brief look. "Yes, we've met."

Ana stared at the black shoes Amanda had lent her. She rarely used heels this high and her feet were already hurting. And she hadn't even started dancing yet.

"Look!" Joaquin pointed at a silver-haired man opening the station's front door. The sounds of violins and drums vibrated in the street. Amanda applauded while Ana restrained her feet from running in the opposite direction. Her sister must have read her mind, for she gripped her arm tighter.

"You're not going anywhere, Ana."

The line moved into a tall foyer where they left their coats and continued through a pair of open doors to a circular dance floor against a raised podium occupied by the orchestra. On the opposite end was a room surrounded by glass windows. Three men wearing headphones stood in front of oval-shaped microphones, chatting among themselves as the dance floor filled up.

Ana slipped to the corner of the room in an attempt to disappear, but Rafael followed her there with his hands buried inside his pockets. He stood beside her without saying a word while Joaquin and Amanda rushed to the center of the dance floor.

The voice of the master of ceremonies caused Ana's heart to start a frantic beating to the rhythm of the drums. An *Otavaleño* with a blue poncho and a long braid shut the door. There was nowhere else to go.

The first song was a conga, a tropical rhythm born in Cuba—like so many others—and one of her sister's favorites. From a distance, Ana discerned Joaquin's arms wrapped around Amanda's waist, twirling her in circles around the dance floor. Ana tapped her feet on the floor. It was an involuntary reaction, stronger than her will or her pride. The music had that effect on her—when nobody was looking.

Joaquin signaled Rafael to come to the dance floor. Ana glanced at the door. It was only a few steps away, but the master of ceremonies had warned them not to leave the room until the contest ended.

A cool hand touched her arm. Rafael was looking down at her. He had the cutest mouth and white, straight teeth. She read his lips for it was too loud in there to hear him.

"Do you want to dance?"

She nodded and let his hand guide her onto the crowded dance floor.

Rafael held one of her sweaty, clammy hands in his and pulled her against him while his other hand rested on her lower back. As the distance closed between them, she smelled the coffee and cigarettes on his skin. They started to move, avoiding each other's eyes. Ana, usually the lead at home, took a step forward in an effort to follow the beat of the song. But the only thing she accomplished was stamping on Rafael's foot.

"I'm sorry," she said even though he couldn't hear her. A frown appeared on his face for a split second before he tightened his grasp on her hand and pulled her closer to him. He took a decisive step forward, and she answered by stepping back. She knew without seeing herself that it had been an awkward, graceless move.

She could dance—Amanda had made sure she learned by the age of ten—but not with a man. She didn't know how to turn gracefully or move her hips the way Amanda did. Especially not in front of a group of strangers or the man she liked.

They continued pulling on each other and stepping on each other's feet during the rest of the song until a tap on Ana's shoulder ended their battle. She was no fool; she had expected to be disqualified, just not this soon. Ana spun on her heels before Rafael said something. She only wanted to disappear, to lock herself in her room for a month. But first she would have to wait until her sister was done charming every man in the room.

Lowering her head, she marched to her corner. Rafael followed her. She could feel his steps behind her, his nearness. How could she ever look him in the eye again? He would never ask her to dance again.

As a bolero started, her armpits sweated. She needed a drink, but she'd rather endure dehydration than walk past Rafael to the table filled with water cups. He was slouching against the wall, not even looking at her.

The dance floor thinned out after two more songs until there were only three couples in the competition, Amanda and Joaquin among them.

Ana's throat tightened with the first chords of "Volver," one of Gardel's most famous tangos. This tango was Amanda and Joaquin's forte. She straightened her back, proud for the first time to be Amanda's sister.

Joaquin shoved his coat to the corner of the room, revealing a pair of suspenders over his white shirt. He lowered his hat over his eyebrows and extended his arm toward Amanda. She held his hand and the space closed between them. She lifted one leg sensually against his and they started to move in perfect coordination. Their footwork was precise, intricate, and impeccable. Not a single mistake made, not a second of hesitation. The other couples were eliminated almost immediately, and now the entire floor belonged to Amanda and Joaquin—it always had.

As the last notes of the violin approached, Joaquin lifted Amanda, reminding Ana of a fairy flying above the crowd. Her beauty was surreal, absurd, only surpassed by the portrait of the Virgin Mary in her parents' bedroom.

A wave of applause blasted throughout the room after the last note was delivered. Joaquin kissed Amanda's hand. She bowed to the audience around her, a radiant smile illuminating her face.

The master of ceremonies approached them with an award in his hands: a small statue of a couple dancing. He handed Amanda the statue and announced over the microphone the grand prize: a dinner for two at Il Napolitano, the fanciest restaurant in town.

Ana rushed to her sister's side and gave her a hug, inhaling Mamá Blanca's hyacinth perfume on Amanda's neck, and feeling her damp back against her hand.

"I saw you dancing with Rafael," Amanda whispered in her ear. "I think he likes you."

Ana glanced at Rafael. He was busy talking to Joaquin. Amanda was delusional, probably due to the excitement of winning.

"Joaquin and I are going to Il Napolitano now," Amanda said louder, and turning toward Rafael, she placed her hand on his arm. "Would you mind taking Ana home?"

Ana pinched Amanda's free arm. Was she out of her mind? Her sister was leaving her at the mercy of a stranger! She pulled Amanda aside.

"Don't do this, Amanda, please. Can't you go to dinner after dropping me home?"

"Of course not. If our father sees me with Joaquin, he won't let me leave the house again."

"But I barely know him." Rafael watched her as he spoke to Joaquin. "It will be unbearable."

"Unbearable?" Amanda laughed. "The house is only ten minutes away. Besides, you like him. What better chance to be alone with him? It's now or never."

"Who told you I like him?" Ana broke eye contact with Rafael and returned her attention to her sister's cheerful face.

"I'm not blind, Ana. And I know he's sweet on you, too. The only problem is he's just as shy as you are. That's why you have to take advantage of this opportunity."

"Wait. What am I supposed to tell Papá Pancho about you?"

"Just tell him I'm at the convent, knitting blankets for the orphanage."

"This late?"

Amanda shrugged. Everything to her was unimportant, uncomplicated. It was Ana's job to worry.

Amanda walked over to Joaquin's side and slipped her arm through his. "Have a good night, you two," she told Rafael and Ana while dragging Joaquin toward the door.

An awkward silence fell between them. Ana ran her hand over her forehead as Rafael drew near her.

"Let's go get your coat," he said.

He led the way to the foyer and helped her into her coat, avoiding eye contact. Maybe Amanda was right. Maybe he was shy. And two shy people couldn't get together unless one of them made the first move. Hesitantly, she wrapped her fingers around his arm. He flinched, but didn't pull away.

They walked outside, careful not to ruin their fragile bond. One wrong move, one erroneous comment could break the magic.

"Did you enjoy yourself?" she asked.

"I'm not fond of dancing." He glanced at her. "But you are."

"Me? Oh, no. It's all Amanda. She can be very persuasive."

"I noticed."

They continued to walk in silence. Ana searched the depths of her mind for something charming to say. *Charming* was the word Amanda used. "You have to charm them," she repeated every time they talked about boys.

Except that there was nothing charming about Ana.

"Ana," Rafael said after a school and three houses of dreadful silence. "I'm going to be honest with you. I've been watching you for a long time. You come from a decent family, and your father has a prosperous business. You seem like a good woman, fond of your house, well-mannered, and decent-looking." He glanced at her. "I'm looking to settle down soon; I've been working at my uncle's store for two years now and I think I can afford the rent of a small apartment." He stopped and held her hands in his. "I'm not looking for a long engagement and I want a large family. What about you?"

Ana was too shocked to pronounce a syllable. Was this a marriage proposal? It seemed more like a job interview. Or maybe this was part of a cruel joke. She couldn't tell if he was smiling, it had gotten too dark.

"Well?"

"I don't know what you expect me to say," she said.

"Are you interested?"

Of course she was interested. She'd liked Rafael for months now. Amanda's words pounded in her mind. "You have to take advantage of this opportunity." If she gave him the wrong answer now, this would be the end for her, and then who knew if another man would ever look at her again. Not with a sister like Amanda nearby.

"Yes," she said.

His teeth shone in the dusk. This was the second time in her life she'd seen him smile.

He softly kissed her hand and her stomach danced in circles. "I'll speak to your father tomorrow."

Ana wasn't exactly sure what she'd agreed to. A courtship? An engagement? Marriage? The only thing she knew was that for the first time in her life a man had picked her over her sister. And it looked like she was going to be the first one in her family to marry. She wouldn't be an old maid, like she'd feared for years. It had been a good day after all.

"So you like it or not?" María Teresa asked Ana as they both studied her reflection in the mirror.

Ana could hardly recognize herself with her hair up. She looked sophisticated and older, which was exactly what she wanted. María Teresa had done a superb job with her bun and makeup.

"It's perfect, Maritere. Thank you."

"Then what's wrong? You don't look like a happy bride."

Ana sighed. Her wedding plans had progressed in a haze. Not her plans, her father's. He'd been so excited about marrying off one of his daughters he'd accelerated the wedding after barely three months of courtship. Rafael didn't mind, and neither did Ana. The entire experience was thrilling, a dream come true. Mamá Blanca sewed her dress, her sisters and best friend were going to be her bridesmaids, and the ceremony would be held at the Iglesia de Santo Domingo. What else could she ask for?

Nothing, really. Everything was turning out just like she'd dreamt. Except for that sudden urge of hers to stop all the clocks in her house, to go back in time, to rethink this whole thing. Just a few weeks, a couple of months even.

She was being foolish, having doubts this late, nearly an hour before the ceremony. This panic freezing her against the chair was probably normal. All brides must feel this way before their wedding. Rafael would be a good provider, a loyal husband. He respected her. He was a gentleman. Everything she'd asked for in a man.

"Anita?" María Teresa said. "You are happy, right?"

Anita. María Teresa was the only person in the world who called her that. She glanced at her friend's shiny red hair—that extraordinary hair that always called attention everywhere she went, as she was the only redhead in town. Ana couldn't hide anything from her. She'd been her best friend since the fifth grade and knew her better than anyone else. Talking to María Teresa was easier than talking to her sisters or her mother, who always judged her and told her what to do.

Ana stood up, tightening her robe across her chest, and walked over to her bed, where her satin wedding gown lay. She sat on the edge of her bed, admiring the sparkling rhinestones encrusted on the belt of her dress.

"You know," Ana said. "*Seco de chivo* is one of the hardest recipes I've ever made. People think it's easy because it's such a popular dish. They serve it everywhere, right? But it's tricky to make. There are so many ingredients, so many flavors blended in, you just can't tell if it needs more salt or beer or *aji*. Maybe you need to add more tomato or onion or *culantro*. No matter how many times I make it, there always seems to be something missing." She focused on the freckles that ran along María Teresa's nose. "That's exactly how I feel about Rafael."

"You're just nervous, *amiga mía*. It's normal."

"The other day he got cross with me because I wore a sleeveless shirt."

"He probably didn't want you to catch a cold. He's only taking care of you!"

"He's not very affectionate. He's never kissed me."

"That's because he respects you," María Teresa said. "But don't worry, that'll change once you're married."

"I don't know. When Amanda talks about boys, she says they have these . . . urges. They always want to kiss and touch her."

"Amanda, always Amanda. You know the kind of reputation your sister has? People are still talking about the dress she wore for the dance contest."

"They are?"

"Yes, *querida*. I know she's your sister, but you're blinded by her. Be happy that you found a man who overlooked her behavior and is still willing to marry into your family."

Ana let out a deep breath. María Teresa was right. She was lucky to have found Rafael. Everything would be fine after they were married. At least she hoped so.

It had been a beautiful wedding. Everyone said so. And she was a radiant bride, according to her mother's friends. With her hand, Ana felt the cloche cap headpiece hugging her head to make sure it was real. Yes, this was her veil and this man in the tuxedo, white bow tie, and matching gloves was her husband. She held Rafael's arm tighter as they stood in the greeting line of the Club de Rotarios's foyer. Faces blended in front of her as they congratulated her. Amanda came by, holding the arm of a tall man with inquisitive green eyes and a regal stance. This must be the mysterious man she'd met the night of the contest, the man she'd been talking about incessantly since that day. But he must have been at least ten years older than them!

"Ana, this is Nicolas Fornasieri," she said. "Nicolas, my sister Ana."

Ana shook his hand, shocked that such perfection existed outside the Renaissance paintings in Alejandra's art books.

"Nice to meet you."

He kissed her hand. "*Bellissima.*"

Ana smiled. Nobody had ever called her beautiful before.

"This is my brother, Vincenzo." Nicolas pointed at a young man resembling himself, who stood behind Amanda. "I hope you don't mind that I brought him with me."

"No, not at all," Ana said.

Nicolas's brother shook her hand.

"Call me Enzo," he said. Up close, he was even more handsome than his brother.

Ana recovered her hand. "Please, make yourselves comfortable. There's plenty of food and drink in the parlor."

Rafael glowered at the newcomers.

After they finished greeting the last guests in line, Rafael asked her to come with him. He led her toward the lavatory, pulling on her arm a bit too hard. He yanked the door open and pushed her in.

"What's wrong?" she asked. "What are we doing here?"

He locked the door behind them. "Who are those men with Amanda?"

"Friends of hers. Why?"

"What were they telling you?"

"Nothing. They just congratulated me."

"No. They were giving you compliments. I heard them. And one of them kissed your hand."

"He was just being nice."

Rafael hit the wall. "No. He was flirting. How dare he kiss you in front of me? It's our wedding day, for God's sake!"

Ana took a step back. She'd seen Rafael displeased before, but not like this.

"It's that Italian, isn't it?" he said.

What did he know about him? "Yes, the owner of Il Napolitano."

"What is he doing here?"

"Amanda invited him."

He drew his brows together. "How dare she? This is not her wedding."

"I don't understand what's wrong with that. He's her friend."

"And Joaquin is mine, and he happens to be my best man."

She caressed Rafael's cheek. "Forgive her, please. There's nothing we can do about it. I can't ask them to leave."

"That sister of yours, I should have known better than . . ."

He removed his gloves and shoved them by the sink. What was he going to say? Did he regret marrying Ana?

"I think Joaquin will understand," she said. "Don't let that ruin our day." She held his hands in hers and kissed them tenderly.

His eyes softened a notch. "You do look very nice today."

This was the first compliment he'd given her. He held her face with her hands and kissed her. Softly at first, but then his tongue broke into her mouth in an aggressive search. She could taste the champagne on his lips and his new mustache rubbed her skin like sandpaper.

"You're mine," he said in a distant, strange voice.

He pushed her against the tiled wall, his hands traveling hungrily about her body, leaving no part untouched. His hand lingered painfully on one of her breasts and the other found her hand and brought it to his crotch. It was hard and warm. She tried to pull away, but he didn't let her. Instead, he raised her dress all the way to her girdle. His hand went directly to her silk panties. He dug his finger inside her most intimate area and rummaged about, as though he were searching for diamonds in a stream.

This was a nightmare, a wedding dream gone bad. She could barely breathe. She needed air, distance. This was not the way she'd imagined her first kiss to be. There was nothing romantic or remotely tender about this fondling.

After what seemed like an eternity, he finally pulled away from her. Still breathing hard, he licked his upper lip with his tongue. "Tonight," he said. "We'll finish tonight."

She shivered. His words sounded more like a threat than a promise.

He straightened his jacket and combed his hair with his fingers. "We need to go back. They're probably looking for us."

"You go ahead," she whispered. "I'll be right there."

"Don't take long."

He walked out the door and left her alone.

Trembling, Ana opened the water faucet and washed her hands, adding more and more soap to her already clean hands. Why had he touched her like that? It had been so dreadful, so vulgar. She didn't even want to think about what awaited her tonight.

She brought her hands to her throat, where a painful lump had formed. Warm tears streamed down her cheeks. This Rafael, the one she'd met in this lavatory, was a stranger. This couldn't be the man she married. She sat on the toilet, covering her face with her hands. What had she done? Who was this savage she'd married?

The door opened behind her, but she didn't dare to turn around. It would be too undignified—the bride crying in the lavatory. She quietly dried her tears with her fingers. Whoever was at the door was watching her and probably didn't know what to do either. After an excruciating moment, the person gently shut the door. Only then did she turn around, confirming that she was alone again. Alone with her reality, for she could never tell anyone the revulsion her new husband had provoked in her.

Chapter 8

At the jewelry store, Rafael was a different man. From a stool behind the counter, Malena witnessed how he assumed an amicable persona who patiently waited for a woman to make a ring selection. He offered several options, praising her slender fingers and good taste. The woman's husband yawned by her side, but his boredom was no obstacle for Rafael to remove another set of rings from the drawer and place them on the counter.

"Mmm . . . I don't know," the woman said. "Maybe a necklace."

Rafael elbowed Javier, whose face emerged from behind the newspaper.

"Necklaces," Rafael mumbled.

Javier folded the paper and shoved it under his arm. From the display case, he removed a necklace with a massive amber pendant. "How about this one?"

The woman tilted her head, considering the piece.

"I think it would match your eyes beautifully," Rafael said.

"Allow me, please." Javier lifted the woman's hair and clasped the necklace around her neck with one swift move. There was undeniable skill and probably years of practice in his deliberate actions—he didn't even drop the paper. He handed her a mirror. "What do you think?"

Eyeing her reflection, she touched the intricate pendant hanging over her bosom. "What do you think, Mariano?"

The husband flinched, as though he'd just woken from a dream. "Very nice, *querida*." He turned to Rafael. "You have a great jeweler."

Rafael patted his son's back. "Yes, we do. Javier is a natural."

Blushing, Javier glanced at Malena.

"Papá . . ."

Javier loosened his tie a notch, his glance shifting from Malena to the counter and back to her. What was wrong with him? What was there to be nervous about? If anything, he should be proud. Malena had no idea he was the genius behind the splendid jewelry in those display cases.

"All right, I'll take it," the woman said.

Both Rafael and the woman's husband exhaled.

"Great choice." Rafael started the transaction behind the cash register while Javier packed the necklace.

The bell at the front door chimed and Claudia walked into the store. She removed her veil, peeking at her father as she did so. Rafael gave her one of those looks—the ones reserved for family members in the privacy of their home.

After the couple left, Rafael turned to Claudia.

"Did you lose your watch or what?"

"I'm sorry, Papá. I stayed for confession."

"Do you have to go to mass every morning? God is probably tired of you already."

"Papá!"

"Confess on Saturdays or whenever it doesn't intrude with your work schedule. We need you here. At least until Liliana learns the job."

What? Malena was expected to work for this man?

Claudia opened a drawer and tossed her purse inside.

Well, if Malena must work here, she would start by reorganizing those cluttered drawers. She'd been itching to do it since Javier opened one of them. Maybe working for the family would alleviate some of the guilt of lying and living off of them.

Rafael faced Javier. "And you! When are you going to clean that damn storage room?"

"Tomorrow."

"No, not tomorrow. Right now." He pointed at the back door. "Now that Claudia's here, you can get to it."

Malena jumped off the stool. "I'll help you."

Someone opened the shop door again—the indecisive woman.

"I changed my mind. I want earrings." She strode toward Javier while her husband stood by the door, looking as if a close family member had just died.

"Go ahead," Javier told Malena. "I'll be right there."

Malena wandered down the hallway, not sure where the storage room was. She heard a muffled noise, the same one from the other day, and opened the door without knocking.

From behind an old wooden desk, Alejandra lifted her head up. She had goggles on and held a small torch and a pair of tongs in her hands. She'd been soldering something, a cross pendant, on top of a rectangular rock-like surface. She turned the torch off and set her tools by a small scale.

"What are you doing here?"

Malena let go of the doorknob. "Sorry. I had no idea you worked here."

Alejandra wiped her hands on her stained blue apron and rested her goggles on her head. Her desk was filled with various types of pliers, hammers, and other tools Malena had never seen before. It was a long room, and there was another desk across from Alejandra's. A kiln sat on a table in the corner of the room. The only source of light, besides the lamps on both desks, was a high window by Alejandra's desk. Based upon how dirty the floors and walls were, Trinidad was probably not allowed in here.

"Are you Javier's assistant?" Malena asked.

Alejandra let out a chuckle, which sounded a lot like Amanda's laughter, except that it was stripped of any joy. "More the other way around. He's *my* apprentice."

"But Don Rafael said—"

"I know exactly what he said."

Malena picked up a silver earring with ruby inlays from Alejandra's desk.

"Did you really make all those pieces in there?"

"Most of them. Javier helps me with the polishing and some soldering."

Malena placed the earring beside a cone-shaped metal tool with a ring inside. "I've never seen a woman doing this type of work before."

"There's a first time for everything."

"Why does Don Rafael lie about Javier?"

"He doesn't want anybody to know the jeweler is a woman. He thinks it would be bad for business."

"Does he also make you dress like a man?"

Frowning, Alejandra lowered her goggles.

"Sorry," Malena said. "I didn't mean to . . . I mean, I like your clothes, they're just unusual."

Alejandra picked up the torch and resumed her work.

The entire family lived off this woman's work, yet nobody ever acknowledged her, including the maid. Didn't they have any gratitude?

Alejandra turned off the torch. "You're still here."

"I'm sorry." Malena walked to the door. "I'm leaving now."

The door across from the workshop was already open. Malena found Javier standing in the middle of a murky room surrounded by boxes, books, and old furniture. The smell of dust and mold was overwhelming. Never in her life had she seen so much dirt concentrated in one place. It gave her the chills.

"Where should I start?" she asked.

Javier pointed at a big cardboard box on the floor. "Why don't you look through that stuff? Throw whatever seems unimportant in that black trash bag."

Malena dragged a chair next to the box and sat down.

"Where were you just now?" he asked.

She opened the flaps of the box. "At the workshop, with your aunt."

Javier's eyes looked darker, almost black, under this light.

"So you know." He opened another cardboard box.

"Why do you take credit for her work?"

"My father's the one who does it." He removed a tarnished lamp from the box. "I can't do anything about it. You must have noticed he doesn't let anyone contradict him."

"But you enable him with your silence."

"Can you imagine what my life would be like if I dared contradict him in front of a customer? I can tell you right now. It would be hell."

"Sure, but I bet next time he wouldn't lie again."

"Maybe."

What a hypocrite she was—judging Javier when she was also living a lie. And her lie was worse than his.

Malena removed a large black notebook from the box at her feet. It seemed like an ordinary accounting book. The writing was somewhat faded and some of the yellowing pages were about to fall off. She wouldn't have looked at it twice if it weren't for one thing.

"Whose handwriting is this?" she asked.

Javier peeked over her shoulder. "I have no idea. Those are very old." He pointed to the date on the bottom of the page. "That was back when my grandfather and Tío Fausto were alive. You can probably throw them away."

Malena looked inside the box; it was full of notebooks exactly like the one in her hand. She examined the familiar writing and scanned the names at the bottom of the page: *Francisco Platas, owner; Fausto Guerrero, cashier; Rafael Dávila, clerk; Enrique Hidalgo, accountant.* But there was no Hugo Sevilla in there.

"Finally someone decided to clean around here."

Malena lifted her head. Alejandra stood by the door.

"You're welcome to help," Javier said.

"Ha!"

"I knew I could count on you." Javier stepped on a cockroach. "Would you at least help Lili figure out if we need those notebooks?"

Malena handed Alejandra the notebook. As soon as Alejandra opened it, her smile faded. She slammed it shut.

"This is trash."

Alejandra left without another word. Malena stared after her, stuffing the notebooks into a trash bag. Whenever she got a chance, she would hide them.

For the next couple of hours, Malena and Javier cleared bookshelves, threw away trash, and moved furniture around, all along engrossed in a conversation about their favorite movies. Her absolute favorite was *Breakfast at Tiffany's* while he favored anything starring James Stewart. For the first time since her arrival, Malena felt normal. With Javier, she didn't have to pretend to be someone else. Since he didn't know much about Lili and her family, Malena could talk without fear of making a mistake. And one thing she was good at was film talk. It had been the only thing she and her father had in common. Once a month, sometimes twice, he would take her to the cinema to watch the latest Mexican drama or American comedy. She would even watch Westerns if it meant going to the picture show on a lazy Saturday afternoon. She'd forgotten how much she enjoyed those conversations with her father about a movie's ending or an actor's performance.

"Do you know Ernesto Albán?" Javier asked.

"Of course."

Ernesto Albán, a local comedian mostly famous for his theater performances around the country, had been one of her father's favorite actors.

"Have you seen his movie yet?"

"No." Her father had promised to take her, but he had died first. There was so much he'd left unfinished. Again came that empty feeling in her stomach and the despair from the first days after his death. She'd been eager to run away from the pain, and she had, just not far enough from her memories.

"You have to see it," he said. "It's funny."

She turned away from Javier and dusted the top shelf of a bookcase with a rag. Swallowing was painful, but it was the only place her tears could go. She cleared her throat.

"I always dreamt of working with him," she said.

"With who?"

"Ernesto Albán."

"You want to be an actress?"

"I did. When I was younger, of course. Nobody can make a living in theater in this country." At least, that was what her father always said.

She'd never voiced her dream before—mainly out of fear that people would mock her—and she didn't know why she'd told Javier, or what it was about him that had inspired her trust.

"Well, fortunately you won't have to worry about money," he said. "You're going to inherit a huge ranch, from what I hear, and you'll probably find a rich husband."

Malena scrubbed harder. She'd never wanted to *find* a husband, rich or poor, but what bothered her the most was his condescending tone. She was about to answer, but a knock on the door interrupted her.

"Lili?" It was Ana's voice. "Oh, here you are. I've been looking for you all over the house."

"Yes?"

"Your mother is on the phone waiting to talk to you."

Chapter 9

Alejandra, 1936

Whatever was wrong with Fausto now? He'd been acting very strange around Alejandra, and she couldn't stand it. Sure, he'd paid her attention while they were having their picture taken, but ever since her sisters had left, he'd run off with the neighborhood kids and left her alone on the swings. If only she didn't have a stupid dress on, she could have run behind them. But her mother had warned her to take care of her *only* outing dress, passed down from one of her older sisters.

She fixed her long hair into a thick braid. She hated her hair. It was yet another source of controversy with her mother. Alejandra wanted it short, but Mamá Blanca insisted that a girl her age should look *feminine*. The word alone made her cringe. Even worse, Mamá Blanca had warned her that soon she would have to wear one of those brassieres her sisters always talked about—as if underwear was the most interesting subject in the world. Alejandra eyed the two protuberances growing from her chest. She couldn't deny it anymore, those things were growing, and according to her ghastly cousin, they were larger than Abigail's. Oh, God. How could that be when Abigail was two years older than her? It must be some sort of punishment for skipping mass.

Well, she wasn't about to waste an afternoon in the park feeling sorry for herself, dress or no dress. She jumped off the swing and followed the trail her cousin had taken with his friends. *His* friends. Not long ago, they used to be her friends too, her *jorga*, as they liked to call themselves. But lately all they did was mock or ignore her.

"Fausto!" she yelled. "Come here, *idiota!*"

The idiot was probably hiding behind one of the dense trees or maybe on top. *Shit!* Nothing was more embarrassing than looking for someone who might be watching you. She glanced at the summit of the *capuli* tree, the one Fausto had taught her to climb when they were small—before he decided she wasn't fun anymore.

Well, she was still fun, and she didn't need a boy to have a good time. With both hands she grasped the trunk of the tree and stepped on the nearest branch. Her skirt swished, and not in a good way, in a torn fabric sort of way. She examined the skirt as best as she could but it didn't look like there was any damage. She continued her climb as quickly as her dress allowed her. See? This was fun. She didn't need *him*. If only it weren't so hot here, her joy would be complete. Her hands were sweating, and so was her back. Come to think of it, she was sweating all over. Oh well, she was almost on top. From there, she would spot those damn boys.

"Señorita?"

A voice called from the bottom of the tree. She looked down, beneath the branches and leaves, at a young man watching her.

"Who are you?" she said. "What do you want?"

"I'm Edgar Carrasco, the new barber's son. We just moved here."

Alejandra had seen the new barber shop across the street and had been curious about her new neighbors, but this was a strange time for introductions.

"Are you okay?" he asked.

"Of course. I've climbed this tree a hundred times before."

"It's just that you're bleeding . . . so I thought . . ."

"Bleeding?"

Alejandra checked her bare arms and legs. This kid must be crazy. She wasn't bleeding; nothing hurt.

She laughed. "All right. Thank you."

"I'm serious. You might want to come down and take care of . . . your problem."

"What on earth are you talking about?"

The boy brought a handkerchief to his forehead and dried it. "Just come down. I'll explain everything here."

Alejandra sighed. Had she cut herself and not noticed? She descended carefully. At only a couple of meters from the ground, she jumped down, landing painfully on her feet.

She stood in front of this Edgar person. He looked about her age, maybe already fourteen, but he was shorter than her.

"So what is this about? Did you just want an excuse to talk to me?"

"No."

"Then?"

"Look, I don't want to embarrass you, but—"

"Alejandra!" Fausto yelled behind her. "What are you doing here? I thought you'd be home already, and what in God's name happened to you?"

He was looking at something on her back. She looked behind her shoulder but couldn't tell what the source of all this uproar was.

"And who are you?" Fausto asked the new kid.

"This is Edgar Carrasco. Our new neighbor," Alejandra said.

"Well, don't you see you're making my cousin uncomfortable?" Fausto said. "Get out of here!"

Edgar took a step back and headed for the pond.

"You shouldn't be talking to strangers," Fausto said.

"He's just a kid."

"I don't care. You don't talk to young men if you haven't been properly introduced."

"Well, if you hadn't left me alone, I would have been properly introduced."

"Stop being fresh with me. Have you forgotten I'm older than you?"

"By six months."

Fausto removed his jacket and covered her derriere with it.

"What are you doing?" she asked.

"Just walk home. You'll thank me later."

"What is it? What's wrong with me?"

"Don't ask me. Ask your mother or one of your sisters."

Hesitantly, she took a step forward. Fausto never called Mamá Blanca "your mother." The fact that he was being so formal meant this must be serious.

Alejandra locked herself in her room, too flustered to face the world again. Her linen pink skirt had a round blood stain on it. Blood, of all things! And not exactly from a cut. This was her period, according to Mamá Blanca. And from now on, her life would change. She couldn't climb trees anymore, or play *fútbol* with the neighborhood kids, or eat avocado during "those days." And of course, she could never mention this to anyone from the opposite sex, including Fausto. No wonder he'd been so awkward about it. He probably knew all along what the damn stain meant! As if things weren't bad enough with her so-called friends already, now she had to put up with this nonsense, the disgrace of becoming "officially" a woman—capable of making babies at age thirteen! She'd never heard of anything more ridiculous or disgusting. She prayed Fausto wouldn't tell them. But what about Edgar? He owed her no loyalty, especially after the rude way Fausto had treated him back at the park.

She threw one of her brushes across the room, then another. Her box of watercolors followed and then her pencils. Once her wooden desk was empty, she crashed on her bed, pounding her fists on the mattress until she'd exhausted her arms.

She must have slept a long time for it was already dark when she woke up. And now her mother was knocking on her door and calling her name. Alejandra told her she wasn't hungry. She couldn't go downstairs and face her family. She could already picture Fausto's smirk across the table. No, it would be too humiliating.

Her mother brought her a bowl of lentil soup and a glass of *avena* that first evening. For breakfast, she left a tray with bread and cheese, and a cup of *café con leche*, but by lunchtime she wasn't so understanding anymore. She forced Alejandra out of the room and made her sit across from Fausto at the dining room table.

Alejandra avoided the sight of her cousin during most of the meal, but once or twice, her gaze wandered in his direction. He didn't look at her once. He talked to everyone at the table, except for her.

After lunch, she followed him to the courtyard.

"You want to play *fútbol?*" she said.

His eyes narrowed. "With you?"

"Sure."

"I don't think you can."

"Of course I can."

"Not according to Mamá Blanca." With both hands, he seized the branch of one of the lemon trees.

"Things don't have to change. I can still do the things I did before."

He didn't need to say anything. Alejandra knew things had changed between them, maybe forever. Unless she could prove otherwise.

"Do you know the circus is coming next week?" she asked.

"Yes."

Holding on to the branch, Fausto kicked his legs up and folded them over it. He let go of his hands and hung upside down.

"I can probably get us tickets," she said.

"You?" He chuckled. "How?"

"I can ask my father."

Fausto laughed. Still upside down, his face had turned red and his straight hair pointed down.

"Good luck with that."

"I have my methods." Although she'd managed to sound confident, she didn't have the faintest idea of how to convince the stingiest man in town to give her money for something as irrelevant as a circus performance.

"The only method that would work would be to take the money from his drawer."

"What drawer?"

"You know that desk in the workshop that's shoved against the wall?"

She nodded.

"Top drawer." Fausto grasped the branch again and jumped down in one swift move. "But of course, you would never dare."

She kicked a rock. Only Fausto had the power to make her this angry.

"Yes I would."

That hateful smirk appeared on his face. "We'll have to see about that."

Without another word, he headed for the kitchen door. She grabbed a handful of soil and threw it at him with such bad aim that it landed on one of the concrete columns in the courtyard instead of his back. He laughed louder.

"You wait and see," she muttered. "Just wait."

***

How hard could it be to take a few coins from her father's drawer? As immersed as he was in his jewelry work, it would be as easy as taking a piece of candy from a baby. He would never notice. She dragged her feet down the hall and opened the workshop's door.

She stopped at the sight of her father leaning against his teak desk, his back arched, his black-frame glasses on the tip of his nose, his calloused hands polishing a silver ring with a piece of sandpaper. Francisco Platas worked ten hours a day in this moldy room—with minimum help from an occasional apprentice—to support his large family. All that sacrifice and hard work so that one day his youngest daughter would sneak into his workshop and rob him. She glanced at the desk in the corner of the room where Fausto said her father kept his spare change.

Papá Pancho, as they lovingly called him, looked up at her.

"*Hija,* what a surprise. Come in." He nodded at a chair beside him, still holding the ring mandrel with one hand and the sandpaper with the other. "It's been so long since you've come to visit me. When you were little you used to spend all morning here until your mother dragged you back into the house. Remember?"

"Yes." She loved it here more than anywhere else in the house, despite the mess and the smell of wax used to mold the pieces. She could watch her father work for hours.

"You're the only one who ever remembers this *viejo*. Unlike your sisters who only come here asking for money."

At least they ask. Alejandra pressed her cold hand against her burning cheek. There was no way she could ask him now. But she needed the money. There was simply no other way.

"People are so obsessed with money nowadays," he said. "Look at all the assistants I've had. Almost all of them robbed me. Either that, or they were too lazy."

"But you like Toño, don't you?"

Papá Pancho shrugged. "He's all right, but he's not family. It's not the same. An employee is transient. Just watch, once he finds a better paying job he'll leave. He has no ties here." He blew the dust off the ring. "I can't wait until Fausto grows up so he can run the store, or until one of you girls gets married so your husband comes to work here."

"Don't look at me," she said. "I'm never getting married."

Francisco Platas seldom smiled, but apparently what she'd said was pretty funny; his smile was so wide that his oversized front teeth, as bright as the keys in an organ, stood out in full contrast with his tan skin.

"That's what you say now. Wait a couple of years and we'll talk."

Alejandra doubted time would change her mind. She already knew she didn't want her mother's life. She despised housework or having to slave around at a husband's every whim. Having children didn't appeal to her either. The way those stomachs grew when they had babies inside! Not to mention the peculiar *method* of getting pregnant, which Abigail had told her about two years ago. Alejandra couldn't imagine kissing a boy, much less having his *thing* inside of her. She'd seen firsthand how dirty boys could be, always farting and burping, allowing lint to lurk between their toes for days. Sure, they were more fun than girls, but they could also be infinitely gross. No, her father would have to look elsewhere for a son-in-law. They could call her a *solterona* all they wanted.

Toño entered the workshop.

"Don Francisco." He stood by the doorway, a pencil stuck over his ear. "Don Pascual needs to speak to you."

"Can't he talk to you? That's why I pay you." He pushed his glasses up with his index finger. "Excessively," he added to himself, or maybe not just to himself.

"I know, S-S-Señor, but he says he has a s-s-special request for you." Oh, Christ. The stutter had begun. It appeared whenever Toño was nervous, which happened to be every time he spoke to Alejandra's father.

"Special request?" The lines on her father's forehead deepened. He hated talking to clients as much as Alejandra hated the idea of robbing her own father. "What does that mean?"

"He insisted, *p-p-patrón*."

With a loud sigh, Papá Pancho left his tools on the surface of his desk and dusted his hands on his apron. He stood up and removed his apron in slow motion—his entire body rejecting the idea of talking to a customer. Without the apron, his thin frame stood out. He didn't have an ounce of fat in his body, in spite of how much he ate, which was more than any other person in the family. He pulled out a handkerchief from his back pocket and blew his nose vociferously. Alejandra giggled.

Papá Pancho walked past Toño, leaving the door ajar and his employee tiptoeing behind him.

Alejandra stood up right away. This was it, her only chance. She approached the desk in the corner of the room and opened the top drawer. The money was there. Enough money for all her *jorga* and Fausto to go to the circus, but she had to be smart. She would only take enough for Fausto and her so her father wouldn't notice. Glancing over her shoulder, she grabbed a handful of coins and inserted them in a tiny purse Mamá Blanca had crocheted for her in pink wool.

After making sure nobody was in the hallway, she snuck out of the workshop. Papá Pancho's voice arguing with the customer echoed in her ears. If only he knew what his perfect child had done, he would never look at her the same way again. Shoving her thoughts away, she entered the house and ran upstairs, two steps at a time.

Fausto's mouth fell open after she dumped the money on his bedspread. He touched the coins, as if he couldn't believe they were real.

"I told you I would do it," she said, filled with a strange sense of pride. For the first time in her life, Fausto looked at her with admiration—not the other way around.

Alejandra couldn't believe she was really here, in this magical world under the white tent. This place was well worth her betrayal. It almost made her forget the guilt she felt every time she was near her father after the Unmentionable Act.

Fausto sat beside her. Things were getting back to normal already. He'd even agreed to play cards with her this morning. He'd taught her a game called *Cuarenta;* except he'd gotten furious when she beat him.

"Beginner's luck," he'd said, sweeping the cards to the floor with his arm.

Alejandra smiled just thinking about it. She loved beating her cousin at anything. And so far, she had the upper hand. They were at the circus, weren't they?

After the acrobat show, Fausto leaned over her shoulder and said, "That's what I want to do for the rest of my life."

She laughed. Fausto, an acrobat? Not according to Papá Pancho's plans.

When the show was over, her cousin made her wait until everyone in the audience had gone before standing up. She followed him down the bleachers to the center of the stage, where three men were already sweeping the floor.

"What are you doing?" she asked Fausto.

"Just follow me, and keep your mouth shut."

He approached one of the cleaning men and asked where the circus administrator was. The man pointed at the shiny red curtains where the performers had come from and told him to ask for Simón. Alejandra followed Fausto through the curtains, only to see the magic fade before them.

The smell of manure was strong here and the ground was sandy; the enchanting elastic woman, now in a blue robe and her hair down, didn't seem so enchanting anymore; the clowns walked around without makeup and the tigers rested in small cages, looking sad. Other performers she'd seen earlier walked past her, oblivious to her presence. One of the acrobats even bumped into her.

"I'm looking for Mr. Simón," Fausto asked again and again, until finally a young man in a sweater-vest and gray knickers stopped in front of them.

"Who are you?" he asked with a coastal accent.

Fausto extended his hand. "My name is Fausto Guerrero, and this is my cousin Alejandra Platas."

The man shook Fausto's hand, surveying the area the entire time. There was an eagerness in his gaze that was very appealing; it was the look of someone who never did things halfway.

"And your name is?" Fausto asked.

He withdrew his hand. "Enrique Hidalgo. What are you doing here?"

"I want to talk to Mr. Simón."

"What for?"

"I want to work here."

Enrique Hidalgo looked younger when he smiled, and he didn't have a lot of facial hair either. He couldn't have been older than seventeen or eighteen. "Doing what?"

"I want to be an acrobat."

He laughed.

Fausto scowled. "What's so funny?"

"It takes a lot to become an acrobat. These fellows start training when they're four years old. What training do you have?"

All of Fausto's training consisted of hanging upside down from trees, and he wasn't even that good at it, in Alejandra's opinion.

"Look," Enrique said, "my *padrino* is a busy man. Don't waste your time." He patted Fausto's back, dismissively, his attention still on the action around them. "Benito, add more chairs to the front row!" he told a man in a blue jumpsuit. "And now, if you'll excuse me, I have a lot of work to do here."

"Fine. But I'll be back tomorrow to talk to Mr. Simón."

Enrique sighed, all amusement wiped from his face. He looked at Alejandra for the first time, sending a wave of electricity throughout her body.

"Alejandra, right? You look like a reasonable young lady. Would you put some sense into your cousin?"

He remembered her name? She nodded; she would nod to whatever he said.

"Look, you both seem like nice kids, but unfortunately I have to go." He patted Fausto's arm. "Good luck to you." Enrique walked past Alejandra and the scent of his cologne masked, for a few seconds, the offensive smells in the area. Alejandra stared after him, mesmerized. She was starting to reconsider the idea of kissing a boy.

"Come on," Fausto said, his fists clenched against his sides.

Alejandra followed her cousin in a haze, deaf to his complaints the entire way back. By the time she arrived home, she had reconsidered her stance on a lot of things.

Chapter 10

Malena followed Ana through the hallway, living room, and foyer, keeping her head low and her shoulders bent as if heading to her own execution. Her mind had gone blank. What, if anything, would she tell Lili's mother? María Teresa would know her daughter's voice well; she couldn't deceive her. If only she could find a way to escape. Before she could flee the house, Ana held the study door open for her.

The unhooked receiver rested on the desk's surface.

"Come on." Ana pointed at the phone. "Your mother's waiting."

Malena approached the phone. She placed the receiver against her ear and heard a woman's hoarse voice at the other end of the line.

"Lili?"

Ana stood beside her, examining every gesture, every feature in her face. Malena's ears burned. She was ready to say "hello," ready to give herself away, but before she could utter a sound, Lili's letter flashed in her mind. Of course, why hadn't she thought of that before?

"Liliana Paz! Answer right now!" María Teresa said. "I know you're there. I can hear you breathing."

Malena looked into Ana's eyes and placed the receiver on the hook.

"What are you doing?" Ana asked. "You just hung up on your mother!"

"I don't expect you to understand," Malena said. "But my mother and I had a quarrel before I left, and I do not wish to speak to her. Please tell her not to call me again."

"I know all about that fight, Lili, but your mother was acting for your own interest. That man is not good for you. His wife is pregnant, you know?"

Damn. Liliana's boyfriend was married.

What had Lili said? *Tell my mother that her plans to separate us didn't work, and that it will take a long time for me to forgive and forget the pain she caused.*

"I'm not sure of that. It could be another one of my mother's plans to separate us," she recited.

"Lili, you can't possibly think that of your mother! She's not a liar."

"Maybe you're right, but I'm not ready to speak to her."

"What's going on here?" Amanda asked from the doorway. She wore her beige coat, a matching pillbox hat, and held a small purse in her hand.

Ana sighed. "Liliana hung up on her mother."

Amanda removed her gloves from her purse. "Well, Ana, that's between María Teresa and Lili." She peeked at Malena. "You look like you can use some fresh air. Do you want to come with me to the restaurant?"

Malena couldn't say "yes" fast enough. Leaving the house was exactly what she needed. She rushed behind Amanda, though not without noticing first the hard look Ana gave her sister before they left the study.

"Don't be disappointed when you see the place," Amanda told Malena inside the taxi. "You have to remember I'm going to remodel it."

Malena peered out the window. She was curious to see the source of yesterday's commotion. Moreover, she was grateful that Amanda had taken her away from Ana's questioning. She beamed at her savior and wished with all her heart she would turn out to be her mother.

"Thanks for coming with me," Amanda said. "You probably noticed my family doesn't trust I can pull this off, especially Rafael." She shook her head. "He thinks women should only obey the men and look pretty. Sometimes I could just kill him. Such arrogance, such airs of superiority! He thinks he's so cultured just because he can finish a crossword puzzle and read each and every word of *El Heraldo*. Never mind they always run the same puzzle or that the paper is only eight pages long!"

"But if he feels that way about women," Malena said, "how does he let Alejandra work for him?"

"It's not that he *lets* her. He didn't have a choice. The jewelry store was our father's and he taught Alejandra everything. My father is the one who put her there and believed in her." She turned to the driver. "Here to the left. Besides, Rafael is not dumb. He knows she's good and everyone likes her work."

"But nobody knows she's the jeweler."

"That was Rafael's condition when he took charge."

Malena thought about Alejandra and the ill-treatment she must have suffered all those years under Rafael's tyranny.

"She's admirable."

"Yes, she is." Amanda glanced at the steep road ahead. "You should have seen her before. She was so different; she would have never allowed Rafael to treat her like this. She was so rambunctious."

"Your mother told me she was in shock after your cousin died."

"Yes. And the shock has lasted more than twenty years." Amanda scowled. "Alejandra and Fausto were close. He grew up with us, like a brother. His mother was Mamá Blanca's sister, Tía Emilia. She was a year older than my mother, but they could pass as twins. She was a curt woman, though, very different from my mother." She crossed her hands over her lap, displaying her perfectly manicured red fingernails. "Tía Emilia and her husband died in a bus crash on their way to Quito when Fausto was seven years old."

"That's terrible."

"When he died, my sister was so depressed she joined the convent."

Alejandra, a nun? "For how long?"

"I don't know, less than a year."

"What happened then?"

"She changed her mind, I guess. I think she just wanted solitude. Everything in the house reminded her of Fausto. I don't think she really wanted to be a nun."

Somehow Malena couldn't reconcile the image of Alejandra as a nun. What if, in reality, she'd joined the convent to hide something? Like a pregnancy?

"Did you see her during that time?"

"No, she didn't want to see anybody. It was especially hard for my mother." She waved her hand. "Oh, let's not talk about that anymore. I don't like thinking of those times. They were hard for everyone." Amanda scrutinized Malena's features the way Mamá Blanca had done the other day. Her perfect eyebrows creased in disapproval. Oh, no, what had she discovered?

"You know?" Amanda said. "You would be a lot prettier without all that eyeliner and mascara, and you don't need the fake eyelashes either." She brought her fingers to one of Malena's curls and pushed it away. "Your hair is gorgeous but it needs a trim and some styling." She glanced at Malena's old shirtwaist dress. "And you definitely need new clothes. I can't believe María Teresa has been so careless about your appearance. She used to be very fashionable when she lived here." She looked outside the window. "Well, I guess the country would do that to a person."

Or growing up without a mother. Malena faced the opposite direction, distraught that her appearance turned out to be so unsatisfactory. She'd never given her looks much thought; she simply mimicked the makeup of her favorite movie stars or whatever she saw in magazines. La Abuela never taught her anything about fashion or hair; her main concern had always been Malena's school work.

"I don't want you to be a *burra* like me," her grandmother would say. "Study hard so you can be a teacher or a nurse, like your mother." Her mother, the nurse. How did La Abuela come up with that lie? It was apparent that none of the Platas sisters were nurses. If only her grandmother hadn't made that up, Malena would not have spent a full year locked in the library trying to memorize the names of muscles, bones, and organs.

"Right here," Amanda told the driver. She turned to Malena. "Welcome to the Madreselva."

<hr />

Madreselva, Amanda explained as they walked into the restaurant, was the name of a plant. More importantly, it was the name of a famous tango sung by Carlos Gardel. Amanda must have thought it natural to name the nightclub after the song.

A transformation came over Amanda as they walked in. A smile illuminated her face, her eyes brightened, and she hummed the "Madreselva" tango.

Malena followed Amanda's glance up, to the tall vaulted ceilings.

"So what do you think?" Amanda asked.

"I think it has a lot of potential. Great chandeliers."

"I love those chandeliers." Amanda pointed at the back of the room. "I am going to raise a big stage there, and hire musicians and dancers."

"Dancers?"

"I placed an ad in the paper today. I'm having auditions all next week."

"Wonderful." Tango dancing had always captivated Malena, even when her grandmother criticized it.

"It's completely inappropriate for respectable women to dance so close to a man," she'd say.

Her father, on the other hand, had always liked it. After La Abuela died, he'd bought the entire Gardel record collection.

"Are you going to dance, too?" Malena asked.

A veil of sadness came over Amanda's expression. "I can't dance anymore. Not like I used to anyway. I had a bad fracture in my leg." She raised her skirt, exposing a thick scar winding from her knee up to the middle of her thigh.

So that was why Amanda limped sometimes.

"Now one of my legs is shorter than the other." She lowered her skirt with a rough motion. "Like some kind of freak."

"Oh, but you're so beautiful, Amanda. That's barely noticeable."

Amanda caressed her cheek. "You're sweet."

"How did that happen?"

"I was in a car accident." Amanda's voice broke, and Malena knew her sadness had nothing to do with the physical pain. "I've never driven since."

There was so much she wanted to know about Amanda. "Can I come to the auditions?"

"Sure, I can definitely use the help." Her smile faded. "This place brings me so many memories."

"What memories?" Malena couldn't believe she'd voiced her imprudent thoughts.

"Oh, nothing important. Memories of an old woman that nobody cares to hear."

"You're not old, and of course I would like to hear them."

Amanda left her purse on top of a table. "No time for that."

"Oh, but I insist."

"Just leave it be, Liliana." She softened her tone. "Come, I'll show you the rest of the place."

Chapter 11

Amanda, 1936

"I knew we were going to win," Joaquin told Amanda from across the table.

Amanda had known, too. All those months of practice, of sneaking out at night with Joaquin, of trying to find a decent place to practice, of begging her mother to make her dress—all that effort had to pay off somehow. And it had. She was finally at Il Napolitano, the new Italian restaurant everyone was talking about. She'd always known that if she wanted to come here, she would have to earn it herself. Expecting Papá Pancho to bring them would've been a fantasy. It was simply not the kind of expense he would incur, even if he had enough money in his safety vault to take the entire family every weekend.

"You looked stunning in there," Joaquin said without taking his eyes off her. He had gotten a haircut that morning and she hated it; there was no curl left, and his nose protruded more than usual. Yet there was something appealing about him, something that made girls melt in his presence. It might have been his long eyelashes and magnetic chestnut eyes, or maybe the way he led girls on the dance floor. He was the best dancer Amanda had ever known, and she would be eternally grateful for everything he'd taught her. How lucky she'd been to meet him during that *melcochada* party four years ago—they'd become inseparable ever since.

"Carlitos would have been proud," he said.

Carlitos, of course, was none other than Carlos Gardel, their idol, who had died last year in an airplane crash. She still cried from time to time remembering that fatal day.

"Are you happy?" he asked.

Amanda looked around the grand salon. Happy didn't even begin to describe her feelings; it was a dream come true. Il Napolitano was everything she'd heard and more. Dinner was wonderful; she had the cannelloni and Joaquin tried the risotto. The music, the wine, those lovely chandeliers and the lighting were enough to make her wish the evening would never end.

"Yes," she said as her eyes rested on a man in a tuxedo standing by the quartet of violinists, staring straight in her direction, sending heat to her face, to her entire body.

Joaquin's voice got lost in the background. She held the man's stare for a moment, and smiled. He smiled back. But Joaquin's cold fingers touching her hand broke the enchantment. She turned to him, irritated, but he apparently didn't perceive her annoyance and had a smile on his face. He held her hand in his, softly, possessively, and pulled out a red velvet box from his jacket pocket.

Oh, no, she had to do something—quickly. She knew how Joaquin felt, but she had always hoped he wouldn't tell her.

She looked him squarely in the eye.

"I'm in love."

"What?"

"Do you see the man with the black tuxedo and the red carnation?"

Joaquin glanced over his shoulder.

"I'm going to marry him," she said.

Joaquin covered the box with a cloth napkin.

Amanda pretended not to see the sadness in his eyes, the frown between his thick eyebrows. She loved Joaquin, but he was like a brother to her; she'd never thought of him in terms of marriage. The day she married, it would be to someone important, someone who would take her away from this small town and show her the world.

She returned her attention to the back of the room, but the elegant stranger was no longer there.

"*Buona sera,*" a husky voice greeted her from behind. "Welcome to Il Napolitano."

It was him.

"Are you enjoying your dinner?"

Madre mía, that Italian accent was so attractive. She twisted a side curl with her index finger. "Very much."

"My name is Nicolas Fornasieri. I'm the owner of this establishment."

Nicolas Fornasieri. She liked the sound of his name. She liked everything about him, including the fact that he was older than he'd appeared from afar—probably in his thirties already—and that he had the most mesmerizing green eyes she'd ever seen.

A short and stout waiter stood beside him with a bottle of wine in his hands.

"I understand you're the winners of the dance contest?" Nicolas said.

"Yes." Amanda locked her eyes with his.

"My congratulations to both of you," Nicolas said and then turned to the waiter. "Bernardo, *per piacere.*"

The man called Bernardo served them two glasses of red wine.

"Please enjoy this drink from my country," Nicolas said.

Joaquin finished his wine in one gulp and set the glass on the table a little too loudly, glaring at Nicolas. For a moment, Amanda thought he was going to break the glass on the Italian's head.

She took a sip of wine.

"Delicious." She boldly looked into his eyes.

Nicolas looked away. An older man nervous at her advances? She wanted to laugh.

He excused himself and left with Bernardo.

Joaquin stood up. "Are you ready to leave?"

"But we haven't had dessert yet."

"I know, but I don't feel so good. I think the shrimp was bad."

"Are you out of your mind? In a restaurant like this?"

Joaquin held her arm. "Come on."

Amanda was not about to let Joaquin's jealousy ruin her only chance with Nicolas.

"I need to go to the ladies' room first," she said.

She headed for the lavatory before Joaquin could do anything to stop her. And what a lavatory it was. It even had a sitting area! She powdered her nose casually, looking in the mirror until the last woman was gone. When she was alone, she took off her bracelet and dropped it near a flowerpot. She finished fixing her hair and left.

<hr />

First thing the next morning, Amanda went back to Il Napolitano to pick up her bracelet. Nicolas sent Bernardo to fetch it while they sat at a table by the piano. The place was closed until lunchtime, but there were already a handful of waiters setting up tables. Nicolas opened another wine bottle and poured half a glass for her to taste.

"Isn't it a little early for wine?" Amanda asked.

"It's never too early for *vino rosso.*"

Eagerly, Amanda tasted the wine. This was a man, not a boy, having a drink with her. How his eyes sparkled when he took that long sip! They stared at each other for a long time, with little to say. She was speechless, bewitched by the intensity of his gaze.

A jumble of Italian brought her back from her trance. A young man about her age, or maybe a little bit older, stood behind her. She had never studied Italian, but she gathered he was asking who she was. And he had called her *bella*.

"Amanda Platas, this is my brother Vincenzo."

Nicolas's brother kissed her hand and looked her in the eye. He was better looking than most men in San Isidro, but he paled in comparison to his older brother. He excused himself, claiming he had an appointment, but it didn't escape Amanda's attention that he winked at Nicolas before he left.

"Monsieur Nicolas," Bernardo interrupted. "*Mademoiselle's* bracelet."

Why was the man speaking French? He placed the emerald bracelet on the table.

Amanda picked it up, but Nicolas quickly took it from her. "Allow me."

The soft touch of his fingers on her wrist as he clasped the lock was enough to send chills down her spine. He was not much of a talker, this Nicolas, but she didn't need another Joaquin, who wouldn't be quiet for more than a minute. Words were unnecessary between them. The curve of his jaw, his moustache—trimmed just right—his exquisite suit, and the bergamot scent of his expensive cologne were enough for her. Add to the mixture the touch of his fingers rubbing the inside of her wrist and she was in heaven.

———◆———

Amanda sat back in Nicolas's 1934 Fiat Balilla with her eyes closed, enjoying his proximity and the now familiar scent of his imported cologne. She'd made a habit of sneaking out of her house every night and escaping to Il Napolitano. She'd meet Nicolas at midnight, after the last client had left, and keep him company while he closed the business. She loved watching him impart orders to his subordinates, smoke incessantly while he counted stacks of money, or argue with his brother in Italian. Amanda had become one of them. The waiters greeted her as she walked in, the black leather sofa in his office became hers, and Bernardo brought her a slice of *tiramisu* or a scoop of *gelato* every night. She usually observed Nicolas in silence—so as not to disturb him—while listening to the sounds of Vivaldi's *Four Seasons* on his phonograph. Nicolas had taught her so much already about music, wine, and the other fine things in life. How much more would she learn from him still?

Nicolas was always a gentleman. The anger he displayed against his brother or employees was never aimed toward her. Every time he directed his attention to her, his features softened and his voice turned kind. He was different from any other man she'd known. For one, he was a man, not a boy. And he never tried to touch her inappropriately or asked her to kiss his earlobes, the way other boys had done. Of course, real men were not obsessed with breasts and hormones, the way Amanda's peers were. Men had more important things on their minds, like managing the family business or raising a younger brother after their parents' passing. Yes, Nicolas had every reason to be different, and she loved him for it.

She often wondered if his parents' untimely death was the reason for the sadness she found in his eyes, in his demeanor, and she vowed to erase that melancholy off of him, to make him happy. Together, they would travel the world, go to the theater, the opera, museums, his homeland, and after they'd had enough fun and adventure, she would give him children, the family he'd lost.

When Nicolas stopped the Fiat—the only Italian car in San Isidro—Amanda didn't open her eyes, hoping to prolong those last moments in his presence.

"Are you sleeping, *bella?*" he asked.

She opened her eyes, recognizing the fabric shop that belonged to Joaquin's father at the corner of the street, one block away from her house. This was the spot where Nicolas parked every night so his car wouldn't call attention to them, so Papá Pancho wouldn't hear the engine outside his house. He held her hand in his, the way he did every night, and kissed it softly.

"Thanks for the lovely company," he said, staring into her eyes.

Some nights, like tonight, she wished he would respect her less, compliment her more, or even steal a kiss from her. She longed to feel his lips against hers, his hands on her waist. But his kiss didn't come, and despite what everyone in town thought of her, she would never make the first move. Not when she was used to having men beg for her love.

Before he could step out of the car to open the door for her, a knock on the passenger's window disturbed their farewell. The blood drained from Amanda's face as she discerned her father's disapproving eyes in the darkness. A deep frown crossed his forehead. How had he found her? Did Ana say something? No, it wasn't possible. Ana no longer lived in the house.

He opened the door.

"Out!" he yelled.

Amanda stepped out of the Fiat, while her father took her seat inside the car.

"Wait for me at the house," he ordered.

Papá Pancho shut the door and pointed forward.

"Drive!" she heard him say. *Maldita sea!* Papá Pancho was treating her like a child in front of Nicolas. He was going to ruin everything! She watched the Fiat drive away, into the blackness of the street, and she forced herself back home.

In the stillness of her room, the minutes went by slowly. Her eyes remained fixated on her bedside clock as its hands marked one hour since the car drove away. Where was her father? Had he killed Nicolas and was now entangled in the tiresome task of disposing of the body? No, that was impossible. Nicolas was twice her father's size, and her father didn't have a violent cell in his body.

A thump downstairs startled her. Her father was home. She brought the covers to her chin, hoping to find protection in the blanket her mother had knitted for her as a child, to become invisible to her father's wrath. She waited in terror for her bedroom door to open wide, for Papá Pancho to march inside and pull the covers off, slap her face, spit on her, call her a bad daughter, an easy woman. But nothing happened. The minutes passed in a nerve-racking silence until Amanda could barely hold her eyelids open.

In the morning, she woke up to the dark figure of her father at the foot of her bed. He stood there in his chocolate nightrobe, his arms crossed in front of his chest. His cheeks appeared thinner than the previous day and bags underlined his eyes.

She sat up. "Papá, let me explain."

But he was in no mood for explanations. "You will marry that man as soon as your wedding gown is completed."

After pronouncing his last word, he left the room. Amanda pulled the covers off her legs, uncertain of whether she'd heard her father correctly, or if she was still dreaming. She stepped out of bed; the floor cold under her feet. Yes, she was awake, and her father had been in her room, and he had somehow persuaded Nicolas to marry her. Or had Nicolas been the one who came up with the idea? It didn't matter. All that mattered was that she was going to be Mrs. Nicolas Fornasieri.

She covered her mouth with her hands for she had an irrepressible urge to yell, to laugh, to tell the world how happy she was. Things wouldn't have been so perfect if she'd planned them. She would marry the man of her dreams and she would live happily ever after with him.

Amanda pulled the heavy wooden door open, hoping her stylish felt cloche wouldn't offend Father Ramón, who favored a traditional veil for the women who walked into his church. She pressed her purse against her new wrap coat, another one of her husband's expensive gifts, and entered the church. The scent of incense was strong, as usual. She'd always wondered about that. Was incense supposed to purge all sins? Or just mask them?

She walked along the nave, the same path she'd followed six months ago, on her wedding day, back when she still believed her life with Nicolas would be a fairy tale.

She quickened her stride; she needed to catch Padre Ramón before he left for his siesta, she needed to talk to him before she changed her mind. And God only knew how many times she'd changed her mind. She slowed down as her doubts kicked in once again. Would she have the courage to tell him the truth? Her secret was too embarrassing, too painful to utter aloud; not even Ofelia or Ana knew. It was times like this when she wished she had Joaquin to talk to. But he hadn't spoken to her since the day she announced her engagement to Nicolas. She'd seen him around, always with a different girl by his side and a contemptuous smirk on his face. If only he knew the truth about her marriage, he would laugh at her; he would say "See? I told you so," or "You should have married me instead."

She found Father Ramón locking the sacristy door.

"Amanda Platas, long time no see. What brings you here at this time?" Father Ramón eyed his wristwatch, wrinkling his large nose. By now, the entire town knew his afternoon siesta was sacred.

"Padre, I need to speak to you. It's urgent."

He sighed, running his palm over the scarce long hairs covering his bald head. "I was on my way out." He examined her face for a moment. "But I guess I can spare a few minutes if it relieves your soul."

She followed his black cassock to the confessional and knelt down, her eyes away from his large silhouette at the other side of the metal screen that separated them. This was infinitely better than having to look him in the eye. She crossed herself and began her confession in a monotonous tone, prolonging her petty sins, her lack of spirituality, her insolence with her parents, anything, before saying what was really on her mind. She paused for a moment.

"Is that it?" Father Ramón yawned.

"No."

"Continue, then."

"I can't, Padre."

He turned to her for the first time. "Why? What's wrong?"

She bit her lower lip. "It's . . . my husband."

"Your husband?"

"I'm not happy with him."

"Does he not respect you?"

"He does, Padre."

"Is he violent?"

"No."

"Is he not a good provider?"

"The best one."

"I thought so, after that wedding."

Father Ramón was right. Her wedding had been the most ostentatious one the town had ever seen. And Nicolas had paid for everything.

"Then?"

She couldn't bring herself to say the words.

"Amanda?"

"Padre, the thing is, Nicolas and I, well, we've never been intimate."

For once, Father Ramón was out of words.

"He's the most benevolent man and a splendid husband, but when it comes to, you know . . . he won't. For a while I thought I wasn't attractive enough, or that he respected me too much, but lately, I've been thinking about something I heard once about men who . . ." She played with her wedding band. "Who aren't attracted to women."

For a moment she thought Father Ramón might have fallen asleep. She glanced at him. His shadow grew larger on the grille—he was definitely awake.

"What should I do, Padre?"

"Well, *hija*." He looked straight ahead. "We all have our crosses to bear. The Lord has sent you your own cross, and there's nothing you can do about it. As you know, marriage is sacred." He used his homily tone now. "You must be strong and patient. You must wait until your husband is ready."

"You think he will be?"

"Only time will tell. But I've heard of cases where it's happened."

His words energized her. She would help Nicolas; she would be patient and sweet, the best wife he could ask for. She just hadn't made her best effort yet. But that would change. She would go to the seamstress right away and have her make her a new chiffon nightgown; make herself irresistible. There was hope after all.

Chapter 12

By the time Malena returned to the jewelry store from her outing with Amanda, most of the boxes had been removed from the storage room. Free of his tie and with his shirt sleeves rolled up, Javier swept the dusty floor. The corner of the room, where she had left the trash bag with the accounting books, was now empty.

"What did you do with the trash?" she asked.

"I threw it out."

Her head started to itch. "But I told you *I* would throw it out!"

"That's okay, I don't mind. You helped me enough."

She had to get hold of those notebooks before they took the trash out of the house! But where did they keep the garbage bin?

"Where were you?" Javier asked.

"Amanda took me to her restaurant."

She'd seen a back door in the kitchen leading to a patio. Maybe that was where they kept the trash.

"How was it?"

"I'll be right back."

She scampered in a mad search for the garbage bin, passing halls and doorways until she reached the empty kitchen, where

114

the pots on the stove indicated that Trinidad was nearby. She went through the back door to a small patio surrounded by a brick wall covered in vines. Three cotton sheets hung from a clothesline in the center of the patio, and a concrete laundry sink sat by the house wall. Behind the kitchen door were two large metal garbage bins.

Holding her breath, Malena dug inside the first trash can. She gagged as her fingers felt all kinds of disgusting textures and shapes: mushy avocados, old corn husks, empty sardine cans. She was *definitely* going to the shower after this. Among moist banana peels and leftover bones, she found a handkerchief. She took it out. Could it be *the* handkerchief? The cause of Rafael's accusations? She examined it; nothing extraordinary about it: white cotton and the letter "E" embroidered with golden thread. She made a mental note of all the names in the house; there were no E's, and her father's initial was an "H," so it couldn't be his. She buried it in her skirt pocket anyway and continued with her search. The black bag was stuck underneath broken eggshells and glass bottles. Good thing the bag had protected the accounting books from the filth surrounding them.

"Can I help you with something?" Trinidad said behind her.

Malena sucked in her breath, inhaling the stench from the trash.

"You scared me!"

"I'm sorry, Niña, did you lose something?"

"Javier accidentally threw some important papers here."

"If you want, I can look for you."

"No. Thank you." Malena lifted the nasty bag. "I already found it. I'd better take it back to him." She went into the kitchen, praying the maid would keep quiet.

The dining room was empty, but there were voices coming from the foyer. She couldn't go to her room! Her only option was the courtyard. She drew the curtains in the dining room so nobody could see her outside, and slipped through the glass door.

Kneeling by a lemon tree, she dug a hole in the moist ground with both hands until her fingers were covered in dirt and a nail had broken. She could smell the trash in her clothes. After making a knot, she placed the bag inside the hole, covering it carefully with the soil to make sure the area looked intact. At night, when everyone slept, she would come back and examine the notebooks. There was something there, she was certain, and she would find out what it was, starting with who had written those books and why the handwriting looked so much like her father's.

Malena could barely recognize herself in Amanda's red sheath.

"I think this one fits you well," Amanda said.

Malena had never worn a red dress before; especially not one with a pencil skirt that so tightly outlined the contour of her waist. She ran her hands by her hips, self-consciously, and felt the fine silk under her palms.

"It's very pretty," she said, watching her own reflection in the mirror.

"I'll do your makeup tomorrow," Amanda said. "None of that black eyeliner."

Malena agreed, but if it was up to her, she wouldn't even show her face tomorrow at Claudia's engagement dinner. Not when her fiancé—Sebastian?—could say something about that indecent hotel where he'd seen her with Javier.

"And that necklace?" Amanda asked her.

Malena grasped the silver sun pendant hanging from her neck. This necklace was the only valuable piece of jewelry her grandmother Eva had given her, and Malena always wore it under her shirts. Coming from Guayaquil, she knew better than to flaunt her jewels, lest someone might try to rob her.

She covered the pendant with her hand, as if anybody who would see her grandmother's necklace would know her true identity. What a fool she was.

"It was a gift from my grandmother." Was Lili's grandmother even alive?

"Let me see." Amanda touched it. "It's so familiar. Did María Teresa wear it before you?"

The door opened and Claudia walked in. She stopped short when she saw them.

"What do you think?" Amanda asked her. "Doesn't Lili look beautiful? She's going to wear it to your *Pedida de Mano* tomorrow."

Claudia sat on her bed, staring at Malena.

"It's settled, then." Amanda picked up a pile of dresses she'd brought for Malena to try on and walked out of the room.

After Malena closed the door, Claudia spoke.

"You're really going to wear that dress?"

"Yes. Why?"

"Well, I don't think it would be appropriate."

"Why not?"

"Well, for one it's red, and someone our age shouldn't wear red. And second, it's out of style."

"But your aunt—"

"I can imagine what Tía Amanda said, but she's older than us. She doesn't know what young women wear nowadays."

Claudia had a point. Amanda had criticized her makeup and false eyelashes when Audrey Hepburn and Angélica María wore them all the time.

Claudia opened her armoire and removed an ivory empire waist dress with a bell skirt. "This would probably suit you better."

She extended it toward Malena. "Go ahead, I won't look." Claudia covered her eyes with her hand as though she were a child playing hide-and-go-seek.

Malena slipped off Amanda's dress and tried on Claudia's. It felt tight around the bust line and pushed up her cleavage.

Claudia peeked. "See? This looks much better." She circled Malena, examining her front and back with a clinical eye and brushing the creases from the bottom of the skirt. "And I think you should keep your eyelashes on, too."

Malena examined her reflection. It was truly a beautiful gown, fancier than Amanda's had been. In her twenty years of life, Malena had never owned anything this expensive. It was a hard choice—both dresses were stunning—but perhaps she should go with the one that was mostly likely to get her unnoticed during the party.

Malena snuck down the stairs, holding onto the rail to prevent a fall; her sense of touch was her only guide in the dark house. At the bottom of the stairs, she felt along the wall until she reached the dining room door. It was ajar.

Pushing in, Malena dug her hand into her robe pocket to extract the candle and matches she'd borrowed from Claudia's drawer. Ever so carefully, she lit the candle and looked about the dining room. The room appeared larger now that it was empty. She couldn't look at the *Last Supper* on the wall. Jesus would not approve of her recent behavior.

She fumbled with the curtains until she found the sliding door leading to the courtyard. She unlocked the latch, but before she could open the door, bright lights blinded her.

She froze in panic. She'd been so close. If only she'd heard the footsteps behind her she could have hid underneath the table, hurried outside, or come up with a reasonable explanation. And now those footsteps she hadn't heard before were approaching her.

A hand rested on her shoulder.

"Lili?"

Javier smelled of alcohol and smoke, the way men smelled when they'd been out all night. Her father had brought that scent home with him a few times. *Her father.* Of course, *he* was the solution to her imminent problem.

"What are you doing here so late?" he asked.

She remained stiff, looking straight ahead, the way she'd seen her father do.

He held her arm. "Lili? What are you doing with the curtain?"

Mimicking her father, she looked past Javier, focusing on his ear.

"I'm cleaning it," she said, certain that he would burst out laughing.

"*Por Dios!*" he said. "You're asleep!"

She fought the urge to laugh. If she did, she would ruin everything.

"Let me help you to your bed."

He took the candle from her hand and guided her to the foyer. She moved slowly, the way her father did after she found him sleepwalking around the apartment. Javier was so gentle it touched her. But her own capacity to deceive disgusted her. She'd never imagined she had it in her.

He opened Claudia's bedroom door and helped her inside. He set the covers aside and helped her lie down. She did her part by closing her eyes, listening intently as he blew out the candle and tiptoed outside the room. She didn't open her eyes until the door closed.

Chapter 13

Claudia's engagement dinner was not something Malena was looking forward to. She wasn't used to social gatherings; she'd only been to a few—usually involving her father's mathematics awards. But the kind of people who attended intellectual events had little or no concern for fashion or etiquette. Malena suspected the San Isidro society was different.

Wearing her borrowed gown, Malena slid her necklace inside the night table's top drawer. She could hear the laughter and music downstairs. Had Claudia's fiancé arrived yet? Aside from her social inadequacies, Sebastian was the greatest reason why she was still locked in Claudia's room. With just one word, one question uttered in front of the wrong person, he could ruin all of her plans. She'd been lucky enough that Javier hadn't said anything about the hotel.

Someone knocked on the door. Malena opened it.

Javier's eyes lingered on her chest for an uncomfortable moment. "My mother asked me to call you. Are you ready?"

She took a moment to respond. "Yes."

The two of them walked together down the stairs—Javier, whistling confidently the entire way down; Malena, holding onto the banister. Maybe it had been a mistake to wear Claudia's dress; she had the mortifying impression that her breasts would make an unpleasant appearance in front of the guests tonight. Why hadn't she picked Amanda's outfit instead?

Everyone was already heading for the dining room. On the last step, Malena tripped with her heel and lost her balance, but Javier seized her arm and broke her fall.

Rafael scowled at them. "You're late," he muttered.

Beside him, a lady in a hazelnut mink coat seriously examined Malena's chest.

"This is María Teresa Paz's daughter," Rafael told the woman. "Liliana."

After righting herself, Malena extended her hand out to the woman.

"This is Ofelia Rivas," Rafael said. "Sebastian's mother."

Ofelia gave her a soft handshake in return. Malena stiffened at the sight of the woman's son looking at her. There he was, Claudia's fiancé. She could only hope he didn't remember the hotel incident.

Sebastian seemed like one of those men who always called attention to himself, even without trying. It wasn't just his size, but also the confidence in his poise. He had the look of someone who understood his place in the world. Only now did Malena realize how truly handsome he was, how perfectly proportioned his facial features were, like the hero in one of those *fotonovelas* her neighbor Julia always read.

There was not much resemblance between mother and son. Whereas Sebastian was tall and sturdy looking, his mother was short and her thin hand gave the impression of a frail woman underneath her gigantic coat. Sebastian's face was tanned, with a green shadow running along his jawline. Ofelia, in contrast, had blonde hair and light skin—according to her neck anyway—since her face was a spectrum of color resembling the frantic brushes of an Expressionist artist.

"Nice to meet you, Señora," Malena said.

As Ofelia removed her coat, she revealed a youthful figure underneath an elegant blue gown. Javier took Ofelia's mink and she waltzed into the dining room with Amanda, without giving Malena more than a dismissive glance.

Amanda glared at Malena's gown. Claudia, on the other hand, gave her a reassuring nod as she wrapped her hand around Sebastian's arm.

"You've met Sebastian, right?" Claudia said.

"Yes."

Sebastian stared at her for an unnerving moment. But instead of an imprudent question, he offered a polite nod and a handshake, much stronger than his mother's had been.

Javier rested his hand on the small of Malena's back and led her into the dining room.

Everyone looked their best tonight, even Trinidad, who had disposed of her light blue uniform in lieu of a black long-sleeve dress with a lacy apron over it; her braid was wrapped into a bun on top of her head that added ten years to her otherwise youthful face. The only one who didn't seem to realize the importance of this gathering was Alejandra, who had chosen a pair of black trousers and a striped blouse for the evening.

After everyone had taken their seats, Trinidad placed a cup of shrimp cebiche on top of every plate. For a moment, the clinking silverware was the only sound in the room. Either Trinidad's appetizer was too good, or the atmosphere too tense with anticipation. The assortment of silverware and glasses puzzled Malena, but she mimicked Claudia's selections, and based upon Mamá Blanca's approving nod, she must have done a good job.

The obligatory subject, the weather, led to the newspaper where Sebastian apparently worked. Once Trinidad brought the second course—a long tray of turkey decorated with peaches and prunes—Sebastian ran his eyes past everyone.

"Well, this may be as good a time as any." He focused on Rafael. "Señor Dávila, by now you know the reason for my visit." He eyed Malena for a split second. "I really would have liked my father to be here with us tonight, but we all know that's not possible . . ."

There was a short silence in the room before smiles faded and people nodded, indistinctly enumerating the list of qualities Sebastian's father had possessed.

"Ignacio was such a good man."

"What a pity!"

"Tragic, really."

"Such a gentleman."

"So good."

So Sebastian's father had died, too. Amanda had said something about the man's illness a few days ago. At least Sebastian had the consolation that his father hadn't ended his own life. The comments around the table reminded Malena of her father's funeral, where strangers had said the same things about him. When people died, it seemed like they turned into saints that could do no wrong.

Sebastian grasped Claudia's hand. "But life goes on, and I would like to start a new one with Claudia." Claudia's cheeks were as red as her nail polish. "If that's all right with you," Sebastian told Rafael.

Rafael produced a wide smile; so wide he looked like someone else.

"Of course it is." He rose and served champagne to everyone. "This deserves a toast!" He raised his glass.

Malena clicked her glass against Javier's, sitting by her side, and then Ana's, before trying the sweet champagne. Her eyes met Sebastian's for a second as he drank.

As the evening progressed, Malena's eyes continued to gravitate toward Sebastian. Okay, so she was not completely indifferent to him. That didn't mean anything. It was normal for a woman her age to admire male beauty, especially since she'd never seen a specimen like this outside a movie screen. Her eyes were glued to Sebastian and Claudia as they sat across from her in the living room.

He whispered something into Claudia's ear and she giggled. Of course she would. If Malena had the attention of a man like Sebastian, she would be giggling, too. Malena could no longer follow Ofelia's conversation. Yes, dinner had been excellent, and yes, she had noticed some streets in San Isidro needed repaving.

Claudia stood up, nodding at Sebastian, and walked toward the piano.

With the first notes of Beethoven's *Moonlight Sonata,* she became the center of attention. Behind the piano keys, there was no trace of that shy girl who seldom smiled and spoke softly. Sebastian's eyes glimmered as he watched his bride play the piano. For the first time in her life, Malena wished she were someone else.

———— ⋙•⋘ ————

Standing in semidarkness, Malena twisted the plastic phone cord around her index finger. With her other hand, she tightened the phone against her ear, listening impatiently to the steady ringing. Julia wasn't picking up. Of course, she was probably asleep—hopefully without her earplugs. The sun had not yet risen, but this was the safest time to call her friend. After last night's gathering, everyone in the house would be sleeping in.

"Hello?"

"Julia? It's me. I'm sorry for calling so early."

"Malena? Where are you? I've been worried sick." It was so good to hear Julia's voice, to talk to someone who knew her real name.

"In San Isidro."

"Did you find your mother?"

"No. Well, sort of." Malena glanced at the door. "Listen, I can't explain right now. Things here are a little more complicated than I thought."

"But how long will you be there?"

"I don't know. A few more days. Have you been watering my fern and picking up my mail?"

Julia sighed. "*Mi reina*, there's something I have to tell you and you're not going to like it."

"The fern died?"

"No, worse." She was silent for a moment. "I didn't want to say anything after your father's funeral because you seemed so shocked, but it may help you now." She paused, dramatically. Julia loved to be the first one to share a piece of gossip. Malena could picture her neighbor's tall bouffant, black roots standing out on her otherwise red hair, like a volcanic eruption in the middle of the night. She might be wearing her silk robe, the black one with fading butterflies, and drying the sweat from the back of her neck with a handkerchief. "The night before your father's death," she finally said, "he got into a fight with a man."

"What man?"

"I don't know who he was. I'd never seen him before, but the two of them were yelling so much I thought they were going to hit each other."

Her father yelling? But he'd had the patience of a saint. Then again, her father had turned out to be a stranger.

"Are you sure?"

"Yes, *mi amor*. I saw them. Hugo was out of control."

Malena's moist fingers had left prints on the receiver. "Julia, could you describe the man?"

"Short, thin, bald."

Bald? Her father didn't have any bald friends. His only friend had been Pedro Córdova. And Pedro had abundant curly hair. He was not thin either.

"He was not bad looking. Probably in his early fifties."

"Did you hear what the fight was about?"

"No. Your father was just telling him to leave."

"You didn't hear his name?"

"No."

"Lili?"

Startled, Malena turned around. She hadn't heard Claudia open the door. How long had she been standing here? Had she heard anything? How could she have been so stupid and careless to call Julia from the house! She hung up the phone.

Claudia tightened her salmon robe across her chest. "Who were you talking to?"

"A friend. What are you doing up so early?"

Claudia studied her. "Looking for you. I was wondering if you wanted to come to mass with me today."

———— ❧ ————

Malena followed the future Mrs. Rivas down the street. Claudia was a mystery to her. Sometimes she was friendly, like last night when she'd helped her get ready for the dinner party, or even this morning, when she'd invited her to come to church. But there were days when Claudia wouldn't say a word to her. She hadn't asked anything else about the phone call. Would she tell Ana? Then again, Lili must have friends. It wouldn't be so unusual that she'd be calling one of them.

The phone call. Malena still couldn't grasp what Julia had told her. Her father had gotten into a fight with a man, a stranger. It seemed so out of character. And who was that man?

Claudia stopped and pointed across the street to a sand-colored house with a pitched roof and a concrete fountain in front.

"That's Sebastian's house."

So this was where he lived. Sebastian had a quaint house with a black metal fence surrounding the property. He must walk by this courtyard every morning, perhaps touching the water in the fountain on his way out. He might be inside right now, maybe watching through one of the windows. She searched for him in the second story, but all the curtains were drawn.

"Are you going to move here after you get married?"

"I suppose," Claudia said. "But I would much rather live away from his mother."

Malena didn't blame her. Ofelia seemed like a difficult woman.

Claudia resumed her walk, rubbing the cross pendant hanging from her neck.

"That is a beautiful cross you're wearing. Did Alejandra make it?"

"No. My grandfather Pancho. He gave it to Tía Abigail on her eighteenth birthday, and she gave it to me before she passed."

"Do you remember her?"

"Of course. I was eleven when she died. She was my *madrina*." There was a deep sadness in Claudia's eyes after she mentioned that Abigail had been her godmother. "My room used to be hers. We shared it."

Malena halted. She slept on the bed of a dead woman?

"Really?" Malena forced her legs to move.

"She was so sweet and beautiful. A great seamstress, too."

The sight of the Gothic church standing proud in the heart of downtown silenced their chatter. Claudia covered her head with a black veil and climbed the concrete stairs of the most ostentatious construction in San Isidro. Malena followed her into the cold, gloomy nave flanked by rows of polished pews. The clatter of her heels echoed on a tiled floor covered with geometric patterns. She wanted to ask more about Abigail, to know everything about her, but she could never find the right words. It was apparent that every time she mentioned her, she brought sadness to those who knew her.

Chapter 14

Abigail, 1936

It wasn't always easy being the weakest one in the family, or more exactly, being thought of as weak only because you were sick as a child. How much longer did she have to pay for having a bad kidney? How many more of these torturous baths?

The place that had once seemed magical to Abigail for its natural beauty and warmth had now become her prison. Now that she'd turned fifteen, it was no longer fantastic to have a waterfall directly across from the pool where she sat for hours so the minerals in the water would restore her health. Neither did it seem extraordinary that said waterfall would be named after the Virgin's mane—*Cabellera de la Virgen*—for the water that cascaded like women's tresses along the mountain. As a child, she'd tried to visualize the Virgin's features somewhere in the mountain's green vegetation. She'd imagined the largest rocks to be her eyes, watching her, protecting her, and a row of bushes to be her nose. The mouth always changed; sometimes it was the shadow of a tree or a dent, and sometimes, despite how hard she tried, she couldn't visualize it at all. With the years, the Virgin's features became harder to find, and then one day, Abigail couldn't see her altogether.

She looked away from the cascade and focused, instead, on the warm green water wetting her calves as she sat by the edge of the pool. Tightening her fingers around the slippery rim, she kicked the water, the People Soup, as she called it, splashing all the heads around her. They glared at her. But Abigail didn't care. She was done with these miraculous thermal waters her mother forced her into three times a week; done with the wrinkled toes and the tight white cap pressing uncomfortably against her forehead; done with the stiff balsa floater imprisoning her chest and the textured polyester of Amanda's old bathing suit rubbing against her growing breasts. She couldn't stand any more sick people around her, or more kids splashing about. She longed to be normal, like her sisters, and go to dance contests, like Ana and Amanda were doing this very moment. And, why not, have her own set of admirers.

Abigail removed her floater and discarded it behind her.

"Are you going to sit there all day?"

Abigail's gaze followed a pair of wet legs to the childish shape of a prepubescent girl with a nose full of freckles and a yellow cap. Oh, great. It was the little brat. She'd seen her before; she was always the loudest and most obnoxious of all the kids in the pool.

Squinting against the sun's rays, Abigail shielded her eyes with her hand. "That's none of your business."

"How come you always sit by the edge with that stupid floater? How come you never swim?"

Abigail stared at her own pale legs—they were never exposed to the sun long enough to get a tan. It was humiliating that this girl, younger than she was by at least four years, could swim. That was perhaps the worst of all her problems with this place—this irrational fear she had of the water.

"You're a chicken," the girl said.

"That's enough," Abigail said. "Get out of my sight, *niñita majadera!*"

She turned her back on the girl and glanced at the people in the pool. But before she realized it, she was among them—*in* the water; face down, wet, light against the thick water; her body loose, *unsafe* without her floater. She kicked randomly with legs and arms, realizing—perhaps too late—that the insufferable girl had pushed her and she couldn't reach the pool wall with her hand. She tried to yell, but a gush of water broke violently into her mouth and down her throat. She coughed, but instead of sounds, she produced an assortment of bubbles, which now blinded her view of the pool's surface. Her body sped downward, toward the bottom, until she could only hear the noises inside her own head, the painful pressure in her sinuses, her ears ready to explode. She couldn't breathe, she'd lost all control of her body; she'd lost her long battle with death, the battle that had started as a little girl with painful injections and hospital rooms. She shut her eyes, now certain this was the end of her life, thinking how unfair this all seemed. But then a force that she recognized as a hand, or maybe two, gripped her arm, her waist, her now loose hair. She felt a bare shoulder, an Adam's apple, an arm, and she held on to a neck with one hand as her body ascended as quickly as it had descended.

Her emergence to the surface was an attack to the senses: a bright light shone in her eyes, yells hurt her ears, the tastes of salt and sulfur scorched her tongue. A pair of hands—the hands that saved her—pulled her slippery arms onto the hard edge of the pool; fresh air filtered through her nose. *Oxygen.* She was breathing again. She shut her burning eyes, lightheaded from the heat of the water, from the movement around her. She was still alive. Or was she not? Someone lifted her up. She was floating. But bodies didn't float; only souls did. She tried to open her eyes, to assess whether or not she was truly being elevated from the pool, but she didn't have any strength left, not even in her eyelids.

In a matter of seconds—or had it been hours?—she was lying on a rough but warm surface. She opened her eyes to see a blurry face leaning toward hers. It was an angel, an apparition of some sort. Only an angel would have eyes that blue, skin so light, a voice so soothing. As her vision sharpened she discerned that it was a man, a young one, perhaps sixteen or seventeen, and he was saying something, except that she couldn't understand him. There were too many other voices mingling with his. He leaned over. Was he going to kiss her? Of course, it was the only way. It had happened to Sleeping Beauty and Snow White. Their princes brought them back to life with a kiss. She shut her eyes, for there was nothing else to do but receive that imminent first kiss of love.

She stiffened as his lips touched hers, but instead of a gentle encounter like the ones Amanda had talked about, he blew air inside her mouth and squeezed her nose with his fingers. No, this kiss, or whatever it was, couldn't be considered a kiss of love by any stretch of the imagination. She brought her hands to his bare chest and pushed him away.

"I'm sorry," he said. "I thought you couldn't breathe."

Oh, but he was an angel, for sure. Never before had she seen such a perfect creature. He was lean and his straight nose was sunburned. His mouth was bright red and still moist. Running his hand across his dripping hair, he asked if she was fine, and the sound of his voice was music.

She focused on his Adam's apple, the one she'd felt under the water, and nodded. Resting her hands on the concrete floor, she attempted to push herself up, but her arms were still weak. Gently, he placed his hand behind her back and pushed her to a sitting position. This close, she could get lost in the brightness of his blue eyes. She wanted to thank him, to ask his name, but Pepe, the pool supervisor, pushed him aside and leaned toward her.

"What happened to you? I told you not to remove your floater!"

It was an unpleasant change of scenery to have this man's sweaty face and his foul breath in front of her. His loud voice hurt her ears.

"I'm sorry," she said.

Pepe yanked her up by the arm and asked if she needed help getting home. Abigail searched for her savior among dozens of wet heads, but he'd disappeared through the crowd as quickly and as unexpectedly as he'd appeared under the water.

Abigail asked the curious bystanders if they knew him, but nobody had seen him before, or had any idea of where he went.

She returned the next day, and the day after, and continued going for the next three months, but there was no sign of him. She could no longer follow conversations or do simple school work. Not even the prospect of Ana's wedding or her new dress excited her. Her mind was occupied with a single goal: to find *him*.

At the pool, she asked about the young man, talking to anyone who would listen, describing every detail, every nuance of his serene face until the point where she couldn't be certain anymore if her mind had fabricated his features. Did he really have that deep shade of blue in his eyes? Had his wet torso really brushed again her chest? Had his mouth been on hers for a split second? She questioned if he'd been real. Had she even fallen in the pool? Pepe never mentioned the unfortunate event again. No one else did. Not even the little brat who pushed her into the pool and never spoke to her again.

No, he had been real. And she would find him. Eventually. It was not a choice; she *had* to see him again.

Chapter 15

Sebastian stared at the breakfast sitting in front of him: a piece of stale bread, a hard-boiled egg, and a watered-down coffee, no milk. Blowing on the coffee was unnecessary; he hadn't warmed it long enough. It was flat-out cold. He bit a corner of the bread, but it was about as appealing as chewing on a shoe sole. The egg wasn't any better; the yolk had turned green from overcooking it. His stomach growled in protest.

"Where is Juanita? I need a strong coffee," his mother said as she walked into the dining room—her hand resting on her forehead, no makeup on, and still wearing her golden robe.

"You fired her."

She tied the robe's belt around her waist. "I did?"

"Last night, remember? She couldn't find your shoes for the party."

His mother sat down. "Of course I remember. She was so incompetent." She sighed. "I guess I'm going to have to find another maid."

Sebastian ditched the bread. "No, you're not."

"What?" Her eyes widened. "Am I supposed to cut down on that, too? You already took my chauffeur and sold your father's car!"

"What do you expect me to do? Papá left me nothing but debt. Besides, a chauffer in San Isidro is unnecessary. One car for the both of us is enough. I can drive you around. Or teach you, if you'd like."

She picked up Sebastian's cup with a bitter laugh. "You expect me, Ofelia Vásconez de Rivas, to drive? I suppose you want me to cook and clean, too?"

"I told you, it would only be for a short time, until I pay off our debt."

She took a sip from Sebastian's coffee and grimaced. "Fire someone from the paper!"

"I already did!"

"I'm not cooking or cleaning. I don't even know how."

He straightened out his collar. "Fine. I'll cook and clean."

Smirking, she pointed at Sebastian's breakfast. "You call that cooking?"

Sebastian rubbed his temple. What was he going to do with this woman?

"Sebas, *mi amor*, think about it. This is a big house. There is no way I can keep it without help." She flashed her red nails.

He sighed. "Fine, let me think about it. But I'm making you a budget."

"Fine," she said, though they both knew she wasn't going to follow a budget. "But let's change the subject. I hate talking about money. What did you think about last night?"

He had nothing to say about last night, at least not to her.

"I thought Claudia looked lovely," she said. "What a difference with that . . . Liliana, Lili, whatever her name is. I can't believe María Teresa raised a daughter like that. Did you see the dress she was wearing? That cleavage, my God!"

Cleavage? Of course, Sebastian hadn't been able to look at anything else the entire evening. He tried to picture what his fiancée had been wearing, but couldn't remember.

"That girl is a walking catastrophe! She tripped twice with her heels."

Sebastian stood up. Hunger was preferable to listening to his mother. He hated the spiteful tone in her voice, the innate harshness women had toward each other. She didn't even know this girl and was already criticizing her.

He headed for the foyer, nearly tripping over his mother's latest purchase: a metal sculpture of a life-sized angel so ugly that initially Sebastian had thought it was the Devil himself—until he realized it was missing the horns and the tail. His mother had bought it the day after his father's funeral. Sebastian didn't understand how she could've thought about her art collection the day after she buried her husband of nearly thirty years.

In the courtyard, he walked by the concrete fountain and absently wet his fingers with the cold water, the way he did every morning.

He'd finally been able to place that girl: she was the one who entered the cheap hotel with Javier. Seeing her with Claudia's brother last night reminded him of where he'd seen her first. And it only meant one thing: Javier and Liliana were lovers. It was just a matter of watching how possessively he held her arm, the way he pulled the chair out for her, and how he constantly paid her attention. But it must be a secret. Rafael and Ana would never consent to having Javier's girlfriend under their same roof. The only logical conclusion was that the family didn't know about their relationship, which was probably why the two of them met at hotels. But why wouldn't Javier just propose? Why would he take a family friend to a hotel, and such a nasty one at that? The other detail that didn't fit into the equation was Claudia's explanation for Lili's visit. She'd said her family had sent her to San Isidro to keep her away from her married lover, yet Javier was single. Or did she mean *another* lover?

Sebastian lit a cigarette, contemplating the circles of smoke as they dissolved with the air. He'd known Javier since their high school days. Back then, his future brother-in-law had had the reputation of being a womanizer. Sebastian could understand that; he could understand certain biological urges, too. But this was different. Liliana was the daughter of Ana Platas's best friend, and yet he was treating her like an easy woman.

What a pity—such a sweet girl. Sebastian had been touched by the way she cared for Mamá Blanca last night—rubbing the lady's arm during dinner, covering her with a wool poncho when she fell asleep in the living room, talking to her in a soothing voice. He'd never known a woman to be so gentle. Not even Claudia.

Sebastian stopped in front of the Iglesia de Santo Domingo as soon as he spotted Claudia's unmistakable gait outside the church's double doors. Sometimes, like today, he had to look at her feet to make sure she was stepping on the ground and not floating. The grace of her movements had always fascinated him. But not today. He didn't want to approach her, especially because that girl, Liliana, was walking beside her.

He waited by the light post until the girls got lost among the crowd, in the direction of the Platas home.

Chapter 16

Malena wouldn't make the same mistake twice. She would *not* get caught sneaking into the courtyard again. She would wait until Javier returned home before leaving Claudia's room. But the wait was excruciating. It was already midnight and he wasn't back yet. Her exhausted body relaxed under the covers and her eyelids closed every few seconds, comforted by the sound of Claudia's soft snores. Did Javier have to go out *every* night? Couldn't he ever spend an evening at home? If only he had a more predictable schedule, she could have been to the courtyard and back already.

As she drifted into sleep, something woke her. Was that the front door? She stiffened under the covers, listening to the noises in the hall: someone whistling and juggling keys, the floor squeaking under heavy steps, and finally, a door shutting.

Once the house was silent, Malena stepped out of Claudia's room with only a candle in her hand. She tiptoed down the stairs and into the dining room, the piece of paper in her brassiere brushing against her skin. That little piece of paper, so close to her heart, was the answer to a question that had been pounding in her head for the past few days.

She stopped in the kitchen to pick up a large wooden spoon from a drawer, then slipped outside. It was cold and the pavement felt rough under her bare feet. She knelt by the lemon tree. The soil was harder than she remembered; digging with the spoon wasn't easy. She set the candle on the ground so she could use both hands and dug deeper, looking around the patio every so often to make sure nobody was around, not that it did much good—as dark as it was. She had no idea what she would say if someone found her out here. The sleepwalking trick probably wouldn't work this time. Worse yet, the black plastic bag was nowhere to be seen. What if someone had found the accounting notebooks and thrown them away?

She scooped with her hands, frantically, almost in a panic, until she felt the plastic bag with her fingers. She pulled it out, tore it open, and took one of the accounting notebooks out. She moved the candle closer to her leg and removed the piece of paper from her brassiere—her father's goodbye note, the last memory of him—and compared the handwriting with the script in the book.

It was identical. The same left slant, the oversized capital letters, the same curly tail at the end of the *s,* the tilted line crossing his *t's.*

On the bottom of the page was the accountant's signature: Enrique Hidalgo. Again, the accountant's signature matched her father's writing. Was it possible that this man, this Enrique Hidalgo, was her father? She knew he'd been an accountant before becoming a math teacher. But why would he change his name?

She examined the date at the bottom of the page. *November 10, 1941,* the year prior to her birth. No, this couldn't be a coincidence. The writing, the timing, the profession, it all coincided, and besides, nobody ever mentioned Hugo Sevilla. Trinidad hadn't even heard the name before.

Enrique Hidalgo must be her father.

The paper trembled in her hands, her fingers numb. Her father had lied about this, too. She hadn't even known his real name. She read his note, the last words he had written to her.

Dearest Malena,

I know I was never the father you deserved. I hope one day you'll forgive me for that and for what I'm about to do. I just can't run away anymore.

I've always loved you.

Papá

Nothing about his deceit, about his lies. She crumpled his note and would have dumped it in the trash if she had one nearby, or if she had the certainty that nobody would find it. Instead, she returned it to her brassiere, fighting her tears. Her entire life was a farce, from beginning to end. Worse yet, she wasn't any better than him. Wasn't she doing the same thing?

Mechanically, she removed another notebook from the bag and leafed through it. The same names and the same writing repeated throughout. Enrique Hidalgo had to be him. She tried to remember what her grandmother had called him when Malena was little, but "*hijo*" or "your father" were the only terms she recalled.

She returned both notebooks to the plastic bag, and her fingers brushed against a soft fabric. *Ana's handkerchief.* She pulled it out of the bag, remembering now Rafael's accusations, remembering now the initial sewn on it. Yes, it was the letter *E*, as in *Enrique*, as in her father's real name.

Before she could draw any conclusions, before she could grasp the full meaning of her discovery, she caught a glimpse of a dim light coming from one of the upstairs rooms. She couldn't tell whose room it was, afraid as she was to turn her head toward the source of light. She froze, like a rabbit waiting for its predator to act first.

With her peripheral vision, she discerned a figure standing behind the curtain, probably watching her, *discovering* her. Her instinct told her to blow out the candle, to run back into the house, to hide, but her body was paralyzed. If she remained still, she hoped, maybe she would become invisible. Seconds passed until she could no longer hold her curiosity. Her need to know was a force stronger than her good sense. She turned her head toward the window, but the figure—if there had truly been one—was gone. The gauzy curtain stirred gently in the night breeze. A second or two later, the light went out and the house turned completely dark again.

Chapter 17

Ana, 1940

The basket was heavy and Ana could feel drops of sweat on her forehead. She squeezed Javier's tiny hand and took longer steps. Only one more block to go. She could've handled the heat or the pain in her legs, but not Rafael's anger. If lunch wasn't ready by the time he got home, she would get the silent treatment—at the very least—and she couldn't stand his indifference. She quickened her pace in spite of Javier's complaints.

"Mami, I'm hungry!"

Ana ignored him. It was already twelve thirty and Rafael expected his food on the table at one. No delays. Javier freed his hand from her grasp and stopped. What now? She squatted to his level. Javier pouted, his eyes watery. Oh, no. Her son's screams would echo all over the block at any second. She had to do something! As she grabbed a pear from her grocery basket, she felt a piece of paper underneath and pulled it out. Without taking her eyes from the paper, she handed Javier the piece of fruit.

"Here *mi amor*, but please hurry up. Papi will get mad at me if we're not home soon."

After Javier grabbed the pear, Ana seized the paper. It was a typed letter.

Ana, she read, *I've lost count of how many letters I've written you, but this is the first one you'll ever see. Perhaps the only one.*

She stood up, confused, and continued to read:

I've tried to ignore my feelings for I know you're a taken woman, taken by a man who doesn't deserve you, but it's useless. The more I try, the harder it is not to think of you. I'm only sorry that I must now burden you with this truth, but I think it's only fair that you know there's someone longing for you, someone who hasn't been able to take you out of his mind since the day he met you; the happiest and the saddest day of his life.

I know I'm wrong. I've often wondered about this fascination of mine with a married woman, and I only come to the same conclusion. There is no one in this town, in this entire world, as kind and generous as you.

I've seen the way you tend to your child and I'm mesmerized by your tenderness. I watch you often, though you never notice me. Please don't be afraid, I would never do anything to harm you or your reputation. I've resigned myself to watch you from a distance.

Today, I finally gathered the courage to finish this letter and send it to you. I don't expect anything in return, just that you know that someone loves you.

Ana read the letter again, quickly, skipping words, her eyes flowing back and forth from beginning to end. An anonymous love letter. For her? It must be a mistake. This sort of thing never happened to her. She slid the note into her sleeve and grabbed her son's hand.

The walk home went by smoothly. Neither the heat, nor the whining, nor the heavy basket could keep her mind off the note. Someone loved her. A man. An admirer. She was the kindest woman he'd ever seen. *Ana*, he'd written, not any of her sisters' names. There was no mistake. She glanced over her shoulder, hoping to see the man who followed her every day to the market, the man who loved her from a distance.

The sidewalk was empty.

Rafael had arrived home early and scolded her for being late. But Ana didn't care. She only had two concerns: to hide the note and to find out who her admirer was. Unless it was a joke. Or maybe Rafael was testing her fidelity. No, he was too unimaginative to think of a scheme like this, or to worry about her at all. Rafael's only thoughts pertained to his work and his resentment toward Papá Pancho for hiring that new accountant, Enrique Hidalgo, three months ago instead of giving Rafael the position.

"And don't even get me started on your cousin," Rafael said, chewing on a piece of *guatita*. "He was late again today, but of course, your father didn't say anything about it or the fact that Fausto still reeked of alcohol when he walked in." His knife sliced through a potato. "I can't wait to find another job and get the hell out of that store!"

The next morning, Ana made an excuse to go back to the market. This time, she wore her nicest outfit: a two-piece tailored brown suit with matching shoes, gloves, and a hat with a long feather; she even wore makeup. Her fancy shoes were unsuitable for the market, but they perfectly matched her attire.

Ana deliberately left her basket on the floor and walked a couple of steps away, pretending to be looking for *corvina* fillets. A child of about ten years of age walked by her basket and dropped a piece of paper inside. She prayed the boy was not her admirer.

Ana paid for the fish and rushed after the boy.

"Wait!" She caught up with him.

"Please don't hurt me, Señora."

"Who gave you that letter?"

"I don't know who he is."

"Where is he?"

The boy shrugged.

Ana looked around; this was her only chance. "Tell him I want to meet him."

The boy ran away. She watched after him, unable to suppress a smile. She'd surprised herself with her request, but she didn't regret it.

The second letter was a short poem. Ana read it until she had memorized every word. After that, her trips to the market were never the same. She couldn't concentrate anymore; she often returned home with half the things she needed. She found ridiculous excuses to go back during the week, only to scan every man around her. She was self-conscious the entire time, certain that he was watching her from a window or an automobile.

Until the day her torment finally ended.

The little boy showed up by the fruit stand and handed her a third note. Not a word was spoken. She waited until she got home to read the note. It was the shortest one. It only had a day, a time, and a place. A date with her admirer. She would finally see him.

On the afternoon of her rendezvous, it rained all day. Ana rushed past the jewelry store, covering her face with her navy umbrella so Rafael wouldn't see her from the window. She had dropped off Javier at her mother's house and was on her way to the other side of town, where the man who loved her waited for her in a little-known café. She hated to worry her mother and tell her lies, but she couldn't come up with a better excuse than a doctor's appointment.

Ana arrived five minutes early. The place was crowded—the perfect way to go unnoticed. She sat in the back of the room and ordered a cup of coffee without removing her gloves. She would only be here for a few minutes, however long it took to finish her coffee. Not another minute. It would be a quick meeting, quick enough to remain inconspicuous. She took a first sip of coffee but it was still too hot to drink, which she was grateful for—it gave her more time.

She watched the people around her, afraid to be recognized, afraid to see any familiar faces in the crowd. She took a deep breath and exhaled slowly. Why should she be ashamed? There was nothing wrong with what she was doing, unless it was a sin to have a coffee by yourself in a public place. She sat up straight, reassuring herself that everything would be fine.

But her conviction didn't last long. It died the minute she saw Amanda's brother-in-law at a nearby table with some friends. Oh, no. What if he saw her? What if he told Nicolas or Amanda? Ana couldn't live with her sister's reproach if she found out about her little escapade. She covered her face with the menu and told herself he probably hadn't seen her, or else he would have come to greet her. Good thing he was so engrossed in conversation; she could hear his voice loud and clear.

Oh, God, what was she doing here? She only hoped He would forgive her. He had to. The Lord only knew how much she had suffered with Rafael's treatment. But this was still wrong, a little voice in her head reminded her. This was a mistake and she'd better leave before this so-called admirer arrived, before it was too late and she *had* something to regret.

"What are you doing here?" a male voice said in front of her.

She would have recognized his voice anywhere. Her legs trembled under the table and her voice was lost somewhere in the depths of her throat, unwilling to come out. Ana lowered the menu.

He glared at her with contempt, hatred even, his eyes sparkled like never before, and for a minute Ana was afraid that Rafael would slap her in front of everyone.

Chapter 18

H er mind was playing tricks on her. Yes, that had to be it. The figure standing by the window had been nothing but a figment of Malena's imagination. Otherwise someone would have said something to her this morning. Not that she had given the person a chance. She had avoided all eyes during breakfast, and eagerly agreed to accompany Amanda to the Madreselva again.

"You look tired," Amanda said as they entered the nightclub. "Did you sleep well last night?"

Malena nodded, though she couldn't remember what a restful night felt like anymore. She'd been thinking about her father all night. About this fake name he used. Which was his real name, Enrique or Hugo? Now more than ever, she needed to stay in San Isidro and find out what was behind all of this.

With Amanda's help, Malena rolled the faded Venetian rug off the floor. It had been Nicolas's pride and joy, Amanda told her. A distant cousin had brought it from Italy amid perilous adventures that he related often and that had the strange quality of becoming more impressive with each telling.

Malena was grateful for the distractions around her: the employees coming in and out of the parlor, the moving of tables and chairs, the piling of trash in the corner of the room. Focusing on simple tasks gave her mind a rest.

A few meters away, one of the new waiters held a ladder for Bernardo while he removed the old curtains. The drapes carried with them dust from the last twenty years, enough for all of them to cough for a full minute.

A slim middle-aged man in a striped gray suit and tilted hat walked into the restaurant. Behind him entered a tall brunette in a tight blue dress.

"Excuse me?" the man said to no one in particular. "I read in *El Heraldo* that you're having auditions for tango dancers."

Amanda stood up and brushed the dust from her hands.

"Yes, I'm Amanda Platas, the owner." She pointed at Malena and Bernardo. "These are my associates, Liliana Paz and Bernardo Meneses."

Bernardo cleared his throat. "*Bernard.*"

The man removed his hat, revealing a thinning crown and long sideburns. "My name is Leonardo Montes. I've been a dance instructor for thirteen years." He rested his hand on the small of the woman's back. "This is my wife, Rebecca. She's also a dancer." Not once did he look at her. She stiffened from his touch.

Amanda walked to the record player. "Well, let's see what you can do."

Rebecca and Leonardo danced to "La Cumparsita" with a grace and skill Malena had only seen in movie stars with names she couldn't pronounce. Their feet moved effortlessly across the floor, Rebecca's skirt twirling around her statuesque legs. Her back was perfectly straight and her neck long and smooth.

Malena sat on the nearest chair to absorb the sensual scene she was witnessing. How she wished she could move like that! But she would probably trip and fall if she ever attempted those turns. She'd never tangoed with anyone but her father, and that had been years ago, when she was still a child. Now, the idea of a man holding her that close was unthinkable. Rebecca and

Leonardo's hips were practically locked together, and his leg fit perfectly in between Rebecca's.

Bernardo applauded as soon as the song was over.

"Thank you, Señor Montes," Amanda said from her seat. "Please write your personal information on that piece of paper." She pointed at a notepad on a nearby table. "I'll give you a call as soon as I make my decision."

Leonardo lifted an eyebrow with arrogance. "As you please."

Stiffly, he walked to the table and filled out the paper. Rebecca stood behind him, all the confidence from the dance gone. They left without saying goodbye and bickered by the front door.

Amanda turned to Bernardo and Malena.

"What do you think?"

They both agreed they were splendid.

"He's a little short, but he can definitely dance." Amanda rubbed her chin with her index finger. "The woman is much too tall for him."

"Try to find a tall male dancer in this town." Bernardo stacked old chairs into a pile. "The only tall ones are the Rivas. Only Monsieur Sebastian, really, now that his *père* is gone."

Something in Malena's stomach fluttered at the mention of Sebastian's name.

"And from what I've heard," Bernardo continued, "he can also dance."

"He can?" Amanda crossed her legs. "Claudia never mentioned it. Not that she would." She paused for a moment. "Now that I think about it, Sebastian took a trip to Argentina a few years ago. Maybe he learned there."

Bernardo folded a faded tablecloth. "But you couldn't possibly ask him, not now that he's in mourning."

"Of course not." Amanda fingered her pearl necklace. "But if nothing else, I think this Leonardo Montes and his wife will do."

"*Madame*, I have to tell you. I was inspired when I saw them dancing like that," Bernardo said. "She reminded me so much of you when you were younger."

Amanda stared at her bad leg, scowling.

"I felt it, too," Malena said. "It must be wonderful to be able to dance like that."

"You don't know how to tango?" Amanda asked.

She hesitated. Did her experience with her father count? "Not really."

Amanda's eyes opened wide. "Well, we're going to have to fix that." She uncrossed her legs and covered them with her linen skirt. "Everyone here should be able to tango."

<hr />

It had been useless to refuse to dance in front of Amanda. When the woman set her mind on something, she got it. And her immediate desire was to see Malena dancing. Tangoing was harder than Malena remembered, but her legs had surprised her. They'd recalled steps that she had thought long forgotten. Amanda told her she had "natural talent" and "good rhythm," and she turned out to be an excellent teacher and lead. But by the end of the day, the woman was noticeably limping.

Malena couldn't pinpoint what it was that she loved about dancing. All she knew was that for a moment, she had forgotten all her worries, she'd felt more alive than ever, and she didn't want it to end—even if her feet felt the opposite way. With all that exercise, she should have been able to fall asleep immediately. But she couldn't. Sleep made her vulnerable, unrestrained, and who knew if, like her father, she talked in her sleep. And Claudia was less than a meter away.

The light of dawn was stealing into the room through the curtains. The bedside clock marked five. No point in changing positions or shutting her eyes any tighter. She sat up, fixed her loose curls in a bun, and tied them with a long strand of hair. Then, she stepped out of bed and slipped into her robe. She needed a tea, a glass of water, anything to refresh her dry throat.

From the top of the stairs, she saw the strangest thing.

In utmost silence, Mamá Blanca, Amanda, and Ana crossed the foyer toward the front door, their heads low the entire time. None of them saw Malena on the stairs. None of them looked back. One by one, they left the house, like zombies in black dresses.

Chapter 19

"I saw your grandmother, your mother, and your Tía Amanda leaving at dawn today." Malena studied Javier as he tightened a bracelet clasp with a pair of pliers. She'd seized the opportunity to talk to him as soon as his father stepped out of the store. "All in black."

Javier didn't lift his eyes from his work. "I know." He returned the piece to the display case, then tossed the pliers into a drawer behind the counter. "Today is the anniversary of Tío Fausto's death. They visit his grave every year and then attend mass."

"Why didn't Alejandra go with them?" Malena knew Alejandra was in the workshop. She'd heard the drone of her drill from the hallway. "I thought she was close to her cousin."

"She was."

Javier led the way to the street and held the door open for her. "She's not a religious woman. And she says she doesn't like to visit the dead."

The two of them sat on a street bench.

"What happened to Fausto?" Malena asked.

He took a cigarette from his shirt pocket. "Someone tried to rob the store and shot him."

Javier's tone was so detached.

"Did they find the murderer?"

"No. Never."

"That's sad."

"Yes." He placed his arm around her shoulder. "It's very sad, being Alejandra's birthday and all."

Malena recoiled, not only from his proximity but also from the news he was delivering. "Today is her birthday?"

"Yes."

"Her cousin was murdered on her birthday?"

"Unfortunately."

"Nobody mentioned anything about her birthday," she said. "Don't they celebrate it?"

"Oh, no."

Malena tugged her skirt over her legs, aware of Javier's eyes on them. "That's not good."

"What?"

"Dwelling on the past like that."

"She doesn't like anyone to acknowledge her birthday, much less celebrate it. We don't celebrate birthdays in this family. Only Claudia's and mine, really. And that was when we were kids."

"Maybe we should bake a cake for her."

He glanced at the cigarette in his hand. "A cake? I don't know. She might not like it."

"Oh, come on. It will be fun."

Javier was about to answer when a female voice from behind the bench spoke.

"I don't think that's a good idea," Claudia said.

Malena hadn't seen her arrive.

"Why not?" Javier said. It was enough that Claudia opposed the idea for Javier to consider it. "Lili is right, Tía Alejandra should stop dwelling on the past."

It was somewhat amusing to see how easily these two got into quarrels. Malena had never had that kind of relationship

with anybody. Would things have been the same if she had
grown up with Claudia and Javier?

Claudia fanned the smoke with her hand. "Well, that is her
decision to make. I can tell you right now celebrating her birthday would be a big mistake. She'll be furious."

"That's okay," Malena said. "We'll take the chance."

⸻

Malena dug her fork into the pile of rice but was too anxious to
eat. Nobody had mentioned anything about Alejandra's birthday yet.

Alejandra hadn't touched her food either. Her short brown
hair curled up behind her ears and her eyes were fixed on her
full plate. She seemed distracted, absorbed in her own thoughts,
perhaps more than usual.

"I have an announcement to make." Amanda broke the
silence in the dining room. Since the day she'd proclaimed she
was going to manage a nightclub, nobody in the family had
spoken to her at the dinner table.

"The nightclub's opening is this Friday." She looked around
the room. "You're all invited."

Ana's fingers tensed on the table's surface. She didn't dare
look at her husband, who'd stopped chewing.

"Are you dancing?" Javier asked.

"No. I hired a couple of dancers."

"Javier, finish your meal," Ana said.

"Well? Nobody has anything to say?" Amanda said.

"I'll go," Alejandra said.

Amanda served herself some mineral water. "How about
you, Mamá?"

The old woman rubbed Amanda's hand. "Depends on how
I feel that day, *hija*."

"And you, Claudia?" Amanda said. "You can invite Sebastian."

"I don't think Sebastian would approve of me going to a nightclub. Besides, I doubt he'll want to go."

"Well, ask him anyway," Javier said.

"Javier!" Ana snapped.

Amanda turned to Ana and Rafael. "I guess your silence speaks for the two of you. That's what I expected."

Javier nodded at Malena from across the table.

"We have a surprise." Javier dragged the legs of his chair back with an irritating screech that forced everyone to cover up their ears—a reaction he seemed to enjoy infinitely.

They brought Malena's pineapple cake from the kitchen and placed it in front of Alejandra. Javier turned off the lights and sang "Cumpleaños Feliz" with a surprisingly good voice. When he finished, Malena applauded—she was the only one.

The room fell silent. Alejandra's face was partially illuminated with the burning candles. A tear slipped down her cheek. After a harrowing silence, she finally spoke.

"Turn on the lights, please."

Trinidad obeyed.

"Thank you, but you shouldn't have bothered." Alejandra stood, without another word, and left the room.

Claudia stared at Malena with a smirk.

Chapter 20

When Malena entered Amanda's office, she was on the phone, frantic over some centerpieces that had yet to arrive. She signaled Malena to sit down across from her. According to Amanda, this chaotic office had once belonged to her brother-in-law, Enzo. Amanda had added her personal touch to the room: a painting of a couple dancing under a subdued light, her portrait of Carlitos Gardel on the wall, and a flower arrangement on her desk. A disarray of papers and folders surrounded the green vase.

"I'm going to have a heart attack before the day is over!" Amanda slammed the phone down. "Those flowers should have been here hours ago!"

Malena didn't even flinch. In the last few days, she'd become used to Amanda's outbursts and she'd learned that when it came to her business, Amanda was not only demanding, but a perfectionist. To expect anything different the day of the Madreselva's opening would be preposterous, especially with only two hours until the reception.

The lines on her forehead softening, Amanda turned to Malena. "I need you to do me a favor. The liquor has been delivered, but as you know, Enzo did wonders for our credit.

The delivery man won't leave the bottles here until I pay him." She grunted. "And I'm such an idiot I forgot the checkbook at home. Would you be a sweetheart and go get it?"

"Of course," Malena said, already standing.

"You're such an angel." Amanda removed her purse from one of the drawers in her desk. "And while you're at it, bring my red dress, the one you tried on for Claudia's engagement party, so you can wear something nice tonight."

Malena would have been happy to forget the dress fiasco, but apparently she had to live with the humiliation forever. "All right."

"I'm sorry, Lili, I meant to take you to the seamstress, but you know how hectic it's been around here." She unzipped her purse. "The checkbook is in my armoire. Bottom drawer." She handed her a key. "And hurry up, please."

———————

Malena entered Amanda's bedroom and went directly to the oak armoire. The checkbook was exactly where Amanda had said it would be. Before she closed the drawer, a half-burned book with a brown leather cover drew her attention. She pulled it out and opened it.

It was a diary. She read the cover.

Diario de Vida de Abigail Platas.

Malena glanced at her watch. Amanda had asked her to hurry, but an opportunity like this might never come again. This journal might hold all the answers she needed. Amanda would just have to wait.

She locked the bedroom door and sat on the bed. She was about to violate another ethical code—one more transgression in her long list—but she hoped her reasons were enough to earn her forgiveness.

She opened the journal with care, assessing Abigail's pretty penmanship, and read.

June 23, 1940

I've never written a diary before. A life as ordinary as mine doesn't deserve to be recorded, but Ana thinks it's a good idea or else she wouldn't have given me this notebook for my 19th birthday. She says it will help with my "melancholy," as she calls it. Well, I'm going to give it my best effort.

In most pages Abigail talked about her frustrations with her family, her dissatisfaction with her job at the jewelry store, and the most recent books she'd read. Malena skipped a few pages until she spotted her father's name.

July 27, 1940

Something strange just happened. Yesterday, Fausto and Alejandra convinced me to go to the circus with them. Any distraction is worth considering in a town like this. The two of them went a few years ago and enjoyed it. I must admit I was impressed with some of the performances.

At the end of the show, we stumbled upon the assistant manager, whom Fausto and Alejandra had met earlier. His name is Enrique Hidalgo.

Enrique looked at me in a way that made me uncomfortable, to say the least. Nobody has made me blush like that since . . . I'm not even going to write that.

After Fausto introduced us, Enrique kissed my hand. He wanted to know everything about San Isidro and Fausto described the town for him. Then Fausto invited him to a game of Cuarenta later on in the evening. Fausto came home very late. I heard him singing in the street at dawn.

This afternoon, Enrique showed up with circus tickets for the entire family but I doubt my father would want to go.

My father can be so obtuse sometimes. He stormed into the store and yelled at Fausto over yesterday's balance being off, right in front of Enrique! Good thing Rafael wasn't there or he would have incensed my father even more. He never misses the opportunity to complain about my cousin. Fausto snapped. Lately, his temper has gotten atrocious. I tried to appease the two of them to no avail. This was one of the most embarrassing moments of my life.

Enrique offered to help clear up the confusion. He said he was in charge of payrolls and accounting at the circus. Papá Pancho was hesitant at first, but something about Enrique's demeanor and kindness made it impossible for him to refuse. He handed him the ledger and the receipts and Enrique figured out the problem right away. My father was so impressed he invited him for dinner, which is extremely strange, since my father hates company.

During dinner Enrique told us funny stories about the circus. He said he's looking for a job somewhere else, that he's tired of traveling so much and smelling like an elephant. This is where the story gets even stranger. My father offered him a job at the store as a bookkeeper and Enrique accepted! So I guess I'll be seeing a lot of him from now on.

Enrique caused quite a stir between my older sisters. Both Amanda and Ana commented on his "good looks."

I guess people might consider Enrique handsome. I find him more fascinating than good looking. Before leaving, he kissed my hand again (briefly). On his way out, he whispered—

The voices in the hallway interrupted Malena's reading. She lifted her head and froze. It was a man and a woman, and their footsteps were getting closer.

Malena leapt toward the armoire while whoever was at the other side of the door fumbled with the doorknob.

"It's locked."

She recognized Trinidad's voice, followed by a knock.

"Lili?" Javier said. "Are you there?"

Malena returned the diary to the drawer and closed the armoire.

"Yes, just a minute, please."

She rushed to the door and opened it. Javier and Trinidad stared back at her, their expressions a mixture of puzzlement and suspicion.

"Amanda just called," Javier said. "She's wondering what's taking you so long to get back."

Malena flashed the checkbook in her hand. "Just found the checkbook."

"You should have asked me if you couldn't find it," Trinidad said.

Malena ran her index finger along the edge of the checkbook.

"Well, you'd better go," Javier said. "Amanda is livid."

From the taxi cab, Malena saw Bernardo and Amanda talking to a man outside the Madreselva. They stood by a truck with its bed filled with liquor boxes. The man entered the truck's cabin and shut the door. He was getting ready to leave!

Malena paid the taxi driver and then removed the checkbook from her purse.

"Wait, here she is!" Bernardo pointed at Malena as she stepped out of the cab.

"Where the hell have you been?" Amanda grabbed the checkbook from Malena's hands.

"I'm sorry, Amanda."

"You've wasted everyone's time!" Amanda signed the check on Bernardo's back and handed it to the man inside the truck's cabin. Then she demanded her key back.

Damn. Malena had been hoping Amanda would forget about it. She dropped the key on Amanda's palm, then followed her into the Madreselva at a prudent distance.

Inside the grand salon, waiters arranged the tables around the circular dance floor while the musicians fine-tuned their instruments on the raised stage.

Malena curled onto a chair in the corner of the room, unsure of what to do. Her mind drifted to the information she'd just learned from Abigail's diary. She was certain now that her father had been Enrique Hidalgo. Nobody knew numbers like he did, and all that circus talk had reminded her of something La Abuela once said about Malena's father. As a young man, he'd dropped out of school and left El Milagro, their home-town, to live with his godfather. Eva's *compadre*, a man called Simón, ran a circus and took Malena's father under his wing. The idea of her father working for a circus had been so incongruent with the man she knew that Malena had always thought her grandmother had invented that fantastic story for her entertainment—except for the times when Papá took her to the circus and his eyes shone with excitement. He was a different man there. So alive. Sometimes she thought he enjoyed the show more than she did. Thus, she never had the heart to tell him she had outgrown the circus a long time ago. The theater, now that was a different story. She could have gone every day. Those outings were some of her fondest memories with her father.

And Abigail had liked him. All the sisters had. If only she could get hold of that diary again. But how? Amanda carried the armoire key in her purse.

Malena sat up straight as Amanda reentered the parlor, followed by Leonardo Montes. She was yelling, gesticulating with her arms, shaking her head. If she was truly going to have a heart attack, it would be now.

"You call her right now!" Amanda said.

Leonardo seemed to be shrinking behind her. "But Doña, she's gone. I don't know where to find her."

They stopped a few meters from Malena.

"This is incredible, Leonardo. Do you know we open in twenty minutes? What am I supposed to do? Dance in her place?"

"I'm sorry, Doña. This has never happened before."

"Couldn't you at least wait until after opening night?"

Leonardo blushed. "I'm a man, Doña. These things . . . just happen."

"Just happen? You accidentally find your way into another woman's bed? Look, Leonardo. I don't care what you do with your private life. But when your wife is the dancer in my show and is missing because she can't stand the sight of you, then it is my problem. So what are you going to do about it?"

Leonardo scratched his head, looking about the room.

When his eyes rested on Malena, she shrank into her chair. She suspected what he was thinking, she could see the idea— that terrible idea—forming in his head. And she knew what he was about to say before he opened his mouth.

He pointed his finger at her.

"What about her?"

Malena shook her head, in a panic. Yes, she'd danced a few times with Leonardo while they rehearsed—at Amanda's insistence—but that didn't mean she was prepared to perform in front of an audience.

Amanda studied her for a moment. "You think she can do it?"

"Yes. She's coordinated enough. I'll lead her. I'll simplify the routine."

They stared at her as if she were a piece of merchandise in a store.

Malena found her voice. "Amanda, I think it would be better if you danced. You are an experienced dancer, and this is your nightclub."

"You seem to have forgotten that I'm a cripple."

"But I'm not a professional, I can barely—"

"That's irrelevant. You're the only one I have."

"But what if Ana or Rafael find out?"

"I couldn't care less about Ana and Rafael now. I have much more important things to worry about. Are you going to help me or not?"

Chapter 21

Hiding behind a golden curtain backstage, Malena peeked at the Madreselva's grand salon as it filled up with guests. The rundown place from a few days ago no longer existed. The chandeliers, now clean and polished, shone like gold. Velvet curtains framed the long windows at the end of the room. The dance floor had been varnished and waxed. The rose center-pieces had finally arrived, adding an elegant touch to the tables. And Amanda's pride, a quartet of violinists, a pianist, and a *bandoneón* player, were performing the most popular tangos.

Amanda looked stunning in a sleeveless long black dress, her back exposed and a slit in her skirt. The tight dress enhanced every curve of her body and a red rose accentuated her fancy chignon. The last touch was a diamond necklace and matching earrings.

She crossed the room to greet Javier and Alejandra as they entered. She hugged each one and led them to the best table.

When Alejandra handed her coat to a waiter, Malena couldn't believe her eyes. The woman wore a long evening gown. A white lace bodice with sequins wrapped around Alejandra's surprisingly generous bosom and her small waist was enhanced by a pink satin sheath ending in a bell-shaped skirt. It was surreal to see her in something other than trousers.

Malena searched for the rest of the family throughout the parlor, but apparently—and fortunately—only the two of them had showed up.

After they sat, Bernardo, in an immaculate black tuxedo, served them champagne, then whispered something into Amanda's ear. She walked to the center of the stage.

Malena let go of the curtain, frightened. She could still escape. The back door was close enough. She could easily squeeze by the busy waiters and disappear without anybody taking notice, spare herself the agony of standing half-naked in front of strangers. She pulled up the straps of Rebecca's red dress, glancing at her deep cleavage. *Por Dios,* this was even worse than Claudia's dress! This dress was so short she could feel the cold air slapping her legs.

She took a step toward the door.

"Where are you going?"

It was Leonardo. She turned and stared at the red rose on his lapel.

"Nowhere."

Amanda's voice through the microphone welcomed the audience to the club; it was a painful reminder that she was counting on Malena. If she left, Amanda would never forgive her. And she didn't think she could live with Amanda's resentment.

Leonardo picked up her hand. "Ready?"

"No, please. Can't someone else do it?"

"Listen, *nena,* stage fright is the last thing I need." He softened his voice and squeezed her hand. "You don't have to worry about a thing. Just follow my lead."

A violin solo played the first notes of "El Tango de Malena." It was their cue—a distressing irony. Of all the popular tangos, they had picked the one that bore her name. Hearing it aloud made her feel more naked, if such thing were possible.

Leonardo pulled her to the center of the stage. Malena's legs stiffened as she reached the dance floor. All eyes were focused on her, on her body. Worse yet, Claudia's fiancé, Sebastian, walked into the club in a black tuxedo. Malena searched for Claudia behind him, in front of him, somewhere among the watchful eyes in the audience. She couldn't find her.

Sebastian sat alone at a table near the stage. His eyes widened as he recognized her. She only hoped he wouldn't tell Claudia.

Leonardo embraced her, resting a hand on her back. She was rigid and didn't follow properly. The dancer stared into her eyes and lifted one eyebrow. She knew exactly what that meant—she'd better respond before the whole opening went to hell. Malena focused on the music and the steps she'd learned. Leonardo made up for her awkwardness with his poise, confidence, and grace.

As the song progressed, Malena grew more confident. She concentrated on the singer's voice, a tenor similar to Juan Carlos Miranda, one of the original singers of this tango. The intensity of his voice transported her for an instant to her living room, to her father singing this song to her. Even though he hadn't been much of a singer, he'd performed with true emotion. He had to be in the mood, though, usually after a couple of *puros*.

For a moment, she forgot that a hundred people were watching her and that she hadn't tangoed in years. But her father's memory faded when she turned in Sebastian's direction. Dim lights or not, he could still see her. And her skimpy dress left very little to the imagination.

He shifted forward.

She could feel Sebastian's gaze upon her. Knowing he was there was enough for her body to tense up, for her dress to stick to her damp back, for her knees to falter. It would be so unbecoming if her makeup melted, too.

When the song ended, Malena let go of Leonardo's grip. *Two more songs and this will all be over.* She searched for Amanda, standing tall backstage. The woman offered her the proud look of a lioness admiring her cub's prowess, and it was all worth it. She'd made Amanda happy. The audience burst into applause. It was exhilarating, the idea of performing in front of a public, of having people's attention and approval. It was one of the reasons she'd wanted to be an actress.

As the first chords of "El Choclo" started, Leonardo's wife entered the parlor. A man in a gray suit walked behind her, holding her hand. Leonardo took a step forward, but Malena grasped his sleeve to stop him.

She rested her hand on his shoulder and danced. Somehow— miraculously—he responded. Leonardo started the routine as he'd done it with his wife, though he was moving faster than usual. He was stiff, mechanical, and would not meet Malena's eyes; his full attention was on Rebecca and her man friend.

As the tempo picked up, Malena had difficulty following Leonardo's lead. She searched his eyes, trying to get his attention, but he was in a trance, oblivious to her limitations. She tapped his shoulder and called his name, but Leonardo didn't respond and led her into complicated steps she hadn't perfected yet: the *sacada*, the *gancho*. She turned backstage for assistance. Amanda and Bernardo were frowning. Malena was not crazy or hallucinating; Leonardo was truly out of control, crazy with jealousy.

Leonardo attempted to lead a *colgada*. She had seen him do it with Rebecca before, but Malena was not ready for it— she had never attempted it herself. Leonardo, however, didn't remember or care. He placed his foot between hers, leaning her to the side. He turned quickly. Malena felt her body dangling at a precarious angle, her foot slipping. She grabbed for Leonardo, but it was too late. They both fell hard on the floor. The polished wood felt cold and slippery on her backside. Her tight red skirt had rolled up, exposing her panties and girdle to all who cared to see. Laughter and booing burst from the audience as she tugged her dress down. They were so loud that the music was no longer audible.

"Nice ass!" a man yelled.

A ruckus erupted from the direction of Sebastian's table. Standing, Malena spotted Sebastian holding a man in a headlock. Meanwhile, Leonardo jumped to his feet and plunged himself toward the man sitting with Rebecca, tackling him and knocking him off the chair.

A brawl broke out. Waiters and customers tried to separate the fighting men. The musicians stopped playing. Other more dignified citizens headed toward the door, and in the center of the stage, Amanda watched the evening crumble in front of her eyes.

Chapter 22

Cesar Villamizar seemed to have lost more hair in the last few weeks. Sebastian suspected he was responsible for the dark circles under the older man's eyes and the pronounced wrinkles across his forehead.

"You wanted to talk to me?" Cesar shut the door behind him, staring at the newspaper in Sebastian's hands.

"Yes."

Cesar's jaw hardened. Sebastian knew the man didn't agree with his new policies of cutting down personnel and changing the paper's focus, and he probably didn't like that he'd taken charge of the accounting either. If it hadn't been for all those years of loyalty to his father, Sebastian would have fired the man already, especially after this.

"Are you going to fire me?"

"No. But I want to know why you ran this article without showing it to me first."

Sebastian tossed the paper on top of his desk for Cesar to see. In big bold letters the front page of *El Heraldo* read: OPENING OF MADRESELVA A DISASTER.

Cesar didn't look at it. "What's wrong with it?"

"Well, for one, I don't see how this is your top story with so many things happening in the world right now."

Cesar sighed. "San Isidro doesn't care about the world."

"Still, I don't think this is newsworthy. Talk about local politics, economy, something relevant."

"Local politics? You mean the mayor's new haircut? That's all that's happened since yesterday in the political arena."

Sebastian hit his desk. "Then use one of the wire stories. People need to know what's going on in Quito or Guayaquil. What is President Arosemena up to? His government is anything but stable."

"What's this really about, Sebastian? Is this about your connection to the Platas family? Or the fact that you got involved in the fight?" He smirked. "You must learn to be impartial, Sebastian. That's the first rule of journalism."

Sebastian fantasized about punching Cesar's face, just like he'd done with the insolent drunk who made that obscene comment about Liliana last night. But he'd caused enough problems already. He didn't need any more.

"People need to know what happens in this town," Cesar said. "Especially after all the hype about the first tango club. You can't pick and choose the news just because they are close to you."

Sebastian knew that, in theory, Cesar was right, but there was no relevance in local gossip or smearing Amanda's nightclub. Sebastian didn't even want to think about Claudia's hysterics now that her aunt's nightclub had been featured on the front page, especially next to the word "disaster," not to mention his own mother. Amanda had been her best friend for years.

"Don't lecture me, Cesar. I'm not the five-year-old who followed you around the paper. This is the last time you publish a story without my approval. From now on, I want to read every single word written in this newspaper before it gets published."

"Might I remind you, Sebastian, that your father trusted me completely? That's why he named me managing editor."

Sebastian crossed his arms behind his head, mimicking his father's arrogant gesture.

"Well, things are different now, Cesar. The sooner you realize that, the better it will be for you. The Ignacio Rivas era is gone."

Cesar's eyes flickered with contempt, but Sebastian was not about to back down. He held his stare and smirked.

Cesar looked away and left the room.

Sebastian picked up the paper again. If this article had any repercussions on the nightclub, it would be his fault. He'd started the fight. Of course he regretted it now, but he couldn't tolerate disrespect, especially toward women, and that jerk deserved all the punches he got. Sebastian rubbed his temple with his fingers. He had to learn to control that wretched temper of his. *Somehow.* As he shut his eyes, the image of Lili in her red dress emerged in his mind. He had no idea that girl was so attractive or that she could move with such grace. It had been a shock to see her there, dancing, looking so beautiful. The movement of her hips, her long legs, and her bare back had been like a magnet.

He opened his eyes again. He had to stop thinking about her. He was engaged and Claudia would be furious when she found out he'd gone to the nightclub after she begged him not to. But perhaps not as furious as Amanda would be after she read the newspaper.

Chapter 23

Almost midnight and nobody had showed up at the Madreselva yet. Covering a yawn with her hand, Malena avoided Amanda's face across the table. Bernardo was already sweeping the dance floor, the musicians chatted among themselves and a group of bored waiters leaned against the wall by the front door.

Amanda set her glass on the table.

"Damn Sebastian! I can't believe he published that story. This is his fault."

Malena wasn't so sure about that. If she hadn't fallen down, this wouldn't be happening, but she'd apologized enough, and Amanda said she didn't blame her. If anything it had been Leonardo's fault, she said. He'd started this entire mess and he'd paid for it. His indiscretion had cost him a job and a trip to the hospital for a concussion after Rebecca's man friend struck him with a chair.

Amanda stood up. "Let's go."

"What if someone comes?"

"I'm not going to sit around and wait all night. Bernardo!"

The man rushed to her side.

"*Oui, Madame?*"

"Tell the waiters and cooks to go home." Her voice trailed off as she looked at something or someone behind Malena's head.

At the entrance stood a tall man with thinning black hair and dark eyes.

"*Buenas noches*," he told Amanda.

Amanda took a few steps toward him and stopped, her shoulders tense, her arms rigid. They stared at each other in silence until she flung her arms over his shoulders and hugged him. He was stiff at first, but eventually raised his arms to her back.

"I thought I'd never see you again," Amanda said. "What are you doing here? I thought you moved to Spain."

"I did. I still live there. I only came to San Isidro to sell my parents' house."

"Good," Amanda said. "We get to have you here for a few days."

Amanda introduced the man as Joaquin Nasser, an old friend, and Malena as María Teresa Paz's daughter. Joaquin didn't appear to know the real Liliana—a small blessing.

"I met your mother when we were youngsters." Joaquin told Malena. "How is she doing nowadays?"

Malena drank from Amanda's glass. It was whiskey and it was awful.

"Fine, I think."

"Joaquin is a wonderful dancer," Amanda told Malena, pointing at the chairs. "We won a dancing contest once."

One of the violinists started playing.

"How's the wife?" Amanda asked Joaquin.

Joaquin undid the button of his jacket before he sat down. "Fine."

"Did she come with you?"

"No. She stayed in Madrid."

The silence lingered between them. Malena had the impression she was intruding in a private conversation.

"Should I bring another bottle?" Malena asked, though Bernardo was approaching them with one already.

Amanda didn't answer. Her full attention was on Joaquin as he looked around the place.

"It's incredible what you've done here," he said.

"All for nothing."

"Don't say that. It will work out."

"You must not know what happened here yesterday."

"I know. I've been here for a few days now."

Amanda tapped her red fingernails on the table. At the first notes of the tango "Volver," Joaquin reached for Amanda's hand.

"Would you dance with me? For old time's sake?"

"I'm sorry. I'm not exactly in a dancing mood."

"Come on, you're going to waste a perfectly good dance floor?" He caressed her hand. "We would have killed for a spot like this when we were young." Joaquin turned to Malena. "Don't you agree with me?"

There was a hint of panic in Amanda's eyes. She placed her hand on her bad leg.

Joaquin stood up, pulling softly on Amanda's arm.

"This is silly, Joaquin."

"Just one dance."

"Please don't ask me that."

He eyed her leg. "I don't care about that."

She conceded. He led her to the dance floor and embraced her, their chests touching. The two of them moved in perfect harmony to the beat of the *bandonéon*.

"Volver" was one of the saddest tangos ever written. It talked about returning to one's first love after twenty years. Amanda had been married once, and her husband had died, but there was something about Joaquin and this encounter that didn't seem like a simple meeting between two old friends. They danced close together, but Amanda moved stiffly, as if dancing were a chore, like sweeping or dusting. So different from the time she taught Malena how to dance. In one of their turns, Malena spotted tears in Amanda's eyes.

A tall man with abundant gray hair entered the nightclub. He was handsome despite his age, which must have been around the same as Joaquin—late forties, early fifties. He stopped by the dance floor and folded his arms across his chest, watching Amanda and Joaquin.

When the song ended, the man applauded slowly and loudly, but his expression didn't reveal happiness. His neck muscles were taut and his eyebrows, those thick eyebrows, were joined so close to one another they looked like one.

"What a beautiful scene!" he said. "*Brava*, Amanda. *Brava!*"

Amanda pulled away from Joaquin.

"What are you doing here?" she said. "You agreed to let me run the restaurant."

So this was the infamous Enzo.

"I did, but it seems there's not much left to run. I see you have better things to do with your time."

Amanda ran her fingers over the sequins of her blue dress.

"So it was true," Enzo said. "All the rumors about you were true. My poor brother! How many lovers did you have then? Let's see." He counted with his fingers. "There was this poor bastard, your father's accountant, probably the milkman and the postman, too–"

Her father's accountant?

Before Enzo could say another word, Joaquin rammed him with his shoulder, sending him into a nearby wall. Joaquin grasped Enzo by the throat and pressed his thumbs into his windpipe.

"Don't you ever, *ever*, talk to her like that again!" he said.

Amanda rushed toward them, as quickly as her stiff leg allowed. "Joaquin, stop!"

The altercation became a welcome distraction to the employees. Cooks and dishwashers gawked at the fight. So did

Sebastian Rivas, who had entered the salon as Joaquin pinned Enzo against the wall.

Enzo's lips lost their color but he managed to reach back to grab a bottle of wine from a nearby table. As he raised it above his head, preparing to strike, Sebastian snatched the bottle from Enzo's hand. Bernardo and one of the waiters pinned Joaquin's arms while the chef took Enzo's.

"*Maledetto!*" Enzo rubbed his neck. "I'm going to kill you!"

Sebastian set the bottle on the table and stood between the two men, his arms outstretched.

Joaquin shook himself loose from Bernardo's grasp. Sebastian gave him a warning look.

"Get out!" Amanda told Enzo.

Enzo looked around the room—he was alone against a crowd. The Italian regained control of himself and adjusted his collar.

"I'll be back for my check."

He stalked out of the restaurant.

Bernardo clapped twice to call the attention of all employees. "That's enough, everybody go home!"

As the crowd dispersed, Amanda poured whiskey into one of the glasses Bernardo had brought earlier. Sebastian looked at Malena, as if noticing her for the first time, and smiled.

"What are you doing here, Sebastian?" Amanda handed the glass to Joaquin. "Did you come to gather material for tomorrow's headline?"

"No. I came to apologize." He ran his fingers along his satin tie. "My managing editor was under the impression he didn't have to get my approval to publish anything, as trivial or damaging as it might be."

Amanda served another glass for herself, without water, and drained it.

"In that case, I hope you took care of him." She set the glass down. "We can't have disloyal employees so close to us."

"It won't happen again, Amanda. You have my word." Sebastian stretched out his hand toward Joaquin. "I'm sorry. With all the commotion, we haven't been properly introduced. I'm Sebastian Rivas."

"Ignacio's son?"

"Yes."

Joaquin patted his back. "Your father and I used to be neighbors. I'm Joaquin Nasser."

"Of course, Señor. My father spoke often of you. You're a diplomat, aren't you?"

"Yes. I was very sorry to hear about his passing. He was a great man."

"He was."

The sadness in Sebastian's voice reminded Malena of her own misery since her father's death. Except that she didn't have the consolation of knowing her father had been a good man, like Sebastian did. She didn't know what to think of her father, especially after Enzo had mentioned him as one of Amanda's lovers. Her father didn't only have a double life, it seemed, but a triple and a quadruple. Understanding what had driven him to suicide—with every new bit of information she gathered— was becoming an impossible task.

"Have a drink with us." Joaquin poured Sebastian a tumbler of whiskey.

Sebastian removed his coat and hung it behind the chair.

"Finally, good whiskey in this town."

He sat by Joaquin while Malena remained standing.

"Would you like some whiskey, Lili?" Amanda offered.

God, no. "I'm fine, thank you."

"Well, don't just stand there. Have a seat," Amanda told her.

Malena sat next to Amanda, avoiding Sebastian's face at all cost. If La Abuela could see her now, sitting with two men at a nightclub while they drank. Bernardo brought more ice and glasses.

"I didn't see your mother here last night," Amanda told Sebastian.

"She wasn't feeling well." He rubbed his chin. "She hasn't been herself since my father's passing."

"Well, losing a husband isn't easy," she said.

Joaquin added ice to his drink.

"So what are your plans now?" Sebastian asked her.

"My plans? Besides getting intoxicated, nothing." She was the only one to laugh—bitterly—at her joke. But maybe it wasn't a joke.

"If you'd like, I can run advertisements for the nightclub all next week, at no cost, of course." Sebastian offered cigarettes to everyone. Malena took one, though the idea of swallowing smoke didn't seem too appealing. "Believe it or not, advertising can be very effective."

Malena held her breath as Sebastian leaned over her to light her cigarette.

"That would be very nice, Sebastian," Amanda said.

"Yes, that's a good idea," Joaquin interjected. "But you need more than that. You need to make people want to come. To believe this is the most entertaining place in town. You have to promote it with more than print advertisement. People have to be moved by dance. They have to see it and want to do it."

Mimicking Amanda, Malena took a drag of smoke. The itch inside her throat was unbearable and despite her attempts to appear smooth and sophisticated, she started coughing.

"Problem is, I lost my star dancers." Amanda patted Malena's back.

"Well, you can get new ones," Joaquin said. "Those two are not the only people in town who can dance."

"No, they're not the only ones, but they're the best. I saw several dancers and nobody came close to them." Amanda stared at Sebastian. "Unless . . ."

Malena set her cigarette on the ashtray. Never again.

"Unless what?" Joaquin said.

"Unless Sebastian helps me."

The glass in Sebastian's hand froze midair. "Me?"

"There's a rumor in town that you can dance. That you learned in Argentina," Amanda said, her words followed by a long thread of smoke.

"That was a long time ago." Sebastian tossed back his drink without catching anyone's eye.

"Your trip was only two years ago. I had not danced in twenty years and still remembered," Amanda said.

"Besides, we can help you with the steps," Joaquin said.

"Please, Sebas, it would only be once." The excitement from days ago returned to Amanda's voice. "We could do it during the New Year's Eve celebration. At the plaza."

"That's a wonderful idea," Joaquin said. "But who would dance with him? Do you have any female dancers in mind?"

Amanda turned toward Malena and smiled.

Malena sank in her chair, hoping to become invisible to all the curious eyes staring back at her.

Chapter 24

Amanda, 1940

In the darkness of the street, the light coming from Nicolas's study shone as bright as the sun. He was awake, and Amanda knew there was no means of sneaking into the house without him hearing the front door. She slowed her pace, trying to come up with a lie good enough for him to believe. Not that he ever complained. That was the hardest part of all, lying to someone who knew you were being dishonest but pretended not to notice.

With trembling fingers, she slid her key into the lock and turned the doorknob. From the foyer of their two-story home—one of the newest and most beautiful constructions in all of San Isidro—she heard two male voices coming from the study. Since they were speaking Italian and one of them was yelling, it was fair to assume that Nicolas was talking to his brother.

Enzo, as usual, was the loudest one. When they spoke this fast, Amanda couldn't understand them, but it was obvious that this wasn't a regular visit. Enzo never came over this late, and although he was an ill-tempered man, she'd never heard him this upset.

Across the foyer was the staircase. Only a few meters away. If only she could cross the study threshold without being seen.

But the study door was wide open. She removed her heels and took a step toward the stairs. Maybe they were distracted enough not to notice her.

"*Sei pazzo, Nicolas,*" Enzo shouted. "*Pazzo e cieco!*"

Enzo darted out of the study in such haste his chest bumped into Amanda's shoulder, nearly dropping her to the floor, as though she'd been struck by a brick wall.

"Oh, here she is!" he said. "The model wife."

Enzo glared into Amanda's eyes with such hatred that for a minute she thought he would choke her.

"*Vai via, Enzo!*" Nicolas told him from his desk.

That Amanda understood, and was grateful that her husband was telling this imbecile to leave.

Enzo slammed the door shut. Amanda hid her shoes behind her back.

Nicolas remained seated, his hands resting on the sides of his leather chair.

"Did you have a good time, *cara mia?*"

Did she? Yes, the best time of her life. But now the remorse was back, the self-loathing, the chagrin. She nodded, eyes moistening. Things could have been so perfect between Nicolas and her.

"*Bene,*" he said. "Now if you don't mind, I still have work to do."

Work. At a moment like this. Of course, work was the only thing on Nicolas's mind. Once she thought it was just devotion, a sense of responsibility to his parents' memory, and she'd admired him for it. Now she knew work was all he had. Work was his excuse, his way of avoiding the truth, his escape.

Sometimes she wished he would just confront her. Tell her what he really thought. How disappointed he was in her, how much she'd failed him. But at other times, she wondered if he knew at all or if he even cared.

She stepped inside the room, playing with the strap of her shoes. A nearly-empty bottle of wine and a glass—just one—sat on his desk, besides his papers.

"Nicolas, we need to talk."

He wrote on a piece of paper.

"I know, Nico. I've known for a long time."

He wrote faster, the ink of his stylograph staining his fingers.

She left her shoes on one of the chairs and rested her hands on the desk.

"Nicolas."

He didn't look at her.

"Amanda dear, this is really not a good time. I have a lot to do."

He was signing papers, writing quickly. She felt like shaking him and forcing the truth out of him. But she could never humiliate him like that. She knew he would never admit to anything. He would rather die first. That was the kind of man he was. He would rather carry his own burdens until he exploded than share them with someone, even someone whom he loved.

Amanda knew Nicolas loved her—as much as he could love a woman, anyway. Just not the way she wanted to be loved. If only he were mean to her, the way Rafael was to Ana, she would have an excuse to leave him. But what excuse did she have? He was the most considerate and splendid husband in town.

What would he do if she left?

She glanced at the wine bottle on his desk. There had been lots of bottles before this one, and she was certain there would be more. His reputation meant everything to him. He was willing to sacrifice his own happiness for it, and he had. She'd seen the sadness in his eyes, she'd heard him pacing in the living room at night, and she'd seen the bottles disappear from the pantry one by one. She couldn't in good conscience cause him any more unhappiness. She loved him too much.

"Good night, *mi amor*," she said, turning around.

She heard him pouring more wine as she left the room.

Chapter 25

Amanda had lost her mind! How could she expect Malena to dance with Claudia's fiancé in front of the entire town? If Ana found out, she would throw her out of the house! Malena submerged the stalks of *toronjil* into a pot of boiling water; she needed to calm her nerves.

"You came home late last night." Ana said behind her. "After midnight."

"I was with Amanda."

"I know, I know." She sighed, serving herself black coffee. "But I don't think a young lady should be out at those ungodly hours." She took a sip. "And I know that's not what your mother wants."

Malena didn't want to think about Lili's mother; neither did she like Ana's threatening tone. Trinidad placed a cup of coffee, bread, and marmalade on a metal tray.

"María Teresa is counting on me to take good care of you. I don't want to disappoint her," Ana said. "She called yesterday, you know?"

Malena eyed the door. Trinidad set a napkin on the tray.

"Is that for Alejandra?" Malena asked the maid before Ana got any ideas about phone calls and such.

"Yes." Trinidad sighed. "She always forgets to have breakfast. That's why she's so thin."

"Is she at the store?"

Trinidad added sugar to Alejandra's coffee. "Isn't she always?"

"May I take it to her?" Malena asked.

Trinidad shrugged. Malena picked up the tray and darted out of the kitchen before Ana could say another word.

⚬

The workshop door was ajar. No sound came from the room. With both hands on the tray, Malena was unable to knock on the door, so she pushed it open with her foot.

Alejandra sat behind her desk with a piece of paper in her hands. She was immersed in her reading and must have not heard Malena for she didn't raise her head.

"Good morning," Malena said. "I brought your breakfast."

Alejandra flinched. Her eyes widened, but as recognition set in, she brought her eyebrows together in a frown.

"Don't you know how to knock?"

"I'm sorry. I didn't mean to scare you. It's just that," she raised the tray, "my hands are full."

The paper in Alejandra's hands was a newspaper clipping and it was wrinkled. Alejandra shoved it into one of the drawers in her desk and slammed it shut.

"Don't ever do that again."

Alejandra's desk was filled with tools and metal pieces, there was no space for the tray. Alejandra pointed at the other desk in the corner of the room.

"You can leave it there."

Malena set it down and brushed her hands on her swing skirt. The room reeked of wax and dust. She wouldn't mind sweeping and organizing here a little bit—the place certainly needed it—but this was not the right time to make the offer.

Alejandra's cheeks were still flushed. What could be written in that newspaper article to make her so uncomfortable?

Malena approached the desk, hands behind her back. With a pair of tongs, Alejandra molded a metal string into a circular shape. She worked fast, too fast for Malena to keep track of what she was doing. She was giving it a new shape now, a petal, and she added other pieces to it—creating sort of a silver flower.

"Amanda said your father taught you his craft."

"That's correct."

Malena couldn't take her eyes off Alejandra's work. "I think that's wonderful."

"What?"

"That your father would have entrusted you with his business. That he believed in you."

"I don't see how that is so strange. That's how family businesses are built, with the contribution of the entire family."

"Yes, but it's usually the sons who inherit the business, not the daughters, especially not the youngest daughter."

"Well, my father didn't have any sons and I was the only one who showed any interest in jewelry."

"Yes, but he had a nephew."

Alejandra opened a drawer, then another, and a third one, without bothering to close them. She pulled out a small torch from one of them. The loud torch that would prevent her from having to hear anything else about her cousin.

"I saw you at the nightclub the other night," Malena said before Alejandra could turn on the torch. "You should wear dresses more often."

Alejandra turned on the torch and soldered the silver petals together.

Chapter 26

Alejandra, 1940

At age seventeen, Alejandra reached the conclusion that she was invisible to boys. Either that or they were afraid Fausto would break their noses if they got close to her. Fausto was her blessing and her curse. Her blessing when he stood up for her when the neighborhood boys complained that he brought her along to play cards or pool. Her curse because he was always on guard when a boy wanted to team up with her or helped her with her stroke at the pool table.

So when they met Enrique Hidalgo at the circus after all those years and he acted as if she were a stain on the wall, she wasn't surprised at all. Even though Mamá Blanca constantly reminded her she wasn't ugly (but what mother would think her child was ugly?) and people often commented on her gorgeous hair, she didn't even come close to her sister Abigail—with that porcelain skin and those almond-shaped eyes. That aura of fragility of Abigail's drove men insane. And it sure had caused the same effect in Enrique.

After Amanda in her late teens, Abigail was the most sought-after girl in town; the Queen of San Isidro. Yet Abigail never seemed to notice how beautiful she was. She always seemed to be in another world. Her nose buried behind a book;

184

undergoing health treatments that involved thermal baths and hospital visits. She even went to a different school. Abigail had practically grown up apart from Alejandra and Fausto. And now that she'd agreed to go to the circus with them, Alejandra wished her sister would have stayed away, in her own little world, wherever that might be.

Initially, Enrique had been polite with Alejandra.

"Yes, I remember you two." He'd pointed at Fausto. "You're the one who wanted to be an acrobat, right?"

Fausto blushed. Alejandra and Fausto hadn't mentioned the circus incident in the last four years, but she knew he was ashamed of it.

"And you," Enrique continued, now looking at Alejandra, sending a cold shiver down the back of her neck. "You're his little sister."

"Cousin," she said, resenting the word "little."

That was as much attention as he'd given her. In contrast, when Fausto introduced Abigail, Enrique kissed her hand. He didn't look at Alejandra once after that.

But the most perturbing thing was to see Enrique at the dining room table, in her own house, after Abigail and Papá Pancho came fussing about him fixing some accounting problem.

Enrique greeted Mamá Blanca and Alejandra's older sisters. For Alejandra, he reserved only a quick glance and a wave of the hand, as if she were a small child who didn't deserve a proper salutation.

During the meal, Enrique exchanged glances with Abigail. Alejandra had been an idiot to think about him during all these years and wonder what their next encounter would be like. In her mind, it had never been like this.

She stared at her uneaten food, stabbing a pea with her fork, wishing she could do the same to one of Abigail's rosy cheeks. Enrique and Fausto took turns telling stories. Enrique's were pretty funny, but Alejandra was not in the mood for jokes. She was the only one at the table who didn't laugh, and she was the only one to leave the room before dinner was over. Nobody seemed to notice; not even Mamá Blanca, who was always on her case, telling her to eat more, to wear some makeup.

Makeup. She stopped by the lavatory and entered. Perhaps that was what she was missing; the mystery behind Abigail's beauty. She opened the medicine cabinet above the sink and took her sister's red lipstick and mascara. Next time Enrique saw her, he *would* notice her.

———✦———

Enrique did notice her, but not in a good way. Alejandra could tell he was trying not to laugh as she stepped into the jewelry store the next day. He rested his chin on his palm and focused on his accounting book.

"What the hell happened to you?" Fausto blurted out from one of the stools. "Are you going to try out for the circus now that Enrique is here?"

Rafael chuckled. Enrique covered his mouth with his notepad. Alejandra removed one of her shoes and threw it at Fausto. Both Rafael and Enrique ducked as the shoe bypassed them before landing on Fausto's forehead.

"Are you crazy?" Fausto rubbed his head. "You could have killed me."

"That was precisely my intention."

"*Loca!*"

"*Imbécil!*"

Abigail, who witnessed the entire scene from the end counter, approached her.

"Come with me, Ale."

Alejandra shook her elbow away from Abigail's grasp.

"Don't do me any favors!" Alejandra rushed to the hallway so Abigail wouldn't follow her.

Her father was walking out of the workshop.

"What's going on here? What are all those screams? And what happened to your face?"

"It's called makeup."

Papá Pancho sighed. "*Hija*, you don't need that garbage to look pretty. You're a natural beauty."

"Well, I'm tired of people thinking I'm a child."

"Being a woman has nothing to do with makeup. But if you must wear it, at least ask one of your sisters to teach you."

Alejandra fought the angry tears threatening to come out. "Papá, if you want to help me, then give me a job at the store."

Papá Pancho scratched his head. "At the store? I have too many employees now. There's Fausto, Rafael, Abigail, and now Enrique. There's not any room there for another clerk."

"I don't want to be a clerk."

"Then?"

"I want to be an accountant."

Papá Pancho smiled. "You? An accountant? But you're an artist, you hate numbers. Besides I just hired an accountant. Why would I want another?"

"And you think he's going to last here long? He worked at a circus, Papá. People like him are nomads. Think about this, if I learn, you won't have to pay a *stranger* to work for you. I'll do it for free."

Papá Pancho nodded toward the workshop. She followed him in.

"What do you propose?" He shut the door.

Alejandra knew she had won the minute she mentioned her money-saving plan. "Have Enrique teach me everything he knows. Once I learn, you come up with an excuse, any excuse, to fire him."

Papá Pancho rubbed his chin. "I don't know. Accounting is not suitable for a woman."

"It's not suitable for gamblers either," she said. "Or overly ambitious sons-in-law, or strangers. Do you want to continue trusting Fausto or Rafael with your money once this Enrique leaves?"

Papá Pancho folded his arms across his chest. "You're right, *hija*. How did I get such a smart daughter? You must take after me." He pinched her cheek. "It's settled then, I'll tell Enrique to start teaching you right away."

Alejandra smiled triumphantly. Let's see if Enrique didn't notice her now.

Chapter 27

A lthough the Madreselva was closed tonight, the lights were on. Malena followed Amanda inside and stopped at the sight of Sebastian sitting by the bar with Joaquin. Malena's hands dampened inside her gloves. Sebastian looked more handsome than ever in that black leather jacket.

Amanda clutched Malena's arm. "You can do this."

Joaquin greeted them. Malena clumsily removed her gloves and shook hands with him. But neither she nor Sebastian attempted to shake hands. She couldn't even look at him. She'd never imagined that one day she would be dancing with Claudia's fiancé. If Claudia ever found out, she would bring the Holy Inquisition down on her!

"Shall we start?" Amanda circled the bar and removed a record from its sleeve. "We're dancing to Gardel tonight, even if people are saying that it's bad luck. Lili, take off that sweater."

Malena removed her pink sweater, aware of Sebastian's eyes on her. He removed his jacket and stayed in a white long-sleeved shirt. Without touching, they edged toward the dance floor. Amanda rushed behind them, giving them instructions on the sequence of steps she envisioned, while Joaquin had suggestions of his own.

Like a mannequin, Malena stood still while Amanda placed her in front of Sebastian, pulling her shoulders back to achieve the perfect pose and telling her how to rest her hand on Sebastian's shoulder. Under her palm, his shoulder felt warm.

"No small talk," Amanda said as a last recommendation. "Just feeling." And then she added, as an afterthought, "That is the secret to tango dancing."

Sebastian seized Malena's hand and held her tight. She took in the scent of his cologne, avoiding his eyes.

Joaquin started "El día que me quieras." Sebastian took a step forward, leading her backwards and then sideways across the floor. They transitioned into pivots, sweeps, and *ochos*. He danced surprisingly well, almost effortlessly. Not with the same skill, experience, and flair that Leonardo did, but he definitely knew the basic tango steps.

For a moment, Malena got lost in the song lyrics. It seemed as though Carlos Gardel was singing to them. She was conscious of Sebastian's fingers on her lower back and his thigh brushing against hers. She liked his closeness, the way her body fit into his. When his hand traveled down her spine, it sent chills throughout her body. She lifted her chin. There was a tiny drop of perspiration above his brow, a nearly imperceptible mole by his nose. Was he holding his breath? Their eyes connected for a split second, and then he stared at her mouth. She lost her footing and stopped. Her face burned. She needed space, air. She took a step back, letting go of his touch.

"What's the matter?" Amanda asked.

Malena fanned her cheeks with her hand. "Nothing. I'm just hot, that's all."

"Well, you'd better not stop like that during the presentation."

Malena glanced at Sebastian's chest moving up and down, his eyes set on her.

"I won't."

Joaquin started the song again.

Malena could barely concentrate on whatever Claudia was saying. Her mind kept going back to the moment when Sebastian held her in his arms. How ironic that she had to help his bride pick a dress for the wedding now.

"What do you think of this one?" Claudia said.

Malena turned to one of the *Burda* magazines lying open on the coffee table. Claudia pointed at a satin gown with a banded waist and a scooped neck.

"It's very pretty," Malena said. Watching Claudia choose her dress certainly seemed like a punishment for dancing with Sebastian.

Ana brought another pile of magazines and sat down across from the girls, next to Mamá Blanca. She eyed the dress her daughter had selected.

"I don't know, *hija*. How about something simpler? Simplicity is more elegant."

"Oh, no. I don't want something simple. You only get married once, and I want my dress to be the most stylish in town." Claudia's words tumbled over one another in her excitement. "My future mother-in-law is a fashion connoisseur."

"But *hija*," Ana said, "modesty is a virtue and vanity is a form of pride—"

"Which is a deadly sin," Claudia recited in a monotone, her cheeks turning slightly pink.

"Claudia . . ."

"Whatever you say, *Madre*."

Mamá Blanca spoke without removing her gaze from her crocheting. "Claudia should be able to decide what she wants, Ana. After all, Sebastian comes from one of the most established families in San Isidro." She lowered her voice, turning to Malena. "Although they're not doing so well now."

"Mamá . . ." Ana said.

"What? Lili is like family now." She renewed her needlework. "Tell her, Claudita."

Claudia cleared her throat. "Well, Sebastian's father got into some risky ventures that lost a lot of money."

"And Ofelia spent the rest," Mamá Blanca added.

"So now my poor Sebastian has to work like a dog to support them."

Malena felt a stab at the word "my."

"We have to find a dress for you too, Lili." Ana handed Malena a magazine. "See if there's anything here that you like and we'll have our seamstress make it for you."

Malena thanked Ana, but doubted she would be here when this wedding took place.

Mamá Blanca pushed herself up. "Lili, would you help me to my room? I'd like to rest for a moment."

"Of course."

Malena helped her grandmother upstairs and down the hall.

"If Abigail were alive, she would have sewn this dress for Claudia." Mamá Blanca entered her room and pointed at the small sewing machine in the corner of the room. "That was hers. The last time she used it was to sew Claudia's first communion dress. Abigail was already sick, but she worked very hard until she finished it. She adored her niece."

Malena strolled toward the sewing machine. Her fingers rubbed the intricate wooden carvings along the cherrywood surface. Four tiny drawers were aligned on its right side. She looked over her shoulder. Mamá Blanca was covering her legs with a wool blanket. If only she could look inside those drawers.

Malena picked up a book from Mamá Blanca's night table. *Los Sangurimas*. Her grandmother Eva would've never approved of such a scandalous novel. "José de la Cuadra is my favorite author," Malena said. "Would you like me to read it to you?"

"That would be lovely. I can barely see that small print."

192

Malena read in the most tedious tone she could muster. Mamá Blanca's eyelids drooped sporadically at first, but stayed shut after a while. Before long, Mamá Blanca was asleep.

Malena set the book on the night table and stood up. She tiptoed toward Abigail's sewing machine and opened the top drawer. It was filled with rolls of thread of every imaginable color. The second drawer was filled with zippers. The third one held needles and pins. The last drawer was full of buttons. Malena touched them with her fingers. A diary, a photograph in the study, and this sewing machine were everything that was left of Mamá Blanca's daughter. Underneath the buttons, she felt a glossy texture—a photograph? A loud snore came from Mamá Blanca's direction. Malena started, but her grandmother's eyes were still shut.

Malena moved the buttons out of the way and spotted a face—a man's face. She picked up the picture, rubbing her index finger over the young man's handsome face. She could tell he had light hair and light eyes. She turned it over and read a name on the back: *Victor, 1940.*

Chapter 28

Abigail, 1940

The bride and the groom seemed to be floating on the dance floor. Abigail wondered if one day she would be in that same spot, dancing with the man of her dreams (for he must be a man—not a boy—by now). And the answer was no. She would probably be there, but not with him. It would probably be another man; perhaps Enrique.

To her surprise, she missed Enrique now that he was out of town for the weekend. He amused her with the stories of his travels, his wit, and his gifts—he brought her a different flower every day—but sometimes she feared she made the wrong decision by agreeing to be his girl so soon after meeting him.

Honestly, she'd been unable to refuse him. Enrique had volunteered to take her and Mamá Blanca to Quito for a doctor's appointment and then he'd invited Abigail to Teatro Sucre to watch a comedy, *Receta para viajar*. Abigail had never been inside a more impressive building. Those Doric columns, those balconies and thick, ornate curtains! She felt like she'd been transported to a neoclassic theater in Europe. And she'd laughed so hard she couldn't break Enrique's heart when he told her she was more beautiful than the leading actress onstage. Not when he bought her a blackberry *espumilla* and lent her his jacket after the play.

That was only part of the problem. The other part was that she'd been bored, tired of waiting for a dream that might never come true, and nervous at the prospect of never marrying.

"Doesn't María Teresa look beautiful?" Ana asked her.

Abigail nodded. María Teresa looked spectacular in her puffy-sleeved organza gown, which contrasted so nicely with her red hair, the envy of all the girls in San Isidro. Ana also looked radiant tonight with her hair in a high pompadour and the close-fitting dress Amanda had lent her. There was something different about Ana lately, not just tonight. She seemed joyful, alive.

Abigail's ponderings were interrupted by an apparition— that was the only way to describe it. The man that had been haunting her thoughts for the last four years stood in front of her, on the dance floor. He hugged María Teresa and took her hand in his. They were both smiling, an evident camaraderie between them. Abigail leaned forward in an attempt to listen to their conversation and accidentally knocked her glass of wine with her elbow.

"Look what you've done!" Ana pointed at the burgundy liquid staining Abigail's mint-colored dress. Ana grabbed a cloth napkin to dry the growing stain, but Abigail couldn't care less about her dress. Her attention was fixed on the man talking to the bride.

Yes, it was him. The same face, the eyes, the shape of his body, so slim and tall. As the band played a new *danzón,* he and María Teresa danced.

"Be still!" Ana told her.

He danced with grace and ease until a crowd shrouded him and María Teresa. Abigail stood up, ignoring Ana's complaints, and strode to the dance floor. The bride's red hair shone from the center of the floor. Abigail squeezed her way through the dancers to reach her, but María Teresa was talking to a woman now, and there was no trace of the man she'd been dancing with. Abigail was about to ask María Teresa about him when Manuel, the groom, took his brand-new wife by the hand and led her toward the wedding cake in the corner of the room.

Like a madwoman, Abigail searched throughout the entire parlor, scanning every face, bumping shoulders with other guests, growing increasingly frantic. Had she been hallucinating?

Her last option was to look outside, on the patio. She pushed the double doors open and walked out, focusing on a man's figure sitting on the edge of the fountain. The full moon and a nearby light post partially illuminated his face. It was him. She slowed her pace, processing the moment, thinking about what she was going to say. She was hesitant to take another step. He looked so peaceful staring at the stars in the sky.

She ran her palms over her long skirt, touching the wet stain on the fabric. Oh, no, her dress was a mess! With her hand she attempted to cover the stain as she drew near him.

"*Buenas noches*," he said.

She stood in front of him, like an idiot, unable to produce a sound, much less a coherent thought.

He looked into her eyes. "It's a beautiful night, isn't it?"

She nodded. It was the only thing she could do.

"Would you like to sit down?" he asked.

She sat beside him. He extended his hand. "I'm Victor Santos Aguilar. And you?"

The touch of his hand was heavenly.

"I guess I'll have to do all the talking," he said. "Are you a friend of the bride or the groom?"

"The bride."

"She speaks!" He smiled. "So am I. María Teresa is my cousin."

Of course, Santos was María Teresa's last name, too. She couldn't believe he'd been so close all these years.

She found her voice. "I'm surprised I've never seen you before. María Teresa is my sister's best friend."

"I've been living outside of San Isidro for the last few years."

She wanted to ask where, she wanted to know everything about him, but it wouldn't be proper. After a moment, she spoke again.

"Thank you."

He raised a brow. "Did you say 'thank you'?"

"Yes."

"Why?" He sounded amused.

"For saving my life in that pool four years ago. I never had a chance to thank you."

He studied her face. "I thought I'd seen you before."

So he remembered her, too, or was he just saying that to be nice?

"I'm glad I saved you," he said. "You've become a lovely woman. A lovely woman without a name."

She giggled. "Abigail."

"Beautiful name," he said. "You rarely hear a Hebrew name in this part of the world."

"My father picked it from the Old Testament," she said. "It means 'God is joy.'"

He uncrossed his legs. "Yes," he said, excitedly. "Abigail was the third wife of King David, if I'm not mistaken, and was known to be a prudent woman."

Abigail wished she could live up to her name, but her present actions proved she hadn't been exactly prudent. She was alone at night with a stranger even though she was committed to another man.

"I trust that you learned how to swim," he said.

"No. Never."

"Why not?"

"Nobody ever bothered to teach me," she said, omitting the most important part—how ridiculously terrified she was of the water.

He observed her for a moment; his eyes changed shades of blue, resembling the ripples on the ocean. She sighed involuntarily, and looked at his hand. No wedding band. Good, but she couldn't be too confident. Some married men didn't wear rings. The movement of the double glass doors caught her attention. Ana emerged from the salon with her graceless gait; her heels getting stuck in the uneven pavers with every step she took in their direction. *Oh, no.*

Abigail turned to Victor. This was her only chance.

"Why don't you teach me?" she said.

"To swim?"

"Yes."

Ana waved at her.

"I don't know, I—"

Abigail stood up. "Tomorrow, at six. It's less crowded in the evenings."

He was speechless.

"Abigail?" Ana stood in front of them. "Rafael wants to go."

Abigail smiled at Victor before following her sister into the parlor.

———⊷———

Abigail arrived at the pool five minutes early. It had been so long since she'd been here, in the Termas de la Virgen, yet she felt as if it had been only yesterday that she'd nearly drowned in these green waters. She recognized the smell of sulfur, the steam emanating from the pool, and the dense air curling up her tresses as it did when she was a small girl. She wrapped her hands around a metal banister that circled the pool and looked straight across at the cascade. She closed her eyes for a moment, listening to the sound of the water falling. Nothing was more comforting, yet so terrifying at the same time—just like finding Victor had been.

It was six already. What if he didn't come? He'd never given her an answer, but he wouldn't stand her up, he didn't seem like that kind of man. The seconds turned into minutes. Ten. Twenty. Twenty-five. Abigail couldn't take her eyes away from her watch, away from those wicked hands moving forward, faster and faster. There were only a handful of people left in the pool, and it looked like they were getting ready to leave.

"Sorry I'm late."

His voice. How could someone go from panic and misery to the greatest state of elation ever known to a human being in a matter of two seconds?

"You came," she said.

"I couldn't have lived with myself if you ever fell in that pool again and there was no one here to save you." He looked at her flower-print dress. "You're going to swim in that?"

She giggled. Then turned around and lifted her hair. "Would you help me with the clasp?"

He didn't answer. She looked at him, over her shoulder. He had frozen, all amusement removed from his eyes. He stared at her back with—was that fear in his eyes?

"Go ahead, I don't bite," she said. So he was shy. She liked that in a man. Usually men—Enrique included—were eager for intimacy, not that she'd ever gone all the way with any of them. "Don't worry. I have my bathing suit on."

He unzipped her dress and looked away. "I'll go change." He picked up his bag from the ground.

Abigail collected her mane into a tight bun and slid a white rubber cap over her head. She waited for him by the edge of the pool. What had she done? Only now did she realize the absurdity of her request. If she was supposed to learn how to swim, she would have to get *in* the water, and she doubted she could bring herself to do that. If her intention was to spend a romantic moment with Victor, she was terribly wrong. Unless he found a panic-stricken, arms-flopping, hysterical girl attractive.

She took a deep breath. She was going to do this, even if it killed her—literally.

Victor reappeared a few moments later in his black swimming trunks. He sure had grown in the last four years. His shoulders had widened, the muscles in his arms were well defined, and a trail of curly hair traveled from his navel to the edge of his trunks.

He dove into the water and swam across the pool toward her in seconds. When he emerged out of the water, Abigail had to pinch her leg to make sure she wasn't dreaming. With that water dripping from his hair, the sun shining on his nose, and his eyes squinting, he looked just like he had as a teenager.

"Get in," he told her.

Get in? Just like that? She eyed the water wetting her feet.

He stood on the bottom of the pool and extended his hand to her. "Come on. It's shallow in here."

She looked at it. Anything to feel his touch again, anything, even death. She held his wet hand and jumped in, shutting her eyes. Her stomach took a leap. As soon as she felt the bottom of the pool with her feet, she opened her eyes, squeezing Victor's hand, both of his hands. He was smiling at her. The warm water pleasantly cradled her body. His gaze dropped to her chest for an instant, and then returned to her face. They stood in front of each other for a moment.

"Let's go deeper," he said. "Don't worry. I'll help you."

Without letting go of her hand, Victor pulled her toward the center of the pool. Her feet fought every step and her breathing became quicker, so quick that her head turned light. Once the water reached Abigail's shoulders, Victor stopped.

"See? It isn't so bad," he said. "Now close your eyes."

She obeyed him.

"Do you feel it?"

She wasn't sure what she was supposed to feel, aside from the panic that he would let go of her hand.

As if reading her mind, he said. "Don't worry, I won't let go."

She let out a deep breath.

His voice was soothing. "See how nice this feels? How peaceful it is."

She nodded.

"Do you trust me?" he said.

"Yes."

"Keep your eyes shut." He placed one arm on her back and lifted her legs with the other, forcing her into a horizontal position. She gasped.

"Now extend your arms," Victor said.

She could feel his hand under her back. His closeness reassured her. She spread her arms, feeling the lightness of her body, the water tickling her ears. A sense of elation took over her body.

"Now I'm going to remove my arm, but I'll still be here."

She stiffened. She wanted to stay like this, with Victor standing behind her.

"It will be fine. I promise." His hand moved away.

She opened her eyes and focused on the clouds above. They were moving, transforming, floating, and the sky was changing colors, giving way to the darkness. Her heart slowed its rapid beat, her body mingled with the water, and for an instant, there was peace and complete happiness.

They met every day for the next three weeks. Victor was kind and encouraging, but above all respectful. Not once did he touch her inappropriately or take advantage of her willingness to please him. To Abigail's chagrin, he always kept his distance, and after that first day, he rarely touched her or stood so close to her again. Sometimes she felt guilty over meeting Victor behind

Enrique's back. She'd rushed into a relationship with Enrique, but she didn't have the heart to break up with him, especially now that he was becoming so close to her family. Well, she would have to do it, as soon as she figured out the right words.

As Abigail's swimming progressed, so did her fear of losing the temporary bond she had with Victor. When she could swim, the lessons would end and she would have to go back to her regular life.

Taking a break from her first complete lap across the pool, she sat on the edge, elated by how much she'd learned. Amazed at the miracle Victor had worked. Removing the cap from her head, she watched him swim in her direction. He always swam behind her—to make sure she didn't drown halfway, she suspected. Her guardian angel. If it weren't for him, she would have died four years ago.

The cold air made her tremble—or was it his presence? She could never tell.

Victor hoisted himself over the edge and sat beside her, his legs keeping a proper distance from hers.

"Good swim," he said. "You're getting really good."

She didn't answer. Getting good had its unspoken downside.

"Are you cold? Do you want me to bring your towel?"

"No. Just hug me, okay?"

He didn't move, his hands remained locked against the pool rim, and his expression seemed somewhat puzzled. One might even say, petrified. She shifted her weight toward him and wrapped her arms around his waist, resting her head on his wet chest. His heart thumped against her ear.

"Don't you like me, at least a little?" she said.

"Abigail, there's something I need to tell you."

Oh, no. The confession, the dreaded confession. He was engaged, he was married. No, she didn't want to hear it. She raised her head and before he could say another word, she kissed him.

He was stiff at first, and backed his head away a little. She held his face with her hands and parted her lips, the way Enrique had taught her. His breathing became heavier and his body relaxed. His hands explored her bare back, pulling her closer to him. She kept her eyes open, to make sure this was real, not another one of her fantasies. She tasted the salt from the water on his mouth.

Slowly, he pushed her down, against the warm floor, and lay over her. He kissed her chin, her collarbone, the space between her breasts and then, abruptly, almost aggressively, he pulled back and sat down.

"What am I doing?" He ran his fingers through his dripping hair.

Abigail sat up, breathing rapidly.

"What's wrong?"

"This is wrong."

"Why? I love you and . . . don't you love me?"

"It's not that."

"You don't find me attractive?"

He chuckled. "Of course I do. That's exactly the problem."

"I don't understand."

"The reason I've been away from San Isidro for the last four years is that . . ." He lowered his voice. "I've been at the Seminario Mayor in Quito."

"The seminary? You're a priest?"

"Not yet."

"Yet?"

"I was going to be ordained a few months ago, but my father became ill and I was granted permission to come here."

No, this couldn't be happening. Not her Victor. "But I don't understand. What kind of priest dances and goes to parties?"

He covered his eyes with his hand. "The kind who promised his father on his deathbed that he would give himself a chance in the outside world. The kind who is trying to make the most important decision of his life."

Then there was still a chance; the decision had not been made yet. She held his wrists and pulled his hands away from his face.

"Then there's nothing wrong with this," Abigail said. "You're only doing what your father wanted."

"It's not that simple. All my life I've wanted this. So did my mother. I made a commitment to the Church, to God."

She dropped his hands. "Then why did you just kiss me the way you did? Why have you been meeting with me? Leading me on?"

"I'm sorry. I didn't mean to. I just wanted to help you."

"You're lying. You know you love me. I feel it."

He was quiet for a moment. "My calling is stronger."

"Your calling? How can you say that when you just kissed me the way you did?"

"To have a calling doesn't mean all your human desires are gone. I'm a man, above all, and you're . . . an irresistible woman."

"Victor, please, forget about that! I can make you happy, much happier than the Church could ever make you." She leaned forward, holding his face in her hands. "Let's go back to what we were doing. I'll teach you what a woman is, and you won't have any more doubts. I promise."

She kissed him again, desperately trying to entice him, but this time, he was impassive. No, this couldn't be happening. Gently, he pulled back.

"Forgive me," he said, drying her tears with his fingers. "You're a wonderful woman, Abigail. Any man would be lucky to have you." He caressed her cheek. "But I can't offer you anything right now. My life doesn't belong to me anymore. So many people are counting on me, on this decision. I'm leaving next Monday. I'm going back to the seminary."

He stood up, almost apologetically, and grabbed the towels. He handed her one, but she didn't take it. She wanted to stay here, alone, in the cold. To punish him by freezing to death right here.

"We should get going," he said.

"You go. I want to stay here."

"I can't leave you alone."

"Just leave, okay? Get out! Go back to your church."

He stared at her for a minute and left.

Abigail looked after him, feeling slightly faint, and then, for the first time in ten or more years, she discerned the Virgin's face in the mountain. She could clearly see her facial features in the dents and trees, and her long tresses in the falling water. And she could definitely see that the Mother of Christ was frowning at her.

Chapter 29

With the holidays, Malena's investigations—her *snooping*—slackened. First of all, she'd been rehearsing every night at the Madreselva. And second, who would have the heart to cause a family scandal during this time of the year? Truth be told, she was enjoying this life too much to even think about going back to Guayaquil. There was nothing waiting for her there—with so many absences, the dean had probably expelled her from school already (not that she minded terribly).

From the early hours of December 31, San Isidro's most enthusiastic citizens had built dummies—called *Años Viejos*—and placed them on small stages framed with tree branches throughout the city. In the plaza, over a dozen dummies were displayed in two long rows. At midnight, they had to be burned to symbolize the end of last year's problems and the beginning of a new year of hope. After the burning, a big celebration would take place at the plaza. Malena had never participated in this tradition. Back home, she'd merely seen the festivities from a taxi or her apartment window.

This year was different. She took a step back, admiring the dummy Amanda and Bernardo had built in the morning with newspapers, pillows, and old clothes. It had a gray-haired wig and a mask of a man with a large nose. The last touch was a bag of spaghetti in his hands.

"It looks just like Enzo," Malena said.

Amanda surveyed her handiwork. "No, it's a better version of Enzo. This one doesn't talk."

Enzo's dummy sat with his arms wide open on a chair. His free hand was placed over a small round table with a handwritten sign that read "Il Napolitano."

"Yes, it's perfect," Bernardo said.

Amanda stretched her back. "I can't wait to burn it." She glanced at her watch. "Sebastian and Joaquin should be here already."

Malena rubbed her hands against the black dress Amanda had given her for Christmas. In only a few minutes, she would be dancing on that stage with Sebastian. The band was playing "La Plaga," and Javier stood beside them, with a guitar in his hands, singing.

"Javier is here," Malena told Amanda.

"Don't worry. He won't say anything."

"Did you know he could sing like that?"

"There's more to Javier than meets the eye." Amanda unzipped her purse and removed her compact. "Don't be so nervous. There's nothing wrong with dancing."

"Tell that to your sister and her husband."

Amanda powdered her nose and returned the compact to her purse. "You seem so naïve, sometimes I don't understand how it is that you dated that man in San Vicente."

Malena averted her gaze. She'd never dated anyone, much less the married man they kept mentioning who apparently was so bad for Lili. If only they knew Liliana was in the capital at this very moment, living her happily-ever-after with the wicked Juan Pablo.

Amanda left her purse on a nearby chair and greeted Joaquin. Malena stayed behind, glancing at the purse. With all the chaos and confusion of tonight's celebration, she might be able to take it. Oh, God, was she turning into a thief now? She just couldn't think of another way to get hold of the armoire key given that Amanda always guarded it like a treasure.

Before Malena could make up her mind, the faint scent of cigarette and mint told her Sebastian was here, standing behind her.

"*Buenas noches,*" he said.

Malena spun on her heels. He wore black, too, and his eyes shone. She hugged her arms.

"You look fantastic!" Amanda told Sebastian. "Now get going, it will soon be midnight."

Malena was conscious of Sebastian's hand on the small of her back as he led her toward the stage. When she crossed in front of the band, Javier's eyes widened upon seeing her there. She stood in front of Sebastian, just like they'd rehearsed.

"Don't look down," he whispered. His eyes were fixed on hers with such intensity she had the urge to look away, but didn't.

As soon as the music started, he wrapped his arm around her waist and pulled her close to him. Then, he held her right hand, softly pressing his palm against hers. She followed his lead effortlessly. The steps weren't hard anymore. Dancing didn't make her nervous; being so close to Sebastian did.

Out of the corner of her eye, she saw a crowd surrounding them, gasping at every turn, applauding. Malena could get used to this attention. This high must be what artists sought in every performance. Approval. Admiration. She felt connected to the audience, free. Nobody had ever been impressed with anything she'd done before—certainly not her father. And the feeling was invigorating.

For a moment, she imagined that it was only her and Sebastian and that beautiful tango, "El día que me quieras," in the plaza. Energized, she boldly looked into his eyes. If she had to do this, she might as well enjoy the moment. So this was what it felt like to have Sebastian's attention. She wondered, too, what a kiss from him would be like.

The rest of the song went by in a haze. Too fast, in her opinion. They remained locked in each other's arms after the melody ended. This might be the last time they would be this close. She couldn't bring herself to let go of his arms. He gently pushed her away, but held her hand as they bowed to the public. A roar of applause erupted around them.

In the microphone, the master of ceremonies praised them and advertised Amanda's nightclub. Then, he started the New Year's Eve countdown.

"¡*Cinco, cuatro, tres, dos, uno, cero! ¡Feliz Año!*"

"Happy New Year," Malena told Sebastian.

He gazed at her lips. Was he going to kiss her? It was tradition, after all. But he simply squeezed her hand. He didn't let go until he spotted Claudia among the crowd, glaring at them.

Malena had never seen Claudia looking this beautiful before, not even at her engagement dinner. She looked older tonight and sophisticated in a light blue sleeveless dress and a high bun. Trinidad, wrapped in a wool poncho up to her nose, stood behind her, like a good chaperone. Sebastian moved a chair out of the way and approached his fiancée. He kissed her cheek. Somehow Claudia managed a smile, but Malena was certain that if Claudia had had a knife nearby, she would have thrown it at her.

Malena searched for Amanda among the heads surrounding her and the small bonfires that had started throughout the plaza. She needed to get away from Claudia and Sebastian.

"I didn't know you were dancing tonight," a male voice said behind her. It was Javier.

"And I didn't know you were singing," Malena said.

"My sister is never going to forgive you for this."

"I know." She watched Sebastian lead Claudia toward the drink stand. She was shaking her head. "How long have you been playing with the band?"

"A few months." Javier's gaze landed on the sparkling pin in the center of her V-neckline.

"You're good."

Sebastian looked in her direction while handing Claudia a plastic cup.

Javier also handed Malena a drink. She hesitated. She never consumed food or beverages from street vendors (typhoid was the last thing she needed).

"Come on, don't be so prudish," Javier said.

Prudish? She liked to think of herself as wary and efficient, thank you very much. Ana and Claudia were prudish, not *her!*

"Would a prudish person dance in front of a crowd?" *Or pretend to be someone else?*

Javier smiled, but didn't remove his eyes from her cup.

She smelled the cinnamon and aguardiente in her *canelazo* and took a sip. It was warm and she could taste the *naranjilla* juice in the mix.

"The band is getting ready to go to Guayaquil in a few weeks," Javier said.

A couple of these drinks and she wouldn't care anymore about having to face Claudia later. "Are you going with them?"

"I can't. You know how my old man is."

"But you're such a good singer, Javi. This might be your one chance."

"Nobody can make a living with music or theater in this country, remember?"

She had told him something similar at the storage room the other day. Things seemed so different now, like anything was possible.

"Make it your New Year's wish," she said.

Claudia was laughing now, and wrapping her hand around Sebastian's arm. It was the *canelazo* for sure. Malena hated to admit it, but Sebastian and Claudia made a nice couple. When Claudia caught Malena watching them, she grabbed Sebastian's face with both hands and kissed him.

Malena drained her drink, wishing Sebastian would push Claudia away. He didn't. Instead, he held Claudia by the waist and responded to the kiss.

"There's Amanda," Javier said, unaware of the pain growing in Malena's chest.

What an idiot she had been to think there was something special between Sebastian and her while they danced. It had meant nothing to him. It had been, like Amanda said, just a dance. He was in love with Claudia, and he would marry her very soon.

Malena followed Javier back to where Enzo's dummy once stood. It was still burning, and Amanda and Joaquin were talking so close to each other that Malena felt uncomfortable interrupting them.

"I'm worried about her," Amanda was saying.

"We should take her home," Joaquin said.

"Who?" Javier asked.

"Sebastian's mother," Joaquin said. "She's had too much to drink."

They pointed in the direction of Ofelia Rivas, a few steps away. Malena barely recognized her. Gone was the classy lady she'd met recently. Ofelia had a glass in her hand, her caramel shawl halfway off her shoulders, her mascara smeared, and she was massacring the bolero "Bésame Mucho" with her screeches.

"We have to tell Sebastian," Amanda said. "Where is he?"

Sebastian and Claudia were no longer at the stand where Malena had last seen them.

Ofelia staggered toward Amanda. "Have a drink with me, *amiga!*"

Amanda wrapped her arm around her shoulder. "Come with me, *querida*. I'll take you home."

"No!" Ofelia shook Amanda's hand off of her. "Leave me alone. I'm enjoying myself for the first time since Ignacio died."

"Fine, then I'll go get your son!" Amanda said. She whispered onto Malena's ear. "Keep an eye on her. I'll be right back."

"I'll go with you," Joaquin said.

Ofelia gulped more aguardiente. *"¡Que viva el año nuevo!"*

"¡Que viva!" answered some drunken male voice from the crowd.

A cluster of townspeople mocked her stance. Sebastian and Claudia approached with Trinidad trailing along.

Sebastian snatched his mother's arm. "Let's go home, Madre, you don't look well."

"No! I'm not leaving!"

Freeing herself from his grasp, Ofelia spun, but her heel got stuck in one of the cement cracks. The woman lost her balance and landed hard on the ground. General laughter followed Ofelia's fall. Claudia smiled briefly.

Glowering, Sebastian helped his mother up.

"¡Mierda!" Ofelia said. "I broke my shoe!"

Malena reached out for Ofelia's free arm. "Are you okay, Doña?" She helped Sebastian pull Ofelia up and wrapped her arm around her waist.

"Let's take her there." He pointed at a park bench. "Trinidad, please bring a coffee for my mother."

They headed for the bench. Claudia followed at a distance. Now that people were dispersing, the band had started playing *pasillos,* which added to the somber mood the evening had taken. Malena sat by Ofelia and slid her hand over the woman's forehead.

"She's very pale."

"I don't feel too good, Sebas, I'm dizzy." Immediately following her words, Ofelia bent forward and puked, loudly, messily, in front of God and everybody.

Claudia covered her nose with her fingers while others around them expressed their disgust with groans and grimaces. Sebastian clenched his fists. Malena hoped he didn't lose his temper again, like he did the evening of the Madreselva opening.

"Sebastian?" she called.

His features softened when he turned to her.

"She's trembling." Malena rubbed Ofelia's back, doing her best to comfort the poor woman. "It's going to be okay." She pulled Ofelia's hair behind her ears and removed her shawl so it wouldn't get soiled.

Sebastian removed his jacket and placed it over his mother's shoulders.

Amanda and Joaquin returned with Javier. An overexcited Claudia explained to them what had happened with Ofelia. Sebastian's jaw tightened.

"I'm going to take her home," he told Malena.

"I'll help you," Javier offered.

The two men helped Ofelia stand and walk away. Still with the shawl in her hand, Malena caught Claudia staring at her. This was going to be a long night.

Malena had avoided Claudia for almost twenty-four hours. Last night, while Claudia changed in the bathroom, Malena had pretended to fall asleep. In the morning, she'd waited until Claudia left for church to open her eyes. And she had practically begged Amanda to take her along on errands all day. But now, as she followed Amanda back into the Platas home, there was no more hiding.

In the living room, Claudia, Ana, and Mamá Blanca worked on the trousseau to the sounds of their favorite *radionovela*.

"Good evening," Amanda said.

"*Buenas noches*," Mamá Blanca responded.

Ana raised her head from her crochet and greeted her sister, but her response was barely audible. She eyed Malena before returning her attention to her needle. Claudia, on the other hand, kept her head low as she cross-stitched a leaf pattern on a towel, as though she hadn't heard them.

"Perfect timing," Mamá Blanca said. "I was just getting ready to go to bed. Would you help me upstairs, Amandita?"

In a panic, Malena turned to Amanda. *Don't leave.* But Amanda was immune to her unspoken pleas. She crossed the living room and helped her mother stand up. Both of them headed for the staircase. Malena attempted to follow, but Ana stopped her.

"Liliana, would you stay for a moment? I need to speak to you." Ana rested her hand on Claudia's lap. "*Hija,* would you be so kind as to bring me a cup of *anís* tea?"

Claudia produced a thin smile and stood up. It didn't surprise Malena that Ana had requested *anís* tea. She worried so much she probably suffered from all kinds of digestive problems.

With Claudia gone, Ana turned off the radio. "I understand you danced with Sebastian last night at the plaza." Her voice was stern. "So far, I've been very patient with you, Liliana. I've overlooked certain behaviors that I know your mother would not approve of, such as going to Amanda's . . . place." She picked up her crochet work and sat down. "But this is intolerable. As you know, Sebastian is Claudia's fiancé. That may not mean much to you being that, well, you know exactly what I mean. But in this family, we respect that."

Sometimes Ana sounded just like La Abuela Eva.

A folded newspaper, *El Heraldo,* sat on the coffee table; a familiar name printed on the editorial page called Malena's attention: Cesar Villamizar.

"I consented to have you stay with us in consideration of my long friendship with your mother, but if this sort of behavior continues, I may be forced to contact her."

Malena raised her head.

"No, please don't contact Ma . . . my mother. I promise I won't go back to the nightclub."

"Stop badgering her." Amanda reentered the living room.

Blessed Amanda!

214

"If there's someone to blame here, it's me," Amanda said. "I'm the one who asked her to dance with Sebastian. Lili was helping me promote the Madreselva."

"Well, that's too bad," Ana said. "You know María Teresa entrusted me with the care of her daughter. In her absence, I'm Liliana's guardian, whether you like it or not."

"Lili is already an adult. She can do whatever she pleases."

"Not while she's under this roof!"

Malena wished she could disappear so she wouldn't have to see the sisters fighting because of her.

Ana tossed her tablecloth aside. "I knew it was a bad idea for you to take over that restaurant. I always knew something like this would happen!"

"What did you expect me to do? Let that damn Enzo destroy whatever was left of Nicolas's business?"

"Stop blaming Enzo! That poor man had to run the business for twenty years, sell your house, and manage Nicolas's fortune. He did everything while you sat here moping over your bad luck!"

Amanda's eyes narrowed. "I can't believe you're siding with that bastard."

"I'm not siding with him. I just think you should take some responsibility for the business's failure."

"That's exactly what I'm trying to do, in case you haven't noticed."

"You could have done it without disgracing this family, or without causing a problem between Claudia and Sebastian!"

"It was just a dance, Ana! It's not like I'm throwing Liliana into Sebastian's bed!"

"You practically are!"

Malena picked up the newspaper and fanned her cheeks with it. This was what she got for pretending to be the mistress of a married man. Now Ana thought her capable of anything. However, posing as Liliana didn't mean Malena had to sit through insults or a morality lecture every day; especially not one coming from someone who might not be entirely honest herself. Ana had crossed the line.

Both sisters turned to her, but neither one said a word.

With the newspaper still in her hands, Malena left the living room. She needed to put as much distance between herself and Ana as possible.

Chapter 30

Ana, 1941

No, this couldn't be happening. *Not now.* Ana sat on the edge of her living room couch to grasp the news Rafael was telling her. He had a radiant smile on his face and a spark in his otherwise dull eyes.

"So what do you think?" he said. "Isn't it wonderful?"

"Your uncle just died and you think it's wonderful?"

"No, *tontita.* It's not that. You know what this means for us?"

She knew. She just didn't want to think about it.

"Tío Román left us his ranch. That means I won't have to work for your father anymore." His brow furrowed. "Stop biting your nails, Ana. It's such an ugly habit."

Ana dropped her hand.

He leaned against the oak cupboard. "We'll finally be free."

"Yes, but it also means we'll be moving away from San Isidro."

"Which is the best part." He opened a bottle of whiskey, the one he'd been saving for the long-awaited promotion at Joyería Platas that never came. "I can't wait to leave this filthy town."

"But the country, Rafael? I didn't think you liked it."

He poured half a glass of whiskey and watered it down. "I don't. But at this point I don't care, as long as it takes me away from here." He extended the glass to her. "Besides, how hard can it be? Raise a few cows, produce some milk and butter here and there. Anyone can do it."

Ana eyed her drink. She rarely drank, but today was one of those days when she needed it. She took a sip—it was hideous. "Where exactly is the ranch?"

"In Tabacundo, north of Quito, on the way to Ibarra."

Goodness. That was so far away, at least a six-hour bus ride. She couldn't go that far, not now that she had the love she'd longed for all her life.

"I can't wait to see your father's face when I tell him I'm leaving, or that good-for-nothing cousin of yours!" He chuckled. "I'm a free man, Ana."

The liquid burned Ana's throat. Through watery eyes, she could see that Rafael was adding whiskey to his glass.

"The only problem is the house," he said. "According to Tío Román's executor, it's in bad condition. The plumbing needs to be redone and there are problems with the roofing. But the house is big enough for all of us."

Ana studied her husband as he gulped his drink. This might not be such a bad idea after all.

"No plumbing? Rafael, how can you even think of taking your family to a house without plumbing?"

"Well, there's nothing we can do but be patient. The renovations won't take long, a few months at the most."

A few months? Ana got excited as the idea took shape in her mind. "How many months?"

"I don't know. Maybe six, maybe more. You know how slow people are here."

Perfect.

She took the glass from Rafael's hands and set it on the end table. Then, she held his hands in hers. "How about this? You go first. Work on the renovations, get the house ready for us, and then we'll meet you there. That way you don't have to worry about us living in those conditions."

"And I'm supposed to be there by myself for all those months?"

"You won't be alone. Tío Román had a foreman, right? And the workers and their families, I'm sure."

"I don't know."

"Come on." She gave him back his whiskey. "You know this is the best solution. You can't subject us to such miserable conditions."

Rafael ran his fingers through Ana's wavy hair and stopped at her cheek. "You know that motherhood has set well with you?"

Ana faked a smile, disgusted by his liquor-tainted breath and the touch of his cold hands. She undid the top button of her collar blouse. It was the price she had to pay, the price for her freedom.

As the bus taking Rafael north faded in the distance, the pressure in Ana's chest released, as though the chains of marriage had been miraculously unlocked. For the first time in her life she was free. And the feeling was exhilarating.

"Isn't this a beautiful day?" she told the woman standing beside her. The woman lowered a handkerchief from her tearful eyes.

"Oh, I'm sorry." What a horrible person she was. In her excitement, it hadn't crossed her mind that someone might be having a sad farewell.

She scurried away from the Terminal Terrestre. She couldn't believe Rafael had agreed to leave without his family. Tío Román's ranch must have been in really bad shape. But she couldn't be too confident, not until she was far away from here, far from Rafael's reach. She took longer steps. She had to hurry lest Rafael changed his mind and returned.

The walk home seemed endless. The apartment still smelled of Rafael, of the unfinished cigarette he'd discarded in the metal ashtray before heading for the bus station, of the black coffee he'd had for breakfast and left on the table. The bathroom still held the humidity from his shower—perhaps the last shower he would take in a long time—and the pine scent of his soap. The facial hair he'd shaved was still stuck on the basin. She rinsed the hairs off, smiling. After today, she wouldn't have to clean up his mess ever again.

She scrambled to the bedroom and removed her valise from under the bed. She neatly folded every one of her blouses and skirts and put them inside, one by one, while whistling "Volver," one of her sister's favorite tangos.

She was going to miss Amanda. And she didn't even want to think about her mother. Who knew when—if ever—she would see her family again.

The ring of the doorbell vibrated all the way to her spine. Rafael! He was back! How would she explain the valise on the bed, the messy kitchen? But no, it couldn't be him; he had a key. Or had he left it behind? The doorbell rang again.

"Ana!" a female voice called out.

Ana's shoulders relaxed a bit. She shut her bedroom door and crossed the tiny living room. Through the peephole, she recognized Abigail.

Her sister was pale and her locks wilder than usual.

Ana opened the door. "What's wrong?"

Abigail chewed on her cracked lips.

"May I come in?"

Abigail sat on the sofa and fumbled inside her purse until she found a cigarette.

"Since when do you smoke?"

Abigail lit the cigarette. "I don't know, a few weeks." After inhaling a drag of smoke, she coughed.

Ana eyed her wristwatch. "What happened, Abi?"

Abigail looked at her through the waves of smoke. "I have something very important to talk to you about."

Chapter 31

Malena pressed the fine silk shawl against her chest as she walked down the street. One name stuck in her mind: Cesar Villamizar, the man from her father's checks. According to the newspaper she'd found in the living room the previous night, he was also the managing editor of *El Heraldo de San Isidro*. It could be the same man her father knew, but it could also be a coincidence. Cesar was not an uncommon name; neither was Villamizar. But still, she had to find out as much information as she could about him. And Sebastian was the only person who could help her.

As she turned the corner, she recognized his two-story house. The black metal fence was unlocked, the water fountain running. She took a deep breath before knocking.

Sebastian opened the door, his tie loose and his sleeves rolled up. His eyes widened.

She smiled. "Hello."

Apparently he was too surprised to answer.

"Sorry to disturb you. I just wanted to drop off your mother's shawl." She extended her hand, offering the clean wrap.

He took the garment from her hand and their fingertips touched for a second.

"Thank you," he said. "You shouldn't have bothered. I could have picked it up."

"That's all right. I wanted to take a walk."

He opened the door wider. "Please come in. I could really use some company right now."

"Your mother is not home?"

He sighed. "She's taking a nap. She's not feeling well."

She walked in. An overwhelming scent of antique furniture reminded her of the university library.

"Careful." Sebastian grasped her arm with his fingers to prevent her from bumping into a bronze statue of a demon in the foyer.

Goose bumps rose on the back of her neck in response to his touch. Sebastian showed her to the living room, where the smell of polished pine became stronger. Though the room was large, furniture pieces jammed next to one another made it appear small. Enormous paintings of hands, feet, wide-eyed people, and a collection of crosses in wood, metal, and glass covered the walls.

"Please, have a seat. Wherever you'd like," he said.

There were certainly lots of choices. Four chairs, an ochre couch, and a rocking chair were available. Malena picked a beautifully-crafted but uncomfortable chair across from the couch where he sat.

"Has the doctor seen your mother?" she asked.

"I'm afraid doctors don't pay house visits for hangovers."

She let his words sink in. Ofelia had been drinking again.

"*Cebiche de camarones* is good for that," she said. "Or so I've heard."

"Unfortunately, shrimp is beyond my cooking abilities."

His cooking abilities? It didn't make sense that as affluent as the Rivas appeared to be, they didn't have a maid to cook for them. Everything here looked so expensive. But Mamá Blanca and Claudia had mentioned Ofelia's outrageous spending habits.

"You have a beautiful home," she said.

He shrugged. "I would prefer something simpler."

As her eyes gravitated toward the dusty coffee table, he spoke again. "It's hard to keep up. Especially now that we don't have a maid. My mother is very hard to please, and she changes maids as often as she changes shoes. If I hadn't been so busy at work, I would have hired someone myself."

He stared at her so intensely she almost forgot what she was doing there.

"Would you like something to eat?" he said. "I was just going to see if there was something edible in the refrigerator. Last time I checked, there was a piece of fish that hadn't rotted yet."

"Fish is my specialty," she said. "Particularly *corvina*. If you'd like, I can prepare it for you."

Sebastian's eyes brightened. "Sure."

In a strange way, Sebastian reminded Malena of her father. For a brief period, right after La Abuela had died, Papá had cooked and cleaned for them. Except that he was always forgetting the stove on or burning anything that went into the oven. And so Malena, at the age of ten, had taken over all housekeeping chores. She'd gone as far as sleeping in her uniform so she would have time to tidy up the house in the morning and not be late for school. She didn't mind, though; her father was a genius and should be treated as such—at least that was the way she saw it then.

Malena followed Sebastian into a minimalist kitchen with appliances that looked more like ornaments than functional objects. Sebastian removed a package wrapped in white paper from the refrigerator and handed it to her.

It didn't stink.

"I think it's still good," she said.

After setting the fish on a pan, she searched the cupboard for spices and herbs. Sebastian leaned on the counter while she picked tomatoes and cucumber from the refrigerator. He followed her every move. Under his scrutiny, she nearly dropped a lemon on the floor, but he caught it just in time.

"Thanks," she said.

She was being ridiculous. She had tangoed with the man. He had held her closer than any other member of the opposite sex and here she was, acting like a high schooler on her first date; so nervous she couldn't think of anything mildly entertaining to say, much less how to bring up the subject of Cesar Villamizar in a casual way.

She found a knife for the vegetables in one of the drawers. "Claudia said you are in charge of *El Heraldo* now."

"I am."

"Do you like it?"

He took a long breath. "I'm starting to. I had to make a lot of changes, but it's paying off. Our readership has gone up."

She fanned her face with a red oven mitt. "I've noticed the paper is thicker, too."

"Yes," he said excitedly. "We have more advertisers now. We subscribe to an international wire service, and are getting a lot of information every day."

"I read an interesting article yesterday about President Arosemena. Something about his leftist tendencies and his drinking problem." Drinking problem? What was she saying? "At any rate, the reporter seemed quite knowledgeable."

He was quiet for a moment. "I suppose he is."

"Has he worked with you for long?"

"He was my father's right-hand man."

So this Cesar must be older. "I imagine reporters must lead very interesting lives, traveling a lot, meeting lots of people."

Sebastian crossed his arms.

She flipped the fish in the pan. "His name is so familiar to me. I think he may have been a friend of . . . my father's."

"Possibly. This is a small town. Everyone knows each other."

"I would love to meet him." She mixed the vegetables in a bowl, adding a dash of salt and lemon. "So I can tell my father about him."

Sebastian arched his eyebrows. He must have thought she went crazy.

"Sure," he said. "Feel free to come by the paper and I'll introduce you to him."

She examined the *corvina*.

"It's ready."

———————

Sebastian ate in silence, which she hoped meant he liked her food. With her index finger, she traced a series of vines embroidered on the tablecloth.

"Are you sure you don't want anything?" he said from across the table. "I should be feeding you, not the other way around. You're the guest."

She couldn't possibly eat in front of him. "No, I'm fine, thank you."

"I guess it's true what they say about the food from Manabí. This is delicious."

Manabí? Oh, yes. Lili was from there.

"You think your mother is hungry?" she asked. "There's enough food for her."

"I doubt it. She hasn't been eating much lately. My father's passing has affected her too much. First, she acted as if nothing happened. She bought things, lots of things." He pointed at the crystal ornaments and the paintings surrounding them. "Then, the drinking started."

Malena wished she could say a magic word to make him feel better, but there was no such thing. Who knew what she would have done if she hadn't found her mother's letter among her father's things? Who's to say she wouldn't have resorted to alcohol herself? "Everyone copes in different ways. Some of us run away." Had she actually said that aloud?

He wiped his mouth with a napkin.

"Who did you lose?"

Time to change the subject. "Tell me about your father."

"My father. Where should I start?" He leaned back. "He was very charismatic and hardworking. Everyone in town knew him. Perhaps his only flaw was he trusted too much. He believed all people were innately good."

"I do, too."

"That explains a lot of things about you."

She wasn't sure if he meant it as a compliment or an insult.

"Enough of that sad talk," he said. "Tell me, are you going to marry Javier?"

His question was so unexpected she was grateful to be sitting down. So he remembered seeing them in the hotel after all.

"Of course not. We're just friends."

He smirked.

She glanced at her watch, without really looking at the time. "I should go. Ana doesn't like it when I leave the house without telling her." She stood. "Please give my regards to your mother."

He pushed his chair back, standing up.

"No, don't get up," she said. "I know the way."

She rushed to the front door, his steps behind her. Feeling the weight of his gaze on her, she stepped out of his house, knowing full well that she couldn't keep up this farce much longer.

Chapter 32

The piercing peal of the doorbell woke Sebastian after midnight. Something terrible must have happened. He stumbled out of bed, barefoot, and hopped downstairs with his pajama shirt slightly opened. In the darkness, he bumped one of his toes into the metal table where the demon-angel stood.

"Maldición!"

The doorbell chimed again.

"I'm coming," he mumbled, feeling the light switch by the door. Nothing could have prepared him for the face at the other side of the door.

Claudia stood in front of him, trembling under her brown coat and pillbox hat, her nose pink and her hands clutching a small leather purse.

"What happened?"

"May I come in?" she asked.

He pulled her in and closed the door behind her.

"What's wrong, Claudia?"

She entered the dusky living room and sat on one of his mother's hideous chairs.

"I'm sorry to come here so late. I know these aren't visiting hours, but I needed to talk to you."

"And it couldn't wait until morning?"

"No. It's very important." She looked around. "Your mother?"

"Upstairs. Sleeping." He sat on the arm of the couch. "So, what is it?"

"Well, I don't want us to wait any longer for our wedding. I spoke to the seamstress and she can have my dress ready in a week."

A week? Why did the mention of his wedding irritate him?

"But the invitations?" he said.

"You can print out new ones at the newspaper."

He scratched his head. "I suppose. But why?"

"I just don't want to wait any longer. I want to be your wife and . . ." She looked at the paintings around them, almost in despair. Standing up, she removed her wool coat and took his hand. "I want to . . . be with you." She pressed his hand against one of her breasts.

Sebastian's mouth fell open. *Had he understood correctly?* Never in his wildest dreams had he imagined Claudia behaving like this. Up until now, she had always cut off his advances. This only confirmed what little he knew of women. He might as well give up any attempts to figure them out.

"I thought you wanted to wait until we were married."

"Yes, I did. But . . ." She sighed. "What difference does it make?"

Maybe he was dreaming and didn't know it. It would be the only explanation for this strange turn of events. Either that, or Claudia had lost her sanity. But her cold hand squeezing his own felt too real for a dream. She brought her other hand to his nape and stood on her tiptoes to initiate a kiss, just like she had done in the plaza during New Year's Eve.

He closed his eyes, from instinct more than anything, because as soon as he felt her lips, another face flashed through his mind. Opening his eyes, he grabbed her by the shoulders and pushed her back.

"What is this really about, Claudia? Is it about the tango incident? I'm sorry I didn't tell you."

"I don't want to talk about that." She undid the top button of her blouse. "Don't you find me attractive? Don't you want to be with me?"

Her fingers fumbled with her buttons, one by one, until he could see her white cotton brassiere. She searched for his mouth again and he kissed her obediently, dutifully—as if kissing her were a chore expected of a responsible fiancé—but his mind was elsewhere, entangled in some complex tango steps with a woman he hadn't been able to get off his mind for days.

Chapter 33

Malena opened her eyes. Claudia's bed was empty. She was probably at the confession room, expelling her guilt over all the rotten things she must have done with Sebastian last night.

Malena kicked the covers off her legs. The thought of Sebastian in bed with another woman—even if it was his fiancée—infuriated her. True, she had no proof that's what they had done, but Claudia had been gone all night, and had arrived in his car at dawn. He had opened the door for her and dismissed her with a kiss on the forehead. What else could they have being doing so late? How could Sebastian forget about her so quickly? She had been to his house that same day and cooked for him! Didn't that mean anything to him?

She shed her nightgown and put on the first old shirtwaist dress she found. Who cared what she looked like anymore?

Claudia wasn't in the living room or the dining room, but the rest of the family was already gathered for breakfast.

After voicing a general *"Buenos días,"* Malena sat across from Javier while the conversation continued as if she weren't there. Mamá Blanca had finally agreed to the dentures and Ana was planning the details.

What am I still doing here?

Nothing was working out. Malena's investigations were taking entirely too long, and on top of everything else, she had gone and fallen in love with Claudia's fiancé. The thought stopped her in the midst of stirring sugar in her coffee. There was simply no point in denying it anymore. She was in love, like an idiot, at the worst possible moment. As if she needed more complication in her life. She might as well confess the truth before she had to witness Sebastian's wedding.

She looked at the faces around her as they continued with their conversation. Maybe this was the moment she'd been waiting for. Why wait any longer? They were bound to find out who she was eventually.

While savoring a piece of papaya, she toyed with the idea of confessing the truth. How would she even start? *I have an announcement to make.* Wasn't that the way Amanda had broken the news about the nightclub? *My name is not Liliana, it's Malena, and one of the women in this family is my mother.*

Her legs quivered. She was going to do it. This façade had been going on for too long. She cleared her throat, but before she could speak, Claudia mumbled a barely audible *"Buenos días"* from the doorway. She dragged herself into the room like a restless soul, entirely in black, no makeup on, and dark circles under her eyes. She gripped the back of Javier's chair.

"How was mass, *hija?*" Ana said.

"I have an announcement to make," Claudia said.

Rafael looked up from his crossword puzzle for the first time.

"Sebastian and I are getting married in one week."

Around the table, a rising murmur of voices asked why, some more excited than others. Malena drained her glass of watermelon juice.

"We just didn't want to wait any longer." Claudia fixed her eyes on Javier's messy hair. "Everything is almost ready anyway."

"I don't have a problem with that." Rafael lowered his reading glasses and gazed at his newspaper. "The sooner, the better."

"But what about the dress?" Ana said.

"The seamstress says she can have it ready by next Friday. I have a fitting this afternoon."

Somehow Claudia didn't look as excited as she should have. Malena couldn't understand why. If it were her, she would've been jumping for joy.

"In that case, Lili should go with you. She needs her dress, too." Ana said.

Great. She'd get to spend all afternoon alone with Claudia.

"Amanda and I have to take Mamá Blanca to the dentist, but we'll meet you girls there later."

Malena ground her teeth. What a coward she was. Only a minute ago she'd been determined to say the truth, but now, the idea of being exposed as an impostor frightened her. After she confessed, everything would change, and she was not ready for that yet.

Chapter 34

Claudia had not said a word since they left the Platas home. She'd been staring outside the window the entire ride to the seamstress's house. The road was bumpy and strident *albazos* had been pounding on the radio since Malena and Claudia had entered the bus. Malena shifted her weight on the seat and faced forward. The bus was crammed and the smell of half-rotten produce and bodies in desperate need of a shower had taken over. Malena refrained from scratching her legs, which had started to itch just thinking about all the germs floating about. She reminded herself they would arrive shortly. The day they'd gone for their measurements, it had only taken fifteen minutes to get there. Then again, Javier had driven them in the Chevy.

The tires screeched and the bus came to a sudden halt. A booming smash sent Malena's torso against the seat in front of her, like a rag doll. The passengers' screams surpassed the music. Then, for the briefest moment, there was silence.

"What happened? What was that?" several voices asked in unison. Rubbing her sore collarbone, Malena turned to Claudia.

"Are you okay?"

The color had drained from Claudia's face. Nodding, she rubbed her chin, which was quickly turning red.

Malena stood to look ahead. Through the windshield, she spotted the side of a small green car, the driver door squashed inward as though it was made out of paper instead of steel.

"It came out of nowhere," the bus driver repeated again and again.

He turned off the ignition and climbed out, followed by a row of passengers.

"We should go," Malena told Claudia, who seemed to be in some sort of trance. She barely nodded and followed Malena out of the bus like an automaton.

In the street, the driver and several passengers attempted to remove a young woman from the driver's seat, but it was impossible to open the door. Another man broke the passenger's window and unlocked the door. With the help of another bystander, they dragged the woman out. Her face and her hair were filled with blood and her eyes were shut. There were pieces of glass and metal all over the pavement.

If only Malena had taken her nursing studies more seriously, she could have helped this poor woman, but she stood there paralyzed, unable to remember the steps she was supposed to take in case of an emergency. *Check for breathing. Roll person onto one side.* She took a step toward them, but Claudia grabbed her arm.

"Let's go," she said.

"Wait, no, I want to help—"

"No. Let's go." Claudia's hands were shaking, her eyes were wide in shock. "Now."

Malena feared that at any moment, Claudia would snap and start screaming like a lunatic. If she didn't faint first.

"But . . ."

Claudia walked past the wreckage with brisk, long steps.

"Wait!" Malena said.

But Claudia didn't listen; she darted down the street as though escaping a fire. What had taken over her? Malena was now running—as much as her heels allowed her to—to keep up with Claudia.

After three blocks, Claudia finally stopped. She held on to a light post, her chest heaving.

Malena placed a hand on her shoulder. "Are you all right?"

She jerked away. "Don't touch me."

"I'm just trying to help."

"I don't need your help."

"Look, I understand why you're upset. That was not a pretty scene over there."

"You don't understand anything." Claudia's voice quivered. She looked at her with disdain, hatred even. "Why did you have to come here? You've ruined everything."

Was this about Sebastian? Did Claudia know how she felt?

"I know what you're thinking," Malena said. "But there's nothing between Sebastian and me, I swear. It was just a dance. We were only trying to help Amanda with her business." She felt a couple of raindrops on her nose. "Look, I'm sorry for dancing with your fiancé, okay? Now can we go help that poor woman?"

"No, you're not sorry. You love to be the center of attention."

The center of attention? How? She'd spent her entire life on the sidelines.

Malena turned around but Claudia gripped her arm. "You're going to listen to me now!"

Malena jerked away.

"I'm not easily fooled like the rest of my family," Claudia said. "I can see right through you. You're a hypocrite!"

"And you're a prude!"

"Better to be a prude than a whore who sleeps around with married men."

Malena crossed her arms to keep herself from punching Claudia in the face.

Claudia pointed a finger at her. "I know all about you, Liliana."

Malena slapped away Claudia's finger. "Look who's talking about being a hypocrite! If you're so decent, then what were you doing last night with Sebastian? Why did he drop you off at dawn?"

She stiffened. "Nothing happened between us."

"Oh, really? Why should I believe you?"

Claudia kicked a stone. Malena wanted to believe Claudia's words, but she couldn't imagine what else the two of them could have been doing together so late. Jagged flashes of lightning broke the gray clouds above their heads.

"It's going to rain," Malena said. "Come on. Hurry."

"No! I don't want to go back there!" Claudia covered her face with her hands.

Should she leave her here? Alone? Malena had never seen Claudia so unhinged.

A loud clap of thunder made both of them jump.

"Do whatever you please." Claudia covered her head with her powder-blue sweater. "I'm going to the seamstress's house."

Damn. She should follow Claudia if she didn't want to get lost. She didn't know this part of town at all. Rushing behind Claudia, Malena prayed the woman in the accident would make it to the hospital alive.

The rain began, and soon it was pouring so hard it was impossible to determine what was curb and what was street, but Malena eventually caught up with Claudia, whose ordinarily pristine hair was now soaked and getting stuck to her cheeks. Claudia stepped hard in a puddle, splashing dirty water on Malena's white swing skirt. Great, it had to be *this* skirt.

Claudia grinned. "Don't be mad. It was an accident."

"With that stupid smile on your face you expect me to believe it was an accident?"

"I'm just doing you a favor, really, as much as you like to clean."

Malena kicked the same puddle and splashed Claudia.

"Of course, such would be the reaction of someone so uncivilized."

Malena scooped up a handful of mud, ignoring the yucky feeling between her fingers, and threw it at Claudia's chest. "I'm tired of your superior attitude."

Claudia responded with a mud ball of her own. In this battle, mud was not the only thing thrown; they hurled at each other every insult they could think of.

So drenched and muddy from head to toe she was barely recognizable, Malena started to laugh. Claudia paused and soon followed suit. It was hard to believe that this was Ana's daughter. If only Sebastian could see his proper bride now! But Malena was more surprised with herself. She'd never made such a mess of herself before, not even as a child.

By the time they arrived at the seamstress's house, they were both shivering and covered in mud.

"Señorita Claudia!" the seamstress said. "Please come in!"

The seamstress, Nadia, was a miniscule woman with cinnamon hair in a statuesque bouffant that made her head look too big for her body. She led them to a bright den where the rain clattered so heavily it seemed like it would crack the skylight ceiling. They stood by a flower-print couch, looking at their ridiculous reflections in a floor-to-ceiling mirror. In the back was a mannequin, a sewing machine, and a variety of dresses hanging from a coat stand.

"Take those clothes off," Nadia said. "I'll go get some towels."

Awkwardly, the two of them stripped off their muddy outfits, or what was left of them. As Claudia removed her panty hose, Malena spotted a piece of fabric sticking out of her brassiere. At first, she couldn't tell what it was, but then she realized

Claudia had been using handkerchiefs as padding to make her breasts look fuller. Malena smiled. She'd never imagined Claudia to be so vain or care about the size of her breasts.

"That's weird," Claudia said. "Tía Amanda has the same birthmark on her thigh."

Self-consciously, Malena rubbed the coin-sized strawberry birthmark on her leg. She'd always despised her birthmark, as hideous as it was, but now the thought of Amanda having one made it somehow more acceptable. Claudia's comment sent her mind wandering, making connections she'd never thought of before. She remembered what her grandmother had told her about her birthmark when she asked about it.

A birthmark like hers, she'd explained, appeared when a pregnant mother had a craving for strawberries that wasn't fulfilled, or if the woman experienced fear during pregnancy.

"Your mother must have one, too." Claudia unzipped her skirt. "I've heard those things are passed down only from the mother."

Nadia reappeared with a couple of tangerine towels and robes for them. Malena snatched one of the towels and quickly dried her legs with it. Then, she slipped into a mint robe with white orchids and peacocks spread throughout.

"You girls may shower here and then I'll bring some nice, warm *agua de tomillo* so you don't catch a cold," Nadia said and disappeared down the hall.

Chapter 35

Amanda, 1941

The room spun in circles around Amanda's head. She took in another deep breath and removed the blankets from her legs as the nausea returned. Her palms were clammy and a cold sweat ran down her forehead. Her body, however, felt like it was burning up. She remained still, hoping it would somehow help her fight the urge to throw up again.

Her bedroom door opened and Nicolas walked in. With him came the smell of wine, which only made her queasiness worse.

"Do you want me to call Dr. Gaitán?" he asked.

"No." A doctor wouldn't help. No one could.

Nicolas sat at the foot of her bed, which surprised her since he always avoided her closeness.

"Why not?" he said. "You've been throwing up all night."

Amanda concentrated on her breathing to control her light-headedness. She sat up and reached out for the glass of water on the night table. He rose immediately and handed her the glass.

"Raising your feet might help." He folded two large blankets in fourths until he created a mountain of fabric. Then, he lifted her legs and placed them on top. His touch, as usual, made her uncomfortable. That was all that remained between them, discomfort.

He was right, though. She felt better now. The nausea subsided. They looked into each other's eyes for a moment. His were red. He'd been drinking. Again.

He rested his hands on his hips. "Do you love him?"

His question was so unexpected she didn't have time to react, much less plan a response. She took another sip of water, making it last as long as possible. So her suspicions were true. He'd always known.

"Not like I love you," she said honestly.

The tension in his facial muscles released.

"Who told you?" she whispered.

"*Cara mia,*" he said. "I've been very unfair to you, very selfish."

She couldn't believe he was the one apologizing. She was the tramp, the bad wife.

He twisted the wedding band on his finger. "I never gave you the affection you needed. It's only natural you would find it elsewhere."

"It was your brother, wasn't it?"

He didn't respond. He continued to play with his ring.

"What exactly did he tell you?" she asked.

Nicolas sighed. "What's the point—?"

"Just tell me," she said, louder than she anticipated. "I deserve to know what people are saying about me."

"He said he saw you a couple of times at Café Viteri with your father's accountant."

Amanda studied her cuticles. "What else?"

"He thinks there have been other men, too."

"How come you never said anything?"

"I'm too much of a coward." He looked at her with such despair, such an intense sadness that she had the urge to hug him, to reaffirm him she'd never loved any man the way she loved him.

"It's not right for me to expect you to stay with me after all I've done." He chuckled sourly. "Or should I say . . . after what I haven't done." It was a statement, not a question. An embarrassing reality, the barrier that separated them. A subject that, without ever having been mentioned, had ended their life together. "I can't continue to be so selfish. You're still young and beautiful. You can still start over with a . . . real man."

She placed her hand on his. "Don't say that. You're the man I love. I'll never leave you." Amanda couldn't even conceive the idea of leaving Nicolas, even when staying with him was just as painful as living without him. She knew this marriage, this façade, and Il Napolitano were the only things that kept him alive. "Besides, it's too late for that," she said. "He's . . . with someone else now."

She flattened the creases on her black nightgown. "Since we're being honest, there's something I've been wanting to ask you," she spoke quickly—before he could ask any more.

He anticipated her question. "No. It's not what you're thinking. I do like women. I always have."

His answer shook her. "Then, what is it?"

He stood up, without looking at her, and took a sip from her glass. "I have a . . . condition, an illness if you will." He paced the room, a series of shadows transformed on his face.

"An illness?"

"It's called hypospadias with chordee. It's a form of—" He faced away from her. "Impotence."

Impotence. Amanda brought her hands to her forehead, both relieved and saddened by his words. Her marriage's failure wasn't her fault, like she had thought all these years.

"I know I should have told you before we got married," he said, urgency and despair in his voice. "But I thought I could get better."

Amanda dared to hope.

"Oh, but we could still see a specialist," she said. "We can go to Italy or the United States. Anywhere."

"The doctors say it's incurable."

"What do the doctors here know? Medicine advances so rapidly."

"Perhaps."

Maybe there was a chance for them after all. "Does Enzo know?"

"Nobody knows, except for the doctors, and now you."

"You should have told me," she said.

"I know. It's unforgivable. But I was afraid that if I told you the truth, you might have told someone else. I didn't know you well, and after your father cornered me into marrying you . . . well, I just didn't want everyone in San Isidro to find out. Besides, I thought it was temporary. I thought the doctors would find a cure."

"I might have married you anyway," she said bitterly. "I was crazy about you then. I couldn't believe someone so perfect existed."

"And he didn't exist. He's far from perfect. He's not even normal."

His eyes lost their usual shine. She wanted to cuddle him in her arms, but as she set her feet on the floor and attempted to stand, the nausea returned. She leaned back.

"Are you all right?" he asked.

She rested her head on the headboard. "Yes. I sat up too fast."

He was quiet for a moment. He resumed his pacing, immersed in thought, tensing his forehead again, struggling with something. He finally stopped.

"You're pregnant, aren't you?"

Amanda shut her eyes, thinking how bizarre it was that her husband would be asking this question in such a civilized manner when he knew full well that the child couldn't be his. She'd never imagined having this conversation with Nicolas. Not in a million years.

"What would you do if I was?" she asked. "Would you raise another man's child?"

Under this light, his symmetrical face looked like it belonged in a museum—next to the sculptures and paintings of the Renaissance masters—those art pieces she'd always dreamed of seeing in person.

"I don't think I could," he whispered. "It would be too humiliating."

A match lit in her core, heat expanding in all directions. She clenched her fists, unable to produce a sound, much less a word. If she did, it would probably be something so hurtful she would regret it for the rest of her life.

"Well? Are you?" he asked.

"What?"

"Pregnant?"

"No. And now, get out. I'm very tired and I want to sleep."

Chapter 36

Teas in hand, Malena and Claudia sat side by side while Nadia mopped the mud from the foyer and hall. Malena had offered to do it herself, but the seamstress didn't want to hear another word about it.

Claudia had grown very quiet in the last few minutes, grasping her terracotta cup as if it were a bird about to escape.

"You know they never let me see my Aunt Abigail after she passed?" she said abruptly. "Or my grandfather?"

Malena leaned forward.

"I'd never seen a dead person before." Claudia reached out for the sugar bowl.

"I'm not convinced that she was dead," Malena said, the image of the wounded woman still vivid in her mind.

"She was. It was obvious." Claudia poured one teaspoon of sugar after another into her tea. Just the other day, Ana had scolded Claudia for consuming too much sugar, but apparently she had no use for her mother's rules at the moment. "She was so young. Couldn't have been much older than us." Claudia took a sip. Then added more sugar. "Life can be over in an instant. Just like that, when you least expect it. It doesn't matter how old or young you are."

Claudia was right. One day, Malena's father had been correcting exams at the dining room table, and the next, he was getting buried in Ciudad Blanca, Guayaquil's most notorious cemetery.

"That's why you have to take advantage of every day, every moment," Claudia said in a distant, uncanny voice.

"All done!" Nadia said, poking into the den. "I'll go get the dresses for the fitting."

Ana and Amanda arrived after Malena and Claudia were done with their fittings and had already changed into some pastel dresses the seamstress lent them. The sisters set their gray umbrellas on the foyer and their wet jackets on the coat stand. Malena stared at Amanda's leg as if she could see her birthmark through the fabric of her pencil skirt. Now more than ever, she wished Amanda was her mother. Maybe she would talk to her about it. Perhaps she'd had this all wrong and the best approach would be to talk to each sister in private until one of them confessed.

Once the Platas sisters had tried their garments on, the four of them left together. Amanda wrapped her arm around Malena and led her toward a cab waiting by the curb.

"Do you want to come to the Madreselva with me tonight?" Amanda whispered so Ana wouldn't hear. "We're dancing *milongas*."

Malena glanced over her shoulder. Ana and Claudia walked a few steps behind, immersed in their own conversation. Well, Ana was the only one speaking.

"Sure," Malena said. Maybe she could talk to Amanda then.

Looking straight ahead, Amanda stopped short and her smile faded. Enzo was heading in their direction.

"Long time no see, *sorella*." His eyes were filled with contempt. "I've heard you are managing to save my brother's business after all."

"I told you I could do it."

He smiled, but his face looked sinister under his hat. "You are persistent. I'll give you that, *cara mia*."

"Don't call me that."

"Oh, yes, my brother used to call you that. The fool."

Amanda eyed Malena.

"Guilt can be a good thing, I suppose," he said. "It has pushed you to do a good thing for my brother's legacy."

"I don't feel guilt," she said. "You should, though, after what you did to Il Napolitano."

"No, I'm sure *killing* my brother was worse."

"Shut up, Vincenzo! You know damn well he did it to himself."

Enzo crossed his arms in front of his chest. "Technicalities," he said. "You might as well have pulled the trigger yourself."

Amanda slapped his face so hard the people in the street stopped to look at them.

Ana caught up with them, catching her breath.

"What's going on here?"

Enzo rubbed his cheek. "Mrs. Dávila, I didn't see you." He adjusted his tie. "I apologize you had to witness a scene like this."

"Mr. Fornasieri." She glared at her sister. "Amanda, what's wrong with you? How dare you hit Mr. Fornasieri?"

"Save it, Ana. I don't want to hear it." Amanda pushed Enzo aside and climbed into the taxi cab.

Malena rushed behind her, leaving the door open.

"Shut the door, Lili!" Amanda said. "They can walk home!"

As the taxi drove away, Amanda faced the side window. A faint rainbow appeared through the ashen clouds. Sunlight shone through the windshield and bounced off the driver's bald head. Amanda's fingers quivered as she lit a cigarette. Malena had never seen Amanda this upset. Not even after the opening night fiasco. The way her legs trembled. The way those tears trailed down her flushed cheeks. Malena wanted to ask her what Enzo meant about Amanda killing his brother. If she understood correctly, they had implied that Nicolas killed himself. But why would he do that? Why would a man with a successful business and a beautiful wife kill himself? She turned to Amanda, who squeezed her umbrella with her free hand.

"Don't say anything, Liliana," Amanda warned her. "I don't want to talk about it. And I don't want you to mention this to anyone. Understood?"

By nighttime, Amanda had regained her composure. Her charming self returned effortlessly, it seemed. But Malena had been nervous during dinner, seeing the angry glances between Amanda and Ana. There had been so much tension in the dining room Malena was certain the other family members could sense it.

After dinner, the women in the family—minus Amanda and Alejandra—set themselves in the living room to finish Claudia's trousseau. Amanda walked down the stairs with her coat on and her purse in her hands. She signaled Malena to come.

Malena set her embroidery aside and followed Amanda to the foyer.

"I don't want to fight with my sister again," Amanda said in a low voice. "So just come with me without telling her."

Malena scratched her forehead. She didn't want any more problems with Ana. She didn't want her to call María Teresa. Nothing good would come from that.

"Go get your coat," Amanda told her. "I'll wait here." She hung her purse on the coat hanger by the door and walked toward the lavatory. "And hurry up."

Malena stood in the foyer, paralyzed. She didn't want Amanda angry at her for not coming with her to the nightclub, but she didn't want to upset Ana either. Yet, no matter what she did, someone would be annoyed. She tried to focus. She hadn't come to this house to partake in family feuds. She had a goal but she'd been letting the sisters' demands distract her. Talking to Amanda tonight might not work; not after the incident with Enzo. Plus, she always got irritated when Malena dug into the past.

The answer to her dilemma stood in front of her. Of course, how could she not see it? Amanda had left her purse on the coat hanger. The purse with the armoire key. Malena scrambled toward it, as quietly as possible, and opened the zipper. She couldn't believe how bold she'd become. Amanda was seconds away from coming out of the bathroom, Rafael could walk downstairs, and Trini could bring a tray of tea to the women in the living room. Malena could hear the *radionovela* loud and clear in the living room. The only thing that separated her from them was a wall.

Malena's fingers flew through Amanda's things: house keys, checkbook, lipstick, mirror, a hairbrush. She heard the toilet flushing. She fumbled with Amanda's things until she felt the armoire key with her fingertips. She took it out and slid it inside her brassiere. She closed the zipper at the same time the bathroom door opened.

When Amanda stepped out of the bathroom, Malena was still holding the purse.

Amanda frowned.

"Here." Malena handed her the purse. "Amanda, please forgive me. I don't think I can go with you tonight. I don't want Ana to call my mother. You understand, right?"

Amanda sighed. "Fine."

She left the house as Malena watched—the cold key pressing against her skin.

Malena could still hear Rafael's muffled voice through the wall and the creak of the wood coming from the hall. Gripping the armoire key in her hand, Malena waited for all the noises in the house to cease. Only after everyone had fallen asleep could she sneak into Amanda's room. But if she waited too long, Amanda could come back.

When the only sound remaining was her own breathing, Malena pulled the covers off. She stepped out of bed, hoping her squeaky mattress wouldn't upset Claudia's sleep, and tip-toed to her roommate's side. Filtering through the curtains, the outside post light illuminated Claudia's face. Her eyes were tightly shut.

Malena crept into the hallway, mentally counting the twenty-five steps that separated Claudia's room from Amanda's. Feeling the doorknob, she opened the door and made her way to the night table. She turned the lamp on and removed the key from her robe pocket to unlock the armoire. Abigail's diary was in the same spot she'd last seen it.

She took it out and sat on Amanda's bed, leafing through the pages.

Abigail talked a lot about a boy she met at María Teresa's wedding. Someone called Victor, whom Malena remembered as the young man from the photograph in the sewing machine. Most of the pages were dedicated to him, even though Abigail said somewhere that she'd agreed to be Enrique's girlfriend. Malena scanned through the pages. She didn't have much time and she had to find something else about her father.

Toward the end of the notebook, she found his name again.

Today, I became engaged to Enrique Hidalgo.
Enrique and I will be married sometime this year.
He's a good man. I should be happy, right?

I must forget about Victor. He doesn't love me.
I will forget.

The rest of the diary was charred black.

A voice as loud as thunder startled her.

"What are you doing with that?"

Chapter 37

Malena dropped the diary to the floor, afraid to turn toward the voice.

There were two vertical lines on Javier's forehead. For a minute, he reminded her of Rafael.

"What are you doing in my aunt's room? Why are you going through her things?"

"Keep it down, please," she begged, heat rising to her face. "I have a good explanation for this."

He folded his arms across his chest. "You do? I would love to hear it."

"I do, but can we talk somewhere else?"

She picked up the diary from the floor and returned it to its spot in the drawer. She locked the armoire, sensing Javier's glare at her. She moved quickly, before he had a chance to do or say something. Turning off Amanda's bedside lamp, Malena quietly dropped the armoire key on the floor, hoping Javier wouldn't notice.

In two steps, she was by his side. The obscured hallway light cast sinister shadows on his face, making his usual peaceful demeanor dark and menacing. She stepped out of the room, followed by this man who'd turned into a stranger in a matter of seconds.

"Can we go to your room?" she whispered.

He led the way down the hall to one of the few rooms in the house she'd never seen.

Javier's room was simple: a bed, a night table, and an armoire in the corner of the room. There was also a chair and a guitar on his bed. He pointed at the chair and Malena sat down. He paced the room.

"Well?" He sounded like a school principal.

She hadn't had enough time to think of a convincing lie. How could anyone explain snooping? The lie might come out worse than the truth. Though Javier seemed upset at the moment, she leveraged the possibility of telling him the truth. So far, he'd been loyal to her. He had never told anyone that her luggage had been in that hotel, or that he'd found her fumbling in the dining room the night she was looking for the accounting notebooks. He hadn't judged her when she danced with Sebastian on New Year's Eve, and he'd gone along with her idea of baking a cake for Alejandra. He seemed trustworthy enough. But then again, he would probably feel more loyalty toward his family than her.

He snapped his fingers in front of her face. "Lili? Are you awake?"

"There's something very important I have to tell you. But you have to swear you won't tell anybody else."

Javier frowned. "Go on."

She rested her hands on her legs. "I'm not María Teresa's daughter. My name is Malena Sevilla."

He stopped his pacing. "What?"

"Sit down." She pointed at the bed. "I have to tell you a long story."

Malena took a deep breath. *Where to start?* Her father, his death, and her mother's letter. She told him everything, including the information she'd gathered since her arrival. He listened intently, tense fingers on his lap, and an increasing look of disbelief.

"I can't believe you lied to us," he finally said.

"I know it's wrong, but I was afraid your mother and aunts would send me away without an answer. I still am."

Javier flopped down on his back, staring at the ceiling. He was quiet for a long time.

"I'm sorry I lied," she said. "But do you see how important this is?"

"Yes. I see that."

She braced herself for the insults she expected would come her way.

He sat up. "So any of them could be your mother, including . . . mine?"

She nodded. "She did have that handkerchief with my father's initial."

"Yes, but that doesn't mean anything. It could have been anybody's."

"True."

"What about Tía Amanda?"

"I don't have much on her, other than the birthmark and Enzo accusing her of having an affair with my father. This afternoon, Enzo implied she was responsible for her husband's suicide."

"Tía Alejandra?"

"Nothing. Although Amanda told me she had been in a convent for some time, which seemed strange to me."

"A convent?"

"She also acted suspiciously when I found the accounting books, remember?"

"No."

"She hides a newspaper clipping in the workshop."

"Where in her workshop?"

"In her desk. She seemed very disturbed by it once."

"Okay. I can look for it. What about Tía Abigail?"

"Well, she was engaged to my father."

He rubbed his forehead. "There's an image that has been in my mind for years. Perhaps one of my earlier memories of Tía Abigail. When I was little, I liked to hide from my mother. One time, I hid in Tía Abigail's bedroom. My aunt came in shortly after, unaware that I was hiding behind the curtains. I still can't believe she didn't see me." He ran his fingertips over the guitar strings. "She had a corset under her dress and when she removed it, her stomach stretched out, and it was huge. I remember thinking it was funny that she was thin everywhere but her stomach."

"You think she could have been pregnant?"

"Absolutely. Unless she had a tumor in her stomach, which she didn't."

Malena's head felt light. She rested it on her hand. "But wait. She had another boyfriend besides my father. Victor. I just read about him. He left her because he was going to be a priest, and so she decided to marry my father." She dropped her hand. "Something doesn't fit in this picture. Why would she give me away if she was engaged to my father anyway?"

"Well, what if her child wasn't Enrique's, but Victor's?"

"But Enrique raised me. I must be his."

"Maybe she didn't love Enrique and didn't want to live with him."

Malena hugged her waist. "Are you sure it was Abigail you saw? It couldn't have been someone else?"

Javier was pensive for a moment. "No. I don't think it was anybody else, but I can't be completely sure. It was a long time ago."

"There's something else," she said. "After my father died, I found a stack of checks written to a man named Cesar Villamizar. I don't know why Enrique was paying him, but it turns out this man works for Sebastian at *El Heraldo*. Do you know him?"

"No. Do you think he may have had something to do with your father's suicide?"

"Maybe."

"This is what we'll do," he said. "Tomorrow, you go to the newspaper and meet this Cesar. Meanwhile, I'll see if I can find that newspaper clipping you saw in my aunt's desk."

She exhaled. "So that means you're not going to tell on me?"

He rolled his eyes.

Malena felt like hugging Javier, but she simply said, "Thank you."

The headquarters of *El Heraldo de San Isidro* were hard to miss. According to Javier's directions, all Malena had to do was find the one building that seemed most out of place in all of downtown. She spotted it immediately, across from the Iglesia de Santo Domingo. Somehow, she couldn't associate this ornate, industrial construction with this town, much less with Sebastian.

The building was as cold and gray as it looked from the outside, with marble floors and unusually high ceilings. After a slow elevator ride to the fifth floor, the doors opened with a squeak. She walked down a long corridor, the walls decorated with portraits of Sebastian's ancestors, the men who'd founded the newspaper. The last frame was a painting of Ignacio Rivas. Even if she hadn't looked at the label, she would have known this man was Sebastian's father.

Malena knocked on a door with a metal plaque that read PRESIDENCIA.

A round-faced woman with a kind smile and wide hips opened the door for her.

"*Buenos días,*" Malena said. "I'm here to see Mr. Rivas. My name is Liliana Paz."

"Follow me, please."

The foyer had a desk and a black leather sofa. Behind the desk was a closed door. The secretary entered the room. Malena could hear their voices, *his* voice, though she couldn't discern what they were saying.

After a minute or two, the secretary returned with Sebastian.

"Lili? What are you doing here?"

She ran her hands over her yellow sleeveless dress—another one of Amanda's gifts. "I was in the neighborhood and decided to stop by and see the newspaper. I hope I didn't catch you at a bad time."

"Well, I have a meeting with my editor coming up." He ran his fingers through his hair, resting his free hand on his hip. Christ Almighty, he looked so attractive when he did that. "But maybe Pamela can show you around? Or if you come back later, I can do it?"

It was tempting. To come back later. To spend that time with him. To see what he did all day. But she had to stay on task. He said he had a meeting with his editor, with Cesar.

"Your editor? Isn't that . . . what's his name? Cesar? My father's friend?"

He raised a brow. "Yes. That's him."

"Maybe this would be a good opportunity to meet him?"

"Sure . . . if that's what you want." He looked surprised, or maybe annoyed, or maybe he was just too busy for all this nonsense. "Pamela, would you call him in, please?"

While Pamela made the phone call, Sebastian turned to Malena. "Would you like something to drink? A coffee, an herbal tea, water?"

"No. Thank you. I'm fine."

His gaze meandered over her body, as if studying her new dress. One of his hands felt his front pocket. He fished for a cigarette from a box of Lucky Strikes.

"Cigarette?"

She shook her head, mesmerized by the grace of his movements, recalling the feel of his hands in hers, his arm around her waist, the smell of his neck. He lit the cigarette and took a drag. As he did, the lines in his forehead relaxed. His eyes didn't leave hers for a moment and the office, the building, didn't seem so cold anymore. But the heat was coming from inside of her. Traveling up her legs, through her core, all the way to her face. Under his gaze, she loosened her satin scarf a bit. Maybe she should have accepted the glass of water.

Pamela hung up the phone and sat in front of her typewriter. The minutes went by slowly, in a silence sporadically interrupted by Pamela's typing. Sebastian stared at Malena through a cloud of smoke. She smiled. And then, as if coming out of a trance, she realized she didn't have much of a plan. What would she say to this man, this Cesar? Was she supposed to speak to him in front of Sebastian?

A bald man walked into the office. He greeted everyone with a general "*Buenos días*" and stood in front of Sebastian, resting his thumbs behind his suspenders. Malena had never seen him before. She'd been hoping that somehow she would recognize him and know exactly who he was.

Sebastian held his cigarette between his thumb and index finger. "Cesar, this is Miss Liliana Paz. She's Manuel Paz's daughter. She says you and her father are good friends."

Cesar studied her.

"Manuel Paz?" He repeated after Sebastian.

What had she done? Exposing herself in this manner in front of Claudia's fiancé? She might as well shout her real name to all who could hear.

"Yes," Sebastian said. "Married to María Teresa Santos?"

"Oh, yes, yes." Cesar smirked at Malena and offered his hand to her.

Say something! This is your chance! But Malena's mind had gone blank. Sebastian must think she was an idiot for sure.

The ringing phone interrupted their awkward silence.

"*Presidencia?*" Pamela said. "Yes, he's here." She covered the receiver with her hand, her nails the color of a ripe tomato. "It's for you, Mr. Rivas. The mayor."

"If you'll excuse me, Lili. I must take this phone call." He grasped the phone. "Señor Alcalde, what an honor."

Cesar was scrutinizing her. "So, Señorita, how can I help you?"

Malena turned her back on Sebastian and Pamela.

"Mr. Villamizar, the truth is my father asked me to talk to you about a friend the two of you have in common. See, my father has been trying to locate this friend for a while now and thought you might know something about him."

Cesar smiled gallantly. "Of course, Señorita Paz. I'd be glad to help. What is his name?"

"Hugo Sevilla."

Cesar's jaw tensed the instant she uttered her father's assumed name. He glanced at Sebastian before speaking.

"I've never heard that name before."

"How strange," Malena said. "I'm certain my father mentioned your name. I think he said something about Hugo owing you money."

"Your father must have me confused with someone else, Señorita."

Malena peeked at Sebastian. He was watching them while on the phone.

"Now if you'll excuse me," Cesar said. "I have to prepare for an important meeting."

He left the office before she could respond.

Sebastian hung up the phone. "Is everything all right?"

"Yes, Sebastian." She extended her hand toward him. "Thank you very much for your time. I won't distract you anymore." They shook hands. She removed hers promptly and headed for the door before he could say more.

She rushed down the hall. Cesar was the one she was looking for. He'd known her father. She could see it in his eyes.

259

But what had been their connection? Was this man involved in his death? She had to talk to Javier. He would know what to do. As she waited for the elevator, a memory flashed through her mind. She recalled her phone conversation with Julia. She'd mentioned something about a strange visitor the night before Papá had died, and she said they'd gotten into a fight. Julia had described him as a bald, thin man in his early fifties.

Just like Cesar.

Now that Malena so desperately needed to talk to Javier, he was busy with a client. Malena squeezed behind the counters and walked toward the back office, exchanging a meaningful glance with Javier. She would wait for him there since Claudia and Rafael were also in the store tending to other customers.

Amanda's voice echoed from the hallway, raised in anger. She was in Alejandra's workshop. Malena entered the storage room and shut the door. From there, she could hear Amanda's voice.

"I know you took it!" she was saying.

"I don't know what you're talking about," Alejandra answered in a cool, controlled voice.

"Well, you're the only person in this house who would have an interest in getting into my things. Or should I say one thing in particular?"

"Have you gone crazy?"

"Stop playing the fool, please. We're too old for these games. We both know you've wanted to get your hands on Abigail's diary for a long time."

Alejandra raised her voice. "You're wrong. I have no interest in that diary."

"Have you forgotten I found you burning it in the fireplace?"

After a short silence, Alejandra spoke. "That was years ago. I told you Abigail asked me to do it. Besides, why would I want to get it now?"

"That's what I would like to know!"

"Amanda. You're being ridiculous. I'm not the one fixated on that diary. I'm not the one holding on to something that doesn't belong to me knowing my sister wanted it destroyed."

Abigail wanted it destroyed?

"I'm not *fixated* on it," Amanda said.

There was a knock on the door. Malena took a leap, thinking for a minute that someone was knocking on the storage room. Neither one of the sisters answered.

"I still don't understand why you hold on to it," Alejandra said.

"It's one of the few memories we have of Abigail."

The knocking grew louder.

"I already told you. I didn't take your key."

"So if it wasn't you, then who took it?" Amanda's tone softened.

"I. Don't. Know. Now, if you don't mind, I'd like to get back to work. I'm busy and I can't stand the smell of your perfume."

When whoever was at the door knocked again, both sisters yelled back.

"What?"

Trinidad's shy voice responded. "Doña Amanda, I found your key. It was lying by your bed."

There was a short silence. Malena leaned her head closer to the door, touching the wood with her cheek. In a muffled voice, Amanda apologized to her sister. Then came the noise of a door shutting, followed by steps, and then the unmistakable sound of Alejandra's drill.

Malena stood in the dark storage room. She couldn't believe the way Amanda had talked to Alejandra. She'd never heard those two arguing like that. It was always Ana who fought with Amanda. Had it really been Abigail who wanted the diary destroyed, or was it Alejandra?

Chapter 38

⚜

Alejandra, 1941

The accounting lessons with Enrique weren't working. Nothing was. Especially now that Abigail had volunteered to go to Tabacundo with Ana to help her get established there. Since they had left—over three months ago—Enrique had been more distracted than usual and Alejandra was frankly sick of numbers. Not even the love of your life was worth all this work, much less a simple crush. But when Alejandra saw Enrique walking into her dining room with the accounting text-book under his arm and those spectacles he wore sometimes, she remembered why she'd come up with this silly excuse to be near him. He *was* the love of her life, and suddenly all this work made sense. She would have studied Quantum Physics if it meant being close to him.

"Shall we start?" Enrique said.

She opened her ledger for him to review her homework. As he checked her numbers, Alejandra focused on the way Enrique moved his lips as he read her work, the way his index finger rested on his forehead, the tiny mole on his cheek. She fanta-sized about him shoving all the books to the floor, grabbing her by the waist, and kissing her passionately on the table.

"Where's your balance sheet?" he said.

262

"Sure."

He turned to her, and they were only centimeters apart. She could smell the mint candy he was sucking. "Your balance sheet."

"Oh." She searched for the paper inside the leather bag by her feet. "Where did I leave it?"

Enrique sighed, and that frustrated look he often gave her—but never to Abigail—appeared on his face again. "Alejandra, I've told you to keep your things in order. It's fundamental when you're dealing with numbers."

She hated that condescending tone he used sometimes, as if she were a child and he was the parent. One day, he would realize she wasn't a child, and he would pay for his indifference.

The doorbell rang.

She jumped up to get it, relieved for the interruption. She scurried through the foyer and opened the door.

It was Edgar Carrasco from across the street.

"Good afternoon, Alejandra," he said, unable to look her in the eye. Since they'd met in the park, so many years ago, he'd always been a little shy around her. Intimidated, almost. He extended his arm, offering her a black leather purse that looked a lot like her mother's. "I believe this is Doña Blanca's. I found it in one of the pews at church. Her wallet is inside."

"Thank you."

Enrique walked out of the dining room in the direction of the lavatory.

Alejandra raised her voice. "I would love to go out with you for ice cream, Edgar, but unfortunately I'm in the middle of class."

Edgar's eyes widened. "I beg your pardon?"

She winked at him. "Maybe another afternoon, yes?"

"S-s-sure." He blushed.

She glanced over her shoulder. Enrique stood by the lavatory door, but he hadn't entered yet.

"Actually, I have a better idea," Alejandra told Edgar. "Why don't you and your father come over for dinner tonight? I'm sure my mother would be delighted." The leather felt stiff between her hands.

Edgar scratched his forehead. "Thank you. I'll tell my father."

"Would seven o'clock work for you?"

"I suppose."

"All right then, I'll see you tonight." She closed the door even though Edgar was still standing there.

Grinning, she walked past Enrique to the dining room.

"Excuse me, *Profesor.*"

<hr />

Mamá Blanca wasn't exactly delighted to have company with such short notice, though she was grateful for recovering her purse.

"What did you expect me to do?" Alejandra opened the oven for her mother. "I couldn't just say 'thank you' and shut the door."

Mamá Blanca placed two chickens inside. "Yes, but you could've at least invited them for tomorrow, so I could fix a proper meal—not this."

"It didn't occur to me."

"What am I going to tell your father?"

"Oh, don't worry about it. I'll handle my father."

Her father's anger was well worth it when she remembered Enrique's astonished expression in the foyer. She wanted to prove to Enrique that she could attract other men, give him a little taste of jealousy to wipe off that confident smile from his face. He must have known she liked him. Only a blind man wouldn't notice. Well, it was time for him to stop being so sure about her. Jealousy would make him realize that he loved her and not Abigail.

It was so frustrating that Enrique was Abigail's beau, espe-cially because she didn't love him. Alejandra had read her sister's diary and knew she loved that *seminarista*, Victor-something-or-other. So why wouldn't she just break up with Enrique? It would have been the moral thing to do. Enrique shouldn't be anybody's alternate. On top of everything else, Abigail had abandoned him without even setting a wedding day; disregard-ing Enrique's feelings for her, treating him as if he were a joke. No, Alejandra didn't feel guilty in the least about taking her sister's beau from her. Really. She didn't.

Edgar Carrasco and his father, Don Tomás, the best barber in town—as proclaimed by *El Heraldo de San Isidro*—arrived five minutes before seven. Both sported new haircuts, prob-ably given by each other, and repeatedly wiped their feet on the foyer rug. Papá Pancho didn't even attempt to look pleased with the neighbors' visit, as unhappy as he was with the invi-tation. ("How much is this going to cost? What am I going to talk about? Don't you know we have inventory today?") But Alejandra had insisted that it was the only decent thing to do after they had recovered Mamá Blanca's purse and wallet and since, as her mother had attested, not a single coin was missing.

They sat around the table in uncomfortable silence until Mamá Blanca asked Don Tomás where he was originally from. Don Tomás's eyes shone as he described in great length the arrival of the first Carrasco to Ecuador, and how some of his ancestors had been direct messengers for the King of Spain. As he spoke, Papá Pancho yawned so widely that Alejandra had to elbow her father, mostly in an effort to put her blood back in circulation again. Fausto laughed out loud, a good thing after he'd been glaring at Edgar since he arrived. Alejandra didn't like how her cousin looked at the barber's son as though he was dirt.

When Alejandra thought she couldn't stand this gathering any longer, Enrique entered the dining room, ledger in hand.

"Good evening." He approached Alejandra's father and handed him the accounting book. "I'm done."

Alejandra perked up when Enrique turned in her direction. She straightened her back and ran her fingers through her loose hair. He looked into her eyes for a brief moment before turning to Edgar. Alejandra touched Edgar's arm.

"So Edgar, what do you prefer: cutting or shaving?"

Edgar gave her the same puzzled look he'd given her in the afternoon. "Cutting."

While Papá Pancho reviewed the book through the spectacles resting on the tip of his nose, Enrique glanced at the faces across the room. He looked more serious than usual. Of course, it had been rude not to invite him, being Abigail's fiancé and all.

As if reading Alejandra's thoughts, Mamá Blanca stood up. "Enrique, please join us for dinner."

"Thanks, Doña Blanca. Maybe some other time. I just want to go home now."

"Looks good, son." Papá Pancho handed him the ledger. "I'll see you tomorrow."

"Well, then, good night to all." Enrique left without giving Alejandra a second glance.

Alejandra followed him through the foyer.

He opened the front door.

"Enrique. Wait."

He gave her a blank stare.

"I just wanted to tell you . . ." She told herself to shut up, she'd already made a mess of things and she obviously had no idea how to win a man's heart, but the words came out before she could stop them. "Not to come tomorrow."

His eyes narrowed. "Why not?"

"Well . . ." She removed the cloth napkin from her skirt's waistband. "I have plans for the afternoon."

"With that barber?"

Was that mockery in his tone?

She raised her chin. "Yes."

"That's fine." He put on his hat. "Maybe we should suspend the classes as you seem to be more interested in"—he paused—"other things."

She followed him outside the house, the blood in her veins boiling. "That's it? You're not going to do anything?"

"Anything about what?"

"About this. About us."

"Us? There's no us. I'm engaged to your sister, remember?"

She sighed. "My sister left you."

"She didn't leave me. She only went to help Ana with her move to the country."

Alejandra was about to tell him about Victor, but something stopped her. "Fine. If that's the way you see it. You're probably right. We should end the classes." She crossed her arms and kicked a stone on the pavement.

He raised his hand, as if he was going to touch her cheek, but dropped it before she could feel his fingers on her skin. "I'm sorry, Alejandra. You're a wonderful girl, and smarter than I gave you credit for."

He patted her arm, as if she were some cute puppy. She recoiled from his touch. She didn't care about being smart or wonderful. Those were not the words she wanted to hear.

"I'm sure you'll find a good man. This Edgar fellow, for example."

"You're a coward, Enrique Hidalgo."

He shoved his hands in his pockets. She went into the house and slammed the door shut.

For the next two weeks Alejandra didn't show her face in the store. And her body couldn't stand it anymore. Seeing Enrique was a physical necessity, like breathing, eating, or sleeping, and she couldn't deprive her body any longer.

She'd gotten a new haircut that morning. It was shoulder-length and her natural wavy hair curled up at the tips. She'd asked the hairdresser to lend her a bit of red lipstick and rouge. This time, though, she was careful not to overdo it. When she arrived in her father's store, she immediately spotted Enrique leaning on the counter, adding up numbers on a piece of paper, tapping the pencil against his chin. Across from him, behind the other counter, Fausto talked to a customer.

She advanced toward Enrique, zipping and unzipping her purse a dozen times. Fausto scowled at her but didn't address her, busy as he was with a counter full of necklaces and a picky woman who asked to see more pieces.

Enrique glanced up and his eyes widened upon seeing her.

"Is my father here?" Alejandra asked him.

"No. He stepped out for a minute." Enrique returned his attention to his long addition.

"Fine then. I'll wait for him in the workshop."

She walked past him to the back of the store. How could she love someone who infuriated her this much? Up until she'd met Enrique, Fausto was the only person who could make her this angry.

She blasted into her father's workshop, uncertain of what to do. From the beginning, her relationship with Enrique—if you could call it that—had reminded her of a bull and a bullfighter. She was the bull trying to catch him from every possible angle, and he was the bullfighter, skillfully avoiding her with his red cape. Or was it the other way around? She could almost hear a massive "*Olé!*" every time she failed in her attempts to get him. Maybe she should just quit while she still had her dignity. Enrique had been so indifferent to her in the store it was obvious he didn't care about not seeing her anymore. He didn't even comment on her new hairdo, whereas she had noticed everything about him, like how well that blue suit fitted him or how exceptionally attractive he looked without his glasses. She grabbed a cone-shaped ring mandrel and threw it across the room. The metal crashed against the concrete floor, breaking the silence in the workshop.

Less than a minute later, Enrique stormed into the room. "What was that?"

Maybe subconsciously she'd been trying to call him. She disguised her excitement behind a scowl. "I just dropped something."

He followed her gaze to the floor, where the metal mandrel lay.

He picked it up and strolled toward her. "So how have you been? I haven't seen you in a while." He placed the mandrel on the desk. "No, that's not true. I saw you yesterday with that barber."

So he had been watching her when she crossed the street to visit Edgar—just to make Enrique jealous. "Yes, Edgar is such a sweetheart, and we have so much in common."

"Oh, I'm sure. Did he give you that haircut?"

"Of course not. He's a barber."

Enrique waved a hand in dismissal.

She leaned on her father's desk and inserted a ring inside the mandrel. "It's so nice to finally meet a man who talks about something other than numbers."

"A man or a boy?"

"Edgar is so romantic." She grabbed a piece of sandpaper and rubbed the rough edges of the ring with it. "He brought me flowers, you know?"

And he had, but the flowers had been for Mamá Blanca in gratitude for dinner the other night.

"I'm glad to hear that. Everyone should find love."

She sighed. "And I have, finally."

He was quiet for a moment, arms across his chest. "Then if you're so in love, why did you come here to see me?"

She sanded the ring harder. "You're so arrogant. I didn't come here to see you. I came to talk to my father."

"You did? What about?"

"About . . . working for him."

He laughed. "That's what you said last time, I believe. Back when you convinced him you wanted to be an accountant."

"Well, I changed my mind." She was sanding so hard now that the dust was filling up her skirt. "I thought accounting would be interesting, but it's not." She glanced up at him. He was standing much closer than she'd thought. "But maybe it's the teacher. Or maybe it's just not my thing." She returned her attention to the ring.

"Then you want to be a clerk, like your sister?"

"No." She definitely did not want to be anything like her sister. As the ring became smoother, the idea became clearer. It was so simple, why hadn't she ever thought of that? "I want to be a jeweler."

"A woman jeweler?" He chuckled. "Your father would never allow it."

"Watch me."

He took another step. His legs were nearly touching hers. She raised her eyes. He was breathing rapidly, as if he were upset. They'd never been this close before, not even when he would explain something to her in the dining room, side by side.

"You were right," he said.

"About what?"

"That day. When you called me a coward."

He placed his hands on top of hers, circling the mandrel. "Are you really in love with that boy?"

"No."

He released one of his hands and caressed her cheek. "I kept wanting to see you as a girl, not a woman."

Her face burned like never before. Good thing the room was dim or he would have noticed. He kissed her mouth softly at first, but with growing fervor as she drew closer to him. She'd never been kissed like this. She didn't know what was happening to her body, why it was becoming so feeble and warm at the same time. In the back of her mind, she could almost hear a crowd yelling *"Torero, torero, torero."*

The door startled them. Enrique took a step back while Alejandra faced her cousin's glare.

"What's going on here?" Fausto demanded.

"Nothing," Alejandra said. "I'm just waiting for my father. Why? What do you need?"

Fausto flashed an envelope in his hand. "You have a letter from Abigail," he told Enrique. "Your future wife."

Chapter 39

Javier barged into the storage room and locked the door behind him. He flicked the light switch on and drew out Alejandra's newspaper clipping from his back pocket, handing it to Malena.

She read the headline in big bold letters. "Jeweler's nephew murdered. Suspect on the run."

"You said your father was Enrique Hidalgo, right?"

Malena glanced through the article. There was a picture of her father, when he was much younger, under the title. "Yes."

"Number one suspect," Javier said.

"This was the article in Alejandra's desk?"

"Yes."

"There has to be a mistake." She paced the room, a little frantic. "My father was not a murderer."

Javier sat on a chair. "Seems to me like you don't know much about your father."

She stopped in front of him. "True, but I know his essence. He would never kill anybody."

"It says here he was trying to rob the store. Maybe he killed Fausto so he wouldn't tell on him."

"But it doesn't make sense. He was an accountant. There would have been easier ways for him to steal other than opening the vault in the middle of the night."

"Good point."

"There's something else," she said. "This article was written by Cesar Villamizar."

"The reporter," Javier repeated, standing. "The same man your father was paying off."

"For his silence." She nibbled at her lower lip. "Cesar found my father. He must have been blackmailing him."

"That's a possibility."

"I met him this morning."

"And?"

"He acted nervous. He denied knowing Hugo Sevilla."

"We must talk to Sebastian."

She could taste the blood on her lip now. "Impossible. I'm not telling him who I am."

Javier ran one of his hands on the now-organized bookshelf. "I wish we still had those accounting books. If Enrique was robbing my grandfather, he would have surely altered the numbers."

"We do. I recovered them from the trash."

"Are you good with numbers?"

"Not at all."

"Neither am I." Javier rubbed his chin. "But Sebastian is. He was the best in my class."

"I don't want to involve him."

"Sebastian is discreet. We won't tell him who you are. Just that I want him to find out if anybody altered those accounting books, an old family mystery of sorts." He took the article from her hands. "It's perfect. I'll check the books with him. Meanwhile, you go to Cesar's desk and see if you can find anything linking him to your father."

"When?"

"I'll ask him if we can meet tonight."

Malena nodded, too shocked to make any decisions.

"Now I'd better return this article to Alejandra's desk before she gets back." Javier walked out of the storage room, leaving Malena lonelier than ever.

———⋊•⋉———

The hall to Sebastian's office seemed gloomier at nighttime. Malena's heels tapping against the marble were the only sounds in the building.

"We can't stay long." Javier held the trash bag in his hands as if it were a pot of gold. "I have to sing with the band tonight at ten."

"What did Sebastian say about me coming?"

"He doesn't know you're coming."

Great. How was she going to explain her presence? Sebastian was not dumb; he would think this whole situation was strange.

Javier knocked on the *Presidencia* door. Sebastian opened it, a cigarette resting between his lips. He raised his eyebrows when he saw her.

"She's helping me," Javier explained.

They walked past the secretary's empty desk into a spacious office. *His* office. Mahogany desk, austere leather seats, no family pictures, merely generic landscapes of Swiss mountains and streams. The place was clean except for the cigarette butts in the ashtray.

Sebastian offered them a couple of chairs in front of his desk and opened the first notebook. They sat there for a long time as Sebastian examined the numbers.

Sebastian flipped page after page, his index finger on his right temple, his stare locked on the numbers, his jaw tightened in concentration. He reminded Malena of her own father when he corrected exams. The two of them had so much in common.

They were both bright, owners of inscrutable minds and inexplicable behaviors. Was this some sort of Freudian obsession of hers? Seeing Sebastian like this, so professional and concentrated on the numbers in front of him, she would have never imagined he could dance the way he did. His love for tango was yet another trait he shared with her father.

As he picked up another notebook, Javier turned to her and nodded his chin toward the door. She stood up.

"Where is the lavatory?" she asked.

Sebastian raised his head. "Down the hall. Left door."

She walked out of his office. She wasn't looking forward to searching for Cesar's desk in this enormous building, as dark as it was. She wished now she had accepted the tour with Sebastian's secretary earlier.

Malena walked down the hall, avoiding the glances of the newspaper founders, yet feeling their eyes on her, probably demanding an explanation from her irregular presence in their halls. She'd never believed in ghosts, but the long faces of Sebastian's ancestors under the dim light made her wonder if they might visit this place from time to time. Her own steps seemed louder now, but there was no one behind her. She concentrated on her task: find the newsroom. Good thing the doors were labeled.

The newsroom was the last room at the end of the hall. The door's creak made her cringe. She turned on the light. A dozen desks were scattered throughout the room with no apparent order or pattern. Every desk had a typewriter and a sea of papers on it. Random sheets littered the floor, broken by a rugged path that wound toward a small office surrounded by glass windows in the back of the room.

Malena zigzagged through the maze and entered the office.

Inside, she turned on another light. The name plaque on the desk confirmed it was Cesar's. She searched through the drawers. She didn't know what she was looking for. Anything that would link him to her father. A bank statement, a letter, a photograph. She spotted his black leather address book and searched for Hugo Sevilla or Enrique Hidalgo. Neither name was in there.

In the corner of the room was a metal filing cabinet with six drawers. She opened the top one, her fingers flying through folders of articles and tear sheets. This was useless. There was too much information here. With so many papers it would be nearly impossible to find whatever she was looking for. The second, third, and fourth drawers had a similar setup and were equally crammed. From what she could see, the articles were filed by date, from the most recent to the oldest. She skipped drawers and opened the bottom one. This one was different. There were folders and envelopes piled on top of each other. She scanned through them until a name stopped her. *Enrique* was written in cursive on the front of a manila envelope.

She pulled it out of the drawer and opened the flap. There was only one newspaper clipping inside. An article from *El Universo,* Ecuador's leading newspaper, based in Guayaquil. She recognized the event in the picture immediately. It was the launching of her father's book, and there was a picture of him standing with Pedro. She read the caption: *Author Hugo Sevilla, left, and his coauthor, Pedro Córdova, right, at the book launch on Friday, September 1, 1961.*

Her father's face was circled with a black marker. There was another paper inside the envelope: her address in Guayaquil.

She returned the papers to the envelope. She didn't need to see anymore. She was certain now. This Cesar, this vile creature working for Sebastian, had been blackmailing her father for over a year.

Somehow, Malena composed herself before returning to Sebastian's office. She'd been tempted to take the envelope with her, but it would have been one more thing to guard from Claudia in the bedroom.

Javier stood as soon as he saw her by the door. "Everything okay?"

Sebastian raised his head and glanced at both of them. "I think I found something."

He turned two notebooks so Javier and Malena could see them. Paired side by side, the only thing obvious was that the handwriting was different.

"Was there another accountant at the time?" he asked.

"No," Javier said.

"The handwriting is different here." Sebastian lifted one of the notebooks. "And the numbers are a little bit off from the previous day."

"What are you implying?" Malena asked.

"That someone may in fact have been robbing the store." He removed his jacket. His shoulder muscles filled his cotton shirt. "We have to look for any notebooks with this same handwriting."

Javier glanced at his wristwatch. "I have to leave. The band starts playing in fifteen minutes."

"You go," Malena said. "I'll stay here and help Sebastian."

"Or we could just continue another day," Sebastian said.

"No," she said.

Both men looked at her, astounded by her tone. But she couldn't stop now, not when she was so close to finding out if her father had been a thief and a murderer. Malena leaned over the desk and grabbed a pile of notebooks.

"I'll take her home after we're done," Sebastian said.

"Excuse us for a moment." Javier gently pulled her outside Sebastian's office.

They stood behind the wall, by Pamela's desk. "You can't stay here," he whispered. "I told my mother I would only keep you out for a couple of hours."

"It doesn't matter, Javi. I have to stay. I found my father's picture in Cesar's office. We were right. He was blackmailing him. Maybe Sebastian knew about it, too."

"No. Not Sebastian."

"I'm not leaving this office until I get to the bottom of this."

After Javier left, Sebastian and Malena worked in silence, looking through the account books, comparing the handwriting. Soon, all the numbers mingled inside Malena's mind and her head felt like it would disintegrate. She sat back.

"Have you had enough yet?" he asked.

"I suppose."

"Did you find what you were looking for?"

She wasn't sure about what he meant.

He stood up and circled his desk. "That sure was a long trip to the bathroom." Had he been in on this too, with Cesar? Maybe he'd known who she was all along. Maybe they'd seen her in Guayaquil with her father. Her chest ached just thinking that he might have had something to do with her father's death.

She grabbed her purse. "Can you take me home now?"

He took a step toward her.

"Why don't you just tell me what this is all about?" he said. "I can probably help you better if I know."

There was a certain menace in his tone.

"Nothing is going on. I'm just trying to help Javier."

"Why the urgency of doing it tonight?"

"Because you're getting married tomorrow." Her voice faltered. "Who knows when you'll be available after that."

He wouldn't look her in the eye. "Why this sudden interest in something that happened over twenty years ago?"

"That's Javier's business."

"And what's your business? Why are you so invested in this?"

She shrugged. "Just trying to be helpful."

"Of course. You have to help your boyfriend."

"I already told you. He's not my boyfriend."

"And the married man is?"

God, Lili's bad reputation loomed over her like a dark cloud.

"I don't have a boyfriend." She put on her coat. "Can we go now?"

"Who are you?" he said.

She froze for a minute. "What do you mean?"

"You're not Liliana Paz."

That was it. He knew who she was. He'd been part of the blackmail.

She patted his arm. "You have an overactive imagination. Now can we please leave?"

She squeezed past him out the office door, leaving the accounting books behind. She circled the secretary's desk and the seating area, nearly running, his steps following her through the hallway. She reached the elevator and entered as soon as the doors opened. He placed his hands on the doorsill to prevent the doors from closing.

"What are you doing in San Isidro?" he said.

"What makes you think I'm not Liliana?"

"Well, for one, you said you were going to tell your father about Cesar, but according to my mother, Lili's father has been dead for five years."

What an idiot she was! She'd assumed all along that Lili's father was alive and she'd talked about him as though he were. She pressed the first-floor button repeatedly as if the doors could somehow break through Sebastian's palms.

She could see him debating whether to walk into the elevator or not. He examined the inside of the elevator, as if he were seeing it for the first time. His eyes focused on its ceiling, a drop of perspiration trickling down his temple.

After a moment, which seemed like an hour, he took a step inside. The color drained from his cheeks as the doors shut behind him. He looked about the tight space.

"Are you okay?" she asked.

He undid the top button of his shirt and loosened his tie.

"What's wrong, Sebastian?"

"I don't like elevators." He ran his palm over his forehead. "I got trapped here when I was small."

She advanced toward him. Never before had she seen him this vulnerable. She held his cold hand in hers and squeezed it. He remained still for a moment, looking at the floor while the elevator started its slow descent.

After a moment, he raised his head. She caressed his cool cheek.

"It's going to be fine," she said.

He glanced down at her, and she became conscious of what she was doing, of his proximity. She had broken an unspoken rule. She had *touched* Sebastian. The only time she was allowed to touch him was when they were dancing.

His arm circled her waist, pulling her close to him. His other hand lifted her chin and he lowered his face. His lips were soft and warm. With his free hand he caressed her cheek, as if it were a precious object. The heat of his body transferred to hers and soon enough, she was responding. She dug her fingers in his hair, then slid her hands down his neck and the curve of his shoulders, barely believing this was real. Holding her face with both hands, Sebastian pushed her against the elevator wall and kissed her possessively, as if he'd been wanting this as much as she had, as if no one else mattered in the world. And at the moment no one else did. She'd never felt this wanted before, this fulfilled. Her knees weakened and she didn't know if they would be able to hold her weight much longer. The more he kissed her, the less control she had over her body.

"I've wanted to do this for so long," he said, his mouth traveling to her chin and neck and then back to her lips.

She wanted to tell him how much she loved him, beg him not to marry Claudia. It felt like the right time, but she couldn't bring herself to do it.

The minute the elevator doors opened, he pulled away from her. He ran his fingers through his hair, the way he'd done that morning, back when she could only imagine what his lips tasted like. The two of them stared at each other, gasping for air, as if they'd just finished a race.

"I apologize." He dodged her eyes. "This can never happen again."

She picked her purse from the floor. Of course it couldn't happen again. Tomorrow he would be Claudia's husband.

They walked out of the building, side by side, toward a blue Ford parked on the back street. The cool air caressed her burning face, offering a minor relief. She was conscious of Sebastian's closeness, more so than before, and strayed away from him as they reached the car. *What* had just happened there? It had been surreal.

He unlocked the door for her, his hands slightly trembling. Inside, he lowered his window and started the car.

"So you're not going to tell me," he said.

She looked at a light post in the street. "What?"

"Who you are."

Malena resented the businesslike tone he was using. He couldn't just pretend that the moment in the elevator had never happened, could he? She spoke without removing her eyes from the light. "I would tell you, if I knew who I was, but I don't."

He turned off the ignition and faced her, puzzled.

"You're right," she said. "I'm not Liliana. My name is Malena Sevilla."

He didn't seem surprised when she said her real name, at least not like Javier had been. He simply nodded, as if he'd been expecting this for a long time, as if he'd known her name all along and was simply acknowledging it.

"I came to San Isidro to find my mother," she said.

The growing shadows of the night made it impossible for Malena to read the expression on his face. Was it anger, curiosity, disdain? She continued speaking anyway. As she told him her story, he lit a cigarette and gazed at the empty street through the windshield. She talked for a long time, so long she was out of breath by the time she was done. Nothing seemed to faze Sebastian until she mentioned Cesar Villamizar's apparent connection to her father. His jaw tensed.

"You don't believe it?" Malena asked.

"What?"

"That Cesar was blackmailing my father? It's the only thing I can come up with."

"No. I believe it." He was pensive for a moment.

"I'm sorry I lied." She studied the slightest movement of his eyes to make sure he didn't hate her.

"You did what you had to do," he said. "But I don't think you'll be able to keep it up much longer."

"What do you think I should do?"

"Confess."

"I don't think I can."

"You will." He started the car. "When the right time comes."

As he drove away from *El Heraldo,* she glanced back at the strange building, knowing she would never see it the same way after tonight. They were quiet during the five-minute ride to the Platas home. Malena remembered the way he'd kissed her in the elevator, the feel of his body against hers. It had only been fifteen minutes ago, yet it seemed like a wall had grown between them since. She glanced at his right hand as he changed gears and his left one as he rested it over the steering wheel. She wanted to memorize everything about him, now that she had him near, perhaps for the last time in her life. If she were a different kind of woman, she might tell him how she felt, or ask him to kiss her again, but a relationship between them was impossible. Especially now that she was growing fond of Claudia.

He parked a block away from Joyería Platas. "I don't want anyone—"

"You don't have to say anything. I understand." There was a hollow sensation in her chest. She was *the other* woman, and as such, deserved a different kind of treatment. She had to be dropped off in the dark, a block away from her house, so nobody would see them. Had her mother lived the same humiliation with her father?

"*Buenas noches, Sebastian.*" She opened the door before he had a chance to do it and rushed outside so he wouldn't see the tears in her eyes.

With every one of her steps a tear slid down her cheek. She cried for Sebastian, for the love she had found and lost on the same night; she cried for her father and the torment he must have lived with Cesar's persecution during that entire year. And she cried over her innocence lost, for she had never imagined her father—the man she admired and strived to please for years—to be a murderer, to have taken someone else's life. She remembered now Mamá Blanca's words when she told her about Fausto's death. She'd called his killer a "despicable" man. Malena couldn't reconcile that adjective with the image of her father smiling at her from across the dining room table. By the time she reached the Platas home, her shoulders shook uncontrollably.

She fought the urge to scream, to hit the door. She'd better compose herself before she walked in. She took a deep breath, drying her tears with her gloves, and removed the key Javier had given her from her purse. Trying to sleep would be useless; she knew that much, especially if she didn't know for sure what had been going on between her father and Cesar. She slipped quietly into the house and headed for the study.

She shut the door and picked up the phone, whispering Pedro's number to the operator.

It took several rings before a raspy man's voice answered.

"Pedro?"

She could picture his big round face and his white *guayabera* shirt stretched over his gigantic belly. He always wore it, and it always had sweat stains under his armpits. The last time she'd seen him had been at the funeral, when Pedro had refused to answer her questions about her father's suicide.

There was a short silence at the other end of the line. "Who is this?"

"Malena Sevilla."

Pedro's voice turned agitated, urgent. "What's wrong? Where are you? I've been so worried about you. Your neighbor said you left town."

"Pedro, I need you to answer me truthfully. Was there someone blackmailing my father?"

Her question was met with silence.

"Pedro, please. Whatever you promised my father, you have to let it go. I need to know."

After a moment, he finally answered. "Yes."

"Who?"

"A reporter who knew"—he paused and sighed—"his real name."

"And what he had done?" she finished.

"How did you find out?"

"That doesn't matter. Tell me, why did he kill himself?"

"That man, the reporter, wanted more money for his silence. He told your father that if he didn't pay more, he would tell the police where he was. The morning of his death, Hugo said he was going to La Previsora to get a loan. He must have not gotten the money."

Malena shivered when she heard the name of the building from which her father had jumped.

"He was so tired of hiding, Malenita. He'd been running away for twenty years."

"Why didn't he tell me anything? I could have helped."

"He didn't want you to think less of him. He didn't want to get you involved. That's why he made me promise not to tell you anything."

"So he killed Fausto. It's true."

Pedro's silence only confirmed her statement.

She brought her hand to her chest. "Why did he do it?"

"That I don't know. I swear. He never said."

Chapter 40

Malena hated to admit it, but Claudia looked stunning in her empire-waist satin wedding gown. The lace sleeves themselves were a work of art and the embroidery of the skirt must have taken hours of labor.

"Isn't she lovely?" Ana asked.

Malena faced the window so neither one of them would see the tears threatening to come out. With her finger, she wiped a black tear rolling down her cheek. Good-bye mascara.

Ana hugged her daughter and gave her a kiss on the cheek. "Are you happy, *hija*?"

"Yes, Mamita."

As discreetly as possible, Malena removed a compact mirror and wiped the smeared makeup with a tissue.

"I'd better go get dressed," Ana said. "It's getting late."

"And you're not going to change?" Claudia asked Malena after Ana left the room.

Malena glanced at the delicate lemon lace gown waiting for her on her bed, the one the nice seamstress had sewn for her. A dress especially made for her. Who would have thought? Ordinarily Malena would have been ecstatic to wear this beautiful outfit. Not today, though.

Malena removed her bath robe and put the crinoline over her undergarments, followed by the sleeveless dress. She wore her silver sun pendant today. She needed to feel her grandmother Eva near her heart; to give her strength during this ordeal.

Claudia was looking at her through the vanity mirror.

"Do you need help with your veil?" Malena asked.

"Not yet." Claudia turned around. "I want to speak to you first."

Malena couldn't read Claudia's detached expression.

"I want to apologize for all the things I told you the day of the bus accident."

"You don't need to. I also said some ugly things to you."

"Can I ask you something?"

Malena didn't like the sound of that, or the serious look on Claudia's face.

"Who is Malena?"

Malena's legs nearly faltered; she held on to the bed pole.

"Malena?" she repeated her own name. It sounded foreign coming from Claudia.

Malena had known it was a matter of time before everyone found out—and Claudia knowing meant *everyone* would find out. But why was this so hard? The thought of losing her place in the family pained her. No more talks with Mamá Blanca, or walking along those squeaky floors, the smell of Trinidad's kitchen, following Amanda across town, dancing at the Madreselva, or that feeling of belonging, of being part of a family.

Claudia stood up and opened her night table drawer. She removed two pieces of paper and handed them to Malena.

Even without touching the papers, Malena knew what they were. Her father's last note. Her mother's letter to her grandmother Eva. How could she have been so careless? She should have tossed both letters, the same way she did with Lili's, and not given in to stupid sentimentalism. She should have seen this coming. She'd seen Claudia snooping before. It was ironic, in a way. There she was, spying on everyone in the house, peeking through drawers and other people's correspondence, when all along, Claudia had been spying on her. Life had a way of making things even, fair.

"I am Malena."

Claudia's eyes widened. She recovered the papers from Malena's hands and read through them, as if attempting to connect the dots. "And who is A?"

"I still don't know," Malena said. "One of your aunts or . . ." She lowered her voice. "Maybe your mother."

"I knew it. The minute I saw that birthmark, I knew you were one of us."

One of us.

"Where is Lili then?" Claudia asked.

"In Quito, with her boyfriend."

"You met her? Are you a friend of hers?"

"No."

"Who else knows about this?"

"Your brother and . . ." she stopped herself.

Claudia finished the sentence for her. "Sebastian."

Malena stared at the wrinkled paper in Claudia's hand.

"You love him?" Claudia asked.

Malena sat on the bed. "Sebastian would never betray you. He loves you and he's going to marry you."

"That doesn't answer my question."

Malena's hands were trembling.

"Last night, you were crying for him," Claudia said. "You must love him."

A knock on the door interrupted the thick silence that had grown between them.

"Please, don't say anything," Malena said. "Wait until after the wedding. I don't want to ruin this day for everyone."

Without saying a word, Claudia opened her door.

Alejandra walked in, wearing an emerald green ball gown. She held a small box in her hands.

"I wanted to bring your wedding present before all the craziness begins," she told Claudia. As she handed the box to her niece, she glanced at Malena, as if she had just noticed her presence. "It was my father's tradition to give a necklace to his daughters when they got married, and I thought he would have liked it if I did the same with you."

Malena looked away, glad to be wearing a wide skirt to cover the tremor of her legs. She could almost hear Claudia accusing her, telling Alejandra that an impostor stood before them.

As Claudia unwrapped her present, Malena could feel Alejandra's eyes on her. Self-consciously, she touched her low chignon. For once, every hair seemed to be in its proper place, thanks to Amanda's magical hands, but Malena didn't like to be the subject of anybody's examination, especially someone she admired, someone like Alejandra.

"Thank you, Tía." Claudia removed an exquisite pearl necklace from the box.

Malena collected her ample skirt with both hands and gave one last pleading look to Claudia before heading for the door.

"I'll be downstairs."

—————

Sebastian, in a black tuxedo, was talking to the priest at the end of the nave. The pain in Malena's chest expanded like a hurricane all the way to her extremities and swept through the tips of her fingers. She sat in the last pew at the back of the church. She doubted she'd be able to sit through the entire ceremony. Did Claudia even want her here anymore?

Sebastian's mother entered the church. Malena hadn't seen the woman since the New Year's incident and was surprised to see her looking so elegant.

Ofelia stopped beside her. "Liliana, right? I never got a chance to thank you for taking care of me that night." She patted Malena's back. "And for washing my shawl."

"You're welcome."

Ofelia looked at her pendant. "I like your dress."

"Thank you, Doña."

Ofelia's approval felt good, even though Sebastian would never be hers. In only a few minutes, she would lose him forever—not that she ever had him.

Ofelia waved at her son. He waved back. His gaze drifted to Malena for an instant. But he quickly diverted his attention to the priest.

During the next thirty minutes, the church filled up. There was no sign of Claudia yet, but it was customary for the bride to be late. As the minutes passed, family members dashed in and out of the church and whispered into each other's ears.

A stiff Sebastian stood by the altar.

After an endless wait, Rafael appeared at the entrance. Malena pressed her fingers so hard against each other her knuckles turned white. She'd been hoping something—anything—would stop this ceremony.

Javier approached his father. Rafael told him something. Javier crossed the nave toward the altar. He stopped by Sebastian, held his arm and whispered in his ear.

What was happening?

The color drained from Sebastian's face. He found Malena's eyes among the crowd and held her gaze for a second. What was going on? Removing his arm from Javier's grasp, Sebastian retraced his steps down the aisle. He kept his head up during the entire walk to the entrance while murmurs grew louder around him.

After he'd left the church, the priest spoke.

"Brothers and sisters, I regret to tell you there's been a problem with the bride, and there won't be a wedding today."

The murmurs grew into loud rumblings all around Malena. On impulse, she exited the pew and hurried after Sebastian.

"Please step out of the church in an orderly fashion," the priest was saying as she darted outside.

In the street, Sebastian had already started his car.

"Sebastian! Wait!"

She raised her skirt and attempted to run after him, but it was too late. The tires of his Ford squealed as he sped down the narrow road.

After a moment, the curb filled up with people, pointing at Sebastian's car, eager to make sense of what had happened. It would probably be a long time before people stopped talking about today. Javier squeezed through the crowd toward her.

"Here you are," he said.

"What happened? Where's Claudia?"

He whispered in her ear. "She ran away."

"How?"

He took her aside. "She told my father to stop the car, claiming she felt sick and needed a bathroom. They stopped at a restaurant and she went inside. My father waited for a long time and seeing that she wasn't coming out, asked the owner to open the door. She wasn't in there anymore. She had left through the window."

Claudia left? She couldn't believe it.

"Now my parents and Mamá Blanca are going home to see if they can find her. My aunts and I are going to the reception hall to cancel the party."

"I'll go with you." Malena clung to Javier's arm, for her preservation instinct told her it would be better to be away from the house when Claudia told the family about her.

The sun was already setting when Malena returned home with Javier, Amanda, and Alejandra. She drew close to Javier as the four of them entered the foyer. She'd imagined yells and hysterical cries welcoming them into the house, but the voices in the living room were soft and mellow.

"They're here," Mamá Blanca said.

There were no signs of destruction to any of the furniture in the living room and Claudia was not there. Ana, Rafael, Mamá Blanca, and a woman Malena had never seen before sat with *aplanchados* and coffee.

Alejandra grabbed Malena's arm, as if to prevent her from taking another step. It was the first time Alejandra had ever touched her. She looked into the woman's eyes. Was that fear in them? There was a strange tension in the room, but she couldn't quite pinpoint what it was. Ana approached Malena.

"Aren't you going to say hello to your mother?"

My mother? Malena was confused. She looked around. Javier looked as equally puzzled as Malena. Alejandra tightened her grasp on Malena's arm.

Malena turned to the redheaded woman sitting by Mamá Blanca. She was pleasant-looking, dignified, and probably beautiful underneath that sunburned skin.

Ana held Malena's hand. "Your mother wanted to surprise you by coming to Claudia's wedding. I know you've had your problems but—"

"Who is this?" the woman asked.

Ana exchanged a bewildered look with Amanda. "Lili, of course."

The woman stared at her. "This is not my daughter."

When Malena realized she was standing in front of María Teresa, she wanted to die of shame. Of course Lili's mother would be coming to the wedding—she was Ana's best friend! How stupid of her not to consider that possibility.

"Lili?" A confused Mamá Blanca turned to Malena.

Malena looked at Amanda, standing beside her, speechless probably for the first time in her life, and then at Ana. It had come to this. The moment Malena had been dreading for weeks. The performance of her life was over.

Rafael's voice startled her. "If you're not Liliana, then who are you?"

291

She could lie again. She'd become an expert of deceit, but what good had that done (to anyone, really)? Her father, her grandmother, the Platas women, everyone had lied. And Malena, in her attempts to find the truth, had become the biggest liar of all.

"My name is Malena. I'm Enrique Hidalgo's daughter."

A silence as thick as glass threatened to cut through Malena's heart. She looked at the faces around her. What she read was disappointment, shock, disbelief. The pain in Mamá Blanca's eyes was so intense Malena was afraid she might never recover from it. The word "despicable" came to mind. Had she suddenly become as hateful as her father to Mamá Blanca?

María Teresa was the one to break the silence. "I don't understand. Where's Liliana?"

"She left with Juan Pablo," Malena said mechanically. "She's in Quito now." She paused and then whispered almost to herself. "I'm so sorry."

"In Quito?" María Teresa frowned. "Did she send you here to take her place?"

"No." Malena ran her hand by her forehead—it was burning. "It was just a confusion, a coincidence."

"A confusion?" María Teresa stood up. "Can you be more specific?"

"How could you lie to us? And why?" There was no trace of the usual sweetness in Mamá Blanca's voice.

"Is this about revenge?" Rafael said. "Of course, that no-good father of yours sent you here, didn't he?"

Malena couldn't get a word out. Worse yet, the reproach in her grandmother's eyes had left her cold.

"Well, speak up! What do you want from us?" Rafael asked. "Is this about money?"

"No!"

"Would you let her explain?" Javier said.

"Shut up, Javier! This is none of your business." Rafael crossed his arms. "Well, Miss Hidalgo, we're waiting."

Malena lifted her chin. "I came to find my mother."

"What mother?" Mamá Blanca asked.

"One of your daughters," Malena said.

Mamá Blanca looked around. "Who? What is she talking about?"

Malena looked at the Platas sisters, who'd turned mute since they entered the living room. At that moment she knew who her mother was. It was so clear now. It wasn't Abigail, the ghost, or Ana, the queen of this house, or Amanda, the tango dancer. Malena's eyes met Alejandra's as hers filled up with tears. Alejandra, the aloof artist, the admirable jeweler, the woman who silently supported the entire family. She had a vision of Alejandra standing in the park. It hadn't been a dream, Malena knew now. It had truly happened. She could see herself on the swing, watching her Grandmother Eva talking to the woman in the feathered hat. Her father arrived then, and called out her mother's name.

"Alejandra!"

She'd glanced at Malena on the swing. For an instant, their eyes had met, just like today, and Malena thought Alejandra was one of the most beautiful women she'd ever seen. She jumped off the swing, scraping her knees, and walked toward her. But Alejandra moved too fast. In the distance, Enrique caught up with her and held her arm. They exchanged a few words. Not long enough for Malena to reach them. Alejandra recovered her arm and entered a taxi parked by the curb.

"One of my daughters had a child with that monster?" Mamá Blanca shook her head, sat back on the couch. "Which one?" She was hyperventilating.

Alejandra took a step forward.

"No, Alejandrita. Not you." Mamá Blanca pressed her hand against her chest, grimacing. She held on to the rocking chair, about to collapse.

"Javier!" Amanda dashed toward her mother. "Go get Dr. Gaitán!"

Javier ran to the front door. Malena stood behind as the women surrounded Mamá Blanca. Her body was numb, her feet glued to the floor. She watched Alejandra in a daze, and smiled. Her mother. She'd finally found her. And Alejandra had tried to protect her. That was why she'd held her arm earlier. But if she'd known who she was all along, why hadn't she approached her? Why had she been so cold to her?

"Trini! Bring some water!" Ana yelled.

A hand clutched Malena's arm painfully. It was Rafael. He dragged her to the foyer.

"Haven't you caused enough damage already?" He looked at her with a hatred that made her shiver. "Enrique Hidalgo is not welcome here and neither are you. You'd better leave before I call the police."

Chapter 41

Ana drew the curtains in her mother's bedroom as Mamá Blanca lay on the bed with her eyes closed, tears rolling down her cheeks. Dr. Gaitán returned his stethoscope to his black leather bag and removed his prescription booklet. As he wrote, he eyed Ana and her sisters over a pair of black-frame spectacles.

"She's going to be all right." His thick mustache covered half of his upper lip. "Doña Blanca has a strong heart."

Ana glanced at her sisters. They were all probably thinking the same thing. *No, Mamá Blanca will never be all right again. Not after what happened.* Alejandra avoided Ana's gaze and studied her short nails. It was so rare to see Alejandra in a dress, with her fingers so clean and those emerald earrings Papá Pancho had made, but it was even stranger to think of her as someone's mother, especially a grown woman. Only now did Ana realize how little she knew of her younger sister. It was a pity not to know someone after spending practically your entire life around that person—not that Ana had been open with her family either.

Dr. Gaitán handed the prescription to Amanda, who stood beside him, arms across her chest.

"Give her this sedative," he said. "So she can rest."

"All right," Amanda said. "Thank you for coming, Dr. Gaitán. I'll walk you downstairs."

"No. I'll go," Ana said. She couldn't stand to be in her mother's presence anymore, not when she had this urge to yell her own truth, the way that girl, Malena, had done half an hour ago.

Dr. Gaitán bowed to all the women in the room and headed for the door, one hand holding his bag and the other one adjusting his bow tie.

After the doctor had left, Ana walked into the living room, where María Teresa spoke with Rafael and Javier.

María Teresa removed a strand of her fiery red hair—it still didn't bear any traces of gray—from her face. "How is your mother?"

"She's going to be fine." Ana forced a smile.

"*Gracias a Dios.*" María Teresa picked up her purse from the coffee table. "I'd better go, then."

"No, please. Stay here. At least tonight."

"Thank you, Anita, but it's not necessary." She held Ana's icy hands in hers. "It's not the right time for company. Besides, I want to go to Quito first thing in the morning to see if I can find Liliana."

Liliana, of course. She had run away with that man and was somewhere in Quito.

"Javi, would you please take María Teresa back to her hotel?" Ana said.

"Absolutely."

María Teresa hugged her and promised to write or call as soon as she heard from Lili.

Holding onto the doorknob, Ana glanced after her friend and son as they vanished into the bleak street. Exhausted, she rested her head against the door. It had been a terrible day and she only wanted it to end.

Rafael's shadow in the foyer startled her.

"I'd better go find Claudia," he said. "She hasn't arrived yet."

Claudia. With all the commotion, she'd forgotten about her. "I don't think she will be coming back any time soon."

Rafael's brows furrowed. How she hated when he did that. "Why?"

"I didn't want to tell you while María Teresa was here, but I checked Claudia's bedroom and her suitcase is missing, along with some of her clothes. She must have returned to the house while we were waiting for her at the church."

He hit the wall by the door. "*Maldición!* What the hell is wrong with that girl? Has everyone gone crazy in this house?"

"Maybe she realized she didn't love Sebastian after all." Ana stared at the wrinkles multiplying in Rafael's face.

"Love? What a stupid thing to say. Sebastian is the best catch in this filthy town, for God's sake!"

She fought a sudden urge to smile. As humiliating as the wedding cancellation had been, she was happy that Claudia hadn't married a man she didn't love. She knew all too well what a mistake that was. She wished she'd had the same courage as Claudia did in fleeing a destiny that wasn't hers.

He glowered. "Are you smiling?"

Ana pursed her lips.

"You think this is funny?" Rafael's voice grew louder. "You probably knew all along who that girl was, too. You're the one who brought her here."

"Are you insane? Why would I do that?" Ana closed the door, looking around the house, wondering for the first time where Malena had gone off to. She walked to the living room, though she hadn't seen her there earlier.

"Where is she? Did she go upstairs?" She headed for the staircase.

"You don't have to worry about her anymore," Rafael said.
That spiteful sneer appeared on his face.

"Why? Where is she?"

Rafael loosened his tie. "I sent her away."

"What do you mean, you sent her away?"

"I told her she wasn't welcome in this house anymore."

Ana held on to the railing for balance. She had to take a deep breath in order to control the heat building up inside of her. "Why would you do that?" Her voice came out hoarser than she'd ever heard it.

"She lied to all of us. She's the daughter of a murderer. Do I really need to explain this?"

Ana tightened her grasp on the banister until she could see her veins. "How dare you?" Her voice was low, but somehow Rafael's expression softened.

"Come on, we don't have to turn this into a fight. I'm exhausted." He climbed the stairs. Ana grabbed his arm.

"Answer me! How dare you tell my niece to leave my mother's house? Or have you forgotten whose house this is?"

He jerked his arm free. "Watch it, woman. I'm not in the mood."

"You had no right!"

"She was a phony, a con artist. Her father murdered your cousin. Have you forgotten that? I was just doing you all a favor, and this is how you repay me?"

"She's Alejandra's daughter!"

"I don't care who she is! I don't want her here. And that's that, end of discussion."

As he turned back up the stairs, Ana grasped a mass of his hair and pulled him down with all her strength. Rafael stumbled down the stairs to her level. For a second, it felt good, but almost immediately her legs started shaking. She would pay dearly for this.

Rafael's eyes looked like they were going to pop out of their sockets. He backhanded her face so hard she fell down the stairs.

He came toward her, eyes flickering like she'd never seen before.

She found her voice. "Go ahead, hit me if you want, but after you're done, get out of this house. I don't want you here anymore."

Rafael suspended his arm in midair. "What?"

Ana stood up, rubbing her cheek with her palm. "You heard me. I want you out of this house, never to return again."

He lowered his arm. "Look, I'm sorry. I lost my control. I shouldn't have . . ." He ran his hand over his forehead. "This is insane. You know I would never hurt you."

"You've hurt me all my life, but it's over, Rafael." It felt good to say those words out loud. She should have said them years ago.

He laughed bitterly. "You're just saying that. You won't be able to stand the rumors. Ana Platas, the divorcée."

"I don't care about that anymore. All I want is peace in my life."

"I'll tell Claudia the truth," he said.

"Do it. I don't care. She's an adult already."

"Your family won't be able to recover from the scandal. First Abigail, then Alejandra."

Ana tasted the blood in her mouth and brought her index finger to her wounded lip.

"This is how you pay me for what I did?" He took a step forward. "After what I did for that no-good sister of yours? After I gave Claudia my last name and treated her like a daughter?"

"You were happy to adopt her. You wanted a daughter, a big family."

"You weren't even good for that, Ana. You could only give me one son." He squeezed her shoulders with both hands. "But I forgive you. Let's just forget all of this."

Amanda's voice came out sharp from the top of the stairs. "You heard my sister, Rafael. She doesn't want you here, and neither do I, or anybody else in this family. I suggest you pack your suitcase and leave. We'll write you a check for whatever expenses you might have before you find another job."

Rafael pulled Ana closer to him. "Anita . . ."

She pushed him away. He stared at her, defeated. Ana straightened her spine, as if the top of her head had been pulled up by a thread, surprised at how small Rafael looked to her now. She'd been so afraid of him all these years, when the solution had been this simple. How different her life would have been if only she and Abigail hadn't been so weak.

Chapter 42

Ana, 1941

It was hard to believe that only an hour ago she'd been the happiest woman in the world. The same streets that had witnessed her bliss now seemed darker, colder. If only she would have packed faster. If only Abigail had arrived twenty minutes later to Ana's apartment, she wouldn't have found her there. She wouldn't have heard from Ana and Javier except for an occasional letter once or twice a year.

Ana slowed her pace as soon as she saw the two-story house where she'd been complete for the first time, the place she'd viewed as her paradise, her salvation. But she had no valise with her, and she didn't have Javier's small hand in hers either. Instead, she had an explanation stuck in the midst of her throat, an apology, a sadness crawling all the way to her heart.

She rang the doorbell, already mourning the excitement she couldn't feel anymore when standing behind this door. He opened the door, almost immediately, and she focused on his beautiful green eyes. The only pair of eyes in the entire world that shone brightly when she stared into them.

"*Amore,*" Enzo said. "You're here."

He pulled her in, and shut the door. She glanced at the two suitcases by the stairs. He drew her toward him and kissed her.

She gave in to that kiss, their last. His hands held her face and his mouth was warm, so much warmer than Rafael's had ever been.

He finally pulled away. "You're right on time. Are we picking up Javier from your mother's house?"

She shook her head, fighting her tears.

"What's wrong, *bella*? Where's your valise?"

She looked down at her purse. "Can we sit for a moment? We need to talk."

"Talk? What happened? Didn't that *maledetto* leave this morning?"

"He left," she said. It was all she could say.

Holding her hand, he led her to a burgundy leather couch that had belonged to Nicolas and Enzo's parents, just like this house. They sat side by side, his long leg touching her knee. He held her hands in his and kissed both of her palms.

"Enzo, *mi amor*." Her voice broke. "I can't go with you. My sister Abigail needs me."

He frowned, and his lovely eyes narrowed. She touched his rough chin.

"Abigail is pregnant," she said. "She's desperate. She's asked me to take her to Tabacundo with me."

"Why doesn't she marry the accountant? Aren't they engaged?"

"Because the baby isn't his."

Enzo's jaw hardened. "But we already had our plans."

"I have to help her."

"Why doesn't she talk to the man who got her pregnant?"

"Because he just got ordained as a priest."

Enzo dropped her hands. "This is ridiculous. Why must we sacrifice for your sister's indiscretion?"

"If I don't help her, who will?" Ana dried her tears with her fingers.

Enzo removed a handkerchief from his back pocket and handed it to her.

"This was a bad idea anyway." She pressed the handkerchief against her wet cheeks. "Can you imagine what our lives would be like constantly running away from Rafael, from my family? We would live like criminals, always hiding, always pretending we were something we were not. It wouldn't be fair to Javier to grow up away from his father, living in such impudence. What would he think of his mother?"

"The same thing I think of her. That she's the sweetest and most beautiful woman in the world." He grabbed her face with both hands. "Come on, Ana. You can't do this. We love each other." He kissed her, but this time, she didn't respond.

He pulled away from her.

"I just can't go through with it," she said.

He remained quiet, staring at a framed map of Italy hanging on the opposite wall, his fists clenched by his sides. She'd only seen him this mad whenever Amanda's name came up. Ana knew well the two of them couldn't stand each other, and it pained her deeply.

She reached out for his arm. "Enzo, please say something. Please forgive me."

Enzo shifted his weight away from her.

"You're still so young, *mi amor*, you'll forget me," she said. "You'll see, before you know it, you'll find someone else, and you'll marry her."

"No. I will never marry. I will never fall in love again." He stood up, almost violently. "Fine, go after that idiot. Pretend you never met me. I'll do the same."

She stood up, gathering her numb body, swallowing the rest of her tears. She returned his handkerchief.

"Keep it. You're going to need it," he said, unwilling to look at her face. "Just like you did on your wedding day."

Ana squeezed the handkerchief. So he'd been the one who walked into the lavatory while she was crying.

"It was just my luck," he said. "To have met you the day you married that *bastardo*."

He walked away, toward the stairs, without looking back.

She released the handkerchief from her fist and stared at the golden *E* embroidered on it. This was all she had left from the man she loved, the only proof that he'd been real, for she had burned all his letters so Rafael would never find them. She brought the fabric to her nose, inhaling his scent, and rushed to the entrance, trying to beat her tears out the door.

Chapter 43

Abigail, 1952

The knock on the door woke Abigail. Lately, it was increasingly hard for her to stay awake.

"Come in," she said, attempting to sit up, but not finding enough strength in her arms to do so.

Alejandra walked into the room, wearing a black dress, like she had for the last three years after Papá Pancho's death in the earthquake of '49.

"He's here," she said.

Abigail shivered under the covers. "Help me sit up."

Alejandra pushed Abigail to a sitting position, then adjusted three pillows behind her.

"I must look terrible," Abigail said.

Her sister avoided her eyes, confirming her suspicions.

"Quick, bring me a mirror, a brush, and some rouge."

In less than a minute, Alejandra returned with the things, including a pink lipstick and a piece of mint candy. Abigail held the silver mirror in front of her face. She was yellowish, her cheekbones stood out and dark circles framed her eyes.

Disgraceful.

While Alejandra braided her hair, Abigail attempted to bring some color to her face.

"Useless." Abigail set the mirror on her lap, face down. No matter what she did, she was still twelve years older and sick. "Just send him in."

Before Alejandra could walk away, Abigail held her hand. It was coarse and callous, like their father's hands had been.

"Thank you for bringing him," Abigail said. "I knew you would do it."

Abigail squeezed her sister's hand and for a moment, that hard expression Alejandra had always reserved for her softened.

"I need to ask you one more thing," Abigail said. "Remember what I told you about Claudia?"

"Yes."

Abigail pointed at the top drawer of her night table. "I wrote about it in my diary. Burn it."

"I will."

Exhaling, Abigail let go of her sister's hand.

Alejandra walked to the door and stopped. Without turning she said, "I'm sorry I've been so hard on you all these years."

Alejandra didn't give Abigail time to respond; she left the room too quickly. But the knot in Abigail's chest released, bringing her a new sense of peace. Her sister didn't hate her, like she'd always thought. Alejandra had forgiven her for whatever it was she did to her back when they were teenagers.

Her moment of peace dissipated as soon as she heard hard steps approaching her room.

His steps.

Alejandra reappeared in the room, followed by Victor in his black cassock.

This was the first time Abigail had seen him wearing it. She had wished he wouldn't wear it here. It embarrassed her to see it. He seemed so different now. A grown man, a respectable man. But he smiled at her with the same kindness of his youth.

He stood by the bed, hands clasped in front of him. A priestly gesture. Did they get trained on this or did it just come naturally? Only now did she realize that Alejandra had left them alone. But this shouldn't surprise her. After Fausto's death, Alejandra's spirit had left her body and she was nothing but a phantom roaming the halls.

Victor was the first one to break the silence. "You haven't changed a bit."

He was lying, of course.

"Neither have you," she said. "You're the handsomest priest I've ever met."

He brought a chair next to her bed and sat down, hands over his lap. "Did you want me here as a priest or as a friend?"

The question alone hurt. A priest or a friend. Those were his only options. Could you even be friends with the one you loved?

"Both." She reached for the glass of water Mamá Blanca had brought her earlier. Victor handed it to her. She drained it, but the thirst remained, as did the pain in her lower back. Her damn rotten kidneys. She set the glass back on the night table, embarrassed by the tremor in her hand.

He followed her gaze.

"Are you happy?" she asked.

He stared at his palms. "It doesn't matter. This isn't about me. It never was."

"Was it worth it?" She rested her palms on her sides. "Your sacrifice."

"It's not that simple."

"I just want to know . . . I need to know if"—she paused, afraid of his answer, afraid of his pity—"if you ever regretted your decision."

He looked up. There was pain in his eyes. "Yes."

She breathed out. He wouldn't lie to her about this, not on her deathbed. Or maybe it was the compassionate thing to do, even if it wasn't honest. She grabbed his hand. It was stone cold.

"Promise?"

He smiled, but his eyes were still sad. "I do. I'm not the same man you met then. I'm not nearly as idealistic." His voice lowered, as though that last part was only meant for himself. But this was all she needed. Just to know that she'd mattered to him, that it hadn't been only her. She squeezed his hand, ascertaining that this wasn't a dream, that he was truly here holding her hand. She kissed it softly.

He stiffened. "You don't have to do that, Abi."

"Why not? Everyone else gets to do it, right?" He wouldn't take this small pleasure from her, not now. She rubbed his hand against her cheek.

He watched her, tightening his jaw. The tears burned in her eyes, begging to come down. As soon as she felt the first one, she let go of his hand. "Enough of that." She dried her cheek with the edge of the sheet. "Time for the priest to come now. Time for confession."

A small crease formed between his eyebrows. "Please don't joke about this."

"I'm not. I called a priest, didn't I?" She licked her dry lips. "I want my Extreme Unction."

"I may not be the right—"

"You're going to deny the last Sacrament to one of your parishioners?"

"Of course not," he said.

He left the room for a moment. When he returned, he carried a leather case with him. Ana followed him inside, holding an empty tray in her hands. She placed the clutter from the bedside table on the tray—medicine bottles, books, and the empty glass. She looked at Abigail through watery eyes, but beneath the sorrow there was something else. Fear?

Victor approached the night table and set his leather case on top. He removed a white tablecloth, a Bible, two glass containers—water and oil—and a long purple stole that he placed around his neck.

Ana stumbled out of the room, reminding Abigail of her sister's clumsy walk the day they met Victor at María Teresa's wedding.

As he sprinkled her with Holy Water, he said a prayer, but she wasn't listening. She just wanted to watch him, to prolong this moment, for she knew she would never see him again after this. He sat down on the chair, ready to listen. It was now or never, the moment she'd imagined for years.

Abigail started her confession, watching his serene expression as she spoke. She talked about the guilt of leaving her loved ones behind, of lying for so many years to her family, of being responsible for Ana's unhappiness. He nodded occasionally, not asking any questions but simply accepting her words. After his shoulders had relaxed, after he'd let out a slow breath, she stopped.

"Is there anything else?" he said.

"Yes." She reached out for his hand, feeling it tense as she touched it. She took a deep breath, and her back hurt even more. "I was in love once." She hesitated. "With someone who wasn't meant to be mine."

He slipped his hand away from hers.

"His last weekend in town, before he left me for good, I went to the boarding house where he was staying."

"What are you getting at?" The man, not the priest, spoke now. His voice was still low, as low as hers, but there was hostility underneath.

"I have a daughter," she said. "We . . ." She stopped herself upon seeing the horror in his eyes, the intense pain taking shape in his expression. He watched her, finally removing the mask of indifference from his face.

"What? Why didn't you tell me?"

"You'd already left by the time I found out I was pregnant. I didn't want to cause a scandal. I didn't want to ruin your life."

"You should have told me." He brought his hands to his forehead. "Where is she?"

"Here. Probably playing in the courtyard."

Victor straightened himself. "I saw her. She was in the living room when I arrived."

Abigail nodded, for she was afraid her voice would break if she spoke again.

"Claudia is her name, isn't it? I should have known. She reminded me so much of my mother."

"She has your eyes," Abigail said.

"My mother's eyes." There were tears in his now. "Things could have been so different if you'd told me."

"No, they wouldn't have. You were meant to do this. I finally see it. You don't belong in the real world, among mere mortals. You have a gift."

"Don't say that. I'm just another sinner. Worse even."

"Please don't blame yourself. It was my fault. I went to see you with a plan. I wanted to stop you, to entice you. I'm the only one to blame here."

He wouldn't look at her. "But I was weak. You didn't force me."

"Stop it, Victor. I didn't tell you this so you could torment yourself."

"Then why? Why this way? You know I can't talk about it now."

"Yes."

"It's cruel."

"It was the only way to protect you. But you needed to know about her."

Victor covered his face with his hands for a long time. When he removed them, his demeanor was stoic again.

"Can we finish now?" Abigail said. "I need my medicine."

Victor went through the motions mechanically. She wasn't listening anymore. The pain was too intense. And she'd wasted all her energy already. He removed a host from a tiny, flat silver case and placed it on her tongue. She smiled when his fingers touched her cheek. He made the sign of the cross with the oil three times. First on her forehead, then on each wrist. She closed her eyes then, and she didn't want to open them anymore, so that he would be the last thing she would ever see.

Chapter 44

Amanda paced back and forth in the living room. She glanced at her wristwatch for the third time in the last minute, but no matter how frequently she looked at it, the hands didn't move any faster. She heard the keys. Someone was at the front door. She rushed to the foyer to meet an unshaven Javier entering the house.

"You couldn't find them?" Amanda asked.

"No. I looked in all the hotels. Nobody has seen either one of them."

"Malena must have left San Isidro," she said. "But I can't imagine where Claudia could be. Did Malena ever tell you where her home is?"

"Guayaquil. But I don't have her address."

Amanda sighed. As big as that city was, nobody could find someone who didn't want to be found.

"We should have looked for her last night." She hugged her arms. "But I couldn't leave my mother. And then, the situation with your father."

Javier returned the keys to his pocket, looking grim.

She ruffled his hair. "Cheer up, kid. Everything will be fine."

"How's Mamá Blanca?"

"Stable, but she refuses to speak."

"And Tía Alejandra?"

"Still locked in her room."

"My mother?"

"She's the only one I'm not worried about."

Javier ran his fingers through his tangled hair. "I'm going to take a nap. I didn't sleep at all last night."

The doorbell startled both of them. It had to be Claudia.

Javier opened the door, but it wasn't Claudia. It was Joaquin.

"Good morning," he said.

Amanda felt her chignon. "Joaquin, what a surprise! Come in."

"I'll ask Trini to bring you some coffee," Javier said, heading for the kitchen.

Amanda led Joaquin to the living room, self-conscious of her mundane appearance, of her embarrassing limp. He must be looking at her stiff leg now, her horrible leg.

She sat on the couch and he sat beside her, too close. She covered her knees with her skirt and suppressed the impulse to cross her legs.

He still smelled of Old Spice, like he did when he was younger, like he did a few weeks ago when they danced together again. They hadn't touched each other since.

"How are things here?" he asked.

"Not well. So many things have happened since yesterday. This family is in shambles. But let's not talk about that now. What brings you here this early?"

Trinidad walked in, yawning. She placed two white cups and a metal pot on the coffee table, then quietly left the room. She would have normally brought a wonderful piece of dessert along, or *avena* cookies at the very least, but this morning even Trinidad seemed to be affected by the hurricane that had swept over the Platas family.

Joaquin took a sip from his *tinto* and set it down.

"I sold my house," he said. "I'm leaving."

Amanda's chest ached, the same way it had twenty years ago when he said those same two words.

She lifted her own cup. "Back to Spain?"

"Yes."

She deserved this—after the way she'd treated him, after how selfish she'd been when they were young.

"That's wonderful, Joaquin. I bet Catalina will be delighted to have you back."

He watched her over his cup, and then placed it back on the saucer in silence. He hadn't really changed that much with the years; he was still handsome, perhaps more than she remembered. His eyes watched her so intensely she had to look away. She swallowed a sip of bitter coffee. It wasn't warm enough. No wonder Trinidad had brought it so quickly.

"That's all you're going to say," he said.

"What do you want me to say?"

"You haven't learned anything in twenty years? You're still as proud as you were then."

He was right. She was still proud, but this wasn't pride. This was something else, not wanting to hurt the person you love again. Or maybe she didn't have that power anymore. Maybe she didn't mean anything to Joaquin now. He was married to someone else after all.

"You probably didn't think of me all these years," he said. "I can't believe I've been such a fool all this time, thinking you cared, but now I realize you're still mourning him. You never stopped loving him."

She shook her head. How wrong he was. But she couldn't speak; her words were choked inside her throat, underneath the big lump.

"I'm sorry," was all she could say.

He stood. "I'd better go."

Say something! Do something! He was putting his hat on, adjusting his jacket. But she couldn't stop him; he was a married man now. He would reject her. She had no right.

"Please don't go yet," she heard herself say. "I owe you an explanation, at least."

He narrowed his eyes, and she saw the hurt in them resurfacing, the way she'd seen it that night, so many years ago, that dreadful night when she chose Nicolas over him.

"You don't owe me anything," he said. "I already know that what happened between us didn't mean anything to you."

"No, you're wrong." She held his hand, and pulled him back to the couch. He sat down, offering no resistance. She still remembered, so clearly, how happy she'd been in his arms, how tender he'd been with her that first time.

"Then why did you stay with him?" he asked.

She served him more coffee. The night he left San Isidro had been one of the worst in her life.

"The night you left," she said, staring at her hands as she entwined her fingers. "I got so sick Nicolas thought I was pregnant." She laughed bitterly. If at least she had been pregnant with Joaquin's child, she would have had something left of him, someone to live for. But she had nothing, except for his resentment and this awkward silence between them. "I shouldn't have let you go. I practically pushed you into Catalina's arms. But I honestly thought that if I left, Nicolas would kill himself."

"And he did, even with you by his side."

The tears filled her eyes, tears of guilt, for she couldn't fix whatever was wrong with Nicolas in the end. How ironic all of it was. She'd wanted so desperately to leave San Isidro, to see the world. She'd been so impressed by Nicolas's status and by his looks that she had married a man she didn't know, someone whom she thought represented her one-way ticket out of an ordinary life.

"You could have had everything you wanted with me," he said. "I would have done anything for you. I would have given you a family and the trips you always wanted."

She'd regretted her decisions a thousand times. Especially after she learned that Joaquin lived abroad, that he had the life she had fantasized about. She could have had it, too. The opportunity had been right in front of her, hitting her in the nose, but she hadn't seen it until it was too late, until it was gone. The tears stinging her eyes made her realize she was crying. Her best friend, her dancing partner, her lover, she could have had it all.

"You were a virgin, weren't you?" he said.

"Yes." Her voice cracked.

"Were there others after me?"

"No."

"What about"—he straightened his tie—"those other men Enzo mentioned, your father's accountant?"

She leaned back. "You should know better than to believe in rumors. Enrique and I met twice at Café Viteri because he wanted to tell me about some irregularities he'd found in my father's accounting books. He suspected Fausto was altering the books and Enrique didn't know what to do about it. But of course, people loved to talk about me then, and Enzo heard about it. He ran to tell Nico about that, too."

"You must have loved him to sacrifice so much for him, though." His voice sounded bitter. "I heard all about your accident. How you ran out of the hospital when you found out he was dead and drove his car outside of town. You wanted to die; you wanted to kill yourself, to go with him." He glanced at her leg.

"I had nothing else to live for," she said. "In the end, I lost both of you. So, as you can see, I was the fool. Not you."

He sighed. "Who would have thought that the beautiful Amanda Platas would live such a tragic life? I certainly didn't. I thought you were some mythical creature among us."

He removed a red velvet box from his jacket pocket. "Remember this?"

Her eyes filled up with tears again. If only she'd been less impulsive then, less selfish, less ambitious. If only she had never won that stupid radio contest.

"I bought it for you from your own father." He chuckled. "With money I saved up after that first year of working at my father's store." He turned her hand over and placed the box on her palm. "I've always wanted you to have it, even if our fate is to be apart."

She ran her fingers over the soft velvet before opening the box. Inside was a beautiful ruby ring. She touched the stone, her favorite, and could almost picture Papá Pancho polishing this ring in his dark workshop. She could visualize Joaquin bargaining with her father, and Papá Pancho being adamant about the set price, shaking his head, the way he used to do with stubborn customers.

She laughed, crying at the same time. Joaquin removed the ring from the box and placed it on her finger. "It fits," he said, smiling for the first time since he'd arrived.

How she loved to see him smile like that, like old times, before all the ugliness and pain grew between them.

She extended her hand, admiring the ring's shine. "I love it, Joaquin, thank you." This was the way it should have been that night at Il Napolitano. How it always should have been. "But I don't think Catalina would be thrilled to know you gave a ring to another woman, especially me. I know she never liked me."

Joaquin shrugged. "I don't think she'll care."

"What?"

"We've been separated for three months now."

Amanda flung her arms around Joaquin's neck and kissed his mouth, his cheeks, his eyelids. He could reject her all he wanted now, push her away if he felt like it, humiliate her in revenge, but she didn't care anymore. He was not going to get rid of her so easily this time.

Chapter 45

Alejandra braced herself as the knocking started again. She wished she could disappear forever. Anywhere would do. As long as Ana and Amanda couldn't reach her and couldn't continue knocking at her door every five minutes demanding explanations.

She lifted the fabric from the canvas and stared at her self-portrait. She was much younger there, barely a woman. She wrinkled the letter in her hand, the one she'd written to Enrique's mother so many years ago and Claudia had found among Malena's things. Her fingers ran over the paper, rubbing each one of its creases, as if she could heal her daughter's heart, as if she could magically erase the guilt she had felt when everyone surrounded Malena in the living room like sharks around their prey.

"Niña Alejandra, it's me."

She rushed to the door and unlocked it. Trinidad walked into the room, shutting the door behind her. Alejandra hugged the maid's thin frame and the tears she'd been holding back for so long released with a choke.

She cried for a long time as quietly as she could. The maid caressed her head, the way she'd done when she was a child and she'd hurt herself, the way she did when Alejandra came back from the convent, empty-handed.

"You're not going to talk to her?" Trinidad asked after Alejandra's sobbing subdued.

"I'm too embarrassed."

"But she came here looking for you. You owe it to her. You owe her an explanation."

Alejandra sat on her bed and dried her cheeks with her sleeve. "You knew it was her all along?"

"No, but I suspected it. She reminded me so much of *mi niña* Abigail."

"You should have said something."

Alejandra returned her attention to her painting and focused on the baby she was holding in her arms. Malena had turned out so different than she imagined her to be.

"She's beautiful, isn't she?"

"*Si, Niña.*"

"Is she in her room?"

"I don't know. I haven't seen her since last night."

Alejandra stood up, fearing the worst. Malena couldn't have left. Not now. As if waking up from a long dream, her body felt energized, strong, the way it had been before. She opened her bedroom door.

Amanda stood outside her room, arms across her chest.

"Where's Malena?" Alejandra said.

"Rafael sent her away last night," Amanda said. "We don't know where she went."

"What? Why didn't you tell me? How dare he?"

"Don't worry about him anymore. He's gone. For good. Ana is getting a divorce."

"I have to find Malena."

Alejandra attempted to walk past Amanda, toward the stairs, but her sister held her arm.

"We'll help you find her. But it's time we have a talk," Amanda said. "Mamá Blanca is waiting for you."

Alejandra knew she couldn't stall this conversation any longer. Twenty years ought to be enough. She followed her older sister to her mother's room, where Ana, Javier, and Mamá Blanca waited.

Chapter 46

Alejandra, 1941

Alejandra could barely control the tremor in her hands, the excitement that urged her legs to get up and skip around the workshop, the need to look at her watch one more time. This was going to be the best birthday of her life. She tried to focus on the pendant she was making—the first one without her father's help—but she couldn't concentrate. She glanced at the clock hanging over the kiln. It was almost ten. In only a few minutes, he would be here, in this workshop, in their secret meeting place. He'd told her he had something for her—a birthday present—but his love was present enough for her.

Uneven footfalls came from the shop. Normally, she wouldn't have heard a thing, but in the still of the night, in her anticipation, her hearing became so acute she could even hear the buzz of a fly in the hallway. She set her pliers aside and stood up, listening. Yes, there was definitely noise coming from the store.

He was here.

She opened the bottom drawer of her father's desk, which he had assigned to her, and removed the small bottle of perfume Amanda had given her that morning. Her first perfume. Finally a grown-up gift! She inhaled the gardenia scent before spraying it on her neck and the inside of her wrists. As a last touch, she sprinkled a few drops of almond oil onto her hands to soften them.

The steps grew louder. He was coming.

She returned the perfume and oil to her drawer and waited by the desk. Five minutes passed, but she couldn't hear his steps approaching. The noises continued in the shop: the fumbling of objects, the squeak of a door. What was he doing there? She left the room quietly, smiling to herself. Today her fate would change. She'd already decided what her birthday gift would be and it had nothing to do with material things. Today, she would become a woman. It was only befitting, after all; today she was turning eighteen years old.

She opened the office door and immediately recognized a male shape kneeling in front of the open safety vault.

"Fausto?" she asked. "What are you doing?"

He turned to her, red-eyed, and a strong smell of alcohol emanating from his pores. In his hands he held a stack of bills.

"You're stealing from my father?"

"Of course not." His speech was slurred. "I'm just borrowing some money."

"At this hour?"

He stood up with an effort and leaned over the vault door. "Who are you to judge me? You've robbed from your father before."

"It's not the same thing. I was a child then."

"Of course it's the same!" He stood up straight. "You took money from your old man to go to the circus. If it hadn't been for that we would have never met that damn Enrique!"

Damn Enrique?

"All right, all right. Calm down," Alejandra said.

"Don't tell me to calm down." He gripped her wrist. "You can be so condescending some times."

"Let me go. You're drunk."

"What are you doing here anyway? Why are you so dressed up?"

She glanced at her fitted beige blouse and pencil skirt.

"You were going to meet him, weren't you?" His grasp was so tight she couldn't recover her arm. She'd seen her cousin angry before, but today there was something else, something intimidating in his glare.

"And what's that smell?" He took a step closer to her. "You're wearing perfume for him?"

"I'm going to bed." She pulled her arm, but couldn't break free.

"What are you doing, Alejandra? He's engaged to your sister. Can't you see he's playing with you?"

Where was Enrique anyway? He was supposed to be here already.

"Abigail doesn't love him," she said lamely. "He's going to break up with her." Her voice sounded desperate, as if she were trying to convince herself more than Fausto.

"That's what he says." He took a step closer to her. "Men will say anything to take a woman to bed." He examined her face. "You haven't gone to bed with him, have you?"

"No," she said, uneasy by his interrogation, by his nearness.

"I don't believe you. You've already slept with him. I'm not an idiot. I know you better than everyone else and I know you want him. That's why you're wearing this outfit, this perfume, to tempt him."

She slapped him as hard as she could, but it didn't faze him. He clenched her wrists.

"You're hurting me!" she said.

He let go of her. She took a step back. She didn't like the wicked gleam in his eyes. It made her feel dirty. She turned to the door, but he slammed his palm against it, shutting it. She ducked under his arm, heading for the desk for there was nowhere else to go. Maybe she should scream, but there was no way her father would hear her from the house.

Fausto followed her slowly, still menacing, still angry, and cornered her between the vault and a wall. She backed up until she felt the concrete wall behind her. He took another step and grabbed her face with both hands, his mouth a breath away from hers.

"You smell so good," he whispered.

"What are you doing?"

"What does it look like I'm doing?" He caressed her cheek softly. "You're meant to be mine. You always have."

She made a futile attempt to push him, but his chest felt like a brick wall against her palm.

"Fausto, what's wrong with you? You're my cousin. My brother, almost."

"No. I'm not your brother." His arm trapped her waist. "And I'm tired of people saying that. There's nothing brotherly about the way I feel about you."

She glanced behind his head, toward the door, praying Enrique would walk in.

He hit the wall, right next to her ear. "You're still thinking about him? I'm going to kill him."

"Fausto, please." She pushed the words out. "You need a strong coffee and a shower. Come on. Let's forget this ever happened."

"No! I don't want to forget." He tilted his head down, holding her face with both hands. "I've waited long enough. I've wanted to do this for years."

She shook her head, trying to escape his grasp, but he had a tight hold of her. She felt like throwing up the minute his wet lips pressed against hers.

"No!"

She brought her hands to his chest and pushed him, but he took a step closer, pressing his body against hers. He held both of her wrists again, and his mouth absorbed hers, making her unable to breathe, much less yell. He held both of her wrists with one hand, and with the other, he fumbled with the buttons on her blouse. Bile rose up her throat. *Enrique, my love, please come, please save me.*

Finally he set her mouth free, and kissed her neck.

"*Maldito!* Let me go! My mother will never forgive you!"

He ignored her and continued opening her blouse.

"Enrique!" she yelled, as loud as she could.

Fausto slapped her cheek so hard she nearly lost her balance. "Shut up!"

He covered her mouth with his palm and pushed her against the desk. She fought him with all she had, legs, arms, hands, but he was much stronger than her. His entire weight rested on her as he lifted her skirt. She pulled his hair, but again, it had no effect on him. He pinned her hands over her head and held her wrists with one hand. Never had she imagined Fausto to be this strong. She stared at the dangling light bulb in the ceiling as his free hand traveled eagerly up her thigh. An uncontrollable tremor took over her body. She shut her eyes; she never wanted to remember her once beloved cousin attacking her like a hungry animal, the heaviness of his sweaty forehead against her chest, his silent groaning, the searing pain tearing through her, the unbearable shame of her father, or worse yet, her mother finding out. If only she could escape her body, detach herself from this nightmare. But the pain was too real, the betrayal too heartbreaking.

Minutes later or maybe hours, she couldn't tell, a ruckus at the door forced her to open her eyes. Fausto jumped back, pulling his pants up. Enrique walked into the room.

"What's going on here?" He turned to her. "Alejandra?"

She sat up and noticed, horrified, that her underwear rested around her calves. She quickly pulled it up.

Enrique glared at Fausto. "What did you do to her, *hijo de puta?*"

He advanced toward him, fists clenched. Fausto took a revolver from the safe and pointed it at Enrique.

"Don't move!"

Enrique stopped. "Of course. Such would be the response of a coward like you."

"Shut up or I'll blow your brains out."

"Fausto," Alejandra said. "Please put the gun down. Don't make this any worse."

Her cousin faced her. "Quiet! I don't want to hear a word from you."

Enrique tackled Fausto, sending both of them to the floor. They fought for the gun, rolling on the floor back and forth until an explosive noise, louder than any other noise she'd ever heard, vibrated through the entire room, making her jump. Enrique lifted his body from Fausto's, wide-mouthed as a red stain grew on the center of Fausto's white shirt. Enrique dropped the gun and stood up. He was pale.

Alejandra gripped his arm. "You have to leave. My father can't find you here!"

"I killed him. I killed Fausto."

"Come on, get out." Alejandra led him to the door. "They'll take you to jail."

"No. I'll stay. I'll tell them what happened."

"No, I don't want anyone to know." She lowered her head and the sight of her exposed brassiere was so demeaning she didn't want to look at Enrique in the eye. She covered her chest with her blouse. "Please."

Enrique seemed to wake from his trance. "That bastard. I can't believe he did this to you, my beautiful girl." He caressed her wet cheek. "He deserved this."

The tears blurred her vision for a moment. "Please go. I'll take care of this."

He hugged her and kissed her forehead. "I'll be back for you."

She watched him go and something told her this would be the end for them, the end of her dreams. Fausto was lying on the ground. His hand rested on his chest now, getting soaked in blood, and he was watching her. She didn't feel pity for him;

he'd had this coming. But the pain of his betrayal was so intense she could barely breathe.

Voices approached the office and she recognized one of them as Papá Pancho's. She buttoned her shirt and tucked it inside her skirt. She stood still as someone opened the door.

"What happened?" her father asked behind her. "I heard a gunshot."

Alejandra faced her father, speechless. Her body was numb. She hadn't thought of what to say yet.

Fausto spoke with the last energy he had left. "It was Enrique. He tried to rob us."

Her father glanced at the opened safety vault. "*Ese maldito,*" he muttered. It was the first time Alejandra had heard her father curse.

"You stay with him," he told her. "I'm going to get a doctor."

Alejandra nodded. It was all she could do. She had no control over her trembling body. She watched her father dart through the door, bypassing Mamá Blanca, who had somehow made it to the jewelry store and was holding on to the door frame.

"Mamá, don't look!" she warned her. But it was too late. Her mother's gaze was locked on the blood coming out of Fausto's mouth.

Mamá Blanca knelt beside her nephew and took his hand in hers.

"I tried to stop him." He swallowed with difficulty. "But he shot me."

Alejandra was too shocked to speak. She knew she had to say something, but if she did, would she have to confess the horrible thing Fausto had just done to her? Did she have to explain she was no longer fit to be anyone's wife? A remnant of what she'd once been?

Mamá Blanca spoke with a hollow voice. "Don't talk, dear, save your strength."

Fausto stared at Alejandra with terror, and she suddenly remembered the cousin she had loved so dearly, her playing partner, and all the times they had kept each other's secrets. What had happened to him? Where had that child gone? He had been so angry and resentful in the last few years. Her throat burned. Her mother took in quick breaths. Fausto coughed blood. Mamá Blanca helped him move his head up and his blood stained her beige nightgown.

"Hold on, *mi amor,* don't die," Mamá Blanca pleaded, tears standing in her eyes. "The doctor will be here in just a moment."

Alejandra watched one of her mother's tears travel from the corner of her eye, down her cheek to her chin, and land on Fausto's arm.

Fausto looked at Alejandra. "I'm sorry. Please don't . . ." he said, but didn't finish the sentence before his head fell back.

Mamá Blanca sobbed quietly. Her beloved nephew, the son she'd always wanted, had just died. And the truth would kill her, no doubt. Alejandra stared at her cousin's lifeless brown eyes fixated on her and she knew then they would haunt her forever.

———⟞⟝———

Alejandra waited until the syringe filled with blood before removing the needle from the old man's vein. He groaned and stiffened as she rubbed his arm with a moist cotton ball, but she barely noticed. She'd become desensitized to pain, especially hers. She was almost grateful for the pain in her lower back. It was her punishment. She deserved it.

Sister Mariana, dressed entirely in white and hiding her hair underneath a white veil, entered the hospice room.

"Alejandra, there's a man waiting for you downstairs."

She instinctively brought her hand to her enlarged stomach. "Did he say his name?"

"Hugo Sevilla."

Alejandra had never heard the name before. "Are you sure he asked for me?"

"Yes. He said it's very important. He said he met you in San Isidro."

Alejandra set the syringe on the night table beside the sick man. Had something happened to Mamá Blanca? She wiped her sweaty hands on her apron and walked out of the room. The hardwood floor squeaked with every one of her steps. She walked slowly, in no hurry to hear whatever bad news waited for her down the stairs.

In the small receiving area, standing by the enlarged portrait of the Virgen de la Dolorosa, stood Enrique. She slowed her pace and uselessly attempted to hide her stomach with her hand. Her gesture directed his gaze to that precise spot. His eyes didn't reveal surprise, only an intense sadness.

She stood in front of him, unable to look him in the eye. She focused, instead, on the full beard covering his face and adding ten years to his appearance. She pointed at the old couch underneath the portrait of the Virgin. They sat side by side, careful that their legs wouldn't touch.

"How did you find me?" she asked.

"Trinidad told me where you were."

"You went back to San Isidro?" she whispered.

"I told you I would come back for you."

Alejandra ran her palm over her forehead. "Did she tell you about . . .?" She glanced at her stomach, involuntarily, for she wanted to pretend she'd dreamt the entire thing.

"No. But I suspected as much." He reached for her hand, but she pulled back. She was too disgusting to be touched.

He removed a long flat box from the pocket inside his jacket. "I never gave you your birthday gift."

She held it in her hands, rubbing the soft wood with the tips of her fingers. She slid it open and found half a dozen brushes of different widths.

"The clerk said they are the best kind," he said. "Made out of weasel hair."

Of course, *pelo de marta* was what they called it. She'd never had brushes like this. They were expensive. She touched the bristles.

"Maybe painting will help you—"

"Yes. Thank you. They're very nice."

He studied her for a moment that seemed to last forever. "You're a nurse now."

"Not really. They just taught me the basics. There aren't enough hands here."

He watched her for an unnerving moment. "You cut your hair," he said, pulling a short strand behind her ear. "It used to be so beautiful."

Alejandra visualized her long tresses on the tile floor of her bathroom, right after she cut them. She brought a hand to her short hair, as short as Enrique's, and an intense anger crept through her veins. "Why were you late?"

He tensed his jaw. Maybe he thought, like she often did, that things could have been different had he arrived on time on that ghastly night.

"You're right to blame me," he said. "This was my fault. I should have been there at ten, like we'd agreed." He tried to touch her hand again, but stopped himself, perhaps recalling her earlier reaction.

"I don't blame you," she said. "It wasn't your fault. I just couldn't help but wonder what had been so important that you arrived to see me thirty minutes late."

Enrique stared at his hands as he interwove them incessantly. "I was playing cards. Fausto left early. I should have known better. But I waited on purpose. I wanted to make sure he got home and went to bed before I went to see you."

Her cousin's name brought an ache to her throat.

"What are you going to do now?" he asked. "With the baby."

"Give it up for adoption, I suppose."

He leaned closer to her, and she could smell his cologne. She had missed it. "Marry me. We'll raise the baby together."

She shook her head. She never wanted to be with a man again, and she certainly didn't want to raise the child of a monster.

"Why not?" he asked.

"Every time I see the baby, I'll remember that awful night." She shut the box. "Besides, you're a fugitive. What kind of life would we have?"

"At least we'll be together."

"It would kill my mother. She despises you."

"If you give your child up, you might regret it one day," he said. "Many women do."

She shrugged.

"Then let me raise the baby." He lowered his voice. "My mother will help me."

Hesitantly, he stretched out his hand and touched her stomach. She flinched, but didn't remove his hand. Their eyes met for a moment, and Alejandra knew then that her child would not be better off with anyone else.

Chapter 47

Sebastian could feel everyone's eyes on him, and he suspected that as he walked by, people pointed at him. Claudia had turned him into the laughingstock of the town, a joke for years to come. But he had to go on with his life, unlike his mother, who'd spent the last two days self-sedated, too abashed to step outside.

He lit another cigarette—he hadn't stopped smoking since he left his house—and crossed the street toward *El Heraldo*. The guard greeted him without looking at him, as if he wanted to spare him the shame of being seen, or maybe he was trying to hide the amusement in his eyes.

Sebastian walked by the elevator. He didn't stop, but was acutely aware of it—more so than ever.

He climbed up the stairs and sighed before entering his office.

Behind her desk, Pamela greeted him while burying her nose behind the typewriter, her cheeks bright red, as if she'd been the one stood up at the altar. Sebastian didn't know which was worse: this attempt at normalcy or people mocking him in the street.

"Pamela," he said. "Tell Cesar to come to my office."

He shut his office door and sat behind his desk, pressing his forehead with his fingers. He didn't feel like talking to Cesar today, but the sooner he took care of that problem, the better. All the drinking from the past two days wasn't making matters any easier.

After a couple of minutes, there was a soft knock at the door.

"Come in," he said.

"Hello, Sebastian."

He raised his head.

"Here's the cover." Cesar set a paper on the desk. "For tomorrow."

Sebastian held his stare. Cesar broke eye contact first.

"Is that all you have to tell me?" Sebastian asked.

"I'm sorry about your wedding?"

"That's not what I mean."

Cesar picked up a stapler from the desk.

"You want to explain to me your situation with Hugo Sevilla?"

Cesar's brow furrowed. "I've never met that man. I don't know why that crazy woman is making up stories about me."

Sebastian banged the surface of his desk. "Don't call her crazy!"

Cesar took a step back. "All I'm saying is she must have me confused with someone else. I've never been friends with Manuel Paz."

"I know. Manuel Paz is not her father. Hugo Sevilla is."

Cesar's eyes widened. "I told you. I don't know what you're talking about. You're making a big mistake."

Sebastian removed a manila envelope from one of his drawers and tossed it on top of the desk. "Maybe this will refresh your memory."

Cesar eyed the envelope.

"My mistake," Sebastian said, standing up. "You must remember him by his real name—Enrique Hidalgo, correct?"

Cesar stared at the name written on the envelope.

"Or are you going to deny that the envelope is yours?" Sebastian said. "I found it in your office."

Sebastian removed its contents: the newspaper article with Hugo's picture, the man's address in Guayaquil.

Cesar's hand clung to the stapler. "That damn woman must have put it in my drawer."

Sebastian clenched his fists. "I told you not to call her names." He took a deep breath. "I just want to know exactly what happened. Were you blackmailing him?"

Cesar seemed to age in front of Sebastian. "I told you. I've never met that man. I don't know what you're talking about."

"A man is dead, Cesar." He picked up the phone. "But maybe you'd like to talk to the police about what really happened?"

Before Sebastian could dial the first number, a cold, hard object hit his forehead before it landed on the floor. He dropped the receiver, bringing his hand to the fresh cut above his eye. The tips of his fingers stained with blood. He glanced at the object on the floor, the stapler, and then looked up. Cesar ran for the door, fumbling with the doorknob. Sebastian darted toward him and seized his shirt, turning him around. Holding his collar with both hands, he slammed him against the door.

"You killed him, didn't you?"

"No!"

"I want the truth."

"I swear I didn't kill him."

"Why should I believe you?"

"Because it's the truth. Enrique was a coward. I didn't have to do anything. He jumped all by himself. He would have done anything not to go to jail."

"You piece of shit."

Cesar pushed Sebastian off of him. "Why do you even care?" He adjusted his collar. "Oh, I know. You're sweet on his daughter, aren't you? That's why your bride stood you up yesterday."

He laughed bitterly. "Too bad I didn't see that coward's daughter earlier, or else I would have made other arrangements with him. She's a doll, isn't she? And I'm sure old Enrique would have given anything for my silence. Money is not everything, you see."

The match inside Sebastian's gut turned into a full flame expanding all over his chest. He clenched his fist and swung, but before launching a punch on Cesar's jaw, he stopped his arm in midair.

"I can't believe my father trusted a low-life like you." Sebastian dropped his arm. "I used to admire you. What a fool I was."

Cesar tucked his shirt back into his trousers.

"You're fired, Cesar. I never want to see you again."

Cesar glared at him, fixing his tie, before he left the office.

Sebastian removed a handkerchief from his back pocket and brought it to his tender wound. It throbbed, but he was most concerned with his twisted life. In a matter of two days, he'd lost his bride, his respectability, and now his editor and right-hand man.

Chapter 48

"Malena! Where's the letter?"

Malena felt like screaming. Between her new boss's demands and the elusive typewriter keys, she would not survive another day in this office.

"It's almost ready, Señor!"

She pulled the paper out of the platen and studied it. The writing was crooked and there were several strokes through-out. She couldn't hand him *this*. What had possessed her to tell Mr. Ramirez that although she'd never been a secretary, she would nail this job in a couple of days?

Despair, really.

She needed money for food and rent, but she also needed to get away from her apartment, away from her thoughts, and especially away from that monster called loneliness. Just like she'd suspected, she'd been expelled from nursing school and this secretarial job was the only thing she could find with her limited skill set.

It had been two weeks since she left San Isidro, and the mem-ories of that place—of her family—still haunted her. Although she'd been relieved that the truth was finally out—the fall had not been as bad as she'd anticipated—the pain of their rejection was a tough burden to carry. It would have been preferable not to meet them at all than to lose them after she'd found them. Especially in such a disgraceful way.

She inserted another piece of paper in the typewriter. Mr. Ramirez had trusted her enough to give her the position (although she suspected his decision had more to do with her legs than her promises). But regardless of his reasons, she couldn't let him down.

It took her ten more minutes to finish the letter, but this time, there were only two mistakes. Mr. Ramirez's nod signaled that it was good enough, for now, and she could go home. In a way, she was glad to leave late. The later she arrived to her apartment, the faster the night would end. She was sick of those long hours staring at the ceiling fan with no more company than her father's records. Her only diversion was Julia with one of her antidepressant teas or a plate of *humitas*. But even her best friend couldn't fill the empty spot in her chest.

Once home, Malena removed her shoes and dumped her purse on the couch, too tired to explore the kitchen and see if there was anything to nibble on. She sat down and rested her feet on the coffee table. She pictured the distraught faces of her aunts, her grandmother, and her mother the evening they found out about her deceit. She pressed her forehead. When would those images leave her mind?

She had to find a way to forget.

There was a soft knock on the door. Thank God for Julia to save her from her misery!

Malena opened the door, but instead of Julia's gigantic hair and a plate of warm food, she encountered Alejandra. She looked older today—maybe it was the makeup—and she was wearing a skirt.

"Good evening," Alejandra said. "Sorry for coming this late, but I just arrived into town."

Malena never imagined having her mother here, in her humble apartment.

Her mother—she still couldn't get used to the idea of Alejandra being her mother.

"May I come in?"

Malena took a step back, still holding on to the doorknob. As Alejandra entered, she scanned the room. Malena stumbled on her shoes and picked up her purse. The one day her mother visited, she had a mess in the living room!

"Would you like a cup of *té de tilo?*" It was Julia's new thing to fight insomnia—though Malena spent every night awake as an owl.

"Yes, please."

Malena followed Alejandra's gaze around the room: to the cracked paint in the spot where wall and ceiling met, to the faded beige curtains that Julia had promised to replace soon, to the red couch where Malena's father used to read the newspaper, to the fan on top of the dining room table making a steady hum in a desperate attempt to beat the heat. Alejandra picked up a hideous black-and-white photograph of Malena as a teenager—the one she'd never brought herself to throw away for her father had loved it—and touched the glass with the tips of her fingers.

"You have a lovely place," Alejandra said.

Lovely? Surely she was just trying to make her feel better. Compared to the Platas home, this place was a rat's hole.

"Thanks."

Malena went into the kitchen and fumbled with the herbs and the teapot, unable to control her movements and her breathing. She dropped the herbs on the floor and spilled the water, but somehow she managed to prepare a decent cup of tea.

In the living room, Alejandra was still holding Malena's portrait. They sat next to each other, cups in hand, and an excruciating silence settled between them. There were wrinkles surrounding Alejandra's eyes, and gray hairs scattered throughout her short hair.

Malena spoke first. "How did you know where to find me?"

"Sebastian had your address. He found it among Cesar Vil-lamizar's things." Alejandra's voice hardened when she mentioned the man's name.

Sebastian was another person Malena had been trying—uselessly—to forget. So he knew where to find her but hadn't bothered to come see her?

"So Sebastian told you about my father? About what that man did to him?"

Alejandra nodded. "I wish things hadn't turned out the way they did for you and your father. I'm so sorry."

"Did you know who I was all along?"

Alejandra stirred her spoon in circles, as if debating whether to take a sip or not. "No. I only figured it out the day of Claudia's wedding, after I saw your pendant."

Malena brought her hand to her pendant and felt it through her cotton blouse. It was there, as always.

"It's the first piece of jewelry I ever made," Alejandra said. "I mailed it to Eva after you were born. I wanted you to have something from me."

"She never told me it was yours." Malena's voice faltered. There was so much she wanted to ask, but she was afraid she'd start crying if she talked more. Now that she *could* cry again, she seemed to do it for the most idiotic reasons.

"I wish I had recognized you when you arrived in San Isidro. I should have known who you were. You have my sister's hair." Alejandra gazed at the lime Telefunken radio on the console table. "And then, you were constantly asking questions, wanting to know everything about us."

Malena took a sip of her tea.

"The day of Claudia's wedding," Alejandra said, "after you left the room, she and I had a talk. She told me who you were, she showed me the letters she'd found in your suitcase, and asked me if I knew who your mother was." She looked up for a second. "I told her it was me. I wanted to talk to you about it right away, but with the wedding and then the cancellation, I didn't have time. And then, that damn Rafael had to send you away. Ana was so upset she threw him out of the house."

"Ana did that?"

Alejandra smiled for an instant.

"But there's something I don't understand," Malena said. "Javier told me Abigail was pregnant. He saw her stomach."

"Yes. She was pregnant, too." Alejandra finally took a sip. "And she had a daughter of her own, except that she had the fortune to watch her grow."

A daughter of her own? Of course, how could she not see it?

"Claudia," Malena said.

Alejandra nodded.

"That's why Abigail asked you to burn her diary, to protect Victor."

"Yes."

"And you? Who did you want to protect?"

Alejandra set her cup on the coffee table.

"Why didn't you marry my father? Didn't you love him?"

"I loved him with all my heart, but I was a coward. I should have fought for our love. Things would have been so different for all of us if I had."

Malena was quiet for a moment. For days, she'd been pondering what she would say to Alejandra if she ever saw her again—planning every word, every question. Mostly, she needed to know if her suspicions about her father were true. But now that she had her mother within touching distance, the words were stuck in her throat. She ingested a generous drink of her tea to moisten her palate.

The words finally came out. "Why did my father kill your cousin?"

"Your father was . . ." A tear slipped down Alejandra's cheek. "Enrique was a wonderful man. You should never doubt his honesty, his integrity, or that he adored you. My cousin . . ."

She clutched one of the flower-print cushions on the couch. "He was what you would call a bad seed. I always considered him a brother, but he didn't love me the same way. As I came to find out, he saw me as something other than a cousin." Alejandra struggled to get the next words out. "That night, when I was waiting for Enrique at the workshop, Fausto came to the store." Her voice broke. "He was drunk. He . . ."

Malena reached out for her mother's hand. "You don't have to say any more. I suspected something like this."

Alejandra dropped her gaze.

The tears stung Malena's eyes. "After I learned that my father had killed Fausto and you confessed you were my mother, I knew he must have had a powerful reason to do what he did. He was a gentle man, but he had a strong sense of justice and he was loyal. He once told me he believed killing was not wrong if you did it to defend someone you loved. That story in the newspaper about the robbery never made sense to me."

"You knew him well, in spite of everything he hid from you."

"Yes." Malena pulled her shoulders back. "And to me, he will always be my father."

"You are stronger than I thought." Alejandra squeezed Malena's hand. "One of the reasons I gave you away was because I was afraid of this moment. I thought the truth would devastate you. I always regretted my decision to leave you, but I was unfit to take care of you then."

Malena stared at her mother's closed fist.

"I tried to find you after your grandmother Eva passed away, when you were still a little girl, but I didn't have any luck. Your father left El Milagro for good, and never looked for me again."

"We lived in many different places. We only settled in Guayaquil a couple of years ago. My father really liked it here."

Alejandra's eyes brightened. "It doesn't surprise me. He always talked about doing something with his life. Sebastian showed me the newspaper article about his book."

341

"Yes, he dedicated a lot of time to that book. I'll show it to you." She attempted to get up, but Alejandra softly pulled on her arm.

"Please stay. You'll show it to me later. Now I want to see you, to know you. I never imagined I would have such a pretty daughter." She cupped Malena's chin with one hand. "Malena," she said. "The name suits you."

"Amanda must have thought of it."

"No. Amanda had nothing to do with it. The year you were born was the year that tango was written. I heard it in a movie while I was pregnant and I immediately fell in love with the song." Alejandra held Malena's hand again—it transmitted warmth. "I don't blame you if you never want to see me again or if you never forgive me. But I want to ask you just one thing, one small favor, if you will."

"What?"

"Come with me to San Isidro. Mamá Blanca wants to see you. She's very sad about the way you left and misses you terribly. She hasn't gotten out of bed since you left."

The truth was Malena missed the entire family, too, but the idea of returning to San Isidro meant opening up her wounds again, the ones already healing here.

"At least think about it," Alejandra said. "I'll come back in the morning to see what you decided."

⸺✦⸺

Malena stepped out of the cab, tightening her purse against her side, adjusting her collar. She hesitated as the cab drove away, but told herself she had come all the way to San Isidro for this, and she couldn't back down. She wasn't the girl who'd come here scared and insecure. She wasn't alone anymore.

Straightening her back, she followed her mother into the house. Alejandra held her hand as she led her into the foyer, the way it should have been when Malena was small.

"Welcome home," Amanda told her from the foot of the stairs, stretching her arms out to her.

"Amanda."

"*Tía* Amanda," she corrected her. The two of them hugged and Amanda kissed her forehead. "We've missed you."

Ana, followed by Trinidad, came out of the kitchen.

"I'm so glad you came," Ana said. "Your grandmother is waiting for you."

Your grandmother. Malena never imagined the Platas sisters to be this welcoming to her after her deceit.

Holding her hand, Amanda led her up the stairs. Malena recognized the scent of the lemon detergent Trinidad used to scrub the floors, the squeaky sound the wood made under her feet. Her legs tensed as she walked past Claudia's door, but continued down the hall flanked by her mother and aunts, and the loyal Trinidad behind them.

Alejandra opened her mother's bedroom door. Javier rose from the chair by Mamá Blanca's bed and smiled at Malena. Mamá Blanca looked up from her knitting. The lines in her forehead released.

"You came." She extended her arms to her. Malena approached her. Mamá Blanca hugged her. "I'm so glad. This house is not the same without you."

Malena realized she'd been holding her breath.

After her grandmother let her go, Malena sat on the bed.

"I'm sorry for what I said that day about your father." Mamá Blanca glanced at Alejandra. "But my daughter already explained some things to me."

Mamá Blanca's eyes filled with tears. The room was silent for a moment, gloomy expressions all around. Malena felt the pressure in her own throat.

Her grandmother caressed her cheek. "You're staying with us, right?"

"I don't know."

Mamá Blanca squeezed her hand. "Please. I don't want to lose all my grandchildren at once."

"All?" So Malena's suspicions were true. Claudia had finally married Sebastian.

"Javier is going to Guayaquil with the band," her grand-mother said.

"Yes," Javier said with a wide smile. "We got an offer to play at a nightclub there."

"That's wonderful." Malena said. She hesitated for a moment, but she had to know, sooner or later. "And Claudia?"

Alejandra spoke. "The day of her wedding I told her about Abigail and Victor, too. She decided to go find her real father. She hasn't been back yet."

Ana's face was surprisingly serene at the mention of Claudia's fate. "This morning we received a letter from her," Ana said. "She said she was fine, but doesn't know when she'll be back."

"So as you see," Mamá Blanca said. "We need you here."

Malena looked at the faces staring back at her, ready to tell them her decision.

Chapter 49

Malena closed her eyes for a moment, soothed by Alejandra's tender hands pinning her hair up. Growing up, she'd always dreamt of having her mother fix her hair like this—maybe if she had, her hair wouldn't have been such a royal mess all the time. Now she wanted to prolong this warm sensation for as long as possible.

"There!" Alejandra said.

Malena opened her eyes and glanced at her mother's reflection in the mirror. They were in the opulent sitting room of the Madreselva restroom, preparing for Mamá Blanca's birthday dinner. Malena's heart soared at the sight of Alejandra's warm smile.

"They shouldn't come off now," Alejandra said. *They*, of course, were none other than her curls.

"Let's hope so." Malena ran her hand over her fresh chignon.

"Thank you for baking my mother's cake," Alejandra said. "And thank you for mine, too. I regret never trying it."

Malena patted her mother's hand. The cake she'd baked with Javier seemed like a lifetime ago. "It was the best kind, too. Pineapple. My father used to love it."

Alejandra's eyes seemed to lose their shine.

Malena stood. "Don't get sad, Mamá." She crossed the thick carpeted area and stopped at the restroom door. "I'll make you another one for your next birthday." She looked back at Alejandra shyly; this was the first time she'd called her Mamá. "We should go back. Everybody is waiting for us."

Alejandra smiled through the tears and took her hand.

Together, they headed for the parlor, where Javier, in a black tuxedo, stood behind a large microphone singing "Volver." Behind him, a *bandoneón* player, a pianist, and a violinist performed.

On the dance floor, Joaquin led Amanda into the *molinete* step, and she managed beautifully—stiff leg and all. There was no other couple who danced with such feeling and poise as they did.

Malena and Alejandra sat with Ana and Mamá Blanca. Malena never imagined seeing Ana in the Madreselva. Yet somehow her aunt seemed to belong there, among all of them, in her gray satin sleeveless dress, absently holding a glass of red wine in her hand, looking around the nightclub.

This was also Mamá Blanca's first time at Amanda's nightclub. She'd been so excited about coming that she'd asked Ana to take her to the hair salon for an updo and was even wearing her dentures—despite how uncomfortable she said they were.

Onstage, Amanda was beaming. Joaquin didn't have eyes for anyone else, as usual, and occasionally winked at Amanda. Malena only wished one day she would find a man who loved her the way Joaquin loved Amanda.

Her mind drifted back to Sebastian. Why did this always happen to her? Why couldn't she just be happy and forget about him? She had her mother, her family, everything she'd always wanted. It was clear the Platas women were unlucky in love, and she was one of them. So she needed to stop being ungrateful, stop thinking about what was missing in her life instead of what she had.

Yes, she would do that. She focused on Amanda's dancing, mentally counting her steps, analyzing the grace and ease of Joaquin's moves, but she couldn't get Sebastian out of her mind. This music and Sebastian were interconnected. She glanced at the door. If only she could see him again. But he was gone. And nobody knew if or when he was coming back. The rumor in town was that he had taken his mother to Quito, to some sort of specialist or clinic. His absence was obvious. *El Heraldo* had only been four pages long this morning and it featured a wedding on the front page. God only knew who was running the paper now (the secretary?).

As the song ended, Bernardo carried Mamá Blanca's birthday cake to the table. The musicians played "Cumpleaños Feliz" while Javier sang. Mamá Blanca clapped when she saw the gigantic chocolate cake with seven candles lit on top, one for each decade.

The Platas sisters gathered around the table, singing to their mother.

"Make a wish!" Amanda said after the song was over.

Mamá Blanca took a moment before she blew out the candles. Malena suspected her wish had something to do with the television sets that had finally arrived to San Isidro and that Mamá Blanca mentioned daily. The salon broke into a loud applause.

Malena watched the faces around her. How very different from the people she'd met when she first arrived, back when Rafael dictated their every thought and action. Back when everyone seemed to be trapped in her own lies, in her own secrets. She was so grateful that the truth was out, as painful as it might have been, and that they'd accepted her. She had a sudden—and stupid—urge to cry. This was ridiculous. She needed to get out before anyone could see her, before she would ruin this moment with her newfound sentimentality.

She walked out of the Madreselva, taking in the humid scent of the air after a long rain, the smell of wet leaves around her, the soft breeze freshening her cheeks and lightly billowing her skirt. She stood by a light post, hugging her bare arms. Maybe one day she'd get used to this Sierra chill digging into her bones, to the beauty of the star-filled sky without the obstruction of tall skyscrapers and pollution, to the idea that she wasn't alone anymore.

It was so odd, and somewhat overwhelming, finally belonging somewhere, being a daughter, a niece, a cousin, a granddaughter. But there was a lingering irrational fear that something—anything—could break the bond growing between them and her.

"Malena?"

She glanced over her shoulder. Sebastian stood behind her, hands buried inside the pockets of his dark coat, his head tilted down, his hair slightly wet.

"You're back," she said. He'd never called her by her real name before.

"So are you."

She squared her shoulders. "Claudia is not here."

He removed a box of cigarettes from his pocket. Then he seemed to think better of it and put it away. "I didn't come here looking for her."

The street light illuminated his face. A pink scar extended over his eyebrow.

"What happened to your eye?"

"It's nothing."

"But you have a scar."

He sighed. "Cesar and I had an exchange of words."

"Looks like there were more than words exchanged."

"He got a little violent after I told him I was going to take him to the police." He let out a slow breath.

"That coward." She fought the urge to touch his scar.

"Don't worry about him. He's gone now."

He reached out and held one of her loose tendrils between his fingers. She shivered from his unexpected touch, uncertain of what to say next. She knew she was being an idiot. Reading too much into things.

His finger traced the outline of her cheek while his eyes remained on hers for a long, unnerving moment. "I went to see you in Guayaquil."

"What?"

"Your neighbor told me you were here. And she fed me the best *humitas* of my life."

Malena brought her hand to her chest. Sebastian had been to her building, he'd met Julia. "Why did you do that?"

"Why?" His husky laughter broke the stillness in the cold street. "You really need me to tell you?" He lifted her chin up. "Because I haven't been able to stop thinking about you." He took a step closer, if such a thing were possible.

The intensity of his gaze made the tips of her fingers tingle. Only once had he looked at her this way, and it had been the most amazing moment of her life. She thought of it constantly, especially when she neared the most awkward building in town.

She forgot what she was going to say. Something about Claudia or his mother. It didn't matter anymore. She was too conscious of his fingers under her chin, of his other hand resting on her lower back, of the smell of rain emanating from his skin, of his lips brushing against hers.

But this was a whole new different kind of kiss. It wasn't that long-awaited, fervent encounter from the elevator. This kiss affected her on a different level. It filled her chest with warmth. It comforted her. Never had she felt more connected to another human being. Never had she belonged anywhere more than here, in this misty street. There was nothing to fear, nothing to lose.

A couple walked out of the Madreselva, followed by the sounds of the *bandoneón* marking the first notes of her tango.

"I want to dance with you," Sebastian said.

"Okay." Holding her hand, he led her inside, walking past her family's table.

Her mother was smiling.

When they reached the dance floor, Sebastian pulled her close. She rested her hand on his shoulder. Their bodies seemed to recognize each other. Every part knew its exact place, its precise movement. Their steps were not perfect, but this dance felt right, and she surrendered to his lead without caring that the entire salon was watching.

She listened to the lyrics, and thought of her father. How much had he loved this tango, and how much sadness it had provoked in him. But somehow the memory of him didn't hurt this time. He would certainly be satisfied to see her today. A grown woman. Whole. Fulfilled. Reunited with Alejandra, the woman he had once loved. Now she understood that she owed it to him, to both of them, to be happy. To live the life they never could. As she glided across the floor, she realized that no matter what came, no matter how the world shifted, she would be okay. She would endure, thrive even. She was part of a family now. And Sebastian would be her partner in the ever-unfolding dance.

Acknowledgments

Many people helped me turn this dream into a reality. Thanks to my husband, Danny, for always believing this novel would get published (even when I didn't) and for pushing me to continue. To Andy and Natalie for sharing their mom with her imaginary friends on the computer. To my parents for feeding my imagination with stories of their childhood and youth, and for inspiring the perfect setting for this novel (including the evening tangos on my dad's portable radio). To my agent, Liza Fleissig, for her undying enthusiasm for this story and for never giving up. To my editor, Maxim Brown, for taking a chance on this novel and for bringing a new level of insight to these characters. Also to the Skyhorse team for their meticulous work and the beautiful cover.

To the brilliant writers who've helped me along the way: Rosslyn Elliott, for reading three different versions of the novel and realizing it needed a new structure to work. To my cheerleader, Susie Salom, who loved this novel from the start and has been one of its most fervent advocates. To Marriah Nissen, friend, agent-sister, and fellow historical writer who has struggled with me on the quest for publication, and to María Elena Venant, my walking encyclopedia who's always there when I need a historical, fashion, or literature question answered. If it hadn't been for you, I might have never written a novel in English. To my early readers: Joycelyn Campbell, for thoroughly questioning my characters and introducing me to the world of the Enneagram; to Barbara Leachman and Don Morgan, for reading a very early and flawed draft filled with ESL errors. To Sandra Toro for always cheering me on and making me a member of her annual writers' conference committee. To Paula Paul, Natalia Sylvester, and Juliet Blackwell for their wonderful blurbs.

Many thanks to my family in Ecuador for their support; to my siblings, Mónica, for her enthusiasm in all my literary efforts, and Alfredo, for helping me with important career decisions. To Ruth Hughes, my unconditional and loyal reader. To Cathy Hughes, for helping me with the kids in those early days of writing classes and conferences. To Gia Worlitzky-Smith for the lovely author photo. To Dr. Elma Gutierrez for answering my medical questions. To Margaret Kipp Chynoweth for sharing her knowledge of tango with me.

Finally, a big thank you to Ximena Reyes for her amazing insight and patience every time we talk about my work; and to Marili Figueroa for helping me plant the first seeds of what would become *The Sisters of Alameda Street*.